KILLING SHADOWS

The Wrong Man Part 3

*take care
from
Michael*

M J ELLIOTT

Published by Compass-Publishing UK 2023
ISBN 978-1-915962-06-5

Designed by The Book Refinery Ltd
www.thebookrefinery.com

A CIP catalogue record for this book is available from the
British Library.

Dedication

Geoffrey Michael Elliott 28.11.1936 – 31.01.2022

Malcolm Renshaw 25.09.1944 – 22.07.2022

This book is dedicated to my father, Geoff, and my father-in-law, Malc, who both passed away in 2022.

Geoff and Malc were men of a different time, men of a bygone era, men of the old school. Two men who lived their lives with dignity and respect – men of the like we may never see again.

Geoff and Malc both inspired and influenced me in different ways through their shared common values. They were two men I would have trusted with my life.

Miss you both. You'll be forever remembered.

RIP

Foreword

I was thrilled and honoured when Michael asked me if I would be willing to write a foreword for this book.

However, after I'd had a chance to think, I realised what a responsibility it was and how much faith Michael had in me. And, thus, I hope I do his faith justice.

During the 26 years we have known each other I have been Michael's boss, mentor (for a short time) and friend. We both share a love for reading and had always harboured the dream of one day becoming an author, which is why my small role in providing feedback has become a passion of mine.

I first met Michael in the summer of 1997. I instantly knew we would get along and he would be a success. Anyone who is willing to break off from a family holiday and travel two hours by car to attend an interview for a new job has my attention from the start.

True to my gut feeling, I was right, and Michael started working for me as a sales representative in the South Yorkshire area within a few weeks. Michael has great qualities – his work ethic, family values and down-to-earth attitude to life and people. This always came out in and out of work, as did his wicked sense of humour. I always enjoyed his company then and still do today. These strong traits shine through in all of his books, none more so than in this recent work, which, in my view, is his best to date.

Through his support career as a funeral celebrant, Michael has developed a fantastic reputation and successful business with wonderful references. This inspired me to take the relevant training course he had written, and I am now a certified celebrant, too. I am pleased, however, that should I ever decide to take up this new career, Michael lives a long way away – I know I wouldn't get much business if he was nearby.

When I first heard of Michael's new venture as an author, I was fascinated as to what he might write about and in what style. I was also nervous for him, knowing how competitive the writing world is and the high standards of both new and established authors.

My own favourite fiction writers include many of the greats. I like a good old-fashioned page-turning thriller or story with great characters. Therefore, when I started reading *The Wrong Man*, I really hoped I would be able to give Michael a positive review. He's always known he'll get my honest and forthright opinion, which is probably why he asked me to write this foreword.

I had no reason to worry because his first novel was a winner from the start. The opening is gripping – and it comes back to play a major part in the later stages of the story, which is in the style of authors I have followed in the past.

I thought Michael's writing would be good, but as a debut novel, *The Wrong Man* is superb – and a great base for the trilogy it has gone on to become. The Pearson family are a wonderful backbone for the books and the strength of the characters allows many stories within a story to develop.

I wasn't sure how you could follow and improve on such a strong story like *The Wrong Man* but Michael managed to achieve this with *New Blood*. The next generation of the Pearson family come to the fore and add to the wealth of characters from the first book. I enjoyed the follow-up even more and could see how Michael's writing and story development was even better. I knew there would be a third novel to complete a trilogy, which, in my opinion, rivals anything out there.

For those who have read the first two instalments, then you are in for a treat because *Killing Shadows* eclipses its predecessors. It's one of the best crime/thriller books I have read and a page-turner you just can't put down. *Killing Shadows* is good enough as a stand-alone story, but I recommend you read *The Wrong Man* and *New Blood* first for maximum effect.

I was privileged to be part of Michael's support team on this project and to read through his transcripts while he wrote the story. Having played even a minor role in the creation of something as special as this gives me great pride – especially since Michael made some additions to his fantastic ending based on my thoughts and feedback.

Michael's consistent source of support and guidance has always come from his wonderful wife, Debbie. It was Debbie who convinced Michael to venture into the writing world – how right she was. On a recent visit to their wonderful home and new life in Portknockie, to complete my celebrant training, I did have some fun with them trying to come up with a title for the book. After much discussion, over many ideas, Michael eventually settled on *Killing Shadows*. When you have finished reading, you will know exactly why he chose it.

Michael has created a family and a storyline that can be concluded as a trilogy, but a part of me hopes there is more to come from the Pearson clan, and even if not as a fourth instalment, then perhaps further books that are based on some of the strong and engaging characters within the Pearson family and team.

I hope you enjoy *Killing Shadows* as much as I did.

I wish Michael and Debbie every success with its release and their new life in Scotland.

Thank you, Michael, for giving me the chance to be involved in the making of your novel and having my name against your foreword.

It has been a pleasure and I look forward to your next masterpiece, my friend.

Paul Gibbons

chapter one

Saturday 11th January 2020 – London

Alice was in London for a girlie weekend. She and her two friends Becky and Wendy, from Mansfield, had taken the opportunity to head to the bright lights of the capital for three nights of fun, staying in a boutique hotel near to Tower Bridge. Yesterday, they drank around Piccadilly Circus, before moving up to Covent Garden to eat. Tonight, they were enjoying the hospitality of the classier drinking establishments of Soho. It was approaching nine o'clock when they entered what was probably the most exclusive-looking place they'd been in since they'd arrived. Alice was surprised they'd not needed a ticket or an invite to get in. The place was full but being such a classy joint, there was still plenty of room to accommodate the rich-looking clientele.

'Bloody hell, Alice, this is a cut above, ain't it?' Wendy said, in awe of the chandeliers dangling from the high ceiling.

'Yeah, well, we are here to enjoy ourselves, aren't we? And like I said, tonight's all on me.'

Alice had wanted to treat her old schoolfriends. Becky and Wendy were both from quite affluent families in Southwell and used to the finer things in life that Mansfield had to offer, which, to be fair, were nothing like where they were now. They'd both moved to Mansfield a year ago, fed up with what they called "living in the sticks". They shared a house on a fairly new estate built on what used to be an old quarry, both worked for the council, and both, except for a week or two in the sun, had never really left Nottinghamshire. This weekend in London was something they'd been so excited about.

Alice had wanted some time away from the family business. She'd had some real shit to deal with recently, having been attacked by a loan shark and his sons, so a weekend on the lash was just the ticket.

'Shall I pick us some cocktails?' Becky asked, plonking her bottom in the corner booth they'd managed to grab, before scouring the extensive range of exotic-sounding drinks.

'Yeah, go on then. I'm just off to the loo,' Alice replied, looking around for the ladies. 'Here's my phone – pay with that. You know what to do.'

'You coming?' she asked Wendy.

'What – again? Yeah, go on then. You OK here?' Wendy asked Becky.

'Yeah. I'll pick the drinks. No problem.'

Alice took the lead and spotted the sign over the far side, which pointed up some stairs. 'Over there!' she shouted over the music, which had just been turned up a notch.

She took in the room, as she climbed the stairs. It was larger than she'd first imagined. Either that or it was a bird's-eye view illusion. She stopped four steps from the top.

'What's up?' Wendy asked.

Alice didn't answer. Wendy put her mouth to her ear. 'I said, what's up?'

'Er, nothing ... just seen someone I know, that's all.'

'What – in 'ere? Who are they? Famous?'

'Eh? No, not at all. Just someone my family deals with.'

'Ooh, who is it, a London gangster? Show me which one it is. I've never seen a real-life London gangster before.'

Alice discreetly pointed with her right hand. 'See that group of five men there, next to that pillar?'

'Yeah.'

'The one second in from the right. His name's Tariq. Nasty piece of shit.'

'Have you met him then?'

'Yeah, saw him a few weeks ago, at the funeral, ya know.'

'Oh, he was there then?'

'Yeah, I nearly got frisked by one of his men.'

'Dirty bastard. Which one was it?'

'None of them there. I only know Tariq.'

'Ooh look, I think they're leaving.'

Tariq straightened his suit jacket. It became apparent that out of the five men, two were with Tariq and the other two were there together. Alice assumed it was a meeting. They shook hands and walked away.

'He must've had a bullet in the leg,' Wendy said, pointing with her head.

'Who?'

'Him in the grey suit. He's limping. See him?'

'Ah yeah. Probably. Mixing with Tariq will get you shot at some point.'

Alice watched them disappear out of the door, totally unaware of the importance of what she'd just witnessed.

chapter two

**A month or so earlier – December 2019,
Papplewick, Nottinghamshire**

Phoebe had just come off the phone with Archie. Benny
Lancashire had been sorted. She sat back in her chair
in the boardroom. The last loose end was tied up. She
smiled as she looked at Alice.

'Here's to the new dawn, sweetheart. Or, as Jez said,
the new blood.'

'New blood, eh,' Alice said, smiling back at her mum.
'Sounds good, does that. I like it. Good old Jez – and
he is old, bless him.'

Phoebe laughed, as did Raquel. 'Aye, but he can
still mix it when he wants to. And listen – old or not,
he'll be invaluable to us in the foreseeable. Don't
underestimate his worth. He's an old head, and old
heads come in handy from time to time.'

It had been just over two months since Phoebe had
ordered the murders of Steven Wallace and Johnny,
Alice's boyfriend. Two months that had flown by, in
which she'd realised how being at the top of a major UK
criminal family took its toll. People were always trying
it on, always trying to muscle in from somewhere,
and she knew she'd never be able to sleep soundly

again. At first, she'd wondered what all the fuss had been about, but that was when she was sweeping clean with a new broom. When the honeymoon period quickly evaporated, she'd soon come to acknowledge how much Frank, and Archie, had had to deal with.

Archie had done good murdering Benny Lancashire. Phoebe had ordered it the moment Archie had rung her, three days before, to tell her he'd come across him in Spain. He'd caused untold damage to the firm, and for that he had to pay with his life. She had no regrets. She found things like that surprisingly easy to cope with. She'd amazed herself at how taking someone's life mattered not to her. They always deserved it, and if she was honest, she revelled in the thrill and power it gave her. Power was one thing she did enjoy about being at the helm. The constant threat of her rivals, large or small, seeing her as an easy target was something she didn't like one bit.

'How is Archie?' Raquel asked.

'Fine. He seems to love it out there, and Sarah and Mary certainly do. He's made a life for himself. I can't ever see him coming back.'

The mood changed. Raquel and Alice looked at each other. They knew how disappointed Phoebe was now Archie seemed to be making no plans to return. When she took over the top chair, she'd hoped he would come back to support her. Having her son at her side would have made the perfect business partnership, but he'd made no move to corroborate that theory. He'd never said he would never return either, but the silence on the subject spoke volumes.

Phoebe did have Alice, though, and while she was no match for Archie in terms of strength and muscle, she had shown her true colours since pulling that trigger and shooting Johnny in the head. She was traumatised at first, but within a few days she made it clear she understood she'd stepped into their world. Alice wanted to be a big part of it. She was a Pearson, after all. A true Pearson at that.

Phoebe was a Pearson by marriage. Alice, along with Archie, was the bloodline. People had been surprised by Alice's brutality. Everyone expected her to crumble, especially after the initial meltdown, but Alice Pearson had found something, as her mum had, that she liked. Power. She'd always been happy to make the tea, file the paperwork and stay on the fringes, but pulling that trigger had made a tingle run down her spine which, at first, she didn't recognise. Now she did, she wanted more of the same.

Phoebe straightened her skirt and raised her glass once more.

'No, it's just us girls. We're the ones in charge now. The three of us, plus Pat of course.'

Pat was still Phoebe's number two and her most trusted.

'Here's to us ladies. We may operate in a world full of testosterone, and we may be the fairer sex and all that shite, but we can be as ruthless as any man – and I challenge any man to dare take us on.'

'Yeah, fuck 'em,' Alice said, laughing. She placed her glass down, untouched.

'Yeah, I'll second that,' Raquel quipped, nearly choking on her wine.

Just then the door flew open. 'It's Jez!' Gloria shouted. 'Quick!'

Simultaneously, Phoebe, Raquel and Alice jumped up and followed Gloria out into the garden. There, lying on the patio, clutching his left arm, was Jez. A man who had been with the family since the 1970s. A man who had been Frank's second for nigh on forty years, and the man who Phoebe was relying on more than anyone to advise her through the coming months and years.

The old head was dead. He'd always said the job would get him and that he'd die in a blaze of glory, probably protecting one of the Pearson family. He'd been involved in more fights, shootouts and criminal activities than anyone else he knew, but Jez Carrington, a criminal stalwart, had dropped dead from a heart attack while holding a gin and tonic and telling Gloria of his up-and-coming trip to Norway to hopefully see the northern lights.

'Jez! Jez!' Phoebe shouted. 'Don't go, Jez! I need you! We all need you. We all love you!'

She stopped shaking him, rested her head on his chest and sobbed. Gloria and Raquel cried.

Alice stared into space. Jez had been her mum's pillar. He and Brian had seen it all. Brian was in the background, very much a soldier, whereas Jez, though always happy being Frank's number two, never courting the top job or the limelight, had carried more clout than Brian. Jez was far more astute. A very valuable asset that had been taken in an instant. Without Jez, her mum had become just that bit more vulnerable. That excited her. It excited her very much.

'Bring it on, you fuckers' she thought. *'Bring it on.'*

chapter three

Tariq Mali got out of his car and his chauffeur closed the door behind him. He'd just been to his favourite restaurant for lunch with his latest bit on the side. Tariq didn't do long-term relationships. He wanted women for one thing only – a fuck. He always made that abundantly clear from the outset. The longest he'd ever been with the same woman was ten weeks and three days but, mainly, it was never more than a month. The only reason he'd been with that one for so long was because she'd previously been in a relationship with Paul Dutton, his rival from South London. That had fucked Paul off, so Tariq had milked it for as long as he could, but even that became a bore soon enough.

He was now meeting with his most trusted at one of his offices in Soho.

Tariq had risen through the ranks to become one of the three most feared gangsters in London – the other two being Paul Dutton and Greg West. Tariq ruled the West End. He'd started off in the early nineties supplying women for hire, which had, over time, through his feared reputation, earned him the title of "king of sex". Tariq controlled the London sex scene and anything else that happened in London's West End. He cared about nothing and no one. He was also very clever in how he dealt with problems behind closed doors, hence why he'd steered clear of a spell at Her Majesty's pleasure. He'd had many a run-in with other main players over the years, but nothing serious. The other top table criminals tolerated him, which suited him as he wasn't someone who mixed easily, or well. He kept out of their way, and they kept at arm's length, too.

The only main face he'd ever have loved to have taken down was Frank Pearson. Back in the mid-nineties, Frank had taken out two of his best customers, Akrad Malik and Barraq Syed. Frank had dropped Tariq like a stone, citing that he didn't agree with how Tariq treated his girls, which Tariq could not understand, given the line of work Frank was in. Frank was major league, far above Tariq in the pecking order. Tariq had let it go to a degree, but he'd always dreamed of taking him out. He'd never had the chance, though, and if he was honest, he knew it would be a war that would result in a lot of casualties. He didn't like the Pearsons, though, and that hadn't altered since Frank's demise. He did attend the funeral, but more as a show of strength and to mingle with the elite. Occasions to make friends seldom came in the underworld. Phoebe, he tolerated, but in his world, women were not to be running criminal families. He would never have allowed that himself, but he stayed out of it, keeping to his own vast criminal empire.

He'd heard about Jez's death and was going to the funeral, again just to shake hands with his fellow associates. He had a few plans that might need the help of some of the main players around the UK, so he was not going to miss a chance to sow a few seeds. Tariq was as ruthless as the next criminal, more so in a lot of ways, but he'd never understood why people made war when they'd suffer casualties. Tariq had built his empire on making strategic moves, when he was in a position of strength. But, as with most businessmen, he was always up for expanding his power and wealth. Without Jez in the frame, a lot of the Pearson contacts and alliances would be weaker, so Tariq was, if nothing else, interested to see how Phoebe would be treated.

When Frank passed away, it was important for Phoebe, in the eyes of the criminal fraternity, to have faces like Jez and Brian at her side. One half of that was now gone. Tariq was curious – curious to see the lay of the land. He had a plan. And watching from the wings had always served him well. Jez had been well liked and well respected. As Frank's number two, he'd always had the backing of the major players. With Jez gone and Archie seemingly liking the sun, Tariq would watch. Just watch and observe. Anything he saw would go in the memory bank. He played the long game. He'd been in this business a long time, so if he saw anything of interest, he'd note it and store it away.

He was now sat waiting for some contacts from Amsterdam. He dealt a lot with his Dutch counterparts.

The sex game made dealings with Amsterdam a necessity.

'Come in, gentlemen, take a seat. We have a lot to discuss.'

chapter four

Saturday 21st December 2019

No one knew Jez had prepaid his funeral plan or that he'd wanted to be buried. Phoebe had assumed she'd be the one arranging things, and that a cremation would be the order of the day. Standing with the hundreds of mourners at Mansfield Cemetery, listening to Archie's speech, she thought again about the events of the past year. She could not believe that in the past twelve months – well, the past seven to be precise – Frank had been murdered, Archie had buggered off to Spain and Richie had, by the looks of it, been murdered by Faye, the manager at his care home, who'd seemingly topped herself by stepping in front of an HGV, though Phoebe had ordered that one. She'd also ordered the murders of Steven and Johnny. And now, to top it off, Jez, one of her most trusted and faithful, had decided to have a heart attack. That was a lot of people from within the family business – people who had, with the exception of Johnny, at some point or other been part of its criminal activities.

Phoebe, however, had had the foresight to realise early on in her reign that she needed to replace those she'd lost, and that included Jez and Brian. They were both going to be her pillars to lean on. Her sounding boards. Muscle, too. But they'd already taken a step back or two. She'd replaced them, in terms of bodies on her team. Her only pillar now was Brian, ever present and ever needed.

It was cold. Phoebe could see everyone was feeling it, especially Pat. He was on holiday in the Canaries when Jez dropped dead. He stood out with his tan.

The men were all blowing air into their hands to keep warm while moving from side to side on the spot. Every top criminal in British gangland was there. Phoebe hadn't restricted numbers, as she had at Frank's funeral. One reason was because, being a burial, it was all outside, so she couldn't really stop anyone from attending. Plus, she wanted as many of her compatriots and rivals as possible there. It would be an opportunity for her to show her strength and get to know the leading players a bit more. She'd seen them all many times but, for the most part, she'd been in the background chatting with the ladies.

Today was different. The last time she'd been in the company of so many of the criminal elite was at Frank's funeral, and she'd only just taken the top seat. Back then, everyone was making it their business to tell her she had their full support, but a few months down the line, things could be different. Of that she was acutely aware. George Burbanks had already, out of a good heart, told her that they'd all be watching like hawks – and any sign of weakness, they'd pounce. She liked George. He was old school, just like Frank. And like everyone else, save for his brother, Ivan, Phoebe was blissfully unaware of the Burbankses' involvement in the war with Fletcher O'Brien. No one knew and seeing as she'd ordered Archie to take out Benny Lancashire, no one other than the two brothers had any idea.

The old-school way was how Phoebe had seen things done, though, and it was a model she liked. One she was trying her best to replicate. She was all too aware that to the outside world it would seem ludicrous to suggest people like Frank, George and herself had a moral compass, but they did and the one thing she was going to do for Frank was carry on the Pearson name in the same vein. It was all she knew in this game. She looked round, saw George next to Ivan, and smiled. They both smiled back. George mouthed 'You OK?' Ivan blew into his hands. Phoebe nodded, smiling back.

'That was lovely,' she said to Archie, as they made their way to the cars.

'My hands are blue, look. I can't feel 'em.' He then, right on cue, clasped his hands and blew hard.

'Straight to Frank's, Phoebe?' Del asked.

'Yeah, straight there, but make sure security have their lists. I don't want any hangers-on getting through. Only who's on the list.'

'No bother. They have 'em, but I'll make a call.'

Del got into the second car with his brother, Michael. His two sons, Ryan and Des, joined them, along with Brian.

'Des, call Brigsy and make sure he has the list. I know he does but just make sure for me.'

'Will do.'

The ride to Frank's was sombre. Even though Frank had been dead for around four months, it was still often referred to as Frank's. Especially when things were serious, like today. It mattered not that it was now Gloria's house. For many, it would always be Frank's place.

Jez had been such a force in their lives, it really was like losing Frank all over again. Jez had been at Frank's side for so long, the wake just had to be there. Des confirmed Brigsy had the list.

The hired help made sure everyone had a glass in their hand. Raquel sipped her wine, while she chatted to Tariq. She'd very nearly met him all those years ago in the mid-nineties when she was checking out the club in Leicester that Frank had taken over from Barraq and Akrad. Fortunately, she'd never had the pleasure as things had blown up before she'd had the chance. Tariq never knew that it was her he had been due to meet a couple of days after Frank had taken the Leicester boys out.

'Never knew you could have a funeral on a Saturday,' he said, between sips of his lemonade.

'Well, you can, but I don't think it's too popular. Phoebe wanted a Saturday as it'd be quieter up there today. I don't believe there were any other funerals today, you see.'

'Fair enough, makes sense. How's things anyway? She copin'?'

'Phoebe?'

'Yeah, who else?'

'Of course she is. Why wouldn't she?' Raquel retorted.

'Fuck me, only askin'. You know, makin' polite conversation and all that.'

Raquel didn't like Tariq. Never had. No one had ever spoken highly of him and to her knowledge, that hadn't changed. He made her skin crawl.

'No need to be polite. Not on my account.'

Tariq felt her animosity. He'd expected nothing less but wasn't going to bite. 'Another?' he asked, pointing to her almost empty glass.

'No thanks, I've already got two waiting,' she replied.

Tariq was finding it increasingly hard to restrain his anger but remembered where he was. 'No problem. Look, I think I'll go and talk to...' – he scanned the room and saw Barney from somewhere up north, Hull maybe – 'Barney, I'll go and chat with Barney.'

'Fuckin' slag,' he muttered under his breath, as he moved away, knowing the noise would mask his words.

His number two, Mo, followed him as he always did.

As he chatted away to Barney and the large fella he now had as his number two, he kept one eye on Phoebe. She held herself well. He was surprised how much presence she had, being a woman. She had authority, of that there was no doubt, and the main players all seemed to be treating her just as they had Frank. That annoyed him. In his mind, she shouldn't even be in the position she was in, never mind holding court with the country's elite.

Alice sipped her lemonade. She'd offered to stay off the hard stuff just in case anyone needed a lift. The funeral directors had been paid to have their cars on hand all afternoon, but Alice was happy to be there if needed. Sarah was sat beside her, with Mary on her knee. She looked so much happier now that she and Archie were in Spain. The constant look of worry had gone. Alice had never really noticed it before, but the move had made her realise how haunted Sarah had always looked. Alice could see Sarah felt uncomfortable with it all and looked largely overwhelmed. She looked for Archie constantly, who it would appear was enjoying catching up with members of the firm. He was shaking hands and hugging the players, who were all telling him to get back home.

Meanwhile, Tariq was quietly trying to gauge his reaction. He was pleased Archie was telling everyone that Spain was just too good to leave right now. Of course, no one noticed Tariq telling him how good he looked on it all and that he was right – Spain was where he should stay.

'I still can't believe it. Jez gone, just like that,' Pat said to Phoebe and Raquel.

'I know, I'm still processing it. It's been a bloody tough year – not one anyone could've seen coming,' Phoebe replied.

'Well, let's just hope it's all behind us now. Time for a bit of stability, eh!' Pat said, raising his pint glass.

'I bloody hope so, Pat. The last thing we need right now is aggro.'

Phoebe scanned the room for her top team. This was a chance for her to see how they looked in this, the most prestigious company of criminality. She noticed Brian, which gave her a warm feeling inside. She knew he would die for her.

Pat was at her side, as he always was. A man she trusted with her life and would swap for no one. Raquel was in her fifties, and as ruthless and respected as any player in the room. She then looked for Del, who she spotted with Ryan and Des, and his brother, Michael, who was close by. Del was a diamond, and his two sons were cut from the same cloth. Michael was just the same. All four were frontliners who could be relied upon in any situation.

Trainer had recently taken over the running of Leeds and Doncaster, and was young, raw and as tough as nails. Cool as fuck was Trainer and a likeable fella. She then looked around for Pēteris, a Latvian who had been with the family for a few years now. He had with him a relatively new guy called Jase, Phoebe recalled, having met him for the first time only a few weeks ago. He was Pēteris's number two, and had held a good account of himself since that first meet, so much so he was now looked upon as an important member of the firm. Phoebe had to quickly recognise those with talent and those with loyalty. She needed brawn and Jase had muscles on top of muscles.

She now also had Gray, who often got called Gary. He could never understand why so many people got his name wrong. He now ran Leicester for Phoebe. Gray was in his thirties and, after ten years with the firm, had recently come to the fore. She looked around the room and saw him chatting with Gloria and forty-year-old Knighty, who now ran Derby. Both Gray and Knighty reported to Del, who oversaw everything on a daily basis and reported to Raquel. It was a solid team. Frank would never have had these new guys at his top table. He would have made them earn it over a far longer period, but Phoebe was different like that. Other than not having the luxury of time, given events of the past seven months, she had the opinion that if you were good enough and there was room for you, then you should have a seat.

There was only one guy missing in her team and that was Archie. That seat had been taken by Alice. She was young, but she had amazed Phoebe with how brutal she could be. Only two weeks ago Alice had walked straight up to a guy in a bar in Mansfield and slashed him with a smashed glass all because he'd said within earshot there was a rumour she was "up for it". He was unaware of who she was, of course, and was just trying his luck with a young lady he quite liked the look of, but he now had a scar that would remind him of Alice Pearson every time he looked in the mirror. Phoebe had intervened and made sure the CCTV was "not working" that day. Del and his sons made sure the fella and his mates had memory loss and couldn't recall who'd done it. Alice didn't fuck about. That made Phoebe slightly nervous, but Alice had the bug, like she did – and that thrill of hurting other people was a rush that was hard to replicate any other way. Phoebe just hoped Alice would use it to the family's advantage and not as a tool to bring aggravation and heartache.

The afternoon was going well. The mood was calm, although Raquel could not help but sense tension in the air. She was an older hand now. Having turned fifty a couple of years ago, she picked up on these things more than most. Experience was an asset, and she knew when there was tension. She couldn't place it, but it was there. Frequently throughout the afternoon, she sought their faces for any sign of aggression. There was nothing. Pat was the only one she confided in, which put him on guard, so much so Phoebe thought he was in a mood, which she was not too pleased about given the occasion. He walked between rooms, chatting as he did, but no matter where he was or who he was speaking with, everything looked calm. He was talking to Pete Porter from Middlesborough – nicknamed Pee Pee because his forename and surname both began with a P – when he heard a commotion from the other room.

'Get your filthy hands off me!' Alice shouted.

Everyone in the snug looked towards the couple of steps leading up to the main living room. A man with his hands up had taken a step back.

'All right, lady, calm down, just a misunderstanding. It's fairly crowded in here, if you hadn't noticed.'

'If you want to cop a feel, at least fuckin' ask!' Alice continued.

'You better calm down, young lady. I might just forget my manners.'

With that, Alice kneed him in the groin. He bent over, reaching one hand for the wall.

'Fuck me!' he wailed.

By now Knighty had him by the back of the neck. Given the kick in the bollocks, he was making an admirable attempt to walk upright.

Del, Pat and Brian arrived on the scene. Phoebe walked calmly over, as did Raquel.

'Get him out of here!' she instructed Knighty. 'Who is he?' she asked, not directing the question at anyone in particular. No one knew.

Tariq appeared from a small group. 'He's with me, Phoebe. I'll sort him. You OK, Alice?' he asked, seeming genuinely concerned.

'Yeah, I'm fine. It was no accident, though. You wanna get rid of him. He'll get himself in real bother one day.'

'Please accept my apologies, Alice.' He then turned to Phoebe. 'I cannot apologise enough for his behaviour. I will ensure he's made aware that it is totally unacceptable.'

Phoebe was just about to accept the apology when Archie came flying through from the other room, pushing his way through the group that had gathered round. Thinking Tariq was the aggressor, he made for him. Brian sensed Archie's intentions and immediately stepped forward to block his path. Archie attacking Tariq was quite possibly the worst thing that could happen right now. If Archie were to lay a finger on him, it would start something that even he wasn't sure the family could cope with. Tariq was a top London face and wouldn't stand by and do nothing if he was struck.

'I'll fuckin' kill ya, ya dirty bastard!' Archie raged, while Brian struggled to hold him back. 'If you touched her, I'll fuckin' do ya!'

Tariq stared at Archie, totally unfazed. Mo, Tariq's number two, on seeing the rage in Archie's eyes, had instinctively stepped in front of his guvnor. Del, thinking Mo was about to make a move, punched him hard on the back of the head, knocking his face into Brian's head, who had by now restrained Archie. Blood poured from Mo's mouth and Brian's head. It was on the brink of becoming a free for all, so Pat and Michael got in the middle to separate the two sides. There was hardly any room to be had, given the number of people now packing the room. Testosterone filled the air.

Raquel now knew what she'd been looking for. She could tell from the man's reaction when Alice first challenged him that it was no accident. This had been orchestrated. She was convinced. By who, she was not so sure, but Tariq's reaction wasn't natural. For one, he'd seemed prepared for Archie's onslaught, as though it had been rehearsed. And two, he was *never* apologetic and certainly not where women were concerned. He looked at women as pieces of meat. He'd always seen them as beneath him.

Things began to subside. Pat and Del told everyone to calm down. Brian continued to hold Archie back. Mo looked dazed and Tariq glared at Archie, knowing full well what the once young pretender had wanted to do. This young upstart was getting above his station. The whole room was now watching, waiting to see who did what. Tariq wouldn't let this liberty go, but decided, for now at least, he would act with composure. He'd find it hard, but the other main players would be expecting him to swallow it and show some class.

Phoebe, who had taken a second or two to piece it together, spoke first. 'Gentlemen, this is not what we are here for. This is to remember Jez, a man we all admired and respected, and I will not have his memory tarnished like this. This stops now. This is Frank Pearson's house, and the place where we chose to remember his dearest friend, and while you are here, as my guests at Jez's wake, you will all act with decorum. Now, please, let's forget this little incident and get back to remembering where we all are, why we are here and take a moment to honour a great man who has lost his life.'

'It wasn't Tariq, Archie, it was one of his men. Knighty has him outside with Des. Tariq was just trying to apologise.'

Brian loosened his grip on Archie, hoping he would listen to his younger sister. He straightened his coat and then held out his hand. 'Apologies, Tariq. I didn't know. She's my little sister. I'm sure you understand.'

For a second or two it appeared Tariq was going to leave Archie hanging, but just before it became uncomfortable, he held out his hand and shook it firmly.

'Family eh!' he said, bringing Archie to him for an embrace.

Archie patted his back, feeling slightly awkward.

'I see the Spanish sun has done nothing to calm your temper. I'm sure you'll always come runnin' if your mum ever needs you.'

Was Tariq suggesting Phoebe would need Archie from time to time or that she wasn't capable without him? Either way she was wise enough to know there was a hidden message in it. She held his gaze till he and Archie broke free of their bromance. Tariq knew she'd recognised what he was getting at.

As Tariq let go of him, Archie replied, 'Nah, she's as tough as any man in this room, Tariq. No danger there.' He too fixed his eyes on Tariq, unsure himself whether there was any hidden message in his remark.

Tariq stared for a moment before reassuring Archie and Phoebe that Lester would be dealt with. He apologised to Alice again and she accepted.

'You shouldn't go around threatenin' to kill people, young Archie. It may come back to bite you one day. Remember the company you keep,' Tariq said, perturbed by Archie's reaction.

'Yeah look, sorry about that. I just saw red. As I said, she's my sister.'

'Hmm,' Tariq replied.

While Tariq had let it go, those who knew him were fully aware of his reputation for playing the long game. Archie needed to look over his shoulder. Frank would have known that. Phoebe, however, was not yet experienced enough to know Tariq's way of doing things.

Del looked at Mo, who was still wiping his mouth. Mo looked at Tariq, who nodded. Mo held out his hand. Del shook it. No words were exchanged.

With honour of sorts seemingly restored to all parties, Tariq said, 'Well, I think that's our cue to go. Be a bit, well, weird if we stayed now. It's been a pleasure, Phoebe, although I'd have much preferred today to be under better circumstances. And I hope this little misdemeanour won't affect our relationship.'

'No reason why it should, Tariq. All sorted now,' she replied sternly, which Tariq noted.

Tariq, Mo and the other from Tariq's main organisation left through the front door. Pat, Trainer and Jase followed, as ordered by Phoebe. They nodded to Brigsy as they turned left out of the door to walk the ten yards to Tariq's car. Lester was untouched, still flanked by Knighty and Des. They nodded to the three guys who were guarding the rather expensive cars that filled the very large driveway.

'Well, maybe Mansfield, or wherever the fuck we are, isn't as backward as they reckon,' Tariq mocked, as he looked Knighty up and down. He turned to Lester. 'No rough stuff out here, Lester. Remember whose house this is, son,' he continued, exaggerating his cockney accent on *son*.

'They must have standards after all!' he laughed.

Knighty looked at Pat. Pat shook his head, as if to say, *'Don't react, stay calm.'*

Pat stood in front of Tariq square on. 'A slightly different Tariq we see out here then.'

'One and the same ... er, Pat, isn't it? You're the one who runs around after Phoebe all day, aren't you? I would say, licking her arse, but I bet her pussy tastes all that sweeter.'

Pat remembered all that Frank had taught him down the years. To whack Tariq now would be the easiest thing in the world, but out here on Frank's drive, he'd be nothing more than a local thug. Pat was better than that and he wanted Tariq to know as much. Plus, taking on Tariq, even in a street-type brawl, was potential suicide. He laughed.

'It tastes fuckin' lovely, Tariq. Now have a safe trip, boys, won't you?' With that, Pat nodded to Knighty who, along with Des, moved away from Lester. 'You never quite did get over Frank making you look small and weak back in '96, did you?'

Pat could see the anger rising from Tariq's boots. He regretted it instantly and wanted to take it back. He knew he'd just lowered himself to his standards. He felt like a schoolkid telling tales. Tariq turned on his heels. He didn't say a word as his driver opened the car door for him. Lester made a gun signal with his right hand, pointed it to Pat and pretended to blow away smoke from the end of his fingers. 'Boom!' he shouted.

Pat remained expressionless, hoping he hadn't just lit the fuse of a fire that would get people burnt. Tariq was no wannabe. And neither Pat nor anyone else would want a war with him. He decided there and then to keep that thought to himself, hoping Tariq would have dismissed it all by the time he pulled onto the M25. He watched Tariq glare at him as the showroom car drove away.

'Get me back to London pronto, for fuck's sake! That fucker there and that fuckin' school kid inside are history.' No one spoke on the drive back towards Mansfield Cemetery and onto Annesley, towards the motorway.

Tariq was deep in thought. He'd instructed Lester to touch Alice up. He wanted to see how Phoebe would handle things, which, to be fair, she did well. As much as he didn't like to admit it, she had impressed him with her coolness and delivery. What he hadn't bargained for was Archie's threat to kill him. A major liberty. If Brian hadn't have stepped in front of him, Archie would have attacked him in full view of the UK top table. Everyone there knew it. Archie had to be dealt with. The fact he now resided in Spain made it more difficult.

Tariq liked to plan for long-term revenge. He would wait, he would think, and he would get his moment.

Archie was busying himself with the expats and that would provide an opportunity at some point. People who needed to know would know that it was as a result of today's show of aggression. Pat, on the other hand, would be easier. He would get what was coming to him. Tariq would bide his time, and when it hit him, Pat would know who it was.

Tariq's driver took the slip road onto the M1. They soon passed the first sign for London. Tariq felt better already. He was on his way home. The north was not for him.

chapter five

The mood was quite jovial when Pat and the others walked back in. It was, of course, the topic of conversation. George and Ivan Burbanks, Greg West and Paul Dutton were curious as to why the whole thing had happened.

'A bit staged all that, don't you think?' George suggested to Greg.

'Maybe, George, but I have no interest in what Mali does. We don't get on, if you know what I mean, so anything he wants to create with this lot are fuck all to do with me. I'm here for Jez and nowt else, fella.'

'Well, mark my words, he's up to something. He's from down your way, so if you want my advice, I'd watch with interest.'

'I don't, George. Never needed anyone's advice. No disrespect, but I'm OK as I am. You know the score.'

George did know the score and was wise enough to know when his company was not wanted.

'Fair enough, Greg.' He held out his hand. Greg shook it firmly, raised his glass and said, 'To Jez.' George nodded in agreement.

Phoebe was in deep conversation with Archie, when she saw Pat walking through the bodies. 'All OK?' she mouthed. Pat put his thumb up, winked and mouthed back 'Sweet', though what he was really thinking was *I fuckin' hope so.*

Phoebe continued talking to Archie. Having pointed out whose head he'd just tried to rip off, they were now discussing Archie never making Frank's funeral. She'd tried to broach it before, but given the distance between them it had been hard.

'I just wasn't in the right place, Mum. I regret it, believe me I do, but it was a bad time for me.'

'He was your grandad, Archie. You'll never get that chance again.'

'I know that, Mum, for fuck's sake.'

'No need to swear at me. I'm only saying.'

'Sorry,' he replied, stroking her left upper arm.

He was angry at himself. He knew at the time he should have been there. Frank was the one man he'd had left to look up to. While Frank was getting cremated, Archie was drinking himself into oblivion to try and block out his remorse. He couldn't put it right and he'd regret it for the rest of his days.

He looked around the room, taking in the men and all they stood for. He'd momentarily missed it all – the power, the adrenaline, the thrill of the life. He then saw Sarah looking at him and almost immediately knew he'd been right to walk away from it all. The life he had in Spain was what he'd wanted all along. Growing up, he'd had no choice – it had been assumed from the day he could walk that he would be part of his grandad's empire and one day take over. That day had come far too soon, of course, and maybe the enormity of Frank's death was what had made him walk away. He knew, though, from the moment he stepped onto that plane to Faro that he was doing the right thing. For the first time in his life, he'd felt himself. Sarah and Mary were the most important things in his life. Only a threat to their existence would ever make him take a backward step into the world he once ruled. He promised Sarah, as soon as she'd landed in Spain, that he would never do anything to put them in danger. They were his world, and his world was not the world it once was.

The afternoon carried on without incident and Phoebe wrapped everything up by teatime. The criminal elite of the length and breadth of Britain shook hands, wished one another a merry Christmas and made their way home. The testosterone left with them and the house felt all the calmer for it.

The drinks continued to flow, with all of Phoebe's top table plus a few select others enjoying a few more stories of Jez. There were so many to tell. He'd been at Frank's side since the 1970s and had had more than his fair share of close shaves over the years. Recalling the tales brought it home to everyone how dangerous their lives could be. Brian and the others agreed it was a fuckin' brilliant life, and not one of them would change it for anything.

Archie kept quiet. No one had asked him if he missed the life. Nobody thought to change the subject either, even though it might be making him feel a little awkward, given he'd pissed off to Spain at such an important moment. The fact no one had given Archie's feelings any thought angered him. For the first time in his life, he felt out of things. It was clear that he'd moved on from this life and this life had moved on from him. He felt insignificant. Even his mum was enjoying reminiscing about the battles they'd had, right in front of him. Archie knew that even a couple of months ago, this conversation would not have taken place with him present. He would have been considered, but now he had to swallow listening to the room talk about how much they loved their lifestyle, how much they were looking forward to the future and how no one gave two fucks about him not being part of it. He didn't like that. He didn't like that one little bit.

chapter six

The next day, 22nd December 2019 – Alice's secret

Alice was up early. She felt fine as she didn't drink at the wake nor after. She had something to do today, something no one knew anything about. It had been her secret for too long. She'd not known how to handle it at first, but she now knew what to do. She hadn't felt she could talk to anyone about it, given the person involved, so she'd put it to the back of her mind, knowing full well the clock was ticking. It had taken her a while to process it and work out how to deal with it. She'd been very blasé but had soon come to realise her initial reaction had been one of denial. Then anger. Why her, why now, why him?

The timing was comical. A month before and maybe things would have been different, but she only found out after she blew Johnny's head off. Two weeks later she first had the thought. She did a test. It was positive. She was carrying Johnny's baby – a child whose father was not only the man she'd shot dead but her cousin. She couldn't keep it. How could she bring up a child, knowing one day she'd have to tell them she'd killed their father? Not only killed him but shot him point blank.

She had no choice and this was why she was angry. Being a mother was something she'd dreamed of since first finding out how children are created. Her motherly instinct had always been strong, but she couldn't bring a child into this world – her world – whose father she'd killed. That could not happen. It would not happen. She would make sure of that. She knew how troubled she'd been when she'd first found out that her uncle, Richie, had played a part in her own father's death. She'd idolised her dad. It had affected her more than she'd realised, so she knew only too well the impact it would have on her own child if they were ever to find out the events surrounding Johnny's death. Too many people knew. Yes, they were people within the family circle, people who were there the night it happened, people she could trust. However, people are not always who they seem – Johnny being a classic example. She couldn't live with the secret. It would destroy her. The only choice she had was to terminate the pregnancy before she started to show. She wore flattering clothes just in case, but she was paranoid about it.

Alice knew she'd changed since that night. Crossing the line and becoming a murderer changed most members of that elite club. The ones it didn't were psychos. Alice wasn't a psycho, but she was angry, vengeful and full of hate – three traits she was unaware of. They played out at times and people commented on them. Alice just thought it was because she'd crossed that line. She just thought it was because she was now a killer.

She did, however, know she enjoyed the new her. She wanted to be part of her new world. It gave her a buzz she'd never experienced. She enjoyed inflicting pain and seeing others suffer, because she was suffering herself. She wanted to kill, because the pain she was experiencing was a result of the decision she'd been forced to make. A decision that was killing her inside. Alice was in turmoil, so everyone else was going to suffer too.

She wiped away her tears and drove to the abortion clinic. The clinic was in Hull, far enough away from her own doorstep. Hull was not their territory. No one other than a few criminal faces knew her there, and she doubted any of them would be working in a private abortion clinic. She drove along the M18, onto the M62, before joining the A63 into Hull itself. Eight minutes later, she arrived in the car park. It was a Sunday. The Sunday before Christmas. There were just two other cars there. One, an Audi A8; the other, a VW Touareg. She suspected they belonged to staff. She locked her car, walked to the entrance door and pressed the buzzer.

'Hello, can I help?'

'Yes, er, my name's Alice Pearson. I have an appointment.'

'Hello, Mrs Pearson. Please come to the top of the stairs and take a seat. I'll be with you in a minute or two.'

'It's Miss Pearson. I'm not a Mrs.'

The door clicked and Alice walked in. It was smart, just as she'd expected. She went up the stairs and took her seat. She waited three minutes before a lady came out of a door to the left.

'Mrs Pearson. My name's Marjorie.'

Alice looked her up and down without getting up. Marjorie looked as though she was in her late fifties. She was heavily made up and had a trim figure for her age. She looked good, although her tan gave away her years. She'd obviously spent a lifetime on sunbeds, which had aged her unnecessarily.

'It's Miss Pearson. I'm not a Mrs.'

'Oh, er, I'm sorry about that, Ms Pearson. My form seems to be wrong.'

Alice stood up, straightened her skirt and looked at Marjorie just long enough to make her feel uncomfortable.

'I'm a Miss. Not a Mrs and not a fuckin' Ms. It's Miss Pearson.'

Marjorie cleared her throat. 'We will not tolerate language like that, Miss Pearson. I have merely made a mistake, for which I am extremely sorry. Now please come this way.'

Alice liked Marjorie. She reminded her of an old-school headteacher. She had authority and clearly didn't take inappropriate behaviour. Alice smiled.

'I'm sorry, Marjorie. I'm just a little on edge. I'm sure you can understand why.' Alice closed the door behind her.

'Hmm. Well, yes, I suppose, but we'll have no repeat, please.'

'No, Marjorie,' Alice replied, momentarily forgetting her anguish.

As she sat in the office, listening to Marjorie go through the formalities, it washed over her again. She then had to wait for two doctors to sign her certificate, trying all the while to stay calm. The sooner it was over, the better.

The next few hours were a blur. She cried, she laughed and she cried some more, but later that afternoon, Alice was no longer carrying Johnny's baby. She had decided prior to going that she would not be staying overnight, even though the price was the same. She wanted out of there as soon as possible and to leave behind any trace of Johnny Wallace, or whatever his real name was. Instead, she checked herself into a hotel and decided she'd get shitfaced. Marjorie had advised her to refrain from alcohol and Alice had, of course, nodded. It had been a while since she'd had a drink and it was Christmas, after all. She'd never been to Hull before and the night was young.

After she'd unpacked her overnight bag, had a shower and applied a bit of lippie, she headed out to the first bar she came to and ordered a gin and tonic. It was a typical modern bar, all straight edges and sharp corners, beautiful glass chandeliers and high tables with tall chairs, and the customary candle in the middle that the staff light the moment you take a seat. The Christmas decorations were tasteful –

minimalistic, but just enough to give that Christmas feeling. Christmas tunes were softly playing in the background. There were couples everywhere. Some male and female, some just female, but interestingly none just male. The only singletons were herself and a twenty-something woman three bar stools away, who looked up and smiled before returning to her thoughts.

Five minutes later Alice was talking to Chloe. A further five minutes in and Alice was listening to Chloe's woes of how a local loan shark was making her life a misery. By the time she'd ordered two more G&Ts, Alice was wondering how she was going to sort the fucker out.

'So, how much do you owe him in total?' she asked, sucking on the lime from her glass.

'Just over four grand.'

'So, why you sat in here spending some of it?' Alice asked, not really caring if that was too full on at such an early part of their conversation. Chloe didn't say anything and played with her straw. 'I mean, it ain't exactly two drinks for a fiver in here, is it?' she continued.

'Look, you came over to speak to me. I don't need you judging me,' Chloe snapped.

'No, but if you wind your neck in, I might just be the one person you were praying would walk through that door.'

Chloe looked quizzingly at Alice, as she sipped her drink, which the barman had just placed in front of her. Alice sucked on an ice cube, waiting for a response.

'What do you mean?'

'What I mean is, this Billington fella – I suppose you'd like him off your back?'

'Well, yeah, course.'

'So, sup up, and once we've had this, you can show me where he is.'

'I have no idea where he is. He comes to me. That's how he operates. No one – well, not as far as I know – knows where his office is. I don't think he even has one. People just know that if you want a loan and you don't want to be filling in any forms, then Billo's your man. Everyone knows about him where I live.'

'And where's that?'

'Hessle.'

'Where's that?'

'Where you from again?' Chloe asked.

'Mansfield.'

Chloe laughed and nearly choked on her gin. 'And where's that?' she asked.

Alice laughed too. 'Miles away,' she said, before continuing. 'So, he's been lending money a long time then?'

'For as long as I can remember. What you doing up here then if you're from Macclesfield?'

'Mansfield, not Macclesfield.'

'Sorry, no idea where either of them are.'

'Well, Macclesfield's nowhere near Mansfield, that I can tell you.'

'So why you here in Hull?'

Alice pondered for a moment. She'd forgotten all about her reason for being there. All of a sudden, she felt tenderness in her midriff. She was reminded. The chat with Chloe all about this Billington guy had taken her mind off things. Rest was what Marjorie had told her repeatedly, especially after Alice had made it clear she was not staying in overnight. Now she was glad Chloe didn't know where Billington worked. To go there now would be stupid.

'You don't have to tell me,' Chloe said, sounding genuine.

Alice decided to confide in her. She was a stranger after all. Who the hell was she going to tell? She needed to talk to someone. No one in Mansfield knew about the baby. *The baby*, Alice thought, realising she hadn't even found out the sex. She hadn't wanted to, although she was sure you couldn't tell at such an early stage anyway.

'I've had a termination.'

'What – a...?' Chloe said, making a pregnancy shape around her tummy.

Alice nodded. 'No one knows, only you. I can't believe I'm telling you, I really can't. Even my own mother doesn't know.'

'Spill it all out, girl. It'll do you no good bottling it up. I'm going nowhere – well, maybe across the road. Lovely cocktails in there. Their Black Russian is amazing. Only place that does 'em.'

Alice smiled.

'Does the father know?' Chloe asked.

Alice flung her head back and laughed. 'No, does he hell! And believe me, he never will!'

'People always tell, Alice, believe me. I'm surprised no one's told Billo I'm in here spending money.'

'No one will tell the father. Trust me, no one ever will.'

'Cocktail?' Chloe asked.

'Why not. I'm staying over. You can tell me more about this Billo guy. He sounds like a nasty fella.'

'He is. His trademark is petrol bombing your house. I'm scared shitless he'll put one through my door.'

'No one grasses I suspect?' Alice asked.

'No one dare.'

'What's his first name?'

'No idea. Just Billo, or Billington. Flash git he is. Flash car, loads of cash on him. Never gives advance warning of his visits. I couldn't tell you when he'll next be visiting me, but I'm on my last warning. I ain't got four grand, no point in pretending otherwise. What will be will be, but these are a reminder.'

Chloe pulled down the neck of her jumper to reveal bruising to her chest and left shoulder.

'Nasty,' Alice commented. 'But don't worry, he'll get what's coming to him. I'll make sure of that, the bastard. Come on, let's go and get those cocktails.'

As she got off the bar stool, she suddenly held her stomach.

'You OK?'

'Tender. It's quite sore actually. I'll sit here a while. I'll be OK soon. Just got off a bit quick, that's all.'

'So I'm intrigued to say the least,' Chloe said, tilting her head to one side.

'Intrigued? What about?'

'How a girl like you can sort out my problem, and to second that, why a girl like you would want to help me sort out my problem?'

Alice picked up her phone. Chloe could see her typing something in the search engine. 'Read that.'

Chloe took her phone and read the first few lines about a guy called Frank Pearson, alleged to be one of the UK's most feared gangland criminals. She scrolled down and read about his recent death.

'Who's this?' Chloe asked.

'My grandad, bless him. Was murdered earlier this year.'

'Fuck me,' Chloe said slowly.

Alice took her phone and scrolled through her photos.

'That was my dad, murdered just over seven years ago.' She scrolled further. 'Look, there's me. That's me at my grandad's funeral.'

Chloe stared at the phone, then looked back at Alice. She giggled. 'Fucking hell, Alice, that is you. So that's your family?'

'Yep. So, as I say, this Billo guy will be sorted no problem. You just leave that to me.'

Chloe bit her bottom lip, in amazement. 'So that's the how explained, but why? Why would you, for me I mean?'

'Why wouldn't I? You need help and bastards like this Billo guy give the likes of my family a bad name. Yes, my family are hardened criminals, but we don't bully people the way he does. He's just a coward. My family aren't like that. My grandad and my dad were honourable. So's my mum. She's the head of the family now.'

'Your mum?'

'Yeah. She's great, is my mum. She'll sort him, no drama. Fancy just a few glasses of wine in my hotel room? I can take it easier there.'

'Yeah, OK, as long as you treat me to a bit of room service. I'll be famished later.'

'You're on. Come on.'

Alice and Chloe sat on Alice's bed. The room wasn't luxurious, which Alice had only come to notice as she listened to Chloe talk. It had been a last-minute thing and the quality of the hotel hadn't been far up in Alice's mind. She was conscious that Chloe would have expected better from the granddaughter of one of the UK's most feared men and wondered whether to explain but surely Chloe would realise that her visit to Hull was about the termination, rather than the wall coverings of her hotel room.

Chloe hadn't given it a thought. She was too excited about her newfound best friend sorting out her massive problem that was Billo. They enjoyed a few glasses of Chardonnay, talked a lot about men, Billo in particular, and giggled their night away. Alice enjoyed Chloe's company. She was easy to talk to. She could tell she'd had a tough upbringing but presented herself well.

Alice found out, later in the evening, that Chloe had had two miscarriages, both in her late teens, when she was with her childhood sweetheart. He was killed in a road traffic accident on the M62 eighteen months ago, which was the reason she owed Billo. She'd borrowed two and a half grand to pay for his funeral. Even though she'd paid a chunk off, with interest, it was now four. She could never see it coming down. The repayments were getting bigger, and now she'd lost her job, she just couldn't afford them. Alice thought about how they had things in common – losing their babies, albeit in different ways, and the fact their boyfriends were dead, again for different reasons. The link, however, was there. Alice was going to help her. First, she needed to find out where this Billo guy was. For that she'd need help. Tomorrow, she was going home to speak to her mum after the top table meeting.

chapter seven

Phoebe was having a cuppa with Raquel at Gloria's. Things had changed slightly with Jez's death, so a "cabinet re-shuffle", as she called it, was needed. Jez was a big loss. She needed to make sure everyone was in place in the right areas. Since she'd seen off Steven Wallace, Del had moved up to oversee Nottinghamshire, Derbyshire and Leicestershire, with his brother Michael as his number two. Raquel was still head of daily operations for the whole business, and Pat Phoebe's number two. Jez had been more of an adviser to Phoebe since Frank's murder, but his presence alone meant his absence was now felt tenfold. Phoebe knew the vultures were hovering. She needed a team stronger than ever – one that was rock solid and wouldn't fracture under pressure.

'More tea, ladies?' Gloria asked.

'Yeah, go on, I'll have another one,' Phoebe replied.

Raquel put her hand over her mug and shook her head to indicate she'd had enough.

'You want one, Archie?' Gloria shouted, walking towards the kitchen door. 'Archie! Another cuppa, luv?'

'Yeah!' he called.

Raquel looked at Phoebe. Phoebe returned the look. This was not going to be easy. It was 9:20. The meeting was called for 10. People would be arriving soon. The only possible late arrival would be Alice. All Phoebe knew was that she'd gone away to see a friend for the night.

Phoebe had decided earlier, over her porridge, that she would wait until the last moment to see if the issue had raised its head. She was hanging fire for two reasons. One, she might not have to deal with it at all. Two, if she did, as much as it would hurt her, it would have to be played out in full view of her team to send a very strong message as to what she was prepared to do for the sake of the family business. Archie was family after all – bloodline – but there was no way Phoebe was going to allow him into the meeting. He'd made his bed and he had to lie in it. This meeting was for the top table only, and jumping ship meant Archie wasn't part of it. Her stomach was churning. Raquel understood the predicament Phoebe was in all too well and said she'd support her decision to play it out if it came to it.

A car pulled up. Phoebe checked her watch. 9:24. She sipped her tea and stared at the door into the hallway.

Alice came bounding in. 'No one here yet?' she asked.

'You look a bit rough. Heavy night, was it?'

'Thanks, Mum. I needed that. But yeah, a few glasses were enjoyed.'

'Cuppa?' Gloria asked.

'Ooh, yes please, I could murder one. Actually, I'll have a strong black coffee. Archie here?'

'Yes, I'm here, sis,' he said, as he came through. 'Ooh, heavy night, was it?'

'Bloody hell. I don't look that bad, do I?'

'Where you been anyway?' he asked, giving her a kiss on the cheek.

'Nowhere for you to concern yourself with. I do have friends, you know. Sarah and Mary here?'

'No, they've stayed over at Southwell. Didn't see much point in them being here while we're all talking shop in there,' he replied, nodding his head in the direction of the boardroom.

Phoebe had kept the boardroom at Gloria's. Frank had ruled from that room and Phoebe saw no need to change it. Gloria was happy as it meant she saw everyone quite frequently.

Raquel glanced over at Phoebe, who noticed but focused on Archie. Her stomach did another turn.

'Well, if it's OK with Gloria, I'll nip upstairs for a freshen-up, seeing as you lot all think I look dog rough,' Alice joked.

'Of course it is, sweetheart. You know you don't need to ask.'

Alice took her mug of coffee and on her way out said, 'Can I have a word, Mum, after the meeting? Need to talk to you about something.'

'Of course.'

Del walked in, followed by Michael, Ryan and Des. 'Morning,' they all said in unison. Gloria boiled the kettle for the fourth time in what seemed as many minutes. They all shook Archie's hand and gave Phoebe and Raquel a peck on the cheek.

'Brian and Pat have just pulled up, too. Shall we go through? Del asked.

'No, let's wait until everyone's here,' Phoebe said.

Over the next ten minutes Trainer, Pēteris, Jase, Knighty and Gray, who'd all met at the club in Mapperley, arrived in Pēteris's car. Gloria made sure they all had a cuppa and took a plate of biscuits through, before returning to the now crowded kitchen.

'All ready for you, Phoebe, luv.'

'Thanks, Gloria. Right, ladies and gents, let's go through.'

Phoebe led the way. Pat followed, along with Brian and Archie. Phoebe heard Raquel cough. That was the signal. She turned, allowed Pat and Brian to pass and placed a hand on Archie's shoulder.

'You'll have to wait in the kitchen, Archie,' she said.

Brian and Pat halted.

'Eh?'

'This is a top table meeting. You're no longer part of things. You know that,' Phoebe replied, doing her best to sound assertive but casual at the same time, as though it shouldn't be an issue.

'You what? Please tell me this is a joke, Mum.'

'It's no joke. You left the family business. You made that clear.'

Archie felt like he'd been hit by a ten-tonne truck. All eyes were on him. He felt like a small child being chastised by his mum in front of his friends.

Everyone found it awkward but admired Phoebe all the same. It was the first time Archie had been back since he'd decided to do a runner. The fact it was because of Jez's funeral made things different. No one wanted to air any feelings on the subject, not at such an emotional and difficult time, but if truth be known, none of them was overly pleased to see him. They all felt betrayed and had made it clear to one another he had no place in the firm.

Alice was sympathetic of course. Archie was her big brother – she just wanted him to be happy. Only Raquel and Pat had told Phoebe how they felt, and if their feelings were replicated throughout her team, this was something she had to do.

Archie nodded his head slowly, in recognition.

'Wow. Just fuckin' wow. Well, I think it's clear how you all feel about me.' He took a step back. 'Not one of you has a fuckin' clue. Twenty-two fuckin' years old I was when I first had the weight of all of you lot on my shoulders. I'm only twenty-three now for fuck's sake and here I am being cast aside. By my own mother.

I never thought I'd see this day come, Mum, but fair play, it's your call. You're the boss now.'

He stared at his mum, who could see he was hurting like hell, and shook his head in despair. Feeling let down and totally humiliated, he stormed out.

Phoebe kept her composure. That was the hardest thing she'd ever had to do. Much harder than ordering someone's murder. Much harder than being the boss of one of the UK's most feared criminal families. And much harder than having to accept her son was not the man he was supposed to be.

'Right, let's get started, shall we?'

Pat and Brian stepped aside to let Phoebe through. The atmosphere was tense, but in the eyes of everyone sat around that boardroom table, Phoebe Pearson had just risen in stature. No one other than Raquel could believe what they'd just witnessed, but every single one of them knew it was the right thing to do – everyone except Alice. She didn't like what she'd just witnessed.

Phoebe Pearson was fast becoming a legend of the criminal underworld.

Archie raced back to Southwell along the A614, swearing at the top of his voice. He, Sarah and Mary were supposed to be staying for Christmas and going back to Spain on the 28th. *Well, everyone could all well and truly fuck off now* he told himself. He was going to book the first flight home. He wanted to be back in Spain by teatime. He turned the final corner to the house and banged the steering wheel for the umpteenth time, when he realised he didn't have the fob for the gates. Another reminder of how he was no longer part of the family.

'Shit!' he shouted. 'Fuckin' shit!' He screeched to a halt. 'Ring Sarah mobile!' he bellowed into his in-car phone system.

'It's me. I can't get in. Open these gates for me, luv, will ya.'

'You OK? You sound annoyed,' she replied, as she pressed the button.

The gates slowly started to open.

'Yeah, fine, but start packing – we're off. Today if we can.'

'Today? What's happened? Something's happened, hasn't it?'

Archie sped towards the house, checking his rear view mirror.

'I'll tell you in a mo. Put kettle on.'

Archie stormed into the house, slamming the door behind him. Sarah hugged him, before cupping his face.

'What's the matter?' she asked.

'I've been outed, that's what. My own mother has outed me from the business. Right in front of everyone, too. Made me look a right prick. Well, that's it, I'm fuckin' done. Take a good look around, luv, as this is the last time we'll see this place. Kiss Southwell goodbye, 'cos we're off and we ain't ever comin' back.'

As much as Sarah wanted to never be part of the family business again, she needed to be his voice of reason. That's what she always did.

'You don't mean any of that.'

'Eh, I do, I fuckin' do.'

'Archie, listen to me. Look, sit down. Come on, I'll make you that cuppa.'

Archie sat on a stool at the kitchen island and swivelled himself round and round as if he were on the cups and saucers at the fairground. Sarah saw a boy with very much a man-sized problem.

'What did you expect your mum to do? Honestly? Put yourself in her position – how could she keep you there, along with everyone else, eh?'

'Oh, so you think she's right to cast me aside like a piece of shit, do you?'

'Who are you really angry at, Archie Pearson?' Sarah said firmly.

Archie stopped spinning. 'What do you mean who am I angry at? Who do you think?'

'Well, I think you're angry at yourself.'

Archie screwed up his face and shrugged his shoulders.

'I'm right and you know it. Here,' she said sharply, passing him his mug of tea. 'What have you always told me? You've always preached about how your dad and grandad ran the family business like a proper business. How they held regular meetings, had people in positions of responsibility, just like a real company. Yeah?'

'Yeah, s'pose.'

'No, "yeah s'pose" about it. That's what you've always told me. So, *let's s'pose*, that it *is* a real business and you as chairman or whatever buggered off without a word and left the running of the business – I don't know, selling footwear – to your mum. A multi-million-pound business. And you bugger off and then tell everyone that you want nothing to do with it. In the real world, can you honestly see anyone, even family, allowing you into a boardroom meeting where they're discussing company confidential information, whenever the fancy takes you?'

Archie looked at her stone-faced.

'Well, can you?' she asked.

He sighed. 'No, I s'pose not.'

'Definitely not, I'd say.' She took his face in her hands once more. 'Look, your mum had no choice. She had to do it. People would've been watching how she handled it. Your mum has done nothing for you to be angry at her.'

She hugged him and he hugged her back. 'Don't leave angry, sweetheart. You'll regret it. Be the bigger person. Accept she had no choice and let her know it's OK.' She pulled away. 'You made the decision to go abroad, Archie. You alone.'

'I had no choice either, you know. Twenty-two years old, I was. You have no idea what I had to deal with. All the pressure and everything,' he replied angrily.

'I'll ignore that remark but see how you flared up when I said you and you alone made the decision to go. I'm proud of you. I couldn't be prouder. That took guts, real guts. The easy thing would've been to stay, but you'd have been staying for everyone else, just to save face. I know you feel weak for going.'

Archie's face changed.

'That's hit a nerve, hasn't it?' Sarah said, staring him down. 'You need to be honest about this whole situation, Archie, or else it will eat you up. Every time someone mentions it, you'll react, because you're masking your real feelings. You're not weak. As I said, it took real guts, real strength to walk away and accept who you are. Accept responsibility for your actions. Own it. Say it out loud.'

'Say what out loud?'

'The truth – as much as it hurts to say it – the truth, Archie. Don't just accept who you are, but who you *aren't*. You are not your dad. You are not your grandad. You are you – the man I love more than anything.'

Archie looked at Mary in her highchair, chocolate mousse all over her face. 'We're bad parents, aren't we?' he said, smiling. 'She heard all of that. All the swear words. I'm sorry, pumpkin, but hey, you'll hear worse.' He kissed the top of her head.

'Let me ask you. Why did you disappear to Portugal?'

'You know why. I just picked it off the departure board.'

'No, I mean why did you go? Portugal is irrelevant. Be honest, why did you go?'

Archie paused. He'd never said it out loud. He'd wanted to but had never managed it.

'Why did you go, Archie?'

He looked her in the eye for what felt an age. ''Cos I was scared. I was out of my depth.'

Sarah said nothing, waiting for him to continue.

'Because I knew without Frank, I didn't have what it took. Whether I would have done one day, I suppose we'll never know, but I was just a kid doing a man's job. With Frank at my side, I could survive. But the moment I saw him lying dead on the ground, I knew the game was up. I needed another ten years to grow into the man my grandad wanted me to be. I'd have carried on while he was alive, even with him in the background. Just him being there was enough. No one will know what it took for me to come back and face everyone. In a way, I'm grateful Jez copped it. It gave me the opportunity, 'cos the longer it went on, the harder it would have been. Everyone's been great, though it eats away at me wonderin' what they're all sayin' behind my back.'

He held out his arms. Sarah walked into them and felt warm and safe.

'And now's the time to stand tall, sweetheart, face them again and just be who you are. No airs and graces, no mask, no nothing. Don't blame anyone else, especially your mum. She needs you. She needs you to be her son.'

Archie squeezed her tight. He put his head to one side on her shoulder so he could see Mary banging her plastic spoon, the sound of a happy child devouring chocolate mousse.

'Am I still packing?' Sarah asked.

Archie thought hard about what she'd just said. He thought about Gloria's house and how his mum had excluded him. Sarah spoke sense and was right about everything, but his grandad, and his dad for that matter, would never have done what Phoebe did. They would never have treated him so disrespectfully. For Frank and Daniel, family always came first. He didn't like who his mum was turning into. He just couldn't swallow what she'd done. It was a step too far.

'Yes. I want to be back in Spain tonight.'

Sarah sighed. He'd regret it but she'd be with him all the way. She kissed his cheek and walked upstairs to pack.

Archie got out his phone and looked for flights. Within the hour, they were on their way.

chapter eight

Phoebe was wrapping up the meeting. Other than the usual family business, she'd slightly rearranged the order of things. Del and Michael were to run the overall daily operations, and report to Raquel. Pēteris was to run Nottinghamshire and Jase to move up and run Doncaster. Trainer now just had Leeds, which he was not too happy about. He liked having Doncaster under his wing but accepted Phoebe's ruling and rationale that she needed a tighter ship – each town needed someone on the ground at all times. Ryan and Des moved away from being heavily involved in Nottingham and became the firm's enforcers. If anyone needed sorting out, anywhere within the territory, it was Ryan and Des that were called upon. This meant that everyone reported to Del, including Michael if truth be known. Del reported to Raquel, and Raquel reported to Phoebe. Pat stayed at Phoebe's side, as always, and Brian as her adviser.

It was a tight ship. One that Phoebe had complete confidence in. The only person without a defined role was Alice. Phoebe just could not find a role that she felt suited her. Alice was growing in confidence, but for some reason she didn't slot in anywhere. Phoebe spoke to Pat and Brian about it, and they agreed she should be part of things at the top, without defined responsibility. Her killing Johnny and her violent flashes had earned her the respect she needed. No one had any beef with her being a senior member. Everyone sort of accepted that as a Pearson, with good pedigree, she was up there at her mum's side. Everyone liked Alice. They looked upon her as the boss's daughter and treated her accordingly, with good reason.

The last item on the agenda was the subject of gun smuggling. Pēteris's friend from Manchester, Janis, who had helped with Fletcher O'Brien, had approached Pēteris at Jez's wake about two contacts he had. Contacts who, it would appear, could supply illegal guns into the UK without any significant issue. Things had become tricky since Brexit. Guns had proven more difficult – metal had a habit of making machines ping. The UK families were doing their own thing, as they always had. No one had cornered the market. Pēteris saw this as an opportunity. He was keen to show his worth and a quick return on the faith Phoebe had shown in him. There was a gap, and gaps need filling.

Janis's two contacts were fellow Latvians called Andris and Valdis. They were also old foes – two criminals who'd been on the receiving end of Frank's wrath around fifteen years ago. Long before Brexit, Frank had cornered the market. They'd met Frank, along with Daniel and Richie, to discuss supplying foreign labour into the UK back when things were just starting to get good. However, things didn't turn out well with Andris and Valdis, who had tried to be the tail wagging the dog. As they swiftly found out, Frank was no dog and always did the wagging. Richie stabbed Valdis in the thigh at the first meeting and although the two sides did end up working together, it lasted less than twelve months before Frank told them to fuck off. Which they did.

Pēteris hadn't heard much of them since. He knew they'd gone back to Latvia after a stint in Wales. Their names had popped up from time to time as they seemed to be involved in dealings with other UK firms. The proposition, however, sounded interesting and extremely lucrative. Dangerous but lucrative. Frank, and then Archie, had always purchased their firearms from UK contacts. They'd never engaged with direct supply from outside, reasoning that dealing with people you don't know too well and don't have history with on such a hot commodity would bring too many headaches. Frank had never liked dealing with people if it meant dealing with individuals whose ethics didn't always match his own. Archie had followed suit. Janis, however, had convinced Pēteris that Andris and Valdis would deal with all the headaches. All they were after was a major contact to act as the link. Pēteris knew Frank would have told him to get fucked with this idea without a moment's thought, mainly due to the two Latvians who were offering to deal with the headaches. Frank was not someone who forgot or forgave too easily. But Phoebe had agreed to it being on today's agenda as a last-minute addition.

'So, tell us all then, Pēteris, how these two guys say they can get the guns into the country undetected,' Phoebe instructed. 'The Channel is a no-go. It's too high profile.'

'The Scottish coast. They want to bring them in via the Scottish coast,' Pēteris replied.

'The Scottish coast is a big fuckin' coast, Pēteris. Any particular area, and why the fuck Scotland?' Brian asked.

''Cos no one ever looks there. Well, not the quiet little fishing ports that I'm on about anyway. All the attention's on the Channel, the big cities and the big ports. They've done it twice now. Well, dummy runs twice. They have a guy on the continent who drives his lorry to a small port somewhere in Denmark, Germany or the Netherlands. So far, they've done it from Germany and the Netherlands. Just a small fishing port or small beach that no one cares a fuck about. Both times they've just sailed over the North Sea into little villages around the Moray Firth, wherever the fuck that is. Anyway, the vessel leaves, and early the next morning arrives somewhere else no one cares about. They've done it both times near "Buckie", or something like that. Anyway, a truck or van will be waiting to pick up the cargo and drive to wherever. No one has scratched their arse, or fuck all. No one looks at a lorry or van parked up – why would they? No one bothers about a fishing boat, and as long as we use different locations here, and on the continent, and operate under darkness, no one will think anything. All we have to do is have the contacts this end for the guns to go to, collect our cut and, well, that's it. We just need to stay under the radar, keep it small numbers, but regular, and keep our mouths shut. Janis reckons his contacts can get as many firearms as we need – handguns, sawn-offs, the lot.'

Pēteris could see their minds racing. 'So, what do you reckon?' he asked them, but looking at Phoebe in particular.

'Who are the two contacts?' Phoebe asked.

Pēteris sighed. 'Ah well, that's maybe the issue.'

'Because?' she asked

'Well, it's two Latvians.'

'I thought it might be. Birds of a feather and all that,' Trainer said, laughing. Pēteris threw him a sarcastic smile.

'And?' Phoebe asked.

'Well, these two guys have dealt with us before. With Frank and his lads back in 2004, I think.'

Brian flung his head back. 'Fuck me, it's fuckin' what's-their-names. One of 'em had a glass eye. Always reminded Frank of Steven Wallace – which did nothing to warm him to Frank, I might add. Anyway, Richie stabbed one of them, didn't he? Is that them?'

Pēteris nodded. 'Ancient history,' he said.

'It didn't fuckin' end well, Pēteris, if I remember correctly. Frank would be turning in his grave. And if I remember right, it was you and some mate of yours at the time who introduced them.'

'Yeah, I know, but I showed where my loyalties lie, Brian. I wasn't to know it would go tits up, was I?' Pēteris replied sternly.

'That rings a bell,' Phoebe said. 'I wasn't involved back then but, yes, I recall them. Why are they interested in getting back in with us?'

'No reason, as far as I know, other than Janis had me as a contact with you guys and, well, saw it as a bit of an earner. They wanted a way in with a crime family and I was that link I suppose, so he spoke to me and, well, I'm putting it on the table,' Pēteris confirmed.

Phoebe addressed the room. 'Hmm. Any thoughts?'

'There's a gap, that's for sure. A real shortage, Phoebe,' Del said, waiting for some support. 'Over the last couple of years, supply has been harder to come by. Well, reliable supply anyway.'

'And it's a good earner. We'll certainly make some money and if we get in first, we can command top dollar,' Pat added.

'There aren't many people who could command the trust of the major players, Phoebe. There's only a handful – the likes of Tariq, Greg West, the Burbanks brothers and us – who could pull this off. No one else would have the trust of the top players. They'd just muscle in and take over their operation,' Raquel butted in.

'Good point, very good point,' Michael agreed.

'But we are respected enough to take this to market,' Phoebe replied. She looked at Pēteris. 'Where are they from?' she asked.

'Latvia,' Pēteris said.

'What – all of them?'

'Sorry, you mean the guns. All over. Some from European eastern bloc countries, but a lot from outside Europe. All around the world. It's begging for someone to take the lead.'

'OK, set up a meeting with them. After Christmas. First week of the new year. Let's see what they have to say. Let me know when it is.'

'Will do.'

'Oh, and before I forget, when are you sorting that new landlord out?'

'Next Saturday was the plan. That OK?'

Phoebe nodded. 'Make sure he gets the message. I don't know who he thinks he is, but he seems to think he's some kind of big shot, doesn't he?'

'He's made noises like "I ain't paying fuck all" and all that, yes, but I assure you he'll get the message all right.'

Phoebe drew the meeting to a close and wished them all a merry Christmas, thanking them for their support during what had been a tough year. She was looking forward to an easier next twelve months. As they made their way out, Alice asked if they could have that word.

'Sorry, Alice, I forgot. Pat, stay behind – Alice wants a word.'

Pat sat back down. Phoebe saw Raquel stall and look. She shook her head, indicating Raquel was OK to go. Phoebe had no idea what Alice wanted to talk about but saw no reason to take up Raquel's time, too. She waited until Raquel had closed the door.

'That must've been hard, Mum – that with Archie,' Alice said, giving her a hug.

'More than you'll ever know, sweetheart.'

Alice pulled away. 'I didn't see it coming and for what it's worth, I think it was wrong. He didn't deserve that.'

'I'm not speaking about it. It's done. It was the right thing to do. Let's leave it there. So how was last night?' Phoebe asked.

Alice paused, knowing Archie was not up for discussion. 'Yeah, it was good, I had a good night,' Alice replied.

'Where did you go?'

'Hull.'

'Hull?'

'Yeah, Hull.'

'Why the fuck did you go to Hull?' Pat asked, obviously surprised.

Alice couldn't tell them the truth. She would take the fact she'd been carrying Johnny's child to the grave. 'Just to see a fella I've met.'

'Will we be meeting him?' Phoebe asked.

'Doubt it. I gave him the push. Not my type in the end. I met a woman afterwards though...'

'Oh yeah? Stepped on the other bus, have we?' Pat said, laughing.

'No, Pat, I haven't, and if I had, it would be no business of yours,' Alice replied.

'All right, calm down. I can see a visit to Hull has done nothing to improve your sense of humour these days.'

'Children, children,' Phoebe said, trying to bring order back to the conversation. 'So, come on, whatever it is must involve this woman you met.'

'It does. Her name's Chloe – lovely lady, in her late twenties. Anyway, her husband died a couple of years ago. Car crash it was. Tragic. So she had to borrow a couple of grand off a loan shark for the funeral. Someone called Billo, short for Billington, I think...'

Phoebe looked at Pat, who shook his head to confirm he'd never heard of him. She returned to Alice.

'Nasty fucker, he is. Trademark is petrol bombing people's houses, she says.'

'So come on, get to the point,' Phoebe instructed.

'Well, this two grand is now something like four and a half and is going up daily. She can't live with the repayments, so she's expecting her house to go up any day. She showed me bruises on her chest and shoulders he's given her, so I thought we could help her by sorting this Billo guy out.'

'No way. Not even discussing it, young lady.'

'What? She's desperate, Mum.'

'Not our problem, Alice. We have enough of our own to deal with without getting involved in matters that don't concern us.'

'But I told her we'd help her.'

'Then you shouldn't have done, should you? You'll just have to tell her you were mistaken, and she'll have to sort her own shit out.'

'Grandad would've. As would Archie for that matter,' Alice said, knowing that would get a reaction.

Phoebe stared her down. 'Your grandad, God rest his soul, did not build this business on getting involved in petty squabbles between loan sharks and waifs and strays who can't repay their debts. You have no right promising the help of this family to anyone, Alice Pearson. No right whatsoever. Don't ever lend the name of this family to anyone again. Not without my permission first. Have you got that?'

Alice didn't reply.

'Have you got that, young lady?'

'Yes, Mum.'

She noted Phoebe didn't react to her comment about Archie.

'Good. Now you make sure you tell this Chloe lady that the Pearson family will NOT be getting involved in her problems. Not now, not ever. And do it sooner rather than later.'

'Come on Pat, we have things to do.'

Pat followed Phoebe out. On closing the door, he put his hand on Phoebe's shoulder. She paused.

'For what it's worth, you were right with Archie. You had no choice, and I'd be amazed if anyone else around that table feels differently.'

'Thanks, Pat. Means a lot.'

'She's his sister, so she's bound to see it differently, but I know everyone around that table would've been relieved and pleased you did that.'

Alice stayed behind in the boardroom. Her mum was right. She'd acted above her pay grade and had only been trying to impress her new friend. She saw the admiration in Chloe's eyes when she told her who her family was and how different she was towards her. It was hard to quantify it, and to outsiders, it wouldn't have even been noticeable, but Alice saw it and she liked it. Even before she'd shot Johnny, when she was very much the tea girl and paper shuffler, she still loved the attention she received just because of who her family were. Since becoming a killer, she was craving that adulation more and more, and yesterday, even though she was acutely aware of what she was doing, she just could not help herself. It had crossed her mind to walk away on first mention of Chloe being in trouble with a loan shark, but she wanted the opportunity to play the big 'un and work out how she would deliver on whatever promise or help she gave her. Even this morning, she more or less knew what her mum's reaction would be but proceeded anyway, hoping her mum would prove her wrong. Now she had to tell Chloe she couldn't help her. Her only other alternative was to take some of the family's men with her, on the proviso it was on her mum's orders, but that would cause even more trouble. Not just for her but for the family. The family she was so proud of.

'I wish you were still here, Dad,' she said quietly, looking up at the ceiling. Alice missed her father, more than ever recently. She thought about the day she found out he'd been murdered in Richie and Marie's house. She thought about the events that unfolded with Richie and how it had all led to her grandad being murdered earlier this year.

'Well, happy fuckin' Christmas,' she said, raising an imaginary glass. She then thought of her aborted child. That made her sad, too. She took a deep breath and wondered when to go and see Chloe. She'd told her she'd be back in touch in a few days, so she had a bit of time. It was Christmas Day in a couple of days. She decided to wait until Christmas was over. She didn't want to spoil Chloe's day. *'I'll go up on the 28th,'* she said to herself. *'Yes, the 28th will be fine.'*

chapter nine

Pēteris was in the car with Jase, Knighty and Gray. They had just set off for the drive back to the Mapperley club. Pēteris was excited. This could well be the big opportunity he'd been waiting for. If he orchestrated this well, it would really elevate him in the ranks of the Pearson business. Pēteris had served the family well. He was loyal and wanted to repay the loyalty he'd been shown over the years.

'Fuck me, pal. I bet you can't believe she agreed to a meet,' Jase said. He was driving, with Pēteris in the passenger seat.

'I'm buzzing, mate. I said to Janis I couldn't guarantee what she'd say, but if I'm honest, I thought their history would be an issue. I wasn't hopeful at all.'

'Well, you can tell your mate that it's looking on, can't you? He'll be buzzing too, I bet.'

Pēteris smiled. 'He will. He deserves a break.'

Pēteris dialled Janis's number. He decided to speak in English, given the company he was in.

'Sveiki, Pēteris. Kā tev iet, draugs?'

'Hi Janis. English please, mate, I have company.'

'Ah OK. How are you?'

'Buzzing, my friend. It went very well. Phoebe is interested. She's asked me to set up a meet after New Year. The first week back. Can you come back to me with a few dates?'

'I sure can. I'm not planning to meet them until after Christmas myself. They're back in Latvia now for Christmas, but I'll try and get some dates off them and come back to you. So what did she say?'

'Just to set up a meeting.'

'What about the previous problems?'

'It got mentioned. Some of the guys were around at the time, but Phoebe didn't seem bothered. I don't think it will be an issue, but just make sure they don't come here thinking they're the top dogs. They need to show respect.'

'I'll try, but you know what they're like. They haven't changed.'

'Fuckin' hell, neither has the Pearson family. If they come trying to call the shots again, it'll only end up like last time, and I'm the one introducing them – again.'

Knighty and Gray looked at each other and both shook their heads. Neither of them knew what had really happened, but enough to know that the likes of Pat, Brian and Del would not take kindly to a repeat.

'Don't worry, Pēteris. I'll let them know. I promise.'

'OK, listen, have a great Christmas and I'll see you soon. This is the big one for us, brother.'

'You too. I'll be in touch soon.'

Pēteris ended the call and turned to Jase.

'Fuck me, Pēteris, I hope this doesn't go pear-shaped. Phoebe will have your balls in a vice. Guns are serious fuckin' shit. If anything goes wrong, it'll be a lot of fucking bird for whoever gets caught in the crossfire ... and doing a stretch in the big house might well be the least of our worries. If you want my advice, mate – and tell me to fuck off if you want – keep your finger well and truly on the button with this one. I know Janis is a mate, but he sounded a bit too blasé for me just then. Don't let him be your undoing, pal.'

Pēteris turned to look straight ahead. He was right. Janis did seem a bit casual. Maybe he hadn't understood the enormity of smuggling guns into the country. For the first time in a long time, he had butterflies in his stomach. He changed the subject.

'What d'you all think about Archie?'

'Right call for me. He made his bed,' Knighty piped up.

'Same here. You can't fuck off like that and expect to be part of the decision-making. If he'd have gone for a couple of days to get his head straight, fair enough, I'd get that, but when he went, he went for good,' said Jase.

'Gray?' Pēteris asked.

'I agree – I can't say otherwise – but he'll be hurting like fuck, and when someone's hurting like that, especially when it's to do with family, they can be dangerous. Phoebe needs to keep him on side at the same time. How she does it is up to her, but for me, he's better a friend than a foe. And with how he's bound to be feeling right now, he could well become a serious foe.'

There was no noise except for the radio. They all considered what Gray had just said. It was a full minute and a half before Knighty broke the silence.

'Burger anyone?'

chapter ten

Tariq Mali was approaching Marble Arch when his phone rang. He glanced at the name. *Hendrik.*

'Hendrik, I hope this is good news.'

'Oh, I would say so, my friend. I know who's after him, and they are not nice people.'

'Excellent. Who are they?'

'Two guys called Dirk and Joris. Heavy duty dope smugglers apparently. Not to be crossed, let me tell you. D'you know them?

'I do indeed. Never dealt with them personally but you can't do as much business as I do over there without knowing who's who. Send me as much info as you have on them. I need to make contact, but I'm driving at the moment.'

'I will, along with my bill.'

'That'll do, Hendrik. I'll be in touch soon. You can then set the ball rolling for me. Have a nice Christmas.'

'You too.'

'We don't do Christmas.'

'Oh yeah, sorry, my mistake. Well, have a nice few days anyway.'

Tariq disconnected the call. He smiled, before turning up his radio and singing at the top of his voice as he drove down Park Lane.

chapter eleven

Phoebe pulled into her driveway and parked up next to Alice's car. Archie's wasn't there. She was nervous and anxious at the same time. *Maybe he's nipped out* she thought. He could have taken Sarah and Mary somewhere. She'd hoped he'd be there when she returned and had tried to convince herself he'd have calmed down if he was – with Sarah's help. If he was in, it was not a conversation she was looking forward to. It broke her heart saying what she did. His disappointment had ripped through her like a knife. While she didn't regret her decision to take the top chair, times like today really tested her limits.

She switched off the engine, sat back in her seat and replayed what she would say when he came back. Above all else, she had to be resolute. If Sarah was in, she'd be OK. Sarah would understand. Pat had let her know how everyone present today felt. They all, without exception, supported her and thought she'd played it right. Pēteris had omitted Gray's comments about keeping Archie on side, simply saying that they thought she'd played a blinder.

'Come on, lady, get it over with,' she said to herself, as she opened her door, thinking maybe Archie was in and it was Sarah who'd nipped out. She'd taken no more than four steps when she looked up to see Alice at the door.

'He's gone, Mum. They all have. Their clothes are gone, everything. Must have gone back to Spain.'

Phoebe stopped. She realised she'd never contemplated him returning to Spain. She took a deep breath and continued to walk towards the door. Alice held out her arms. Phoebe dropped her bag and hugged Alice tight, cherishing the warmth only a hug from a child can give. They rubbed each other's backs for a good minute. Phoebe broke free and went to speak, but Alice beat her to it.

'It's OK, Mum. It's OK, I understand. Though I said he didn't deserve it, he shouldn't have buggered off like this without making it right. Let him be. He'll come right.'

Phoebe smiled in appreciation of her daughter's kind words. 'Thanks, sweetheart. I'm sure he will.'

She knew Sarah would have had no say in the matter. If Archie said they were going, then go they would. She just hoped she'd play her part. That's what the women in this life did. It's what she'd done, what Gloria had done and it was what Sarah would do. Phoebe just wanted her son back. Not her son, the top UK criminal, but her son, Archie. She would've preferred him to be at her side, or even better, for her to be at his, but that was not to be. Phoebe knew it and accepted it. It didn't stop her longing for it, though.

She and Alice walked in together, straight through into the living room. Phoebe suddenly felt warm and cosy. The Christmas decorations, the huge tree – she loved this time of year, always had done. And even though it would be another one without her Daniel, Archie leaving under those circumstances was not going to spoil it for her. She was determined to have a good Christmas.

She kept things small on Christmas Day. After the year they'd had, she wanted a close family Christmas. The only people for lunch were Alice, Gloria, Marie, Brian and Raquel. She invited Brian and Raquel since they had no one else, no long-term partners to spend the day with. Pat had his current lady on his arm, Paige – a Geordie lass he'd been with on and off for five years, so he was loved up in Kingston Park, over the Tyne Bridge. The other main members of the firm were with their families. The day went well in Southwell. Everyone apart from Gloria had a stroll through town before lunch, stopping off for a drink at The Admiral Rodney. Gloria had insisted on staying home and creating a lunch that would have probably fed the whole of Southwell. They marked the occasion by raising a glass to those whom the family had lost and those who were absent. The list was longer than anyone could remember – it had gone from only Daniel to Frank, Jez, Paul and John and, by way of absence, Archie, Sarah and Mary. They even raised a glass to Richie.

No one could have known this calm was not going to last. One mighty storm was brewing, but before that showed its face, they had a bit of a strong breeze to sort out first – a breeze called Billo.

chapter twelve

Friday 27th December 2019 – Marbella, Spain

Archie ordered another whisky. He'd already had enough, but he was in a drinking mood. He'd been on a downer ever since he left Gloria's. Christmas Day had been OK. He and Sarah had just had a quiet day in their villa with Mary. It's what they'd wanted and it had been a happy day in the midst of the cloud that hung over Archie.

He was in a casino down a side street just outside of town. One that only certain people were invited to. Since arriving in Spain, he'd associated with a few English villains on extended stays in the sun and had already earned a reputation as an enforcer. That meant he had no real responsibility, didn't have to think for others and just had to channel his aggression. He was good at it, too. Archie was a good fighter, a brawler with a strong punch. He also had his family's name to ride on. Everyone knew of Frank Pearson out there. He was one of the greats, and being his grandson meant Archie didn't have to try too hard to gain respect or offers of work. No one seemed bothered he came out when he did. He'd put his cards on the table and just said it hadn't been the right time for him, and that knocking heads together or collecting debts was more his line of work. People had accepted it and work had been plentiful and taken him all over Spain. It was work he enjoyed and which had allowed him access to this exclusive casino.

As well as realising he was good at enforcing, he'd come to realise he was quite a good gambler. He'd won a fair few grand of late. He'd never had any urge to overdo it, though – he knew when it was time to quit. Tonight he was eighteen grand up. He'd cashed in and was having one final drink to end the night.

'You're a fuckin' lucky fella, Archie lad!'

Archie recognised the voice but looked around anyway. 'Hugh, how are ya?'

Hugh held out his hand. Archie shook it. 'Not as good as you. I've been watching ya. You must be over twenty grand to the good tonight.'

'Not quite, Hugh, but close enough. I've cashed in, though.'

'Good lad. Important to know when to knock it on the head. Too many don't and they're the ones the likes of you end up going after.'

'Yeah, I've lost count how many people I've had to have a word with, or worse, having lost money in here, or places like it. Keeps me earning, though.'

'Good Christmas?' Hugh asked.

'Quiet, but yeah, good. You?'

'Same. My lady always insists on me staying in on Christmas Day. Does my fuckin' head in, but it's only once a year. Listen, I'm off. Got a young blonde waiting for me.'

Archie laughed. 'OK, mate. Enjoy.'

'Oh, I will, Archie lad, I will.'

Hugh was a dope dealer from the South West of England. One of the biggest in Europe at one point, but he took a one-way ticket from life in the West Country a few years ago. He was technically on the run from a very nasty criminal operation in the Netherlands, which he didn't always try to hide. Everyone knew it would catch up with him one day, but to Hugh it was an occupational hazard of the drug game. Until a hitman put a bullet through his head, he'd continue loving life. He'd shag anything that moved, as long as it had a vagina – which he was about to do tonight by the sounds of it – and sniffed, snorted and smoked anything on offer. If the hitman didn't get him, the lifestyle would. Archie liked him, though. He had a good heart deep down and was a good contact to know. He knew everyone and everyone knew him, hence why it was so strange he was still breathing. If the boys from the Netherlands wanted to come after him, they wouldn't have to try too hard to get wind of his whereabouts. Archie reckoned on the fact he was so likeable that no one had breathed a word of him residing in Marbella.

He watched Hugh take the hand of a blonde lady, who he guessed was in her mid twenties. He smiled at how Hugh would probably need a breather halfway through. He had to be in his fifties and looking at the way she held herself, Hugh was in for one hell of a ride.

He sipped his drink and checked his watch. Eight thirty. He wanted to be home for nine. He knew Sarah didn't like him drinking and gambling. The eighteen grand would do nothing to impress her. She wasn't bothered about money and Archie liked that about her. He knew he'd hit the jackpot with her. She would be with him whatever and for that he was grateful. He couldn't even contemplate where he'd be now if it wasn't for Sarah. The way he felt after his mum outed him, he could've easily spiralled out of control. He had spiralled to a degree, but Sarah and Mary kept him from falling over the cliff edge.

Tomorrow he had nothing to do. He'd enjoy the day off, spend it with Sarah and Mary and see if a job came in. He loved the thrill of the chase. Loved it when he tracked them down and loved it when they always tried to pay him off. Archie was good for his word. His clients knew that, and it was something that was worth its weight in gold.

chapter thirteen

Saturday 28th December 2019

Alice had messaged Chloe to say she'd be up for lunchtime. Chloe asked if she'd sorted anything. Alice told her she'd tell her all about it when she got there. Alice drove along the A63 looking at the Humber Bridge in front of her in the distance. She came off at the Hessle turn-off. From Boothferry Road, the sat nav said half a mile. She was nervous. She'd more or less promised Chloe she'd have some sort of plan by now. Chloe would be expecting her to have found out where Billo operated from and to be turning up with a couple of heavies to sort him out. But it was just her, and there was no plan.

She drove into a nice estate that was maybe thirty years old judging by the style of the houses. Lots of semi-detacheds with small 4x4s in the driveways. Full of people who wanted a Range Rover, but couldn't yet afford one. There had been a sprinkling of snow, and the pavements had children's icing sugar footprints on them. She turned into a cul de sac and pulled up outside number 18, failing to notice the large 4x4 parked a few yards away. She took a deep breath. She reminded herself that she didn't really know Chloe anyway, so if she took the hump, she'd just have to live with it. She could just hop in her car and drive straight back to Nottinghamshire.

She knocked on the door. No answer. She knocked again. No answer. She looked around but couldn't see anyone. She knocked for a third time. A broad man, in his mid to late forties, with dark hair and plenty of bling answered. Alice could tell he would have been a good-looking bloke in his day. He looked her up and down and smiled. She didn't like him undressing her with his eyes like that. Before she knew it, he'd grabbed her by the hair and was dragging her inside. He threw her into the living room, where she found Chloe, her face covered in blood.

'Who the fuck is this bitch?' he shouted.

Chloe looked at Alice, for some sort of instruction. Her mind was racing. Should she tell Billo who Alice was or keep her mouth shut and receive another slap across the face?

Alice gave nothing away, so Chloe replied, 'Just a friend, she's just a friend.'

'Mmm, a very nice friend too,' he said, looking her up and down again.

Alice didn't say a word, as she tried to assess the situation. Aside from the man letching over her, there were two others in the house – one in the same room as them, who a bath would do the world of good, and another who came in to tell the guy with the bling that he'd not found anything. They both looked like they were in their twenties, the one who'd just walked in being the elder of the two.

'Billo, I presume?' Alice said.

'Ah, you've heard of me. I'm impressed.' He took a step forward and stroked her cheek. 'Not local, though. Not with an accent like that. Where are you from, beautiful lady?'

'That's none of your business. Now if I was you, I would leave while you still have a chance of seeing your next birthday. Believe me, you don't want to mess with me or my family.'

Billo laughed a hearty laugh. 'How many times have I heard that line!' He turned to his two lackeys. 'How many times have we heard that, lads? Everyone's a big shot. Everyone's got a dad who can kick the fuck out of me.' He laughed again, then put his face right into Alice's.

'But guess what, no one has. No one. Can you see?' He stroked her face again but this time carried on to the outline of her breast.

Alice spat in his face. 'You'll regret that,' she said.

Billo casually wiped the phlegm away and said nothing. She spat again. He wiped his face with his sleeve a second time and said, 'Not as much as you', before slapping her hard again and again until blood was pouring from her nose and mouth. He pulled her back by her hair. As she screamed, he spat right into her mouth, which he closed with his other hand.

'Swallow that, you fuckin' bitch!'

Alice paused, keeping eye contact the whole time. Billo loosened his grip. She spat it out right into his face.

'Fuck off! My family will kill you for this!'

Billo threw her against the wall and wiped away her spit for a third time.

Chloe got to her feet. 'Leave her alone! It's me who owes you. Leave her!'

The guy who needed a bath grabbed her and put his arm around her throat.

'Knife!' Billo barked at the third man, who'd come back in the room. He took out a knife and passed it to Billo to take by the handle.

'Hold her!' he ordered. The third man grabbed Alice and held her in the same way Chloe was being detained.

Alice breathed heavily. She'd never been in a situation like this before – not on the receiving end anyway. She'd seen this scenario play out, of course, but only when she or her family were in control, like Billo was. She now understood what it must feel like being faced with a knife. She was frightened – not to the point where she was going to break or become a blubbering wreck – more, like what she used to hear her grandad talk about. Frank would always say fear was good because it kept you in control. What she was experiencing now was adrenaline.

Chloe was crying, pleading for them to stop. She was scared shitless and that was the difference between them.

Alice stayed calm. Afraid but calm. She stared Billo down.

'You, young lady, should never have come here today. I have no idea who you are and I couldn't give a fuck who your family are either. So you bring 'em if you want. I suspect you won't, though – no one ever does. Full of shit, all of ya. No one spits in my face and gets away with it. Fuckin' no one.'

He slapped her hard with the back of his hand, then took the bottom of her jumper and pulled it towards him. He placed the knife through the wool and sliced downwards. Then, with both hands, he ripped it open.

'Nice bra.'

Without shifting his attention, he placed the blade on her right cheek and slowly brought it down to her neck. He applied just enough pressure to leave an imprint without breaking the skin.

'Shall I cut your throat, beautiful lady?' he asked with a smile, fully enjoying the control he had not only of Alice but the entire room.

Alice fixed her gaze but stayed quiet. Billo was impressed by her courage.

'I think you need a lesson in manners, young lady. A lesson you'll remember well.'

He increased the pressure and brought the knife down, making a two-inch cut above her cleavage. Alice's breathing quickened. She wanted to scream, but she wouldn't give him the satisfaction. She gritted her teeth, refusing to make a sound.

'That,' Billo said, spitting in her face, 'is a little something to remind you of me every time you look in the mirror when you've got ya kit off.'

He smiled before spitting at her once more. He held out his right hand for his sidekick to retrieve the knife, who then wiped the blood from the end and placed it back in his pocket.

Billo flung Alice onto the chair. She could see the cut wasn't deep but it hurt like hell and there was blood running down into her bra. Suddenly, Billo whacked Chloe around the head. She screamed. He whacked her again.

'You have twenty-four hours!' he bellowed. 'Twenty-four hours or else the place goes up!' He knelt down and squeezed her chin with his right hand. 'I'll not tell ya when, bitch, but I'll make sure for certain you're in when it happens.'

Billo and his two lieutenants then slammed the door behind them as they left.

'I'm sorry, I'm so sorry!' Chloe screamed, tears streaming down her face. 'I couldn't warn you. My phone's upstairs, but they wouldn't let me leave the room. I'm so sorry, Alice.'

'Don't worry, silly. It's not your fault. I kinda knew the score, didn't I?'

'Let me see. Let me see what he's done to you,' Chloe said.

'It's not too bad. I feel like I've done ten rounds in the ring, but this,' Alice said, looking at her wound, 'stings more than hurts to be honest. He could have cut me deep, but he didn't.'

She opened her jumper to reveal the blood.

'Your face...' Chloe whimpered.

'I'll live,' Alice replied, trying her best to make light of it all. 'Who were the two guys with him?'

'No idea. They always tag along, though. Never say much, just carry out his instructions. You shouldn't have spat at him. I can't believe you did. I'd never have the guts to do owt like that.'

'Look, forget all that. What I was coming here to tell you was, I had a word with my mum, but she was having none of it. Doesn't want to get involved. She says she's got enough shit of her own to deal with.'

'Oh,' Chloe said, lowering her eyes to the floor. 'That's that then.'

'Hey, not so fast. Things have changed now, girl. Look at me. There's no way he'll be allowed to get away with this. No way.'

Alice lifted Chloe's chin. 'I know what I said the other day, and I know you might not believe me this time, but trust me, Billo is on borrowed time.'

'But no one knows how to find him. Like I said, he just appears when someone needs a few quid.'

'Chloe, you have no idea what my family can find out. Trust me. My mum will make a few calls and we'll know where Billo is soon enough. There's no danger.'

Alice wrapped her torn jumper around herself. 'You can't stay here. Come with me back to Mansfield. You can either stay at ours, or Gloria'll put you up. Yes, Gloria'll look after you. I'd never forgive myself if he torched this place before we got to him.'

'I have an interview tomorrow.'

'Fuck that, Chloe. Look, you need to come with me. I can only guarantee your safety if you come with me. Please don't stay here.'

Chloe paused a moment then said, 'OK. Let me pack a few things.'

'Good. You do that and I'll make sure the coast is clear.'

Chloe ran upstairs. Alice looked at the cut and told herself, again, it wasn't as bad as it looked.

'Have you got any plasters or anything?' she shouted upstairs.

'Er, if I do, they'll be in the cupboard next to the washing machine.'

Alice found a plastic tub containing paracetamol, TCP, plasters, ibuprofen and what looked like remnants of a cough medicine bottle. She placed the largest plaster she could find over her wound. It hurt more than she'd anticipated, but she refrained from shouting out.

Chloe came back to the kitchen. 'You OK?'

'Yeah, you?'

Chloe nodded.

'Come on then, let's go.'

chapter fourteen

Pēteris was walking through Titchfield Park in Mansfield with Ryan and Des, the firm's newly promoted enforcers. He now ran the whole of Nottinghamshire, which included Mansfield, Sutton and Kirkby. He was having trouble with a town centre boozer and the guy who ran it, who wasn't local but had been giving it the big 'un since taking the place over. Someone was getting above himself. Today they were going to teach him a lesson.

'Why do they always think they can get away with it, eh?' Pēteris asked Ryan.

'No idea, mate, but they never learn. Same old shit, every time. Everyone thinking no one'll notice when the numbers don't add up. Frank had it, Daniel had it and Archie had it. The same old shit to deal with. Mind you, it keeps us on our toes.'

'Always seems to happen when there's a shift around. I'm sure we wouldn't have this to deal with if I'd not taken over Nottinghamshire.'

'Maybe not. Coffee before we go?'

'Yeah, come on.'

They walked towards Titchfield Park Café, hoping it wouldn't be closed for the festive period. When they got closer, they saw the lights on.

'I wonder where the world would be without drugs,' Pēteris said philosophically.

'Fuck knows, but us three would be a fuckin' lot poorer, that's for sure,' Ryan replied.

'Yeah, but does narf cause some fuckin' aggro though,' Pēteris continued.

'Narf? You're beginning to talk like a local.'

'I know, me duck,' Pēteris replied, laughing.

'You said it causes aggro. Sounds like you're pissed off. Where did that come from?' Des asked.

'No, I just think about it a lot. Take this guy we're seeing today. He's a new landlord, and thinks he can cream some off the top by dealing his own gear in his pub. It's always the drugs that cause the problems. I mean, trying to diddle our share of his profits is one thing, but thinking he can deal his own gear – that he buys from wherever it is he comes from – amazes me. I just think without drugs, there'd be a lot less aggravation in life.'

Des looked at Ryan, who returned the puzzled look.

'I have no idea what the fuck you're goin' on about, Pēteris, but what do you want in 'ere?'

'Coffee, just a normal coffee.'

'Three coffees, please, duck,' Ryan asked, while Pēteris and Des went and sat down.

'Milk?'

'Please.'

'Fancy a tea cake, you two? I'm gonna have one.'

'Yeah, go on then, just butter for me, please,' Des replied.

They drank their coffee, ate their tea cakes and after chatting to the young lady behind the counter for around twenty minutes, they'd almost forgotten why they were in town. Pēteris wouldn't normally be on a job like this. He would have left it to his man in Mansfield, a guy called Darren, but because he was new in his post, Pēteris felt he needed to show his face and let people know he wouldn't tolerate it. He told Darren to stay with his family. It was Christmastime after all and he had three young children to be with.

'Come on then, let's go before he gets too busy,' Pēteris instructed.

They set off into town to go and see a guy called Richard. He was a new gaffer of one of the town centre pubs, who thought he was something. "Wannabes" Frank used to call them. Think they're tough, but behind the charade they're just sheep in wolves' clothing. Like others before him, Richard seemed dissatisfied with the family's running of things and had decided to bring not only his southern wit with him but his supply of drugs, too. All he had to do was buy the drugs off Darren and his boys at the agreed rate. That was it, nothing hard or too difficult to understand, but he thought he knew best. An establishment like his should have been dealing far more than it was. The last few weeks had seen his buying patterns diminish to an unacceptable level, even though he'd only been in the post a few months.

Frank, and maybe Archie, would have given him a chance. Only one, but at least he'd have got that. Phoebe, however, insisted there were no second chances. Today, Richard would be sorted out and left in no doubt as to how things would be from now on. Phoebe's instructions were clear. She wanted more than just a few slaps.

It was surprisingly quiet for a Saturday, the Saturday between Christmas and New Year. The three of them walked in. There were about twenty customers scattered about – all men, all having an early drink. A barmaid was serving a punter. Richard was at the end of the bar reading a newspaper. Pēteris took up position next to Richard. He leant on the bar, looking straight ahead of him. A few seconds later, Richard looked up. Taking note of the man before him, he turned to step off his stool, where he bumped into Ryan and Des.

'Going somewhere?' Pēteris asked.

'I've got at least twenty witnesses in here, fellas, so unless you're stupid I don't think anything's gonna happen here, is it?' Richard said, smugly.

Pēteris smiled and nodded – a clear signal to Ryan, who headbutted Richard full in the face, splitting his nose.

'Fuckin' hell!' Richard shouted, his face in his hands.

'Upstairs, gents,' Pēteris instructed.

They frogmarched Richard through the door marked *Private*. Pēteris looked around the room, aware that every one of the punters knew exactly who he was. He looked at them, as if to give them an opportunity to say something. No one spoke; most keeping their heads down in their pint glasses.

'Richard said he has twenty witnesses in here. Did anyone see anything?'

No one said a word. Some shook their heads.

'Just carry on drinking, gentlemen. There's nothing to see.'

He then took a roll of used notes from his pocket and gave the barmaid £140 in twenties.

'Get everyone a drink, including yourself. Any change is yours.'

He then disappeared through the same door.

chapter fifteen

Alice rang her mum as she came off the M18 at the A1 junction.

'Hi, are you at home?'

'No, I'm at the designer outlet at Junction 28. Thought I'd see what bargains there were to be had. It's heaving. Where are you and are you OK?'

'Yeah I'm fine.' Alice then paused.

'Are you sure?'

'Well, no, not really, Mum, to be honest. I have Chloe with me. That Billo guy was there when I arrived. Him and two others.'

'Shit. Has he hurt you?'

'Yeah, but look I'm OK, just a bit shook up now the adrenaline's worn off.'

'What did he do? Tell me, Alice, what did he do?'

'Can you meet me at home?'

'Er, yeah, of course. Er, no, go to Marie's. I've got her and Raquel here with me. It's nearer. Tell me, are you OK? How long will you be?'

'About half an hour. And, yes, I'm fine, Mum, but you aren't gonna be happy when I tell you.'

'OK, we're leaving now.'

chapter sixteen

Pēteris walked into the upstairs living quarters. It was spacious and nicer than he expected. Richard was in the living room, guarded by Ryan and Des.

'Anyone else up here?' he asked.

'No. My missus is out shopping. Love a bargain, don't they, women?'

Pēteris sat down. The others remained standing.

'So, I reckon you owe us a few grand, fella. A good few grand.'

'Look, I'll get it. I just need a bit of time.'

'Shame that, 'cos you ain't got time. Now when we last discussed this little issue with you, we made it clear – well, Darren did, I believe – that you were to buy no more drugs for distribution anywhere from here to Timbuktu. Remember that little conversation?'

'The pub trade ain't what it used to be. People drink at home more nowadays, so the opportunity for me to sell any gear is non-existent.'

'Do you really want me to go downstairs and ask every one of your punters whether you've sold them any drugs recently? Do you?'

Richard sighed. He didn't want that. He'd been dealing a shitload.

'So, going on your predecessor, I reckon you owe us at least ten grand, maybe more. But my boss will settle for ten. Season of goodwill and all that.'

Pēteris walked over and poked his finger in Richard's face. 'You've been dealing your own gear in here, I hear.'

He then turned to Ryan. 'Did you hear that – "dealing your own gear in here, I hear"?' Pēteris laughed. 'My English is now so good I'm making up my own rhymes.'

Ryan and Des laughed. Richard didn't. The bravado had all but disappeared. This was the first time he'd felt afraid. The two previous visits hadn't been violent. The first one a reminder; the second a friendly warning. No violence, but a stern word in his ear. However, Pēteris had to deliver. He was new to this level of responsibility, so had thought it best to take it to Phoebe directly. She said he had to take action – and swift action at that. No warning, just a very clear message.

Pēteris continued. 'So, a round ten grand. Mrs Pearson would be happy with that.' He then leant forward. 'Ten grand now and you get away with a minor beating.' He then whispered, 'But don't tell Mrs Pearson that bit.' He sat back in the chair. 'A minor beating is not something she'd be happy with, but for you, I'd keep that from her. Our little secret, so to speak. But...' he said, raising his right forefinger, 'you've also got to tell us who's supplying you. We need to teach more than one lesson over this little misdemeanour, and if you don't have the ten grand, then I'm afraid you're gonna take a severe beating today.' He stood up and leant into Richard's face. 'And we will be back in two days' time when you will receive further punishment – unless the ten grand, with interest, is paid. Do you have ten grand, Richard?'

'Look, guys, I don't have anywhere near that fuckin' amount. You must know that, but look, I'll have it by next weekend, I promise. But I can't tell you anything about my supplier. He ain't from round here – he ain't nothing to you. I'll tell him I can't have any more, so problem solved, eh?'

Pēteris could sense he was trying his best to mask his fear, though his voice gave it away.

'Oh no, Richard, problem far from solved. We *will* get our money, but your supplier has to be dealt with. They know whose toes they're treading on. For that show of disrespect, they must pay. It's how it works – you know that. Nothing personal. But you will tell us. If not here, then we have a very nice lock-up half an hour away, where we can inflict serious pain. Believe me, Richard, you do not want to go there.'

Pēteris turned to Ryan and Des. 'Gentlemen, I will wait for you downstairs.'

Richard made an attempt to get up but Ryan punched him back down. By the time Pēteris had opened the door to the stairs, Ryan had punched him twice more. Pēteris descended the steps two at a time and the noise of the blows subsided. The bar was slightly busier now. The chatter all but stopped on seeing who'd walked into the room. Pēteris sat on a stool and asked for a glass of water. He sipped it, intrigued by their nervousness. By the time he'd finished, Ryan and Des were at his side, slightly, but only slightly, out of breath.

'Anyone seen Richard?' Pēteris asked loudly. The talking stopped. 'Anyone seen Richard?' he asked again, looking at two men who were in the bar when he first walked in. One shook his head while the other said, 'No, not seen him all morning.'

'Shame. Well, if you do see him, tell him we'll catch him another day. Yes, tell him we'll be back. It would be good to catch up with him.'

Pēteris, Ryan and Des casually walked out of the bar onto the street. The pub stayed quiet for a few seconds before the drinkers returned to conversation – about what had just happened.

Richard didn't come down for the rest of the day. His wife, Dawn, tended to his bruises. His torso was sore and his head was sore, but that was as much from Dawn's whining as it was from the blows.

All day, he thought about two things: how he'd get ten grand by Monday, and his brother, Patrick. Having to take a thirty-minute car ride to fuck knows where was too much for him, so he grassed his brother up. Patrick lived in Bristol, two miles from where Richard had left to come to Mansfield, and had dealt most of his life. Richard had tried to get him off that treadmill, but the "respect" his brother thought it gave him always won in the end. He was a bit of a face down there, but no one of any real influence outside of the large estate he operated from.

Richard now wished he'd listened to his little voice. The voice that told him not to buy drugs from Patrick. The voice that told him he wouldn't get away with it for long. The voice that had been proven right. The same little voice that was now telling him NOT to warn his brother. He thought Ryan and Des would take pity on Patrick, being family, but that wasn't going to happen. He shed a tear, as he recalled what their dad had always said. *'Take responsibilty for your actions, boys. Your decisions alone will take you where you end up.'* He wiped the tear, wincing as he did, and hoped that whatever was coming Patrick's way would be the final lesson he needed to get him out of that shithole of an estate for good.

One thing he did know for sure, though, was that there was no way he was taking another beating. Dawn would have to tap up her mum and dad. They'd have to bail him out for a third time. He just prayed she could persuade them to cough up again.

chapter seventeen

Alice turned into Blackscotch Lane in Berry Hill. As she pulled into Marie's drive, she couldn't help but think of her dad. This was where he was murdered. Her beautiful dad, whom she had such fond memories of.

'Wow, lovely house,' Chloe remarked.

'Bad memories, though. I'll tell you about them one day, but come on, let's get in.'

Phoebe came running out, followed by Raquel.

'Shit, Alice, what has he done? Come on, let's get you inside.'

'Mum, this is Chloe.'

Chloe was like a rabbit caught in the headlights.

'Hello Chloe. Come on, you look just as bad.'

'Hello Mrs Pearson.'

'Call me Phoebe. Come on.'

Chloe followed, unaware who the other lady was.

'In here, sit down. Marie's got the kettle on.'

'Hi Alice. Ooh, that looks sore.'

'It is. Chloe, this is Marie and that scary-looking lady's Raquel.'

Raquel smiled.

'Hi. I'm really sorry to bring this to your door. I really am, but—'

'Chloe, just sit down next to Alice. Let's get a tea. Then you can tell me all about this guy.'

Phoebe looked at the cut on Alice's chest.

'You OK?' she asked.

'Yeah. As I said to Chloe, I'll live.'

'Well, I know what I said before Christmas about not getting involved – but now we are. Well and truly. Does he know who you are?'

'No. I did tell him he'd be wise not to cross me and that he wouldn't want to upset my family, but he just came out with the usual shit about how he hears that all the time and all that. He has no idea who we are.'

'OK, so I guess he was there when you arrived and that you two are a result of him not getting what you owe him?' Phoebe said, directing her eyes at Chloe.

'Er, yes. Look, I don't expect anything. Honestly, I can just go back and see what happens. This is not your fight,' Chloe replied, trying her best to sound humble.

Phoebe liked that. 'Well, it is now, young lady. What's his name, this bloke?'

'Billo.'

'Well, Billo has made it our fight, and it's one he'll wish he'd never started. How much do you owe?'

'Four grand, give or take. I only borrowed two, to pay for my husband's funeral. I've had a bit of a bad time, financially, so my credit rating wasn't too great and I just didn't have the money at the time.'

'OK, so where can we find this Billo guy?'

'She's no idea,' Alice piped up. 'No one seems to know where he springs up from, do they?'

Chloe shook her head. 'No. No one I know knows where he lives or where he operates from. He just appears to give someone a loan – or a beating.'

Phoebe took her tea from Marie, who passed the others round.

'Do you want me to make a few calls?' Raquel asked.

'No, I'll do it,' Phoebe said. 'These two OK to have a shower and freshen up, Marie?'

'Course. You know where the bathrooms are, Alice,' Marie replied.

'You can then bring Chloe to ours,' Phoebe said.

'OK, great. I thought she might stay at Gloria's but that's great if she can stay with me.'

'Better if you're together, and better that you're together at ours.'

Alice and Chloe left to have their showers.

'They've taken a serious one there, Phoebe,' Raquel said, shaking her head in disgust.

'They have that. I can't believe the bastard cut her. My Alice. He'll fuckin' pay for that.'

Phoebe picked up her phone and rang Pat, who was still in Geordieland.

'Pat, it's me. Listen, I need you down here.'

'I'm due back in the morning.'

'What time?'

'I'm leaving first thing, so lunchtime. Why, what's up?'

'That Billo guy Alice was on about after the meeting last week...'

'What about him?'

'She went up today to tell her new mate up there, Chloe, that we weren't getting involved, but this Billo guy was at Chloe's house. He's given Alice a fair seeing to and he's cut her chest.'

'I'm on my way. I'm leaving now.'

'See you soon.'

Phoebe then rang Barney, the main man in Hull. He was well liked, well respected. He'd taken Hull by the scruff and sorted the state of play up there. He wasn't in the Pearsons' league but a decent face all the same.

'Phoebe. Nice surprise.'

'Hi Barney. You got a minute? Need to talk.'

'Yeah, go on. What can I do for you? Sounds serious.'

'It is. What can you tell me about a guy called Billo?'

'Billo? What's he to you?'

Phoebe sensed aggression in Barney's voice. Aggression that wasn't there when he first answered the phone.

'What can you tell me about him?'

'What's he to you?'

'He's hurt Alice.'

'Right, well, I'm sorry to hear that. Is she OK?'

'Not really, but she'll live. I need to know what you can tell me because I'll be paying him a little visit.'

'Now just hold on. Hull is *my* patch. I say what happens here, so if Billo needs a lesson, I'll be the one givin' it, not you, so wind your fuckin' neck in.'

'I'm not sure you understand me, Barney. He attacked and cut my daughter, so excuse me for being a little perturbed. Now tell me what you know and leave me to deal with him.'

'I don't know who you think you are, Phoebe, but you ain't no Frank Pearson, so stop trying to be. I run Hull and let me tell you straight, Billo's a known face around here. I've known him a long time, so for the sake of repeatin' myself, you ain't dishin' out no beatin'. Stick to Sherwood Forest and ridin' on Frank's coat-tails. You'll always be in his shadow, no matter who you think you are. This ain't women's work, Phoebe. You should've stuck to making the tea. Now I hope I've made myself clear. Keep the fuck out of Hull.'

Phoebe waited a second or two before responding. 'So I assume you're not going to tell me where I can find Billo then?'

Barney laughed. 'Fuckin' hell, she's got it.'

'Well, that's not what I expected, Barney, but as you say, Hull is your patch. Sorry to have troubled you.'

Phoebe hung up and tapped the top of her phone to her lips as she pondered.

'I think I heard most of that,' Raquel said, knowing what was coming.

'You ever been to Hull?' Phoebe asked.

'I have as a matter of fact, yes. Only once. Richie took me to see the Stags play years ago. Only saw the inside of a few pubs and the new ground, though.'

'Well, you're going to see a bit more of it now.'

Phoebe dialled Del's number. 'Del, meet me at Gloria's with Ryan and Des at seven. We have a problem in Hull.'

chapter eighteen

Barney swivelled in his chair. 'Fuckin' silly mare. Stick to making the tea!' he shouted. He had a habit of talking to himself, did Barney. He always reckoned he got more sense that way. He stood up and looked out the window. 'Who the fuck does she think she is? Only been in this game five minutes and she's wanting to call the shots. Ha. Well, not on my fuckin' watch, lady.'

chapter nineteen

Phoebe rang Pat back once she'd put the phone down from Del and filled him in on Barney. Pat was amazed at his behaviour. He'd known him a good few years and had never had him down as that kind of guy. He'd always found him OK to deal with, but he was evidently trying to flex his muscles. Men like Barney were still living in the eighties. They didn't appreciate a woman running a prominent UK criminal family. Thankfully, as far as Pat knew, the top table were all modern men. Even the older guys like George and Ivan Burbanks and Rory from the West Midlands were fine with it. Phoebe was unique in that she was a top table member. Pat struggled to think of another woman, save Raquel, who commanded such respect in their world.

As he approached Scotch Corner on the A1, still wondering why Barney had appeared so prehistoric, he gave a moment's thought to when he shot Simon Kelly.

He checked the time on his dashboard. He should make it for seven. He planned to take a leak stop at

Wetherby Services and grab a sandwich. If the roads were clear, he'd have time for a coffee. If not, he'd motor on. The one thought on his mind now was finding out where this Billo guy lived. Ringing Barney to reason with him was out of the question.

He then smiled as he thought of old Norman. *'Yes, old Norman. He'd know for sure.'* Keeping one eye on the road, he checked through his contacts to see if he still had his number. He smiled again. 'I hope you're still alive, you old bugger,' he said out loud, as he pressed the green dial button.

Norman was an old friend of Frank's from years back, a main face around Teesside back in the day. He'd married a lovely lady from Brough, just outside Hull, and when he called it a day, they retired to Beverley. He chose Beverley because of the racecourse. He loved the gee-gees, did old Norman, and he never missed a trick. He knew everything and everyone in Teesside and East Yorkshire and, as far as Pat was concerned, he'd not lost his nose for a wrong 'un as the years had rolled on. Pat was sure Norman would know of Billo.

'Hello?'

'Hi, is er, Norman around?'

'He might be. Depends who wants him, though.'

'Pat. My name's Pat Steadman. I know Norman from years back. Is that, er, erm, Eileen, isn't it?'

'It is. I remember you, Pat, I think. Derbyshire was it?'

'Close enough. I'm from Nottingham. One of Frank's lot.'

'Ah, old Frank. Really sorry we missed the funeral. We were on holiday, you see. Malta we went. Lovely place. You ever been, Pat?'

'Er, no, I haven't as a matter of fact, but I hear it's lovely, like you say. Is, er, is Norman there?'

'Yes, sorry, I know you must need a word. NORMAN! NORMAN! Pat Steadman on the phone!'

Pat could hear Norman in the background. 'Pat? Bloody hell. I'm coming!'

'Pat, is that you, you old devil?'

'Hi Norman. How are you?'

'Top of the bill, Pat, top of the bill. You?'

'Fine, mate.'

'How's Phoebe doing? She OK?'

'Yeah, but we have a slight problem I thought you might be able to help us with.'

'Thought so. So who or what do you need help with?'

'A guy called Billo in Hull. Know him?'

'Oh yes, I know him all right. Tried to put the frighteners on one of the fellas at the bowling club. Not of our class, Pat.'

'Do you know where I can find him? He seems to be rather elusive.'

'I do. He lives in Howden, half hour from here. Nice gaff, but keeps his nose clean out there. No one would have any idea about what he does to earn his cash. That way, not many people know about him, or where he lives. I'll text you the address. Mum's the word though, eh.'

'Mum's always the word, mate, you know that. Listen, thanks pal. I owe you one.'

'Another one?'

Pat laughed. 'Yeah, add it to the list. I'll pay you back one day. Take care, Norman, and look after Eileen.'

'Always, Pat.'

Pat loved Norman. One of the old school. He promised himself he'd call and see him one day.

He rang Phoebe. 'I've found him.'

chapter twenty

Marbella, Spain

Archie was fired up this morning. He would normally have a lie-in on a Sunday, but today he had a job on and needed to hit the road. It'd been another late one last night, and he felt a little rough. He was getting grief from Sarah for his late nights, but his trip to the casino had yielded a further eight grand. He was making more money gambling than he was collecting, but he loved the thrill of his day job. Violence was what he knew. He was brought up around it and now he had no expectations on his shoulders, he could do as he liked. His clients didn't care a fuck what he did to the debtor as long as he collected. Collecting debt was bread and butter for him, but he liked it when he was asked to do some real damage, as he was going to do today.

The guy he was after had pissed off a main London face, and it was through their contacts on the Costas that Archie had been given the job. He often didn't know who he was working for in the UK, only who he had to track down. The various well-known villains on the Costas were the ones who dished out the work. It was always last minute. This job had only come in yesterday teatime from Hugh, who wasn't normally someone who gave out jobs like this, but Archie didn't question it. He just took the work and took the pay. All he was told was that he needed to do the job today and to make sure he took a piece with him. He was ordered to "shoot the fucker" if necessary. Archie, though, only planned to give him a severe kicking – and maybe a bullet hole in his leg for good measure. Getting the money was the real issue.

Apparently, this fella had fucked off abroad with a load of cash after a drug deal, thinking he was untouchable. All Archie knew, along with a photo of him on his phone, was that his name was Gregory. He'd been seen in a seaside town called Isla Canela, a four-hour drive away, not far from the Portuguese border. He liked a drive when he was doing a job. The fresh air, open road and sunshine made it all the more pleasurable. He was taking Sarah and Mary with him, and planned to drop them off for a walk around the nearby town of Ayamonte. Isla Canela was only ten minutes further on – a small marina-type holiday destination full of apartments and hotels. If this Gregory fella proved elusive, he'd just book them all into a hotel and stay over until he found him. Sarah accepted this was what he did. She'd hoped he'd walk away from the life for good, but collecting and beating people up was a price she'd live with to keep him away from the family back home.

'You ready then, luv?'

'Been ready for ages, haven't we?' she said to Mary, as she picked her up. 'Daddy takes ages getting ready, doesn't he?'

Archie slapped Sarah's bum before locking the door behind them.

chapter twenty-one

Barney locked his car door and walked towards his office. He was a car dealer by trade. He'd started out before he left school, selling a few bangers here and there that his uncle got for him. He never asked where they came from and no one ever told him, but it allowed him to make his way into the motor trade. This had, over some years, introduced him to criminality, which had eventually led to him becoming the main face in Hull. He'd completed a couple of stretches inside but for the last ten years he'd kept on the outside. He still had a large second-hand car business that was a mask for a lot of his criminal activities and he still operated from his portakabin offices. He'd always been happy there, everyone knew where to find him, and so he'd seen no reason to change. He had Hull sewn up, so no one came looking for him for the wrong reasons. His reputation locally made sure of that. Today, however, it would be his worst nightmare.

He'd just taken a seat to wait for Scratch, his number two, to arrive to discuss some business, when in walked a familiar face.

'Phoebe,' he said, startled. She stepped aside to allow Raquel to enter, then closed the door.

'Is it Ladies Day at Beverley today? I didn't know,' he said, as he took his feet off the desk.

Neither Phoebe nor Raquel commented. Raquel stayed rooted as Phoebe slowly walked over to him. She checked her watch while looking for changes in Barney's expression. It was there. The inquisitive look – the look that told her his mind was racing.

'If you stay a bit longer, you can meet my man, Scratch. He's only been with me a few months, but he's a fuckin' legend. Came over here from Cumbria, he did. Had to get away sharpish. Nasty fucker is Scratch, but you'll love him, and he'll certainly love you. You've aged well, Phoebe, I'll say that. I could be tempted myself—'

The door burst open and Scratch, looking worse for wear, came bounding through. It was obvious he hadn't intended on entering at such a pace. His face was bloodied and he was panting how any unfit, overweight man would, having been on the receiving end of Ryan's fist. Ryan followed, flanked by Des, Del and Jase. Pat calmly brought up the rear and closed the door behind him.

'Sit down, Barney,' Phoebe ordered.

Barney did as she asked. His cockiness evaporated. 'Look, I don't know what's going on here, but whatever it is it's nowt to do with me.'

Phoebe smiled and looked at Scratch, who was still breathing heavily. She couldn't help but think what poor woman would have him humping away at her night after night. He looked like someone who'd always been overweight, and had probably been a decent scrapper in his prime. He had a few scars to show he'd seen enough action, but looking at him now, it was evident he'd eaten too many pork pies and his best days were behind him.

'It is everything to do with you, Barney. You must recall our chat last night. You know, the chat where you told me—'

Phoebe put her right forefinger over her lips to mock him. 'Oh yes, where you told me I was no fuckin' Frank Pearson and I should go back to making the tea. That was it, wasn't it? Oh yes and also that I should stop riding on Frank Pearson's coat-tails. Yes, that was it. Remember?'

'I was only messing, Phoebe, you know, just having a bit of a crack. No harm done. I ain't got no beef with you.'

'You may not have, but I have with you. Firstly, you need to understand that you're right – I'm not Frank.' She went and sat on the edge of his desk and crossed her leg so he'd see a decent amount of thigh. 'But, thing is, Barney, once I've finished showing you exactly who I am, you'll wish I was. You see, Frank would have come here and walloped you around this shitty little office of yours, but me, I'm just the old tea lady, so I can't do that. I need men like Des here and his brother, Ryan, to do that for me, and they won't be happy with a few slaps.'

She stood up, swivelled his chair round and straddled him. She could feel him, even in his current predicament, getting slightly hard. She raised her eyebrows and stared into his eyes. He knew what she was referring to. She then stroked his cheek with her perfectly manicured nails. 'And neither will I, Barney, my man. Neither will I.'

Phoebe got up and walked towards Pat, who was still minding the door.

'How far my men go, Barney, will all depend on how quickly you tell me where I can find Billo.'

'Er, er, look, Phoebe, you don't need to do this. I have my own men, too, you know. I ain't no fuckin' soft touch. I don't want a war with you guys, but you ain't marchin' in here and treatin' me like this.'

Phoebe looked at Scratch, who had by now just about regulated his breathing. 'Scratch, pass me your mobile, please.'

'Eh?' he said, perplexed.

'Your mobile,' she repeated, holding out her hand.

Scratch put his hand in his pocket and passed it to her.

'You know all about these men Barney mentions. If you want, I'll let you ring them. Bring them here. Bring it on, as they say.' She handed him back his phone. 'But only ring them if you're sure it's something you can win. Do you think Barney has the manpower to take me on, Scratch? Do you? It's your call.'

Scratch looked at his phone, then looked at Barney. Barney said nothing, waiting to see what his man would do. Scratch placed his phone back in his pocket. He looked at Phoebe and slowly shook his head.

'Wise move,' she said, as she motioned with her head to give her men the cue.

Barney stiffened as Ryan lifted him from his seat. Des punched him twice in the stomach. Scratch, give him his due, stepped forward but Des whacked him hard in the side of the head, knocking him into the filing cabinets.

Phoebe looked at Jase. 'Burn it,' she instructed.

'You fuckin' touch as much as one car in this place and I'll fuckin' kill ya,' Barney shouted, as Jase left the office to retrieve two canisters of petrol from his car.

Still shouting what he was going to do, he was bundled into a car. The rest followed, Pat making sure Scratch posed no threat.

Phoebe looked at Jase. 'Torch it.'

By the time she'd got into her car, the portakabin was alight. Ryan was in the back, with his gun stuck in Barney's side. Barney said nothing as his only legitimate source of income went up in flames.

'I ride no one's coat-tails,' she said.

Barney dropped his head, knowing he was in serious shit.

Scratch was in the car behind, sandwiched between Del and Pat. He wondered what the fuck he'd gotten himself into. He'd started working for Barney not long after arriving from Barrow-in-Furness. He'd been into crime from the day he could walk, but had left Barrow sharpish eighteen months ago after putting a copper in hospital after a fight. Cumbria Constabulary were still hunting for him. Scratch was a wanted man, but having put on weight since arriving in Hull and shaving his head, he'd managed to evade being caught. He met Barney when he single-handedly decked five local fellas who'd taken exception to his accent. Barney offered him a job and, given his loyalty and capabilities, Scratch had grown through the ranks to emerge as Barney's right-hand man.

He'd never, however, seen anyone like the Pearsons. He now realised what that top table he'd heard of was all about. He'd known of the Pearsons for years – anyone who was anyone in the world of crime did – but this was the first time he'd had the pleasure of meeting them in the flesh.

An hour and fifteen minutes later they were at a lock-up in Askern, just outside Doncaster. Raquel was tying Barney up on a chair in the middle. Scratch wondered why he wasn't being tied to his. He decided to keep quiet. He'd learnt over the years that sometimes it was best to keep your mouth shut.

Alice had two old metal irons that looked like something out of the 1930s warming on a hot plate. She'd been at the lock-up half an hour, having dropped Chloe off at Gloria's. She did not want to miss today's proceedings – if all went according to plan, they would have Billo in their sights soon enough. Chloe had wanted to tag along but Phoebe had insisted that if Alice wanted to be there, she had to leave Chloe behind.

Barney was still mouthing off. 'I fuckin' know people! You better fuckin' kill me 'cos I'll kill the fuckin' lot of ya once this is over!'

Phoebe nodded to Ryan, who socked Barney full on the jaw and quickly quietened him down. Des wrapped his arm around his throat and pulled him back from behind. Barney struggled while Raquel undid his jeans and pulled them down around his ankles. Des let go.

'What the fuck!' Barney cried.

'Now then, Barney. We have the little issue of Billo to sort out. You said to me yesterday, even after I told you what he'd done to Alice, that I was to leave him to you and that I was to keep out of Hull.'

She turned to Alice. 'Come here, sweetpea.'

Alice walked over, carrying one of the hot metal irons with her glove. Barney stiffened and tried to push himself over with his feet. Des was still behind him, putting enough pressure into his back to keep him sat upright.

Wide-eyed, Scratch didn't utter a word. He'd begun to wonder if he'd been forgotten about. He hoped he had.

'Show Barney what Billo did to you, sweetheart. It's a nasty cut.'

Alice bent forward, putting her face into Barney's. 'See what he did to my face, the bastard? And look at this,' she said, as she pulled her V-neck jumper down. 'You can't see it, can you? Can I just put this on your knee a minute?' she asked, before placing the sizzling-hot iron onto his thigh.

Barney screamed as it burnt his flesh.

Alice dropped the glove onto the floor. 'Can you see it now?' she asked, using both hands. 'Look, he cut my skin. Look, Barney, he cut my skin.'

Barney screamed some more. Alice looked at her mum. 'He doesn't arf make a lot of noise, doesn't he?'

'It might have something to do with that iron,' Phoebe said, nodding towards Barney's thigh.

'Oops. Sorry, Barney, you should have said.'

'FUCKIN' HELL!' he shouted.

'I think you need to even them up,' Phoebe said.

'Yeah, you're right, Mum. Looks a bugger, dunnit?'

Alice swapped the irons over and placed the second one onto his other thigh. Barney screamed the full ten seconds she held it there.

'There, that looks better. I think you might need a bit of cream on them, though, Barney. Twice a day, morning and night.' She laughed as she replaced the iron.

'Now then, where can I find Billo?' Phoebe asked.

'Howden. He lives in fuckin' Howden.'

'Thank you. Thing is, we knew that last night. I just needed to know you'd grass. No one likes a grass,

Barney, but I knew you would. Now we only have to sort out the grovelling apology you owe me. No one talks to me like you did yesterday and gets away with it.'

'Fuck you!' Barney shouted in defiance.

Scratch was silently willing his boss to keep his fuckin' mouth shut, fearing he might be next. He still couldn't believe he'd been allowed to sit on the sidelines, totally unscathed.

'Now that's something you definitely won't be doing,' Phoebe said, as she nodded to Raquel, who threw her the other glove.

Phoebe bent down, iron in hand, and waited for Raquel to remove Barney's boxers. Barney closed his eyes and prayed while she hovered the iron over his flaccid knob. He wanted to scream but knew he'd never hold his head up in East Yorkshire again.

'Phoebe, please,' he begged. 'Please, enough!'

She flicked the end of his dick, which made him flinch.

'It's just a five-letter word, Barney. Begins with S and ends in Y.'

'I'm sorry!' he shouted. 'I'm sorry!'

Phoebe replaced the iron.

'Don't ever tell me I should be making the tea again, Barney. Do we understand each other?'

'Yes, for fuck's sake, yes!'

She turned to Jase. 'Drop him back in Hull. Anywhere will do.' Jase nodded. 'Take Ryan with you and meet us at that garden centre by the Howden turn-off. We'll wait for you there.'

'What about him?' Pat asked, nodding over to Scratch.

Scratch had impressed Phoebe when he stepped forward to help his boss in the portakabin, knowing full well he was heavily outnumbered.

'Bring him with us.'

Pat was puzzled but indicated to Del and Des to look after him. Scratch couldn't help but feel guilty, seeing his boss crying in pain. He looked as pitiful as his penis. Scratch wondered how Barney would ever recover from this. What would the future hold for Hull's criminal underworld now the top man was seemingly at the end of his reign? He couldn't look Barney in the eye when Del and Des escorted him out of the lock-up. Scratch realised he'd just bore witness to the gap between those at the top and those who thought they were.

chapter twenty-two

After a coffee with Sarah and Mary and making sure Sarah had a few euros with her, Archie drove into Isla Canela. He was surprised at how small the place was. There was a small marina with a few bars and shops, a lovely long stretch of beach, a handful of hotels and a lot of what looked like holiday apartments. He parked up at the marina and walked into the first café bar he saw. It was fairly quiet, with a few locals mixed with a handful of British holidaymakers enjoying some winter warmth. It was a comfortable 18 degrees.

'Still water, por favor,' he asked the young girl behind the counter, who looked Eastern European.

He sipped the water, enjoying the coolness on his throat. Two women, who he assumed were English, gave him the eye. Both looked late thirties, early forties. He smiled back. The dark-haired one played with her hair suggestively. He knew if he wanted it, he could be fucking her before his ice cubes had melted. He smiled inside at how easy it was to get propositioned in this world. He was not the sleeping around type, though, and looked away, hoping that would give her the message. He turned his attention to the young girl behind the counter.

'How's your English?'

'Good. I speak it well. How's your Polish?'

'Crap. As is my Spanish. You seen this guy around here?'

The girl looked at the photo. 'No, sorry, I haven't.'

'What about your friend?' he asked, nodding towards her colleague, an older girl, but still only in her late twenties.

'Puedes mirar esta foto, María?'

María came over and took a look, then shook her head.

'She doesn't know him.'

'OK, thanks anyway,' Archie replied, as María left to serve coffee.

He looked up to see the flirty brunette at the bar paying for her drinks. He knew she knew he was staring at her, but she continued to look straight ahead. He wondered if she was annoyed at his rebuff. As she turned to return to her seat, she said, 'He stays at one of the apartments over the road. Scottish, he is.'

Archie jumped off his bar stool and joined her and her friend at their table.

'You know him?'

'Not really. Seen him around for a couple of weeks, though.'

'D'you live here?'

'Only in wintertime. It's Rebecca's place – well, her and her fella's but only us girls come in the winter.'

'A long time to be apart from your fella, Rebecca, especially at this time of year. Christmas and all that.'

'It's how we like it. He's married to his job, you see.' She took a sip of her coffee. 'And we ain't into Christmas.'

'Fair enough. My name's Chris by the way.'

'Chrissie,' the brunette said, holding out her hand.

Archie instantly wished he'd picked a different alias. Chrissie and Chris were just too alike.

'Spooky,' she said. 'Maybe it's a sign. A sign that we just had to cross paths.'

'Yeah, maybe. I don't mean to be rude, ladies, but I need you to show me where this guy lives.'

'What's it worth?' Rebecca asked.

Archie sighed inside. Everyone always wanted something. Even two bored housewives in a small seaside resort in southern Spain wanted something from him.

'Look, I ain't giving anything. All I want to know is where he lives. You offered the information, so let's not play games eh!' he said sharply.

They got the message. Archie was in no mood to be played. Chrissie looked at Rebecca, who sipped her coffee again.

'Number 3, ground floor, in that block over there.'

Archie glanced over. It looked pretty nice – not the kind of place your average Brit abroad would stay. It certainly didn't look like the kind of place you'd find kids jumping around in the pool on their inflatable dinosaurs.

'Thank you. Much appreciated. Get yaselves a drink.'

Archie dropped fifty euros on the table.

'Thought you weren't "giving anything"?' Chrissie said, whipping the fifty-euro note away.

Archie said nothing and drank the last of his water. He placed his glass on the bar and thanked María and the younger girl, before telling the two ladies who'd be having a few cocktails on him later to have a nice day. He walked over towards the apartments, checking the photo of Gregory on the way.

Chrissie and Rebecca watched him until he disappeared around the corner, both thinking what they'd like to do to him given the chance. Neither spoke for a good few minutes, enjoying the tingle their thoughts gave them.

chapter twenty-three

Phoebe, Pat, Del, Des and Raquel were waiting at the garden centre with a round of tea. Alice was outside on her phone to Chloe, making sure she was being well looked after by Gloria, who had mothered her as though she were her own daughter.

Scratch had been allowed to go to the loo alone. Phoebe trusted him. She couldn't put her finger on why but she was drawn to him. Del was watching the loo door. Scratch had no way of communicating with anyone. Des had his phone. They were all nervous that he'd escape through some window. Everyone except Phoebe. She knew he'd come walking back through the door any second.

'They're here,' Pat said, on seeing Jase's van pull into the car park.

Everyone apart from Del instinctively looked out of the window. He remained focused on the loo door. A minute later, Jase, Ryan and Alice walked in.

'Where's Scratch?' Jase asked.

Pat looked towards the toilet door, when Scratch then came through doing up his flies.

Jase nodded. Pat did the same in return.

'Right, gentlemen, let's go,' Phoebe instructed.

'I'll just grab a drink,' Jase said, bringing out a handful of change from his jeans pocket. 'You want owt?' he asked Ryan.

'Yeah, can o' pop or something. Owt'll do.'

Two minutes later they were on their way to Howden. If Barney thought he'd had a rough ride, Billo was in for a right treat.

chapter twenty-four

Archie knocked on the door of number 3. No answer. He knocked again. Still no answer.

'Ha ido a por un periódico. Volverá pronto,' he heard from down the corridor.

'Sorry, erm, do you speak English?'

'He gone for paper. He be back soon. Every morning he go. He get paper and he read on balcony. Every day.'

'OK, thanks. I'll wait for him. Thank you.'

The guy put up his hand in acknowledgement and continued out of the block and over the road.

Archie looked around for a suitable place to wait where he could see Gregory's front door. He saw a bench looking out onto the beach – so that was facing the wrong way. He glanced further along and spotted a bench facing into the marina. He looked at Gregory's front door. It seemed perfect. He'd be able to see anyone coming and going. He checked his jeans waistband. His piece was still there. He chuckled at what Chrissie and Rebecca would have thought had they known he had a gun on him. It amazed him how Joe public had no real idea what went on in the world he operated in. He took a seat and quietly watched the block of apartments. His thoughts turned to his mum and his sister. He wondered when he would see them again. Who'd make the first contact? He still could not accept or forgive his mum for doing what she did.

He thought back to when he was at his grandad's side, and the weight and expectation he had on his shoulders. He never thought that within four months of being a leading UK figure, he'd be sitting on a bench in Spain waiting to kick the fuck out of some wannabe he didn't even know who'd fucked off with a boatload of cash. Back in August, he was destined to be one of the top table. He had pedigree and was respected throughout the UK. He wondered whether he'd have stayed the course had he been older. Would he ever have been the right man to run an empire of the magnitude Frank had built up? He thought of his father and how, if he'd not been murdered, he'd be the one running things, leaving him to be groomed for the right time.

It angered him he'd not been given that time. If he was honest, he was angry at his grandad for thrusting him into that position so early on. Frank should have known, but he was a proud man who put so much emphasis on the Pearson name. It had to be a Pearson at the helm. A bloodline. He wouldn't have accepted anything else. If Archie hadn't been around, or had maybe been a few years younger, he'd have just carried on until Archie was an adult. In Frank's eyes, if you were old enough, you were ready. You were a man once you left school, so Archie never really had a choice. The baton would have been passed to him regardless. He could never have said no. If Frank were alive, Archie would still be in Nottinghamshire being the man Frank wanted him to be.

Despite everything running around his head, he was still of the mind that Phoebe had no right to do what she did. No matter how it was cut, she'd cast him aside. That hurt Archie more than anything. He yearned for her to call him. He wanted his mum in his life, like she'd always been. She was a softly spoken, genteel figure who, through the life her family led, had grown into a woman ruling in a man's world. He respected that immensely. Not only for her journey but for being the only woman in the UK to head a criminal family. And from what he'd witnessed so far, she was more than a match for any man who considered her an easy target.

You needed nerves of steel. Nerves his grandad possessed in abundance. Nerves his father had. Nerves he sometimes lacked. It was Frank's presence that had kept them there on more than one occasion. He thought about the battle with Fletcher O'Brien and how he'd have been lost without Frank at his side – lost at what to do, lost at how to do it and, in the end, he'd have probably lost in battle, too. Archie knew what he was at this stage of his life, and that was a follower. He wasn't a natural leader. He needed someone with those nerves of steel at the front. Someone like his mum.

A wave of sadness washed over him as he thought of how he could be running the family business at his mum's side if he wanted. It'd be a perfect match, but he was no longer sure it was an option. She couldn't welcome him back at her side now. She'd look weak. She should have stepped up while he was still there, straight after Frank's death. Archie knew he wouldn't have welcomed it, though. He'd have looked weak. He was the heir apparent – it had to be him. Frank had already placed him at the top, so making way for his mum to take the job was never going to be an option. That's why he'd ended up in Spain, and that's why he was here waiting for this Gregory fella to make an appearance. He wasn't the man everyone had wanted him to be. He'd accepted that and was comfortable with it. He was just angry at everyone else for not accepting it, too.

He came out of his trance to see Gregory unlocking his front door. He wasn't alone. 'Fuck,' he said out loud, striding over the road. 'In for a penny, Archie lad,' he muttered, before breaking into a jog.

He knocked twice. He recalled Frank telling him more than once how being scared was a good thing. It kept you focused. The trick was to not let anyone sense your fear. The adrenaline was certainly keeping Archie on his toes now.

The door opened. It was Gregory. Archie punched him hard in the face, then twice more in quick succession. They were now in the open-plan living room. The other fella stood rooted to the spot.

'Where is it, Gregory? Where's the money?'

'What fuckin' money?'

'Don't fuck me about.' Archie took out his pistol and forced it into Gregory's mouth. 'The fuckin' money, Gregory! Don't make me ask twice.'

Archie couldn't make out what he was saying, but Gregory was shaking his head. He saw the other fella move and turned his head. Gregory grabbed Archie's arm. The gun went off.

Gregory's head splattered all over the wall behind him. Archie let go. Gregory fell to the floor.

chapter twenty-five

'It's a decent house, nice area, so he must do all right out of threatening women,' Del said, leaning forward to see the house in full view. 'Crime does pay then, no matter how you make ya money.'

Phoebe surveyed the area out of both side windows. 'Wait here a minute,' she instructed, as she got out the car. She wanted to get a feel for what kind of people lived there. It looked the kind of road a company director would live in. Large five- or six-bedroom houses, decent driveways with double garages and plenty of space between each house. The kind of house a senior manager would love to buy but couldn't afford – and have to be content with something similar but far cheaper. These houses were individually designed, well made and oozed quality. Nothing like her place in Southwell, with its acres of land, or Frank's place in Papplewick, but houses most would be proud to own. It was a quiet cul de sac, where people showed off their expensive family cars. This was a clear sign it was the festive period – most people were at home. As she turned to walk back to her team, she wondered what was in the double garages. Certainly not the family motor. More likely, examples of the families' busy outdoor lifestyles. She noted the large, expensive motor parked in Billo's driveway, which suggested he might be in. She opened her door and took her seat. She turned to Scratch, who was sat quietly next to Ryan.

'How well do you know Billo?' she asked.

'Not to have a drink with, but well enough I s'pose.'

'Well enough that he'd take a call from you?'

'Er, well, he'd probably wonder why I was ringing him. I've never rung him before.'

'Ring him. Tell him you need to come and see him. Make something up. I want to know if he's in.'

'He'll know I'll have set him up. I'll be finished in Hull.'

'I wouldn't worry. Billo won't be any bother to you after we've finished with him. But if you don't make the call...'

'What shall I say?'

'That's up to you, but I'd suggest you try your best. You saw how Barney ended up.'

Scratch thought for a moment. He had no choice. He then scratched the top of his head.

'That how you got your name?' Ryan asked, laughing.

'It is actually. Just a thing I do when I'm thinking. Got the nickname at school and stuck ever since.'

'Give him his phone, Des,' Phoebe instructed.

He rang Billo's number. It rang three times.

'Yeah?'

'Billo, it's Scratch, Barney's man.'

'Ah, fuckin' hell, Scratch. How are ya? I didn't know whose number this was. I'll keep it now I know it's yours. What's doin', fella?'

'Er, are you in at yours? I just need to come and see you. Got a bit of business I think you'll be interested in.'

'Business? Does Barney know about this?'

'No, he doesn't, and for fuck's sake, don't tell him. This could make us both very rich, Billo. I need this. I need a man like you with me. Just give me ten minutes of your time. You won't regret it.'

'OK, Scratch. You have me intrigued. You know where my gaff is?'

'Yeah, Barney pointed it out a few times. You there now?'

'Yeah. I'll be here for the next couple of hours, then I need to go and see a bitch in Hessle. You can come with me if you like.'

'I might well do that. See you in twenty.'

Scratch ended the call. Des took his phone.

'Well done. Nicely played,' Phoebe said.

She liked his ability to sound very convincing while lying through his teeth. No wavering in his voice, no nervousness and no stuttering.

'Right, I'll lead with Raquel, as before. You guys follow close behind, but make sure Alice follows us in on her own before you lot come charging in. I want to see the fear on his face when he realises who we are.'

Phoebe got out and signalled to Raquel. She saw her speak to Alice before getting out.

'Alice knows what to do,' Raquel said, as she walked with Phoebe the twenty yards to Billo's front door.

'What do you think to Scratch?' Phoebe asked.

'In what way?'

Phoebe tutted. 'Not in *that* way. You know, just as a man to have on your team.'

Raquel frowned as she pondered. Phoebe rang the doorbell.

'Not sure. Why, what you thinking?'

'Don't know myself,' she replied, as the door opened.

'Hello. Sorry to bother you but do you know where Alice Pearson lives?'

'Who?'

'Alice Pearson. Do you not know her?'

'No idea, but I'd certainly like to get to know you two.'

Phoebe heard footsteps behind her and turned.

'Ah, here she is. Look, it's Alice Pearson. You know her, don't you – Frank Pearson's granddaughter? You must've heard of Frank Pearson?'

Phoebe returned to Billo, whose eyes had widened. He tried to slam the door but Phoebe and Raquel put their hands and feet in the way. Billo pushed harder. Together, they were able to keep the door open wide enough to see the fear in his face. Alice was now at the door, unaware that Pat, Del and the rest were on the driveway. They'd left Scratch in the car, still with a gun in his side.

'Hello Billo. We meet again. I did tell you not to mess with me and my family, didn't I, and if I recall correctly, you said, and I quote, "I have no idea who you are, or who the fuck your family are. I couldn't give a fuck. So you bring 'em if you want. I suspect you won't, though – no one ever does. Full of shit, all of ya." Well, surprise! I've brought them. Ta-da!' she said, with a theatrical wave.

Alice felt like the most powerful woman on earth. How pleased she was to have moved on from taking notes and making the tea.

Billo, looking as though the life had drained from his body, shot off. He had no idea where he was running to as he charged through his house towards the utility room at the back. His heart was pounding. *The fuckin' Pearsons* he thought, as he grabbed a large bunch of keys from the kitchen worktop. He fumbled for the key to the back door but his hands wouldn't work as fast as his brain wanted them to. He had too many keys, far too many. Some he had no idea what for.

'Fuckin' keys!' he shouted, looking up to see Des's silhouette the other side. He glanced back into the kitchen, through the open door from the utility. Phoebe was there, hands on hips, smiling and shaking her head.

'There's no point in running, Billo. There's nowhere to run. You, my friend, have come to the end of the line. That was a very naughty and foolish thing to do to my Alice. Very naughty indeed. For that, well, I think you have an idea.'

'I didn't know who she was, honest. I'd have never ... you know ... never touched her if I'd known.'

'And that's supposed to make it all right, is it? So if poor Alice was not a Pearson, you'd have cut her regardless, would you?' Phoebe took slow steps towards him. 'You really should have picked a different career path. Bullies always get what's coming, and for you, I'd say it's long overdue.'

'Phoebe!' Jase shouted.

Phoebe took two steps back to see Del marching through from the hall with a scruffy-looking young man. The bloke looked Alice up and down and shouted 'BITCH!'

'Ah, you've met this ... this awful young man, have you, Alice?' Phoebe asked, not taking her eyes off him.

'Oh yes. He was one of the younger men I was telling you about. He was there. He was the one who held me while that bastard cut me.'

'You lot are fuckin' dead! I'll come after every one of you! Tell 'em who we are, Dad.'

Phoebe laughed. 'Dad!' she shouted. 'Well well, Billo, we have struck it lucky today, haven't we?'

'Shut the fuck up, Son,' Billo ordered.

'Eh?'

'Keep ya fuckin' mouth shut.'

Phoebe could see the young man had no idea who they were. She walked through to the hallway to look at the photos on the wall. She smiled at the family album, which told her all she needed to know. Smiling back at her was Billo, his scruffy son and another, slightly older-looking, lad. Another son she presumed.

'Jase, go to the car and tell Scratch I need to know the names of Billo's two sons. Tell him we have the scruffy, younger one here. I need to know his name and the whereabouts of the other one.' She looked at Des. 'Give Jase Scratch's phone.'

Billo lunged forward, making straight for Phoebe. Del tightened his grip on his son, who'd made a feeble effort to show he could be aggressive. Pat immediately stepped in front of Phoebe and hit Billo square on the jaw. Phoebe didn't flinch. Des now had Billo in his grasp.

'Fuckin' Scratch. I fuckin' knew it, the grassing bastard. You touch a hair on either of my son's heads and I'll hunt you down. Your time is up, lady. This is a fuckin' man's world. No room for tits and make-up.'

Phoebe glared at Billo for a few seconds, before asking Alice to look at the photo.

'Is that the other one?'

'Yep, that's him.'

Phoebe gave Jase the nod, who made his way to the car.

'Take a seat, gents. We now wait for son number two. Either he comes to us, or we go to him.'

chapter twenty-six

Isla Canela, Spain

'FUCK!' Archie shouted. 'FUCK! FUCK!' He looked at the other guy, who now had his hands up against the wall.

'What's your name?'

The guy didn't speak.

'What's your fuckin' name?' Archie asked again, taking a step towards him, his gun outstretched in front of him. 'Your fuckin' name,' he said slowly.

'Craig.'

'Right then, Craig, me and you need to find the money that I came for – and quick. Any ideas?'

Craig shook his head.

Archie thought hard. This was a disaster. He needed the money. Without it, he had a serious problem. He had no idea who the ultimate client was, only that he was a London face – and that could be so many people. He couldn't see it being Tariq, Greg West or Paul Dutton. They'd have their own men do it. Guys would be falling over themselves to gain credence with London's elite. It had to be a player further down the ladder, but evidently someone who had enough savvy to get the criminals residing in Spain to dance to their tune. The fact Gregory was dead wasn't an issue. He was told to kill the fucker anyway if he wanted to, but only after he'd got hold of the money.

'Well, start fuckin' lookin', 'cos if we don't find it, I ain't gonna be happy, and I might just start shootin' again.' Archie ordered Craig into the bedroom. 'Look under the mattress and under the bed.'

Craig did as he was told, while Archie looked in the wardrobes. He was flicking through the neatly hanging shirts, to look behind them, when the weight of a king-size mattress knocked him sideways. He threw it back onto the bed, focused on the room and realised Craig had done a runner. Archie legged it out into the street. The fact he had a gun in the top of his jeans hampered his run. He looked up the street before swivelling 180 degrees to look down towards the beach.

'FUCK, FUCK, FUCK!' he shouted, as he ran back into the apartment. He stopped when he saw Gregory's body – he'd left the front door open. He couldn't risk anyone coming in, so calmly closed it behind him. He sat on the sofa, rubbing his face, trying to think what to do. He had to search for the cash. For the next twenty minutes he went through the whole apartment. There was no money. Wherever Gregory had stashed it, it wasn't there. He sighed. He then realised that no one had come knocking since the gun had fired. It had been nearly half an hour. That meant no one had called the police. No neighbour and, it would seem, not Craig. *Who the fuck was Craig and why was he here?* he thought. If it wasn't for him, he wouldn't have the problem he now did.

The Spanish guy had said Gregory went for his newspaper every day. Archie looked around. There were no newspapers anywhere. This didn't feel right. Something was wrong with this whole job. Hugh had given him the instruction only yesterday, yet he'd not mentioned anything about it previously. Was it really feasible for Hugh not to have known about it? Why the big rush, and why the insistence on taking a gun? Normally Archie had a couple of days to get things sorted for a job. Three at the most. Time was not a luxury in this world, but twelve hours' notice was unusual in itself.

And why was Craig there? Why did he go for Archie when he had the gun in Gregory's mouth? So many things were rushing around his head. He thought about how coincidental it was that Chrissie and Rebecca were there in the nearest café to Gregory's apartment and knew where to find him. He stood up and stroked his chin, then went into the bathroom to clean himself up. He dried his hands on the towel, convinced he needn't worry about his DNA or any evidence of him being there. Something told him no forensics would be done.

He walked back to the café bar. It was no surprise that Chrissie and Rebecca were no longer there. Archie walked in and ordered a coffee. The Polish girl served him.

'Back so soon?' she asked.

'Yeah, I was hoping to talk with the two ladies that were sitting there earlier. You must know them. Do they come in here often?'

'I have no idea. I have never seen them before. I thought they maybe only arrive today or even yesterday. I have no idea. If I see them again, I tell them you came here looking for them.'

Archie replayed in his mind the events in the bar earlier. He shook his head slowly, annoyed with himself as he realised Chrissie, if that was her real name, hadn't even looked at the photo when she'd told him she knew Gregory.

'Nah, it's OK. I don't think they'll be back.'

chapter twenty-seven

Craig had run out of the apartment, turned right, and just kept going. He leant against a lamp post, struggling to get his breath. His chest hurt. He bent over, putting his hands on his knees.

'Fuckin' hell!' he said out loud, which he'd said inwardly numerous times since bolting out the door. This had gone badly wrong. "Just make sure he's at the apartment," the guys had said. No mention of anyone getting their head blown off. How he wished he'd not come down here for Christmas.

He was from a little village called Thatcham, just outside Newbury. He worked in a coffee shop back home, but had come out to work the local bars and restaurants on the Costa Almeria about eighteen months ago. He'd got into a bit of dealing here and there to make some extra cash, after befriending some of the local main dealers. This had resulted in him getting in over his head, which he now regretted. He knew one day he'd be asked to do something he didn't want to do. That day had come yesterday, when two guys had approached him and ordered him to make the acquaintance of a guy called Gregory and to make sure he was at his apartment in the morning. That's all he was told, except to make sure he didn't fail because "The Boss" would not take kindly to him messing things up. Craig had no idea who The Boss was. He didn't want to know, especially now Gregory had had his head blown off.

Having started to panic that he wasn't going to get an opportunity, he'd casually bumped into Gregory the previous night. One thing he'd not been told was that Gregory was gay. Craig spent most of the night averting his advances. He was sure Gregory had been suspicious this morning. Either that or he had the hump because Craig wasn't offering anything sexual. It had been a bit awkward and Gregory had stormed off, but Craig had managed to persuade him to come back to the apartment, but only after making out he was sorry and was just nervous about his "first time".

His phone rang. 'Where are you?'

Craig didn't recognise the voice. It wasn't either of the two guys from yesterday. Of that he was certain.

'I'm on the road somewhere to Ayamonte. Who's this?'

'Wait there.'

He slowly placed his phone in his pocket. His stomach began to churn. *Who the fuck was that?* he thought to himself, as he finally started to get his breath back. He sat down against the lamp post, and thought about the coffee shop on the square in Thatcham. He thought about his schooldays at

Kennet School, his Saturdays spent hanging around Newbury, and the dreams he had to make it big in the world. It all seemed such a long way from here. He had no idea why he was asked to befriend Gregory, why he'd been asked to make sure he was at his apartment this morning, or who the guy was who shot him. He decided there and then that if he somehow managed to get out of this alive, he was going home. He quite liked working in a coffee shop. It was easy. He would open his own when he got back. He'd managed to save a few quid. He'd have a few tables outside and make it traditional. His staff would wear black with white petticoats and carry cakes on a tray, and he'd kit it out with a vintage feel. He then remembered that his savings pot was not that big, but he told himself his ambitions were.

He heard a car and looked up. It sailed past. He looked down the road towards Isla Canela and the hotels in the distance. It looked more than a mile away, so he reckoned he'd run further than he first thought. He noticed a car approaching. It started to slow down. This must be whoever had rung him. He stood up and it soon stopped right beside him. The passenger wound down their window.

'Craig?' he asked.

'Yeah, that's me. I'm—'

Craig never finished his sentence.

Forty-seven seconds later, a second car came to a halt, right where Craig lay dead. Archie got out and looked at the body of the man who'd run out of the door.

'Well, that didn't take long, lad.'

Archie now knew for sure he had a problem. And that it was not just about the money he'd failed to get. Money that was probably never there to be had in the first place.

chapter twenty-eight

Jase came back into the house, with Scratch's phone in his hand. 'Son number two is called Francis.'

'Francis?' Del asked.

'Yeah, not your usual name for a money lender, is it, but yeah, Francis.'

'Where is he?' Phoebe asked.

'He's currently on "a little job", as he called it, somewhere over east Hull. I have no idea where it is, but Scratch does. An estate full of tower blocks apparently. Says it's about twenty minutes from here. Scratch told him he needed to see him about some business and old Francis said he'd wait for him there.'

'Right, gents, let's go,' she said. 'Where are your car keys?' she asked Billo.

'Yeah, like I'm gonna tell you.'

Phoebe smiled. 'You, my friend, are in no position to decide what's going to happen. You marked my daughter. I have no hesitation in ordering your death right here right now, plus the death of that poor excuse for a man you call a son over there. And to top it off,

I'll kill Francis as soon as I meet him. Either that or you tell me where your keys are. It really is your call.'

'Hanging up in the kitchen. You know the make and model, so it shouldn't be hard.'

'Pat, you go in Billo's motor with Des, Jase and these two. Keep your gun on them both, Des. Del, you with me and Alice. Raquel, you can drive the other car with Ryan and Scratch. I don't think Scratch will be any bother.'

They left without saying a word. Raquel led the convoy, with Scratch giving the directions. They pulled into the estate to meet Francis. It was grey, with grafitti on every wall. She got out of her car and looked around. It was cold and totally uninviting. There were people walking out of the alleyways and walkways between the tower blocks. All in hoodies. No one looked up. No one gave a shit. She poked her head into the car Raquel was driving.

'Ring him, Scratch. See where he is.'

For the second time in less than half an hour, Scratch rang Francis's number.

'Hi, it's me. I'm here. Which one you in?'

Phoebe watched Scratch's body language. He held her gaze. She liked that.

'OK, I'll come up to you. Wait there.'

'That one there,' he said, pointing to the middle of the three blocks. Fourteenth floor. Said he'd wait for me on the landing.'

Phoebe pondered. She looked up, trying to work out the fourteenth floor. She had a good view of the front and left-hand side. She could see the stairways and the landings. It was all outside in the open.

'Del, take Jase with you – and Scratch.'

Del got out, walked to the car Jase was in and gave him the instruction. Scratch got out, tucked his T-shirt into his jeans, pulled his coat down and took a deep breath. He still couldn't believe what had happened so far today. He wondered how Barney was doing and if he'd ever see him again. He looked over to see Phoebe giving Del and Jase what he assumed were further instructions. She walked over to the car Billo and his son were in.

'Scratch! Here! Time to go!' Del shouted. Scratch obeyed orders and quickly walked over.

'When we get up there, we'll hang back. You can meet Francis and keep him talking. Just get him comfortable, but remember, if this goes tits up, she'll blame you.'

Scratch nodded. A pang of fear rose in his stomach.

The climb up to the fourteenth floor was a long one. The wind blew through the stairwells. It was damp and the landings were littered with rubbish. There were blankets and carrier bags under the stairs and it stank of urine. It was evident rough sleepers were taking shelter from the elements. As they reached the stairs to the fourteenth floor, Del tapped Scratch on the shoulder. He was breathing heavily. Del put his right forefinger to his mouth, indicating to Scratch to be quiet. Del then whispered, 'Keep him talking on the landing. Do NOT make eye contact with us when we appear. That clear?'

Scratch nodded. Del motioned for him to continue. He got to the landing. Francis wasn't there. Scratch did what he did when he was thinking – scratched his head. He took in some deep breaths, sensing how nervous his breathing sounded. He hoped Francis wouldn't notice.

Phoebe and Alice were stood at the rear of the car Pat had driven Billo in. The rear windows were both down. Pat and Des had guns pointed at Billo and his son.

'He's up there, Billo, can you see? Fourteenth floor. I'm sure he'll put up a fight. He's bound to, isn't he, being your flesh and blood and all that? Keep watching – I'm sure we'll be able to see the fracas.'

'I'm gonna fuckin' hunt you down, lady, you mark my words. I'll hunt you down if it's the last thing I do.'

'Shush, you'll get yourself all stressed. Just watch that fourteenth floor landing. I want to see who comes out on top. Don't you?'

'Fuck you.'

'Why do men always say that when they have nothing else to say? I reckon it's to mask how afraid they are.'

She turned to Des. 'Don't you, Des?'

'Definitely.'

'Fuck you,' Billo's scruffy son said.

Des chuckled. Billo kept his eye on the tower block.

'That's it, keep watching,' Phoebe said.

Scratch was getting very nervous. *Where the fuck was Francis?* He was thinking about ringing him again, when he heard a voice.

'You should get down the gym, Scratch. Fuck me, you've put on weight. How are ya?'

'I was OK till I met you. I'm at my fighting weight. Don't you worry about that,' he replied, mimicking a boxer and throwing a few punches. It seemed the right thing to do, plus it relaxed him a little and took his mind off why he was there.

'So, what you got for me? And where's Barney? He OK?' Francis asked.

'Yeah, you know Barney, always comes up smelling of roses. Just got a bit of business I wanted to see about putting your way. You and your dad of course.'

'So why not see my dad about it? You know I'll only have to run it past him anyway. You sure everything's OK?'

Scratch saw Del and Jase appear behind Francis, and even though he knew he wasn't to avert Francis's attention, he just couldn't help it. Francis clocked it, and spun round, just as Del and Jase grabbed him.

Billo watched from below, as if in slow motion, his son being thrown over the top of the fourteenth floor landing. He followed Francis as he fell for what felt an age. He could hear him calling out as he flapped his arms, fruitlessly trying to stop his fall. Even from a distance, Billo heard the thud of his eldest son hitting the concrete. For what was no more than a couple of seconds, but what seemed like forever, he stared open-mouthed. He was brought from out of his trance by Phoebe saying 'I'd have taken the lift, but some people are in such a rush these days'.

Billo screamed – as any parent would, realising their offspring was gone forever. He wailed like a child. His younger son sat in eerie silence, tears streaming down his face.

Phoebe motioned to Alice to return to her car. She then looked Billo straight in the eye, offering nothing to him as he snarled like a rabid dog. She turned on her heels.

Scratch looked over the side, to see Francis's body on the ground below – his head pouring blood, his body lifeless. All he could hear was Billo crying out for his son. He saw Phoebe walking back towards the car she'd arrived in. Alice appeared to be looking up at them. She stood there for a second or two before following her mum.

'Scratch, time to go,' Del ordered. 'Scratch, for fuck's sake, it's time to go.'

Jase pulled Scratch away from the wall he was gripping with his hands. He followed, running down the stairs two at a time. The motors were revved up and once all three of them were back in their seats, they screeched out of the estate. Scratch said nothing, as he looked back at the body laying all alone on the concrete. No one had come out. Scratch wondered how long it would be before someone noticed.

As they drove out of Hull and onto the A63, Billo continued to shout about what he was going to do to them all. Billo had no idea where he was going. Once he'd stopped shouting, he looked at his younger son. He watched him snivel and wipe his snot on his dirty sleeve, his chin stuck into his chest.

Just under two hours later the convoy pulled into the lock-up in Arnold, or Frank's Place, as it was now called. A place where torture and death had been administered many, many times over the years. Men had been brought here kicking and screaming. Men had been brought here full of bravado. And men had been brought here scared shitless. Every one of them had experienced pain – death even – at the hands of those who loved to inflict it. Frank liked to use outside help to do the torturing. He'd never been one to get his hands dirty, and was very happy to pay others to do it for him. Bonnie had always been his first choice when occasions like this arose, but Bonnie, save for coming out of retirement to maim, torture and kill Steven Wallace, was well and truly a man of leisure these days. A man whom the underworld missed, for no one tortured quite like Bonnie. But, as with all walks of life, when a vacuum appears, someone or something fills it.

That someone in the East Midlands and the North of England was a man named Victor. He always insisted on being called by his full name. He'd been known to refuse work if anyone called him Vic. His name was

Victor and if you wanted someone to experience real pain – following Bonnie hanging up his pliers for the last time – Victor was your man. He'd worked alongside Bonnie for the last couple of years, perfecting his craft. Victor wanted to be the heir apparent. Bonnie had given Victor his seal of approval, which had meant a lot of work coming his way. He was now the undisputed king.

Victor had received a call from Phoebe late the night before, asking him to make himself available for today and maybe tomorrow. Trainer, who'd travelled down earlier, let him into the car park. He watched Victor set up his tools of the trade. Some he'd seen before, but there were a few that were new to him. Trainer asked Victor what they were for, but he refused to say – citing trade secrets, as if he was some sort of magician.

Des walked in first, followed by Billo and Ryan. Billo's son followed, with Jase behind. Del waited outside with Raquel. Pat, Phoebe and Alice brought up the rear. Trainer shook everyone's hands. He was glad to see them because he was itching for some action.

Billo and his son were seated in the middle of the room. Billo looked like a man possessed. He'd gone from sobbing like a child to spouting obscenities, telling anyone who would listen what he was going to do to them – seeing your offspring thrown from the fourteenth floor has that effect on you. Whether he'd contemplated dying that day no one could be sure, but the fact he still thought he'd be exacting revenge suggested he felt he'd still be breathing tomorrow morning. His son had remained tight-lipped, either hoping it would bring some sort of leniency or because he'd had the fight knocked out of him.

'Who the fuck's this? Bonnie's understudy?' Billo shouted at Victor, who completely ignored him and concentrated on the one paying him his wedge.

'Victor. Thank you for coming so promptly. I know it was short notice,' Phoebe said, shaking his hand.

Victor was impressed by the firmness and shook it multiple times before letting go.

'A pleasure, Phoebe, and may I say how sad I was to hear of Jez's death. I'm sorry I couldn't make the funeral, but I hope you received the donation I sent. I had hoped to go, but in this game, as you know too well, sometimes I get called upon at short notice.'

'Can we do away with the fuckin' arse lickin' and just get on with whatever you plan on doin'? I have business to attend to tomorrow, so fuckin' get on with it!' Billo spat.

Everyone ignored him, although most of the guys present were waiting like coiled springs to give either of them a whack.

'I understand completely and, yes, we did receive your generous donation. He was a good man.'

'A fuckin' legend, Phoebe. I haven't done much for you guys but the bits I did for Frank, and latterly Archie, gave me the pleasure of getting to know him. And let me say, his legacy will be with us for a long time to come.'

Billo started to hum and pretended to play the violin.

'I apologise for the arrogance of our guests, Victor, but I'm sure you'll shut him up soon enough.'

'And I'll enjoy every fuckin' minute,' Victor said, smiling through very white, straight teeth.

'Gentlemen – and ladies,' Phoebe said, addressing the room, 'let the fun commence.'

She then turned to face the door. 'You joining us, you two?'

'What about Scratch? He's in the car on his lonesome.'

'Shit,' Phoebe said, putting her hand over her mouth and giggling like a teenager. 'I forgot about him. Bring him in, Del. He might enjoy it.'

Victor gave the nod to Trainer to tie Billo and his son to their chairs. He looked at Alice to give her the floor. Everyone knew she needed her moment. She took the few steps towards them and looked at the son.

'What's your name?'

Billo told him to keep schtum before he had the chance to answer. He looked at his dad, unsure what to do. The arrogance he carried with him daily was gone. He was certainly a young man who lived on his dad's name. He turned to face Alice and tried hard to appear unnerved. Everyone could see through it, except for Billo, who was determined to see his son as he wanted to see him.

'Your name. What's your name?'

The sound of the kettle on the worktop in the corner clicking was like a bomb going off. No one had noticed Alice filling it. She held out her hand. Billo's eyes widened. He knew what was coming. His breathing quickened. His son looked over, unaware of why his dad suddenly looked so afraid. He looked back, and saw Raquel pass the kettle to Alice, steam coming out of the top. Reality hit him like a juggernaut. He tried desperately to wriggle free from his chair. Ryan moved behind him to stop him from toppling back.

'Marcus, my name's Marcus.'

'Too late,' Alice said, as she poured the kettle into his lap.

He screamed, as the scalding water seeped through his baggy jogging bottoms.

'Never a good idea to play the hard man with such a poor hand to play with, Marcus,' Alice told him, before looking at Billo, who immediately shut up.

'Sorry, what were you saying, Billo? I didn't quite catch that.'

Panting, he said, 'Look, I'm sorry. I'm sorry for what I did, I'm sorry for any disrespect. I'll do anything, but please let us go. He needs a hospital.'

Alice looked at Marcus. 'Oh do be quiet, Marcus. I can't talk to your dad with all your wailing.' She then looked at Billo. 'Well, I said you'd be sorry, didn't I, and to be fair I think you are, but this is a big boys' game and, like Marcus, you're too late.'

Billo yelled, as she poured the remaining contents of the kettle over his head. Marcus cried his eyes out, seeing his father reduced to a blubbering wreck. Billo was on the verge of passing out. Only the thought of what was yet to come kept him conscious.

Scratch stood at the back, astonished at what he was witnessing. He couldn't understand how he'd kept out of the line of fire. Alice replaced the kettle and took her place next to Phoebe. Victor rubbed his hands as he took centre stage. He picked up a club hammer and tapped it into the palm of his hand. The weight of the hammer end was evident.

'Could someone please remove their shoes and socks?'

Trainer stepped forward. Phoebe raised her hand.

'Scratch,' she said, turning round to face him. 'Do the honours.'

Scratch walked forward without hesitation.

'You fucking grass!' Billo shouted.

Scratch stopped and looked him in the eyes. His blistered face looked terrible, with large, seeping sores. He felt for him but he had to show strength. He ignored the comment, bent down and removed Billo's footwear. Billo kicked and tried to make it as difficult as he could. Scratch removed his socks, before doing the same to Marcus, who cried and asked him to stop.

Victor then bent down on one knee in front of Billo and whacked him hard on his foot, breaking his big toe and two others. He repeated the blow on his two smallest toes. To his credit, Billo hardly made a sound. He did the same to his left foot before administering the same blows to Marcus. He stood up to give them a moment and take a swig of his mineral water. He then, with the same hammer, smashed both of their kneecaps. This time, Billo wailed. He was still saying how sorry he was and was now pleading with Victor to stop.

For the next half an hour, Victor tortured the life out of them. They each passed out at least twice. Victor was swift in his methods whereas Bonnie took his time, mainly for his victims to endure as much pain as he could give them. Victor didn't hang about. Fifty minutes after Trainer had tied them to their chairs, they were both dead. He did it all, except for the boiling water and their cuts to the chest. That, Alice did herself to even the score.

Victor cleaned his tools and packed them away neatly in his bag while the others chatted as though nothing had happened. Pat made a call to confirm the disposal of the bodies. People were en route. Billo and Marcus would be gone without trace before the sun had set on this festive Sunday.

'Here's your payment, Victor, and thank you again for coming at short notice,' Phoebe said, passing him a large brown envelope.

'Anytime, Phoebe. See you all soon, I hope,' he said, waving goodbye. He walked out, still able to hear the chorus of 'See you, pal' and 'Yeah, see you soon, Victor'.

'Scratch,' Phoebe said, 'you know, I almost forgot about you today. Maybe that's because you could be a fit for us. I like the fact you stepped forward to help

Barney this morning. I like the fact you've caused us no aggro and the way you did what you did earlier. Fancy a job?'

'Er, well, I work for Barney, Mrs Pearson. He's been good to me, you see. I need to see if he's OK. I owe him that much. I hope you understand, but thank you for the offer.'

Phoebe smiled. There was just something likeable about him.

'Please do not make me come and find you. I really would not enjoy that.'

'I won't, and thank you for your understanding.'

'I like your loyalty, Scratch. The offer's there on the table if you ever change your mind.'

'How will I get home?'

'Trainer will drop you off on his way back to Leeds. But remember, you need to make sure Barney keeps quiet about all of this. Any whisper and I'll come for you. Don't let loyalty be the death of you.'

Scratch nodded. Today, he'd seen the difference between the top table and the rest. In just one day, he'd witnessed more about the main players than he ever had in his life. They walked the walk and he reckoned he could walk it with them. He owed Barney, though, and couldn't bring himself to leave him. He didn't know what the future held for his boss. It would take a lot for him to come back from today and remain at the top in East Yorkshire, but Scratch owed him enough to be at his side while he tried.

'Right, gents, Pat has arranged things for these two. Ryan, Des and Jase, you three wait until they've been and things are sorted. The rest of us will get off. But have a good New Year all of you and see you all in 2020.'

'Hey, anyone know what the crack is with this virus in the news?' Del asked.

'No idea. Sounds serious, though,' Jase replied.

'They reckon it could be a pandemic or something,' Del continued.

'Well, as long as it doesn't reach here for New Year's Eve,' Trainer said. 'I'm out on an all-dayer. Can't fuckin' wait.'

chapter twenty-nine

Richard's wife, Dawn, came through with his phone in her hand. 'It's Gemma.' Gemma was Patrick's wife. She never rang to speak to Richard. His stomach churned.

'Hi Gemma,' he said. It still hurt to speak. 'Everything OK?'

'Don't pretend you don't know, you piece of shit. He's in hospital. They beat the shit out of him. A black guy and two white men. Burst in here, they did. How the fuck did they know where he lived?'

'What – bloody hell. How bad is he? Look, it's nothing to do with me.'

'Oh fuck off, Richard. Funny how they all had Nottinghamshire accents. Coincidence, was it?'

Richard didn't know what to say. He couldn't admit his involvement. He wasn't one to own up to things like that.

'You could've at least warned him. Some fuckin' brother you are. Anyway, thought you should know. But don't bother coming down, he wouldn't want to see you. You're just a waste of fuckin' space.'

The line went dead.

Dawn heard it all. She looked at her husband in despair. 'For fuck's sake, Richard, for once in your life stop trying to impress people. Be done with it all. Have a quiet life. Next time someone could get killed. I can't do this any more.'

Richard sat back in his chair and sighed. He'd wanted to warn his brother but knew if he did, he'd get the beating himself. He hated who he was and now his brother would hate him, too.

'Fuck you!' he said, directing it at Gemma.

He decided after New Year, he'd go to Bristol to make peace with Patrick. He would own his actions and tell Patrick exactly what happened. He'd take the consequences but at least for the first time in his life he would own his own shit. Dawn was right. It was time for change. 2020 was going to be different for Richard. This was just the wake-up call he needed.

chapter thirty

Marbella, Spain

Hugh was sat looking out at the ocean. It always relaxed him, and he needed that right now. The last couple of days had been a nightmare. His worst nightmare. He'd dodged a bullet for long enough, but now it would appear things had come home to roost. His past had finally caught up with him.

The thing that rankled him was that he had no idea how his acquaintances in the Netherlands had tracked him down, or who had given them the information for that matter. This Hendrik guy was not someone Hugh knew. He'd made a few calls, but no one was offering anything. That was annoying him, too. Someone out there must know of this Hendrik fella. Someone always knows something. The criminal fraternity was too large and diverse for anyone who was anyone to be totally off the radar.

Hugh wasn't scared as such. If his life was in danger, he'd have had a bullet put through his head Friday night. He'd left Archie to bounce the young blonde up and down on his cock, but it hadn't turned out as he'd imagined. She, it transpired, was a plant. No sooner had he got his knob out, than three guys made their appearance. One of them being Hendrik. They had the chance to blow his head off, but his friends from the land of windmills and clogs must have had ulterior motives.

There had to be a reason why he was allowed to live. A reason that meant more to them than his life. One that involved him sending Archie off on a job at such short notice. This was not his bag. It's not what he did. He'd never been asked to send Archie, or anyone else for that matter, off on a job – ever. Having a gun pointed at your temple makes you do things you wouldn't normally do, though, especially when your dick's hanging out. The blood had drained from that quicker than a speeding bullet.

All he knew was that the men who came to see him with Hendrik were mainstream. You can always tell the ones who are the real deal, and these were no amateurs. He was in a quandary and he didn't like it one bit. He'd thought of doing a runner but was told he was being watched. He wasn't prepared to take the chance.

His phone rang. It was Hendrik.

'We have a problem,' he said.

'What d'you mean?' Hugh asked.

'Archie shot the guy he was going to see. Fuckin' blood everywhere. It's a right mess.'

Hugh had no idea who it was that Archie had been sent to sort out, other than his name being Gregory, who lived in Isla Canela. He was as much in the dark as anyone else. He didn't have a clue that Gregory was just an innocent guy who happened to be in the wrong place at the wrong time. Picked at random. All Hendrik had been instructed to do was to have a target for Archie to go for. There was never any money to be extracted. Gregory had been totally unaware of why Craig had befriended him. He just thought he was a young man struggling with his sexuality.

'Did he get the money owed?' Hugh asked.

Hendrik needed to play the game. 'Did he fuck. That's problem number two. Not only did he not get the money, he fuckin' shot him through the head. It's being sorted, but my boss has had to pay a rather large wedge to keep this under the radar.'

'Fuck. Archie's gonna be in the shit then,' Hugh replied.

'As are you, my friend. As are you.'

'Eh? Now you can fuck off. This was nowt to do with me. All I got told to do was send Archie on the job. That was it. It ain't my fault if he fucks it up. That's down to him.'

'You seem to be forgetting one tiny detail, Hugh.'

'And that is?'

'The two men I brought with me work for the very men that have been after you since you fucked them over. I can keep them from blowing your brains out, but only if you do what I say. My boss has their trust. He's known them a long time, but one word from him and, well, you'll look like Gregory did after Archie left.'

'Who do you work for?'

'None of your business. Sit tight, Hugh, but remember, if you try and do a runner, we'll find you. No matter where you go, we'll find you. You are very lucky to be alive. Do as you're asked and you might just get out of this with the slate wiped clean. I'll be in touch.'

'Wait, what about—'

The line went dead.

'Archie. What about Archie?'

Hugh flung his head back. 'Someone has fuckin' grassed me up!' he shouted. 'Fuckin' grassers. I fuckin' hate a grass.'

chapter thirty-one

Ayamonte, Spain

Archie was outside a café bar in Ayamonte with Sarah and Mary. Sarah knew something was up. She could always tell with Archie. He'd tried to hide it, telling her the job had gone smoothly, but she knew differently. He was distant. He had things on his mind. Things that were at the moment more important than her and Mary.

'Look, let's just go. You're not enjoying it. Whatever you have on your mind, you need to sort it out, and experience tells me you won't sort it out here sat in the square sipping coffee.'

'I told ya, everything's fine. Come on, let's have a little wander down there. We've not been down that way yet.'

'We have. It leads out to the little fountains. Trust me, we've been down it – me and Mary – twice. Come on, I want to go.'

Archie sighed. 'OK, if you insist, but honestly, everything's fine. I'll drop you off when I get back and then I'll go and pick up my wages from Hugh.'

'Hugh? Working for Hugh now, are we?'

'Yeah, just a one-off job I think.'

'You've never done work for Hugh before, have you?'

'No, but as I say, it's just a one-off. Bit of a favour really.'

Sarah pondered as she picked Mary up and sat her in the pushchair. She knew Archie was worried, and now she knew the job had been for Hugh she was worried, too. She'd never seen Archie like this after doing a job, so that coupled with being the first one for Hugh made her think. Sarah didn't like coincidences. Didn't believe in them. She was a realist and was rational about things. Everything had a reason for happening. An action always had a reaction. There was always a consequence for anything anyone did. Coincidences just did not exist, and Archie looking stressed and Hugh giving him his first job was no coincidence. Two and two were making five and Sarah did not like the feeling she had in her stomach.

Archie hardly spoke while they walked along the cobbled and tiled streets. Sarah could see the cogs turning. Archie was a man with a lot on his mind. She decided to give him space. The last thing he needed was her giving him any more to think about.

chapter thirty-two

Since the call from Hendrik, Hugh had been thinking hard about this whole affair. He just could not work out why he was still alive. He'd fucked the Dutch over good and proper, so why the fuck they would allow him to carry on breathing was a complete mystery. He paced up and down his balcony, periodically looking over to see if anyone was in his grounds watching him. He didn't see anyone. He wondered if this Hendrik guy was playing him. Hugh had no idea if he was for real. Maybe the Dutch hadn't tracked him down. Maybe Hendrik, who he thought was Dutch too, had just decided to use that as a way to get Hugh to play to his tune. Hugh being a wanted man was no real secret. Hugh hadn't exactly kept it quiet. He never really knew why he'd not kept his mouth shut about the whole sorry mess, but Hugh being Hugh let his mouth run way with itself at times, especially after a few cocktails. It dawned on him he could be being played like a fiddle.

He walked quickly into the bedroom. His wife was still having her nap, snoring her head off as usual. He looked at her and smiled. Although he'd shag anything that moved, he loved her dearly. She did his head in, but she was a diamond. A lady he was thankful for and would do anything for. Except stop shagging anything that moved, that is.

He quietly grabbed a few clothes and went into one of the spare bedrooms. He pulled out a suitcase from under the bed and stuffed the clothes inside. He stopped zipping it back up and put his palm to his forehead, realising what he was doing. Why the fuck was he going to the trouble of packing a suitcase when all he was going to do was walk out with it to see if anyone was watching him? He needed to know if all this was for real, although the muse of taking off was just a smokescreen. He decided to leave the clothes as they were, in the suitcase. He checked over the balcony one last time. The light was starting to fade. The street on the other side of his hedge seemed fairly busy. He could see car headlights and hear passers-by. Nothing appeared out of place.

He walked out onto his very neat driveway, onto the street, stopping to look both ways. He decided to turn left. He'd walked no more than a hundred yards when his phone rang. It was Hendrik.

'Where the fuck you off to? Holiday, is it?'

Hugh stopped in his tracks. He looked around. He decided to keep walking. It was about ten seconds before Hendrik spoke again.

'I said, where are you going?'

Ten seconds was a long time. Hugh suspected it wasn't Hendrik watching him. 'What am I wearing?' he asked.

'Don't fuck with me, Hugh. Just walk back home and sit tight. This is your last warning.'

'Tell me what I'm wearing,' he repeated.

The line went dead. Hugh stood rooted to the spot. He knew he was being watched, but not by whom. His heart was racing. He expected a bullet at any moment. Within seconds, a car raced towards him. He saw it just in time to jump out of the way over a wall onto a tennis court. He heard the car make contact with the wall, before screeching away. His suitcase was now about thirty yards down the road, his clothes strewn everywhere.

His phone pinged. *That was a warning. Next time you will be shot. Dirk*

He climbed over the wall, shaken but unscathed. He walked briskly to pick up his clothes, knowing this was for real. Dirk was one of the guys he'd done over. One of the two men who wanted him dead. He was in the shit. If they were in cahoots with a UK top man, and they were prepared to let him live, then whatever was behind all of this was big business – more valuable than he was to them dead. He could only assume what Hendrik had told him about Gregory fucking off one of the main men was true.

He walked slowly back to his villa, leaving the suitcase behind. It was beyond use. He headed up the steps and back into his lobby, where he placed the clothes on the floor and sat on the chair he'd often sit on to do his laces. He then took the clothes upstairs with him, where he could hear Morag snoring from the landing. He smiled as he walked in. There she was, catching flies.

Suddenly, he dropped his clothes and stumbled backwards. Scrawled on the mirror in his wife's bright-pink lipstick was "Joris". Joris was the other guy who wanted him dead – Dirk's business partner.

'Fuck,' he said quietly. 'Fuck, fuck, fuck.'

He heard a knock at the door. Morag stirred. He needed to get the message from off the mirror before she saw it. He spun round looking for a cloth. All he had was the clothes he'd brought back. He wiped the mirror. It smudged. 'Fuck,' he muttered for the umpteenth time. Morag rolled over and was sound asleep once more. Whoever was at the door knocked again. This time louder. He decided to leave the mirror and go answer it. He was sure he could hear his heart pounding through his chest. He took a deep breath and opened the door.

'Archie. Thank fuck—'

'Glad you're pleased to see me, 'cos you might not be in a minute.'

'Come in, go through. Morag's having a nap. So, you get the money?'

Hugh knew the answer, of course, but had to play dumb. He needed to hear Archie's side of the story.

'Bit of a problem there, Hugh, I'm afraid.'

'What problem? Just tell me you've got the money.'

'No. There was no money to be had. Not a penny. Well, not a euro, but you get my drift.'

'So, what about Gregory?'

Archie tried to gauge Hugh's body language, for any telltale signs that he was part of this charade. But Hugh gave nothing away. He appeared genuinely surprised at the revelation. He was an old fox, though, was Hugh. But as good as he was at masking pretence, he could not mask his surprise – and relief – at seeing Archie at the front door. That was a massive giveaway. Hugh either never expected him to return or was expecting someone else. Someone he evidently didn't want to see. Archie wasn't sure which, but he was sure Hugh knew more than he was letting on.

One thing Archie had learnt from his grandad was that knowledge was power, and power was king. Frank had always drilled it into him that if you let your friend or foe know what you know, then they know as much as you. He would always follow it up with "You can go a long way in this world, Son, by keeping your mouth shut".

Archie decided he would keep Hugh at arm's length.

'Gregory. Hmm. Gregory. Well, that's another problem, 'cos I shot him.'

Nothing. Then, after a window of a second and a half, Archie had his suspicions confirmed. It took Hugh that long to get back in character.

'What? You did what? For fuck's sake, Archie, why did you shoot him? Fuckin' hell, this ain't good. We'll never get the money now. It was all about getting the dosh back for whoever ordered this. We have no idea who we're ultimately dealing with here, lad. This could be a major fuckin' fuck-up. People will be coming for you. Maybe me, too. For fuck's sake, lad.'

Archie wanted to applaud. If he hadn't had any suspicions, he'd have maybe bought that little outburst, but he was nobody's fool. Certainly not Hugh's.

'It is what it is, Hugh. There was no money there and I only shot Gregory by accident. He had a friend there with him. Craig, his name was. Anyway, I have Gregory, gun in his face, doing the usual, when Craig, for some reason, takes a step towards me. Somehow my trigger finger twitches and, well, Gregory's all over the wall.'

'Who else knows about this?'

'Well, you. You gave me the job. I came straight here. Who else would I talk to?'

'Yeah, fair enough. Well, look, I'll have to report this back and wait for any fallout, but I'm telling ya, be on your guard, 'cos this won't be looked on lightly.'

'I'm telling ya, Hugh, there was no money...'

Archie was going to follow it up with 'And I don't just mean no money at Gregory's place, but no money period', but he stopped himself. He didn't want to give Hugh any indication that he had doubts about the whole job.

'What were you gonna say just then?'

Archie thought quickly. 'Er, I was just gonna ask who you were expecting, 'cos you seemed surprised to see me. You looked like you'd seen a ghost when you opened the door.'

'Ah, no one, I just didn't expect you to be here, that's all. Expected you tomorrow.'

'I suppose there's no wedge for me then?'

'Is there fuck! No result, no wedge, lad. That's how it works. That'll be new to you 'cos you've never not delivered before, have you?'

'No, first time, and first job off you as well. Funny that, eh?'

Hugh threw him a look. An inquisitive "what do you mean by that?" look. A look that said Hugh was curious and a look that told Archie he should have listened to his grandad.

chapter thirty-three

Phoebe, Alice and Raquel stopped off at Gloria's in Papplewick on the way back from Arnold. It was where they retreated to when they needed to take a break and chill, plus Alice wanted to fill Chloe in on the day's events.

Gloria had been at Frank's side for so many years she was one of the family. As usual, she was making a huge pot of tea, while listening to the finer details of the day. Chloe was mesmerised when Alice, with clear delight, told her what had happened to Barney, Francis and then Billo and Marcus. While she was grateful that Billo was no more and that her debt had been wiped clean, she couldn't help but feel scared shitless. She was sat with three ladies who it appeared would, and could, kill you without a second's thought.

Only Gloria was what she would describe as "normal". They'd had a lovely day together. Gloria had taken her to Newstead Abbey for a walk around the grounds and a sandwich and a drink in the tea room, before coming back to sit by the warm fire with a glass of mulled wine. It had been cold at Newstead Abbey, but the Christmas theme had more than made up for it and she'd really appreciated the walk. Gloria had told her all about Frank. She felt as though she knew him and could really tell how much Gloria loved him. She'd shed a few tears when recounting what happened to him. She also told Chloe what life had been like on the edge of the family, why she'd never stepped over the line and why, even though they did things like they'd done today, they were all loyal people who lived by their own code – which was difficult for the outside world to understand. How could anyone comprehend throwing a man off the fourteenth floor of a building and pouring boiling water from a kettle into their lap?

Chloe realised that as much as she liked Alice, she didn't want to remain in touch once she'd returned to Hull. She'd forever be frightened of saying the wrong thing – and hearing the click of the kettle. They'd invited her to stay for New Year, but she'd politely declined, saying she'd head back home the next day. Alice said she'd take her.

After the girlie chat, Raquel made her way home and Alice took Chloe back with her to Southwell. Phoebe, however, needed a bit of time to herself. A lot had happened today. A lot had happened in recent months. She'd not had a moment to reflect since Frank's murder. She didn't want to go back with Alice and Chloe, didn't even want to offload on Gloria. She just wanted to be on her own.

Pēteris had set up the next meeting with the Latvians for a week or so. New Year was only a couple of days away. Things were going well in general. Del, along with Michael, and under Raquel's supervision, were running a well-oiled machine. Yes, they had their problems to sort – often daily – but running a criminal empire, that was only to be expected. She didn't foresee any trouble over the New Year period. She had a good, solid team that had her back.

She drove down Southwell Road West, towards Mansfield. At the lights at the junction with Little Carter Lane, she looked over towards Carlo's wine shop, where she used to call in for a bottle of 20/20 in her early days of being old enough to drink. She smiled. It brought back good memories. She drove down towards Ratcliffe Gate and a warm feeling came over her when she saw The Brown Cow. It had been a regular of Jez's. He'd loved a pint of real ale in there in the last few years. It was a place he'd retreat to for a quiet moment and it seemed the perfect place for her right now. She pulled into the car park, but as usual it was full. She pulled out and parked on Ratcliffe Gate. On walking in, she turned left into the snug. It was busy. Lots of people enjoying a festive night out in between Christmas and New Year. She spotted a chair in the corner. It looked perfect. She noticed a few faces recognise her. She decided to have a drink to Jez and ordered a pint of dark stout. The description said it had a hint of chocolate. She had no idea if she'd like it, but this was where Jez used to come, to have a moment on his own, and why she'd chosen to go there. She wanted to drink to a great man whom they'd buried only days ago. She laughed inside, wondering how she'd manage a quiet moment, it was so busy.

She took her seat in the comfy chair and realised that even though the place was bouncing, she could be alone with her thoughts. No one was looking at her now, too busy in their own worlds. Maybe on seeing she was alone, their attention faded, but whatever the reason she was grateful. She sipped her drink, and was surprised at how much she liked it. It had quite a burnt aftertaste, which she recalled Jez commenting on when drinking stouts and dark ales. She'd never thought much about it but now she was drinking it she could see the appeal. She sat back and looked out into the crowd. Her mind wandered. She was looking right through the people in front of her, oblivious to their presence.

She thought about Daniel. The man she should be drinking with right now. She thought about the life he'd led, how he'd be the kingpin now and she'd be the dutiful wife. She was angry, which she'd not realised till now. She'd suppressed so much feeling about his death over the years, but now Richie was gone, too, she had no one to channel her hate towards. She was glad Richie was dead. He was a bad apple and if it weren't for him, her Daniel would still be alive. But, for all the hate she felt for him, she was grateful to him for saving her from being raped all those years ago. Maybe he wasn't such a bad apple after all – well, not rotten to the core anyway.

She thought about how she'd taken the top job after Frank had passed, and shook her head slowly at how much she'd changed. She'd become ruthless. People had commented on it. Take earlier – she wasn't convinced Frank would have taken all three lives today. He'd have given them one hell of a beating and maybe scarred them for life, but kill all three, she wasn't sure. People had to realise that brutality was the only weapon she had right now. She was still early in her reign. People were still trying to take liberties. Barney had called her a tea lady. Billo had said there was no place for tits and make-up. She didn't have muscle, didn't have the brawn to give out beatings herself. She had to be brutal. More so than any man. She had to show the criminal world that being a lady didn't mean she was a soft touch. She had to go overboard at times. People needed to know that if you stepped out of line, you paid dearly, especially if it involved her own. Alice was kin and she'd do anything to look after her family.

She thought about Archie. How she missed him. How she wished more than anything that she hadn't had to do what she did. She didn't want to cut him off, but for him to accept you're either in or you're not. No half measures. It was hard for her to do. She cried a tear as she sent him a message through her thoughts. *Love you, Son.* She wondered what he was doing now, hoped he was OK and thought about who would make the first call. She decided that she would ring him on New Year's Eve to wish him all the best.

Her thoughts returned to Alice. The quiet assassin. She couldn't believe how much Alice had changed. Just a few months ago, she was making the tea, shuffling paperwork and taking notes. She was now a killer, who revelled in inflicting pain. Phoebe was worried that it would all go wrong. Alice had a tendency to try and be the joker in situations like today. She'd make light of what she was doing. Earlier, she'd told Marcus to "shut up whining", having just poured boiling water into his lap. That was her mask. Phoebe was sure of it. Alice wasn't dealing with what she'd done. She'd murdered Johnny, blown his head off in fact, and it looked as though she was searching for that same adrenaline rush it had given her. Going from a tea lady to a killer is a huge jump – one that, in normal circumstances, would need counselling – but Alice was trying to be more brutal with every situation. It was like she had no filter. Phoebe wondered where it might all lead. She could be a loose cannon, Alice – one that could go off in the wrong direction. She might need curtailing. Phoebe needed to ensure she didn't spin out of control. For someone in Alice's position, this could well spell danger and catastrophe.

As she savoured the burnt aftertaste, she decided she'd try and talk to her. Therapy was a no-no. Even with her clout, Phoebe didn't know anyone in the counselling world who would break their own code of practice. With what Alice could spill out onto the therapy table, a call to the Old Bill would most certainly follow. They would have to break client confidentiality then.

She came back into the room and watched the people of Mansfield having a good time. She had another half to top up her glass before making her way home. That hour or so had done her the world of good. Watch out, world.

chapter thirty-four

New Year's Eve 2019

Archie was at the casino, having a bad night. He was twelve grand down. His luck seemed to have deserted him. No one had said a word since the other day. Hugh hadn't been in touch, although Archie had clocked him there in the room tonight. They'd made eye contact, but no more. He could sense Hugh was being evasive. Normally he'd have been over by now, with his larger-than-life character filling the air space.

'I'll call it a day, Félix. It's just not my night.'

'OK, Señor Archie. You no lucky tonight, eh?'

'No luck tonight, pal. I'm not in the mood anyway. Too much on my mind. I can't seem to concentrate properly.'

'You need good lady. Your wife is Sarah, yes?'

'Yes, that's right. How do you know that?'

Archie was puzzled. He'd never mentioned Sarah in the casino. She'd never been in either, so how Félix knew of her made him curious.

'I heard Mr Hugh talk about her the other night. He was with two men. They ask about you. They ask about your wife. I hear Hugh tell them about her. She sound very nice. I hear Hugh say she worth one. They all laugh. What does that mean, Mr Archie?'

Just like that, Archie was off his stool, striding over to Hugh. The room seemed empty all of a sudden – he had no one but Hugh in his sights. Hugh saw him and raised his glass in acknowledgement. Archie hit him hard full on the jaw, knocking him into the group of men behind him. His cocktail glass flew threw the air, hitting a middle-aged woman on the forearm as she tried to protect her face. Archie said nothing as he picked Hugh up. The group had parted, making way for Hugh to fall to the floor. He headbutted him in the face, splitting his nose, and held onto him to ensure he was still in his grip.

'Who the fuck were you talking to about my wife?'

Hugh wiped the blood from his nose and mouth, and checked to see if his nose was broken, which it wasn't.

'Who the fuck was it, Hugh? Who are you in with?'

'For fuck's sake, lad, get your fuckin' hands off me,' Hugh replied, as he managed to get his hand around Archie's throat, which was more to keep him at arm's length than anything.

Archie removed Hugh's hand. He could see the number of hardened criminals that had congregated around them. Everyone was waiting to see how things would unfold. He remembered what his grandad had taught him: remain calm, remain in control.

He let Hugh go and said very calmly, 'If anyone touches a hair on her head, I'll come for you. And I'll kill you. I thought you were a friend, Hugh.'

Archie turned to walk away.

'You have no idea who you're dealing with,' Hugh said, straightening his tuxedo, in an attempt to regain some level of composure.

Archie stopped and turned back round.

'And neither do you, Hugh.'

That hit a nerve. He expected Archie to want to ask again, but that spoke volumes. A few of the men nodded in admiration of Archie. He was happy he'd left Hugh pondering and that he'd remembered Frank's advice.

He then heard Hugh shout, 'They'll be comin' for you, Archie! I'd run if I was you! You're outta your depth, lad!'

Archie walked down the stairs, Hugh's words ringing in his ears. He'd run away once before. He wasn't about to do it again. That had been about running away from responsibility, expectation and those conditions of worth Sarah kept telling him about. It had never been about fear of anyone else, only fear of expectation. Whoever it was that was behind all this could come. He'd be waiting. He just wished that Sarah had never been mentioned. That was not how it was done in their world. Maybe they were getting the rundown on Archie and his life to know their target's inner circle – that would make sense. He'd done the same in the past. Take Fletcher O'Brien. He and Frank did their homework on Kat, but only to understand the dynamics of Fletcher's inner world. That was good practice. It was homework. Part of the planning of taking out any target.

"Taking out" – was someone really trying to take him out? Who and why? He didn't have beef with anyone. He'd not upset any of the criminals here in Spain or back home. Well, not to his knowledge anyway. The only upset he'd had was with his mum. He stopped dead. Thinking about that made him feel as though the bottom was going to drop out of his stomach. He saw a bench and sat down. Rubbing his face, he thought about what he'd said, about how his mum had so coldly cut him off, but then he thought about the life he and his mum had enjoyed together. There was no way she would do something like that, was there? He thought about how cold she'd become, how brutal and ruthless she now was, and how she seemed prepared to do anything to show the world that she was as competent as any man in running a criminal empire. But this? No way, he told himself. She wouldn't. It was ludicrous to even think it. He was being irrational, paranoid even. It was madness.

'She's your mum,' he whispered to himself. 'She wouldn't do that.'

No way, he thought. *No way.*

His phone rang. He looked at the screen in amazement. Mum. His mind raced. She'd not been in touch since he'd left. Why was she ringing now? Had Hugh been on the phone to her? Had whoever was behind sending him on that wild goose chase been in touch with her? Did she know he'd just headbutted and smacked Hugh? This was too much of a coincidence. She had to be involved. He felt sick. He pressed "Decline". He needed to think. His own mum. His heart rate quickened.

'Mum, please, no,' he mumbled.

He then remembered Sarah and raced home. He lived three-quarters of a mile away. That was around six minutes for Archie. He needed to get back. If calls had been made in such a short space of time that had triggered his mum ringing him, anyone could have reached Sarah. He needed to get back fast.

***

Phoebe looked at the screen on her phone. She knew she'd been declined. 'Oh Archie,' she said. 'I just wanted to wish you Happy New Year. I miss you.'

Gloria came and put her arm around her. 'He'll come round, luv. It'll just take time, that's all.'

Phoebe sunk her head into Gloria's ample bosom. She felt like a child needing a warm cuddle. Tonight, on New Year's Eve, it was just the two of them – Gloria thinking about Frank, the love of her life, who'd been taken from her far too early, and Phoebe about the son she'd now lost forever. The lady who'd been on the arm of the King of the East Midlands for over thirty years and the lady who now ruled that very same kingdom were both wondering the same thing – had it all been worth it?

***

Archie couldn't get his key in the door fast enough. He was panting, having run all the way back. Hearing him fumbling with his keys, Sarah opened the door. Archie put his arms around her.

'Is anyone here? You OK? Has anyone been?'

Sarah broke free. 'What? What are you going on about?'

'Has anyone been here tonight? Anyone at all?'

'Archie, you're scaring me. No, no one's been. I haven't seen or spoken to a soul.'

Archie took a deep breath as he closed the door. 'Sorry, I just get paranoid sometimes. Ignore me, I'm just being silly.'

'Er, just a moment. That's not you being silly. Now at least do me the courtesy of telling me if my life's in danger. I'm a big girl, you know. Don't you dare keep anything from me.'

'Look, honestly, it's just me being silly. I thought I saw a car, a dodgy-looking car, drive away. That's all. Seemed to be going a bit slow for my liking. It was nothing, I'm sure. Paranoia, that's all.'

Sarah was not convinced. She knew he had things on his mind. She knew to keep her distance whenever he had a lot to cope with. She'd had enough practice after all. His life at the helm had given her enough experience of that. She had to trust him, though, and if he said it was nothing, she'd try and accept that and think no more of it. Experience had again taught her that was not an easy thing to do. She had Mary to think about. Nothing would convince her to put her daughter's life in danger, but for now she'd do the dutiful thing and not add to his problems.

'OK. If I see anything I think is out of the ordinary, I'll tell you,' she said. 'But Archie,' she continued, 'that little bundle of joy in there is the most precious thing in our lives. Nothing comes before her. Not even you.'

'I know, I know. Trust me, everything will be OK. You know it's a hard world we live in.'

'I do, believe me, but we don't have to ever make it harder than it needs to be. Anyway, how was the club?'

'Usual, although I had a bad night. That didn't help my mood.' He decided to leave out the tussle with Hugh.

'Shall we toast the new year?' Sarah asked, taking a bottle of wine from the fridge.

'Yeah, come on. Just me and you. Let's snuggle down and forget the woes of the world for once. Next year will be our year.'

'What – again?' Sarah replied, laughing.

'What shall we toast?' he asked.

'Family,' Sarah said. 'Family.'

Archie glanced at his phone on the worktop and thought of his mum. Had she maybe rung just to wish him all the best? He wanted to believe that but his thoughts wouldn't allow him to. When he was running, he failed to hear the text that came through. *Happy New Year to you all. Thinking of you. Tried to ring, but I assume you're out partying. Love you all deeply, Mum xxx*

chapter thirty-five

4th January 2020

Hugh was on his way to a club that had just opened up. It was a new venture of one of the local Brits, a very good acquaintance of his. He was looking forward to tonight. His friend had assured all the honoured guests of the opening night that there'd be "plenty of sex, drugs and whatever else took your fancy". Sex and drugs took Hugh's fancy at any time of the day or night, so he was looking forward to getting his dick wet more than once tonight. For a man of his age, he could still do a good few hours, as long as the ladies he was mixing it with were able to keep it hard.

He walked briskly, whistling, sometimes breaking into song. The club was down a side street set back from the main drag, just far enough away to be close to the action but secluded at the same time. He heard footsteps – footsteps quickening at a pace that alerted him to possible danger. He listened. There was more than one person behind him. Before he had a chance to turn his head, he had a man either side of him. He stopped and glanced from side to side. The two men now accompanying him along the largely empty street were the same two men who'd accompanied Hendrik when he'd first come to see him.

'Please, carry on walking. We will walk with you,' the slightly taller one on Hugh's left insisted.

Hugh slowly put one foot in front of the other. The guy had a Dutch accent. Hugh was nervous.

'What can I do for you fellas?'

'We won't beat about the bush, Hugh. We work for Dirk and Joris. You remember them, yes?'

'Of course. Please give them my regards,' he replied sarcastically, which they noted.

The guy to his left gave Hugh a little dig in the ribs.

'You are lucky to be alive, my friend. We have another job for you.'

'And that is?'

'Come,' the taller guy said, motioning to the black car that had slid very quietly alongside them.

Hugh put his brakes on.

'Please. Come.'

Hugh had no choice. They walked him to the car, where the passenger door then opened. He couldn't see who was inside.

'Please,' the taller guy said, motioning for Hugh to get in.

'Get in, Hugh,' came a voice from the car. A London accent. A voice he didn't recognise.

Hugh climbed in, unsure who he was going to meet. Next to him in the back was a very well-dressed man waiting to shake his hand.

'Tariq Mali,' the guy said. 'We have business to discuss.'

chapter thirty-six

Two days later – 6th January 2020

Archie was in a bar overlooking the beach, waiting for Hugh. He'd not seen him since the clash on New Year's Eve, mainly because Archie had not been out much. He'd been too concerned about leaving Sarah and Mary on their own. He knew it couldn't continue – he had to earn a living. He couldn't be seen to have disappeared from the scene, especially after what had happened with Hugh. He needed to show his face, maybe answer questions about what was going on with the two of them. Archie was worried, though. He'd heard nothing since shooting Gregory and returning empty-handed. He'd been expecting a visit from someone, anyone, to try and make sense of that whole little job. The silence was concerning. It made no more sense than why he'd been sent to see Gregory in the first place. Someone was playing him and he needed to know who.

He'd worked through his irrational thinking of his mum being behind it all. Having played it out over and over again, he'd come to the conclusion Phoebe wasn't responsible. She was his mum and even though she'd hurt him, probably more than she realised, she'd never do that to him. Of that, he was now convinced.

The text on New Year's Eve had helped. He'd thought of ringing her, or even answering her calls, but he couldn't bring himself to. His pride wouldn't allow it. He knew Sarah spoke to her. She didn't know he knew, and if he was honest, he didn't want her to know he knew. He was comfortable with that – it made him feel better thinking Sarah was keeping it from him. That ticked his box. The macho box. The box that said he was in the right by not giving in. He knew deep down it was all silly and pushed the thoughts deep into his subconscious. As long as he was out here in Spain, he could cope with it all. No one here gave a fuck and he was allowed to do his work without any interference – well, up until the last job of course.

That last job was one he wished he'd never accepted. He knew the lack of contact from whoever was behind it didn't bode well. One day it would come and when it did, it would be the day he rued breaking all contact with his family.

Hugh had rung him yesterday, saying he wanted to meet. He said he wanted to make up and explain what was said about Sarah. He told him it was all innocent. Archie had agreed to meet because he wanted to see if Hugh knew what was going on behind the scenes. Plus, he liked Hugh and would much prefer him on side. That way, he had more of a chance of getting wind of anything or anyone coming over the horizon.

He became aware of someone nearby. He saw a hand in his peripheral vision. It was Hugh. Archie stared at him for a few seconds before holding out his hand.

'Thanks for coming, lad.'

'It's only 'cos I like you,' Archie replied, smiling.

Hugh called the waiter over, ordered a coffee for himself and Archie, then looked at the sea. The waves rolled in and he stared at them long enough that Archie began to wonder if he was ever going to speak.

'You OK?' he asked.

Hugh ignored him and continued to stare. Archie did the same.

'See the waves?' he eventually said.

'Yeah.'

'No matter what we do today, lad, they'll keep rolling in and they'll do the same tomorrow. They've done the same thing since time began and they'll continue to do so, long after man has left this earth.'

He then paused. Archie listened intently, not knowing what Hugh was going on about.

'The sun will set tonight and rise again tomorrow. It always has done and always will, long after we've been and gone. Nothing we do will change that. All we can do is influence what we do in between.' Hugh turned to Archie. 'And whatever that may be, it will set again tonight. The waves will continue to roll in. Man cannot change that.'

Archie held his stare, unsure what to say.

'Sometimes we're able to change and influence what will happen to us, lad, but other times, things happen or will happen that we are powerless to stop. Like the sun and those waves there – they will continue regardless.'

He let the waiter serve their coffee. He picked up the receipt the waiter had placed under his saucer, doing nothing with it before placing it back down.

'What I'm trying to say, lad, is that our own destiny is out of our hands. Our time comes to us all. We all have our own sunset but sometimes, no matter how we try and influence it, it will come at that time regardless. I know I fucked up when I decided to fuck the Dutch over and come here to the land of sun, sea and sangria. I knew my sunset would come. So no matter what I do now, the sun will set on me when others decide it's time.'

Archie tried to make sense of what Hugh was saying. He looked back to the sea and Hugh allowed him time to process what he was trying to tell him. They sipped their coffee in total silence. Archie had only ever really been in Hugh's company in clubs and casinos. He'd only ever seen the loud, confident Hugh – the Hugh who bounced young fit blondes up and down on his dick, the Hugh who snorted anything going and the Hugh who was the life and soul of the party. He'd never seen this side of him. He wondered if Hugh was trying to tell him that he was sorry for something he was about to ask him to do, and that regardless of the outcome, he was a dead man. Was he saying he knew his days were numbered and that nothing he could do would influence him being shot dead at the end of it? Was he telling Archie he'd accepted his own fate, that he was powerless to influence the outcome, but that

Archie could still influence what happened between his own sunrise and sunset?

'So what do you want me to do?' Archie asked.

'Kill me.'

Archie almost choked on his coffee.

'Come again?'

Hugh looked around. The place was quiet. Being well out of holiday season, and the sun behind the clouds, made for a near-deserted place. Hugh looked out to the waves once more.

'You've upset a major face, lad. He wants you dead. That job I gave you – well, it turns out it was all a farce. This face had "bought" my debt from the Dutch. He knows of them well enough, apparently, so paid handsomely. Means I owe him now. He used me, of course, as a way to get to you. There was never any money to retrieve. Poor old Gregory was just a normal fella in the wrong place at the wrong time when they picked him out. They never thought you'd kill him, though.'

Hugh turned to Archie before continuing. He'd expected a response after that last comment, but Archie didn't look at him.

'They thought you might put a bullet in his leg or something, but they knew full well you'd return empty-handed. The other lad – I forget his name...'

'Craig,' Archie said. 'His name was Craig.'

'OK, Craig, well, he was a lad who'd gotten in over his head. You know the type, they do a bit of dealing, think they're part of the scene and before you know it, they're indebted to whoever's pulling their pisser. Two unnecessary deaths.' Hugh shook his head. 'Two early sunsets.'

Archie contemplated his situation. He'd often mocked people for becoming philosophical or spiritual on impending death. Hugh had never been either, so he smiled for a moment at how he was now looking at life and all its meaning.

'So, the fact you didn't recover the money means this face can now look on it that you owe him. He was even talking about how you'd stolen his money – you know, found it and kept it for yourself. I had to stop myself from laughing. He was being serious at the time – trying to convince himself, I think. Thing is, this was after he'd told me there never was any money to be had. But you know how it is, Archie. Sometimes you've just gotta play the game. So you owe him. He's making out you've shafted him, so he's put a price on your head.'

'And he's asked you to do it.'

'Spot on,' Hugh replied.

They looked at each other. Only one of them was coming out of this alive.

'How long you got?' Archie asked.

'Forty-eight hours.'

They both returned to the sea.

'You've got forty-eight hours to kill me, lad and for fuck's sake make it quick.'

'Why you doing this?' Archie asked. 'Why not do the job?'

'How old are you, Archie?'

'23.'

'Your sun is still rising. Fuck me, it's not even ten o'clock in your world. My sun is heading towards sunset. How old do you think I am, son?'

It was the first time Hugh had referred to Archie as "son". It was always "lad". Frank had always called him Son. It gave Archie a warm feeling inside.

'52 maybe.'

'Not bad, lad. I'm 53. I've been dodging a bullet ever since I came here. I know full well if I take you out, they'll give me the bullet next. There's no way anyone has bought my debt without some sort of agreement to shoot me dead after it's all over. The Dutch would've insisted on it. Either way, I'm getting one in the head, son, and I ain't taking you with me. This way, you have a way out. My exit's blocked. There's no fire escape for me.'

Hugh turned to Archie, who was looking at him warmly.

'Anytime over the next two days. Don't let me know. Just do it, and then fuck off. Don't make him look for you here.'

'Who, Hugh? Don't let who?'

'A guy called Tariq Mali. You'll know him, I'm sure.'

Archie said nothing. He looked at the direction of the waves, but unlike before he wasn't really aware of them.

'You do know him, don't you?' Hugh asked.

'Oh yeah, I know him all right. I last saw him less than a month ago. Why does he want me dead? Did he say?'

'No, and I didn't ask. You know the score.'

'Yeah, I do.'

Hugh didn't need to do this. Few in their world would. They'd do anything to save their own skin, but here was Hugh sacrificing himself for Archie, a man he'd only just got to know.

'You're a good man, Hugh.'

Hugh laughed. 'I'll take that, lad. Not many would agree.'

They sat in silence for a moment.

'I don't want to kill you, Hugh.'

'You have to, lad, 'cos if you don't, I'll kill you.'

chapter thirty-seven

Hugh had been gone for over half an hour. Archie hadn't moved. He'd ordered another coffee and was sipping it while he processed what he'd heard. As much as he was concerned about the price on his head, he was more relieved that it wasn't his mum behind all of this. He apologised in his head, knowing he should never have thought it.

He couldn't, however, fathom out why Tariq wanted him dead. He ran through all the dealings he'd had with him, which, to be fair, were very few. Other than at Frank's and then Jez's funeral, he'd only ever met Tariq once, in London. Frank had introduced them as part of Archie's "coming of age", as he used to call it. He'd done the rounds of the UK's top table to make sure Archie knew who was who. Frank always told him to make sure he kept his friends a lot closer than his enemies. He also used to tell him to keep his enemies closer, so, as always, Frank had all angles covered. The only thing Archie could think of was the business at Jez's wake, but he couldn't comprehend how Tariq could be so offended that he'd put a price on his head. To Archie, it was something and nothing. Handbags at five paces and all that. He stroked his chin, as he racked his brain. Nothing. It had to be that – his spur of the moment threat to kill him.

He then recalled Tariq saying: "You shouldn't go round threatening to kill people, young Archie. It may come back to bite you one day. Remember the company you keep." Archie hadn't forgotten the "young Archie" comment, but the more he thought about the look in Tariq's eyes, the more he was convinced that was Tariq's reason for wanting him dead. It had obviously disrespected him more than he'd realised.

Archie thought about what his grandad would have done. Would Frank have ordered someone's murder in retaliation for a threat to kill? He thought about how public it had all been and who had witnessed it, and concluded that in a similar situation there's no way Frank would've allowed a young man like Archie to have made a threat on his life so publicly without retribution. But would his grandad have put a price on the head of a man in Archie's position? He wasn't so sure. Tariq taking Archie out would have been like Frank taking out a son of one of the top players. Suicide. It would start a war. But then again, he reasoned, him being out here in Spain, cut off from the family, made him a far easier target – certainly one that came with less risk. Who would know? Only Hugh knew the score outside of Tariq's inner circle. Except for the Dutch outfit of course. Archie couldn't help wondering if he'd have this price on his head if he was still the head of the family, or even at his mum's side.

He had to take his hat off to Tariq, though. He'd played Archie good and proper. To get Archie to "fuck up" a job gave him a valid reason for taking action. People knew he'd returned empty-handed – that was no secret. A failure like that got round the criminal fraternity quickly. His phone hadn't rung since. But Archie had played the game. He'd not made it known he'd suspected it was all a set-up. That would not go down well at all. It'd be seen as passing the buck and not taking responsibility for your failures, and that would be frowned upon. He'd had to make out that he'd fucked up, not done his homework and had moved in too quickly. People had asked who was behind the job as certain fractions were hovering to see the fallout. Archie had played his cards close, telling anyone that asked for information that it was between him and his employer. He'd not even brought Hugh's name into it, although his attack on Hugh the other night had started tongues wagging.

Archie felt like he had the weight of the world on his shoulders. He had his own life to protect, including the two people he cared for most, and he had this dilemma with Hugh. Archie didn't want to kill him. For all the violence he'd been involved in throughout his short life, he wasn't prepared for something like this. Hugh was a friend – a loyal friend, as he'd just proven – but Archie didn't feel like he had a choice. It really was Hugh or him.

He continued to sit deep in thought about how he'd got there. He looked back on his childhood. He remembered the times with his dad, though his happiest days were spent with his uncle Richie. He recalled the days at The Stags, the home games and the away days. He remembered how violent it was at the matches and how his uncle was held in such high regard.

He reflected on his father's death and how never getting revenge on the people who did it tortured his grandad. It ate away at him. Now he was older, Archie could see how Frank had taken out his anger and frustrations on Richie. He knew his grandad regretted what he'd done to his son. For all his grandad was in this world, deep down, he would have turned back the clock if he could. Archie watched the waves roll in, as he tried to process that part of his memory. Even Frank Pearson, a criminal legend, had regrets. He'd be telling him to make peace with his mum. *"Don't have any regrets, Son, make peace while you can."*

He smiled inside as he wondered why people were always able to tell others what to do but found it so hard to do the very same thing themselves. He knew the only reason Frank failed to publicly admit his regrets around Richie was for fear of looking weak. He had to save face, which was evidently more important than letting people know how he truly felt about what he'd done. Saving face and being comfortable about how people see you are very powerful emotions. At times they override everything else.

Archie was fully aware of how he was behaving over his mum. He could quite easily go home, front it out and be whoever he wanted to be, whether that was part of the family business or not, but he just could not bring himself to do it. The hurt he'd felt when his mum had cast him aside was greater than any desire to make amends. Phoebe had done no wrong, of course, as Sarah had tried to tell him. She was only doing her job – looking after the family business – but much as he tried, he could not forgive her. He was her son and that alone should have meant she understood his reasons for getting on that plane to Faro. She should have supported him unconditionally. He was kin, which, to Archie, should have made all the difference. He couldn't see that Phoebe *had* supported him, by letting him get on with his life as he chose. She could have told him he should be at her side but, no, she allowed him to be who he wanted to be. He couldn't see it of course.

Archie had never felt so sad in his life. A tear ran down his face, as he thought about killing Hugh and where he should take his family next. He couldn't stay there. Hugh had told him to fuck off once he'd taken him out and fuck off, he would. Where to, he didn't know, but one thing he *did* know was that Tariq Mali would never have the satisfaction of hunting him down. He remembered Bonnie's words after Tariq had left Jez's wake: "He plays the long game, Archie. Don't ever let your guard down." Archie had forgotten about that until now, believing it had been put to bed with honour on all sides intact. Archie was twenty-three years old. He had a long life ahead of him and he could play the game as well as anyone.

He dropped enough euros on the table to cover his tab and walked to his car. He felt for Sarah, and Mary too, though being the age she was, she didn't know what was going on. Innocence could be bliss. She'd go wherever her mum and dad took her. He got in and, before putting on his belt, thought about the conscious mind – how, without consciousness, we would all be just like Mary. Being conscious of our surroundings and people's behaviours had a lot to answer for. He looked at the vast expanse of water in front of him, and wondered why early man had ventured into the unknown. It would have been terrifying for the first people to have made something that floated, rowing out towards the horizon, not knowing where they'd end up. Was it curiosity or was it their desire to add to their lot? Did greed make early humans venture out to sea to conquer other lands? Or was it to settle a debate as to whether the earth was flat?

Archie took a deep breath in and said out loud, 'Fuck knows, but it's all led to where I am now.' He started his engine and added, 'And fuck knows where I'm going next.'

chapter thirty-eight

'I knew this would happen, I just knew it,' Sarah said in despair, looking out of the balcony window.

Archie had kept enough from her of late, so he'd sat her down and told her the whole lot. She knew the last job had come from Hugh, but she hadn't known it was a set-up nor that Tariq had used it to legitimise Archie as his target. She'd laughed out loud at "legitimise", realising how ridiculous it sounded, but in their world, it was as legal as you got. She'd seen similar circumstances play out closer to home when Frank, and Archie, had wanted to take a certain course of action. She recalled being told how Frank had taken over Leeds all those years ago, because Gerry Clarke, the guy who ran Leeds at the time, had taken a major liberty. Frank therefore had a legitimate reason to take him out and muscle in. She could handle all of that – it came with the life – but she'd broken down when Archie had told her about his dilemma with Hugh.

'Knew what? That we'd have to move quickly?' Archie asked.

'No. Well, yes, if you like, but I was talking about Hugh. You can't kill him.'

'I have to. It's him or me.'

Sarah sobbed again. Archie took her in his arms. 'You told me to tell you everything.'

'Yes I know, but...'

They sat and held each other close. Through the gap in the door, Archie could see Mary playing in the other room. He thought about how innocent she was and how it would all be taken away from her. Before long, she'd be aware of the life her family led, and that made him sad. But this life would always find him, always draw him in. The adrenaline rush he felt on a job, or back when he and his grandad would be sorting out the shit, couldn't be replicated. Mary would just have to live with it and accept it. There was no other life for him.

As he squeezed Sarah close, he considered how he was going to deal with Tariq. Yes, he would fuck off from here, but was he running? Fuck no. Archie would strategically place himself somewhere else. Tariq didn't know he knew. He would once he'd taken Hugh out, but by the time news of Hugh's death landed at Tariq's door, Archie would have gone, and Tariq wouldn't have a fucking clue where to find him.

"Play the long game, Son, play the long game," he heard Frank say. Archie had all the time in the world. What he didn't have was help, and that was the only thing that concerned him.

chapter thirty-nine

Archie had slept surprisingly well considering his mind had been racing when he'd first laid his head on the pillow, and he'd only woken up once. He'd left a few moments earlier.

Sarah was packed and ready to go. Everything they needed, all they held dear, was in just one suitcase. It amazed her that, even with the wealth they had, she could put everything that meant anything to her in such a tiny space. The rest was material – or, as she told herself, immaterial.

She'd been sombre since waking up. Today was not only the day they moved on, knowing a bullet in the back of the head could come at any moment, but the day Archie did what was necessary. She couldn't make sense of any of it. She knew people had to be taken out sometimes, but this, with Hugh, just seemed avoidable. She'd tried to talk to Archie about it, but he'd told her he couldn't risk Hugh staying alive. Even though Hugh had shown his loyalty with his act of selflessness, the only person Archie could trust in the world they operated in was himself. He'd explained as much to Sarah, who'd taken umbrage, until he'd stopped digging and told her she was exempt from "the world we live in".

He'd also told her to ditch the phone she used to keep in touch with his mum. She hadn't realised he knew about that, but, as he told her, he knows everything. She tried to explain it was crucial to have that contact, but Archie insisted they couldn't afford anyone knowing where they were going, not even family. Someone always talked. Something would slip and that slip could be the one thing to give Tariq a heads-up. Archie had made it abundantly clear that she was to have no contact with anyone from their previous lives – well, not until Tariq was taken care of at least. And taking care of Tariq was going to be the biggest thing Archie had ever undertaken.

***

He wanted to be at Hugh's early. He knew Morag took a mid-morning stroll every day. She would walk along the beach before calling at the local bakery for fresh bread. It was a favourite of Hugh's. He'd told Archie it reminded him of his childhood – his mum had always baked her own bread. He sat thirty yards away and waited, laughing as he recalled Hugh telling him he'd use Morag's stroll as a chance to have a shower and wash his dick of the previous night's shenanigans.

It was forty minutes before he saw Morag, hair in rollers, come out through the gate. She lit a fag and walked briskly in the other direction. Archie checked his hand gun. It was loaded with a single bullet. He locked his car and walked towards Hugh's villa, which was set back. The roof was visible from the other side of the road. It was quiet. A few cars passed in both directions, but save for the odd person ambling along the seafront, there was no one about. He walked through the gates and took in the size of the villa. He'd been a couple of times before, the last time being when he'd called round after the job that never was, but he'd never really noticed how big the place was. He knew it had eight bedrooms and as many bathrooms, but he'd only ever been in two rooms. He also knew where Hugh left the spare key. Hugh had told Archie it was easier to find the spare after he'd had a skinful and a few lines than fumble about in his jacket or trousers.

The key was exactly where he suspected it would be. Instinctively, he looked behind him, and then left and right. He quietly opened the door and walked through into the large hallway. He couldn't hear anyone or anything, but if Hugh was the creature of habit Archie thought he was, he'd be in the shower. As he approached the top of the stairs, he could hear Hugh singing, which he found strange given Hugh suspected he'd be gunned down at any time. He stepped across the landing to what he guessed was the master bedroom. The bed was unmade and Hugh's singing was unmistakably coming from the ensuite.

He sat in the chair adjacent to the window and waited. Within two minutes, the singing stopped. He heard the shower switch off and the sound of someone drying themselves.

Hugh stopped dead when he came out into the bedroom to find Archie sat with a gun pointing directly at him. He dropped the smaller towel he was using to dry his hair, before making sure the large one was secure around his waist.

'Well, fuck me, I thought you'd at least do it with me not knowing. Want to see the fear in my eyes, do ya?'

'Surprised to hear you singing, Hugh. Didn't think you'd be so chirpy, what with you knowing within forty-eight hours you'd have a bullet in your head.'

'I made my peace yesterday, lad. I'm OK with it. Acceptance is a wonderful thing.'

They stared at each other for what seemed an age. Hugh's breathing quickened. Archie noticed. Hugh didn't. Archie stood up and stared a little longer. He admired Hugh's resolve. It was hard not to.

'I ain't gonna kill ya, Hugh. I'm no cold-blooded killer. I've killed before, you know that, but always for a reason. I'm comfortable with all I've done in my short time. The beatings, the maimings, the killings – they've all sat comfortable with me. But this? It'd haunt me for the rest of my days.'

Hugh didn't respond.

'In this gun is a single bullet,' Archie said, walking towards him and placing it on the dressing table.

'I'm gonna walk along the landing and if I get to the end, I'll walk down the stairs. If I get to the bottom,

I'll know I'm safe.' He looked Hugh in the eye. 'If you want to take me out, Hugh, and do what's been asked of you, now's your chance. No hard feelings. It's the world we live in. If I walk out that front door, I'm outta here. You told me I need to fuck off, and that's what I intend to do.'

He stuck out his hand. Hugh shook it.

Archie walked out of the bedroom, reached the top of the stairs and paused. He wanted to look back to see if Hugh was at his bedroom door, gun in hand, but decided against it and walked down the stairs. He got to the bottom and paused again, before making for the front door. As he approached the gates, he heard a single gunshot.

'Hugh, no!' he said out loud, turning to face the house. Hugh using the gun on himself had never entered his head. 'Fuckin' hell, Hugh,' he muttered and bowed his head.

Archie walked out the gate, keeping his head down as he went back to his car. The road was still quiet. He glanced to see if Morag was coming from the other direction, but she was nowhere in sight. He drove away from the scene in an orderly fashion, not wanting to draw any attention to himself, but pleased that no one had any inclination as to what had just taken place. He wanted to be far away by the time Morag returned. He did not want to hear her screams.

chapter forty

Pēteris was driving through Nottingham city centre. He had Janis with him in the passenger seat and Valdis and Andris, who he'd picked up from Newark train station, in the back. They'd flown into London three days ago and taken the train up earlier that morning. He was nervous. Today could be the day that cemented his position in the business. He was a top table member and even though he'd been a loyal employee for so long, he still felt he needed something like this to give him the legacy others had. Valdis and Andris had a reputation for being difficult and that had led to the falling out with Frank fifteen or so years ago. Pēteris wasn't sure they'd mellowed an awful lot. They gave the impression they thought they were a cut above everyone else. To most people in their world, perhaps they were, but you treated the Pearson family, even without Frank at the helm, with respect at all times, no matter who you were. This was not a lesson Pēteris was convinced his fellow countrymen had learnt.

They chatted away in Latvian, to pass the time really because everyone sensed the tension. They all knew the purpose of today's meeting. Valdis and Andris knew what they wanted from it. Pēteris and Janis were praying for an amicable outcome. The meeting had been delayed by a week due to business Valdis had to take care of back home – personal business that couldn't be left, which Phoebe had been comfortable with.

Pat drove Phoebe and Brian into the car park of the main club. The only other member of her team to be present was Raquel, who was already there. Del was at the club, but would stay out of the way. It was 10:15.

'Right, let's have a quick recap of things before they get here,' Phoebe said, walking to the entrance. Her phone rang. It was Alice.

'Hi.'

'Hi Mum, just letting you know the train's delayed by an hour or so, so we'll be late getting into Newark. Problem on the line at Peterborough or something.'

'OK. How was the weekend?'

'Good. Had a great time. Knackered, though. I'll probably sleep most of the way back.'

'Well, don't miss your stop, will you?'

'No, I won't. Hey, I saw Tariq Saturday night.'

'Tariq? How was he?'

'No idea. He didn't see me. He was with some fellas. It looked like a meeting of some sort, or maybe some guys he was trying to impress. Anyway, see you later.'

'Yeah, safe trip.'

Raquel arranged the drinks before joining them in the main meeting room, which was ample for accommodating everyone. Del was there, for now.

'You two still wary of all this?' Phoebe asked Pat and Brian.

Brian spoke first. 'All I know, Phoebe, is last time, they were not people to deal with. Yes, I know it was a long time ago, but people seldom change. I'd be very cautious about entering into business dealings with them.'

Phoebe turned to Pat.

'I can't disagree, I'll be honest. I for one will take some convincing if we proceed, but if that's what we decide to do, you'll have me on board one hundred per cent.'

'I've had them checked out and, as you say, it seems they can be problematic. Irrational, someone said, but they are big players back home in Latvia and have dealt with some of the top firms over here. Direct dealings, I'm not sure. Via a third party, I understand.'

'That's another thing that makes me nervous,' Brian replied.

'And what's that?' Phoebe asked.

'If they've dealt with major players since Frank fucked them off, why us?'

'It's a point that niggles me too, I've gotta say,' Pat added.

'Hmm ... I know what you mean. That's a question I want answering.'

'Maybe it's as Pēteris said and it's just Janis that's the link. Maybe nothing more than that. Had Janis had connections elsewhere it would be someone else meeting them today. We could be trying to find something that isn't there. I mean, if their dealings around the country have been third-hand, I don't suspect they know anyone of any real influence well enough to make this kind of introduction. Just a thought,' Raquel pointed out.

Everyone pondered what she'd just said. This was something Pēteris had reiterated since first putting the opportunity on the table.

'Fair point,' Pat said, slowly nodding his head.

'Well, I think we tread with caution, and suspect lies and mistrust until we feel comfortable otherwise,' Phoebe said. 'But we should still be respectful,' she continued. 'We don't want to spoil things if it is indeed a good opportunity.'

Everyone agreed.

Pēteris pulled into the car park twenty-five minutes later. The meeting was scheduled for eleven o'clock. He found himself treating Valdis and Andris like royalty. He failed to recognise his behaviour until he found himself opening the car door for Valdis. *What the fuck are you doing?* he thought, as he closed it.

'Right this way, gentlemen,' he said, purposely speaking in English to ensure they did the same.

Neither of his guests replied, as they followed him into the club. Del was on hand to greet them. Of course, they looked older, but he recognised them right away.

Del watched Valdis to see if he walked with a limp. He couldn't recall which leg Richie had stabbed him in, but Valdis gave it away, ever so slightly dragging his right leg, which Del couldn't help but find amusing.

'I think you may remember Brian and Pat,' Del said, on bringing them through. Pat and Brian shook their hands firmly, keeping eye contact the whole time. Brian, in particular, was dying to mention Andris's glass eye, but remained professional. Still neither of their guests said a word.

'And this is Mrs Pearson,' Del said, introducing Phoebe.

'Mrs Pearson, it is an honour to meet you. I don't recall meeting you the last time we did business together,' Andris said, as he shook her hand and then kissed it.

'No, me neither. I know you dealt with Frank, but I wasn't really involved back then.'

'Er, this is Andris,' Pēteris said, given Andris hadn't introduced himself. He knew Phoebe wouldn't know who was who.

'Apologies,' Andris continued. 'And this is Valdis.'

'A pleasure, Mrs Pearson.' He shook Phoebe's hand but didn't kiss it.

Phoebe was immediately aware of the duo's dynamics. Andris was the talker, the charmer, whereas Valdis was the quiet one who stared. It was a classic scenario, a bit like good cop, bad cop, which she was used to managing. It made her smile.

'Well, would you like a drink? Tea, coffee, or something a little stronger?' Phoebe asked, as she sat down.

Valdis looked at his watch. 'Coffee for me, please.'

'Yes, for me, too,' Andris confirmed.

Del left the room to organise the drinks with one of the staff, before continuing with his work.

'So, let's get down to business – the business of guns. But, firstly, I need something answering. Why us?'

Andris noticed Phoebe's approach. No small talk, direct, and rather cold in her delivery. His tone changed from his warm greeting moments earlier. 'You do not want it?' he asked, matching her abruptness.

Pat looked at his boss, waiting to see her reaction.

'Whether we want it or not we will decide in due course. Firstly, I want to know why us.'

Andris paused. The meeting from fifteen years ago came flooding back, as did Richie stabbing Valdis. He became acutely aware he was outnumbered once again. He looked at Janis, gesturing with his hand.

'This gentleman here, a very good friend of ours,' he said, 'made our acquaintance some time ago. It's funny how fellow countrymen find each other, don't you think?'

The room was uncomfortably quiet. Andris gave an awkward clear of the throat before continuing.

'We trust him. We approached him with an opportunity. We knew, with all respect, it was out of his league, but we also knew he operated in and around Manchester. I'll be totally honest with you, Mrs Pearson, we had hoped Janis would be in a position to make an introduction to the Burbankses, but he said he had no real links there. As I am sure you know, he had more dealings with Mr O'Brien, God rest his soul. He told us he had a major contact with your good selves, the Pearson family. That, of course, is our mutual friend Pēteris here. We know Pēteris from years back, but for obvious reasons had lost touch, and even though our business dealings with your family ended on bad terms last time, we were prepared to let Janis make the re-introduction. We believe in what's gone is gone. The past is the past. We can only influence the future.'

He leant forward. 'We have a very lucrative proposition, Mrs Pearson. You and your organisation are one of only a handful in the UK who could handle it. One of a select few who would be allowed by the other big players to, how you say, facilitate it.'

He turned to Pēteris and asked him in Latvian if that last sentence made sense. Pēteris confimed in English that it did.

'Do you not know any other UK firms well enough to make a direct approach?' Phoebe asked.

'No. The other UK firms of your kind are not people we have had direct dealings with. We needed a, how you say, go-between. When Janis said he knew Pēteris well, and had worked with you in the past, we thought it would be a good idea to try and build bridges. We would like to build a bridge, Mrs Pearson.'

There was a knock at the door. Raquel stood up. It was Tina bringing the drinks. She placed three pots of coffee and three pots of tea on the table, before bringing through a tray of cups and saucers, milk, sugar and a plate of rather nice-looking chocolate-covered biscuits.

'Thank you, Tina,' Raquel said, before closing the door behind her.

'OK, so what type of firearms are we talking?'

'All sorts,' Valdis said. 'Handguns, semi-automatics, the lot. We can get whatever you want. No questions asked.'

'So, have you actually brought any into the country yet? Pēteris mentioned places in Scotland,' Brian asked.

'Yes, we have done three dummy runs, just to make sure we knew the routes and could get onto shore quickly and easily. We have done two runs now with merchandise. No one bothered us.'

'Where did you come in?' Raquel asked.

Andris looked at Janis, who cleared his throat.

'When they brought them in the first time they landed near a beach in a place called Cullen and then the second time the next village along, a place called Portknockie.'

'Port what?' Pat asked.

'Portknockie,' Janis replied.

'They have some funny names up there, I'll give 'em that.'

'And where are these places?' Phoebe asked.

Janis bent down, taking a laptop from his bag. 'I'll show you. Do you have wi-fi?'

'Yeah, here, I'll put the details in.'

Janis stepped back to let Raquel enter the information. He sat back down and tapped away. 'Here you are, this is the area. This is Cullen.'

Phoebe moved next to Raquel, who in turn moved aside for Brian and Pat to take a look.

'It's a long fuckin' way,' Pat said, before exhaling a deep breath.

'What it is, my friend, is out of the way. The kind of place people go for holidays, not to bring in merchandise like this.'

'Fair point.'

'I think we need to pay the area a visit first,' Phoebe said. 'We need to understand the area, the landscape and the routes in and out. It looks remote – we need to know what we are dealing with.'

'Who do you suggest goes?' Brian asked.

'Me, Pat and Raquel will go. I want to see this place first-hand.'

She turned to Andris. 'Once we have visited the area and are happy with it, we can talk further. We need to talk financials, quantities and how, if we do proceed, you don't deal with anyone else in the UK.'

'Of course, Mrs Pearson. We will meet you up there. When are you planning to go?'

Phoebe sat down and looked at her diary.

'Ten days' time, Thursday 23rd. We'll stay two nights.'

'Then we will do the same.'

'Let us know where you intend to stay. We will stay somewhere different.'

Andris looked at Valdis. He knew he'd take this as a snub and was conscious of him causing a scene. Valdis shook his head slightly as if to assure him it was OK.

'Fine, Mrs Pearson. We will let Pēteris know.'

'Make sure you have some examples of the guns with you. We want to see the quality. Having them up there to show us should confirm that the area is a good area to work from,' Pat said.

Again Andris looked at Valdis, who remained expressionless.

'We would normally show you examples here. I had suspected that would take place at our next meeting, not out in the open.'

Pat sat forward. 'If you want us to work with you on bringing firearms into the country up there in Jock Land, then you shouldn't have any issue having the merchandise on you when we are up there, should you?'

'OK, we will do as you ask. Does that conclude our meeting?'

Pat looked at Phoebe.

'Yes, thank you, I think it does. We shall see you in ten days' time.'

Pēteris took a silent sigh of relief. It had gone well. A little tense, but without any stabbings, so maybe the first brick had been laid. He looked at Janis, who looked out of his depth. Janis was a hard man, a great fighter, but this was a different league for him. Pēteris winked at him. Janis smiled and nodded.

Raquel saw them out. She grabbed Pēteris by the arm before he walked out into the fresh air.

'Keep a close eye on them for fuck's sake, Pēteris. I have a little nagging voice that just won't go away. If this goes pear-shaped, it could be you finished around here. You need to understand that.'

'I do, and I will, don't worry. I'm not planning on letting this go wrong.'

Raquel nodded, as she let go of his arm.

'Thoughts?' Phoebe asked.

'I'm still cautious of them. Something feels off,' Pat commented.

'Brian?' Phoebe asked.

'They seemed OK. Certainly less bolshy than last time. I can see they've mellowed a bit and have more of an understanding of how we do things over here. Let's see. I couldn't stop thinking of Frank, though, when I saw the glass eye. Frank really didn't like him for that alone, poor fella.'

Phoebe smiled. 'Yes, I can see why. I couldn't help but think of Steven while I was speaking to him.' She paused. 'And I assume the other one limped because of Richie?'

'Yeah. Strange they want to deal with us again, innit?' Brian laughed.

Phoebe shook her head while smiling at the same time. 'OK. For now, we keep this between us – well, between our top table. It needs to be kept under wraps. We cannot be advertising our product until we have it. Understood?'

Everyone nodded.

'We are going to have to see the level of interest at some point, though,' Raquel stated, trying to help.

Phoebe had never been involved in anything like this before. Importing firearms was a massive step up. Even Frank would've had his work cut out.

'I'm aware of that, Raquel, thank you, but for now we don't even know if we're going to proceed.'

Raquel took the hint, but felt she needed to labour her point. 'Yes, I know, but we need to understand the dynamics of things here.'

'Meaning?'

'To my knowledge, no one has ever done this before. I think we need to ask ourselves why. The main firms in the UK all do their own thing. It's how it's always been. I don't know why, but it has. Are we sure we would have a market? Would the others buy from us – a rival so to speak?'

The room went quiet. Phoebe sensed everyone was looking for a leader. This was where Frank would've come into his own. People had followed Frank since he was a young man. He'd always had that natural air of authority. Phoebe, for all her grit and determination, didn't possess that. This was when she needed Archie. Even though he'd shown he was not a leader of Frank's ilk, she would've loved to have him as a strong pillar to lean on. She looked around the table. They were all loyal people, who would die for her, but she felt lonely. Right now, she needed someone to lean on. Pat was her number two, but he wasn't Archie. Archie was kin and, like in any walk of life, kin often made the difference. She looked at Pat.

'What do you think, Pat?'

'It's a fair point, although I fail to see why the others wouldn't buy if the price and merchandise were right. It's business after all. If there's money to be made, I can't really see the issue. We have enough respect in this world to make this work. Don't you agree?' He looked at Raquel in particular.

'Yes, I'm sure we do, but the last thing we need is grief with the likes of Greg and Rory.'

Phoebe interjected. 'I can't see there being any grief. All we are doing is providing a product. I think we say and do nothing until we feel the time is right. Let's just see what transpires. For now, we keep our mouths shut. We don't want anyone outside of our top table getting wind of this. We wait until we have the merchandise before we take it to market. Agreed?'

Everyone agreed.

'Janis knows and he ain't even part of our firm,' Pat commented.

'Yes, I know, Pat, but that is unavoidable. He knew before we did. Speak to Pēteris and make sure Janis gets the message loud and clear. And I mean loud and clear.'

Pat nodded.

'Right. For now, we assume they're good for their word. If we keep the tension, it will only create mistrust, and despite our previous dealings with them, that will not be good for business.'

'On a different note, anyone heard anything from Archie?' Brian asked.

Phoebe shook her head sorrowfully. Brian looked at Raquel, then at Pat.

'Nothing. I'm gutted to be honest. I've tried him a couple of times – well, more than a couple – but no reply. I've texted him, Facetimed and all that shit, but nowt. Fuck all,' Pat said, upset.

'I take it you've still heard nothin'?' Brian asked Phoebe.

'Not a thing. He's declined my calls and not replied to my texts. I used to know he'd read them but now it doesn't show. He must've taken that function off.'

'You still speakin' to Sarah?' Pat asked.

'No. Her phone doesn't connect. She's off all social media. Seems like they've just vanished off the face of the earth. Since that last text, where she told me they were moving on, I've heard nothing. I can only assume Archie got to know of the second phone she had. I just have to hope they're OK. What else can I do? It saddens me deeply but I can't change it. It is what it is and I just have to accept it. I just hope they're happy.'

Silence engulfed the room. No one knew what to say.

Phoebe continued. 'He was muscle for hire, as you all know. He was earning decent money and making a decent reputation for himself. We know he's worked for a couple of faces in the UK, who have spoken highly of him. But since I got that text and made a few enquiries, no one's heard from him. Word is, that a job went wrong. That's all I know. But last time he was seen, all appeared well. He had that fallout with Hugh, big dope dealer of yesteryear, but I don't know him. They're saying Hugh shot himself. Maybe Archie was involved in some way and needed to get away. I wish he'd just come home. He could do his work here.'

'He can hold his head up over there, though, Phoebe.'

'He could here! He's done nothing to be ashamed of!' she snapped.

Pat held his hands up. 'I take that back, but you know what I mean.'

'Well, I don't want to hear it. If you have nothing good to say, say nothing.'

Phoebe looked at Raquel. 'We're done here, Raquel. Pat, let's go.'

Brian pondered whether to break the news that Archie had rung him last night. He'd been glad to hear from him but at the same time he wished he'd not bothered. They'd had a good chat, but he'd been sworn to secrecy. He wanted to know his mum and Alice were OK. Of course, Brian told him all was well. He didn't mention anything about Barney, or Billo, or Alice getting cut. Archie didn't need to know. That prompted Brian to tell him that if he wanted to ring anyone, he should ring his mum. Archie said he wouldn't, so Brian made it clear he was not to ask him about family business. He wasn't going to risk the wrath of Phoebe. The Pearson name meant too much to him to go behind her back. He felt awkward about the call as it was, as though he was being disloyal to her. He was tempted to tell her, but then he'd be letting Archie down. He'd given him his word that he'd keep it between the two of them. Even though it pained him to see Phoebe so upset, he decided to keep it to himself. That way, he'd at least know how Archie was. He just hoped he was making the right call.

chapter forty-one

Central London

Tariq was in his office, feet on the table, talking to Mo, his number two. He had two other members of his top team with him: Si, so-called because he was a psycho, and Roach, a late twenty-something hard man from the Home Counties.

'Where the fuck is he, eh? Someone must fuckin' know. He ain't disappeared off the face of the earth, has he?' Tariq bawled. Not being able to locate Archie was seriously bothering him.

'No one knows a thing, Boss. It's like he's just, well, fuckin' vanished,' Mo replied, conscious that was not the response his guvnor wanted.

'Fuckin' magician, is he?'

'I'm just sayin', that's all. We've asked every fucker we know.'

'Well, we ain't put pressure on Miss Silky Knickers, have we? She'll know something,' Tariq replied.

'Word is, they don't have contact, Boss. None at all. Since he fucked off after the wake, she ain't seen or heard from him.'

'Someone must 'ave. That sister of his will know something, the fuckin' whore. Fuckin' hate the lot of 'em. I should've taken out Frank all those years ago.'

Mo looked at Roach and then Si, who returned the glance, though they were wary of Tariq spotting it. They all knew it rankled their boss that he'd rolled over and swallowed Frank fucking him off like a little boy all those years ago. He'd brought it up loads of times over their years together. They knew he hated not having the balls to at least make Frank know he'd been out of order. Time had not healed the wound. Tariq felt it was a slur on his position. No one else cared a fuck. Everyone, including his rivals, knew he was out of his league taking on Frank at the time. But not taking him on had made Tariq feel weak, and that was something he couldn't deal with.

'We're just gonna have to wait and see when and where he turns up,' Mo said, hoping his guvnor would see sense.

Tariq glared at him, and took his feet off the desk. 'That, my friend, is what concerns me, 'cos he might well turn up 'ere and you fuckin' lot have no idea where he is. I want him found. I don't care how you do it, but find that fucker before he finds me.'

The three of them exchanged glances.

'And if he finds me, he'll have you three in his sights, too, so bear that fucker in mind.'

He put his feet back on the desk. 'We wouldn't have this problem if that twat Hugh had done his job. If you want something doing... Anyway, what time are our two Latvian friends getting 'ere?'

'About six o'clock, Boss,' said Si.

'Right, well, I've got a young filly who needs a good seeing to, so you three fuck off and I'll see you back 'ere in a couple of hours. And bring Lester with ya.'

Si, Roach and Mo left Tariq to it. He had a quick shower before spending over an hour with the brunette, who rode him till he had nothing more to give. After a second shower, he prepared himself for the meeting with the Latvians. He was keen to hear how their meeting had gone with Phoebe. He couldn't believe he was about to pull off getting the Pearsons to import a shipment of firearms. The market needed someone to take the reins. London, as with the rest of the country, had always looked after itself, with all the top outfits doing their own thing. Tariq wanted to be the top dog in this market. Greg West and Paul Dutton seemed happy with the way things were. Tariq had tentatively broached the subject with them both, on separate occasions, to see how the land lay. They'd both insinuated they were happy with the current arrangements, and harboured no desire to shake things up. Tariq saw this as a way to get a shipment for free and to take the Pearsons out. He knew Phoebe wouldn't breathe a word of her little venture to anyone outside of her inner circle. An operation like this could not be advertised until they had the product safely in their hands. Only then would they take the firearms to market. No one else of any note had any idea. Once

Tariq knew where the Pearsons were planning on storing them, he would take them out and take the shipment for himself. It would appear to the outside world they'd been double-crossed by whoever they'd bought the gear off. Word would get out where it had come in from and where it had landed. Tariq would make sure it looked like Phoebe and the rest had been gunned down by some foreign outfit from Latvia. Tariq would sit on the shipment for however long he had to, before slowly introducing his new line to the market, making out, of course, he'd only thought about it after learning what Phoebe had been up to. He would then be ahead of the game, with his standing at the top table and no one trying to muscle in on his operation.

Tariq Mali would be the kingpin in the world of fireams and that would make him the top gangster in the UK. And, to top it all off, he'd have removed the Pearson family once and for all. He'd have finally put to bed the memory of Frank Pearson making him look small and weak all those years ago.

Lester showed the Latvians up. Tariq greeted them warmly and invited them into the office he used for meetings such as this. His main office was for him and his employees only. This one had an expensive rectangular oak table and high-backed chairs with neatly placed red cushions.

'Drinks, gentlemen?' he asked.

'Er, whisky for me, thank you,' Andris replied.

'Same here. Lovely,' said Valdis.

Tariq nodded to Lester, who did the honours.

'OK, so you know Mo and Roach, but this is Si, one of my most trusted. And, of course, you already know Lester.'

Everyone nodded, rose slightly from their chairs and shook hands and smiled.

'So, how did it go?'

Valdis spoke first. 'Excellent, Mr Mali. They seem very, how you say, up for it.' He smiled.

'That's good to hear. Good work.'

Valdis took his glass of whisky from Lester and placed it on the table before continuing. 'They are visiting the area we spoke about in ten days' time. Mrs Pearson wants to see the area before we proceed.'

'Why?'

'She just said she wants to get to know the area before she commits, to see the, er, what did she say?' He turned to Andris, who took over.

'She wants to see the lay of the land, to see the roads in and out of the area, and, of course, the areas where we'll be landing. I can understand it, Mr Mali. She will be suspicious of us. Remember, our last dealings with the family did not end well. She will be cautious. And nervous, too.'

'Hmm, yes, I suppose it makes sense,' Tariq replied.

'We will meet her up there. It is what we would normally do. She seemed pleased with that,' Andris said.

'Good. Good idea.'

Valdis looked at Andris, who knew the reason for the glance. Andris continued. 'They want to see samples.'

'See what?'

'They want us to take samples of the merchandise with us, so you'll need to supply us with some for the trip.'

'For fuck's sake. Yeah, OK, we'll sort it with you beforehand. It's no issue.'

'There's just one other thing, Mr Mali. We have never spoken about what we do after we have handed the shipment over. What are your intentions after the goods are in Mrs Pearson's possession? Will you still need us?'

Tariq had been waiting for this. From their body language and questioning at previous meetings, he already knew they wanted to know what the plan was moving forward. He was surprised it had taken them this long, though.

'That is not your concern, gentlemen. Your role is to get them to take the bait and to bring the merchandise across the North Sea. You are then to ensure it's in their possession, and on its way back to that shithole of a place they reside in. The one thing you must do is know its final location. It'll be somewhere near where they live, so just make sure you find out.' Tariq leant forward. 'Because, let's be crystal clear, my friends, without that piece of information, you two do not get your fee.'

'Er, now Mr Mali, that was not the agreement,' Andris said.

'Well, it fuckin' is now, gents. No final destination, no money.'

Both Andris and Valdis stared hard at Tariq. Mo readied himself and glanced at Si, who glanced at Roach.

'In that case, we have no deal, Mr Mali,' Valdis said, knowing Andris would back him one hundred per cent.

'Really?' Tariq replied, nodding at Lester.

Lester took a seat, having been at the back of the room since doing the honours with the drinks. He took out his phone and played a video. Both Valdis and Andris looked on in horror seeing their two wives sat in a restaurant enjoying a meal.

'That, gentlemen, was last night. See how easy we can get to your family? Now do we have a deal?'

Andris spoke first. 'We do, Mr Mali. We have a deal.'

Tariq clapped his hands. 'Excellent. I thought we would. Now then, let's have another drop of whisky to celebrate.'

Valdis stood up. 'It's OK, Mr Mali, we're done here. We'll be in touch after the trip to Scotland.' He looked at Andris as a sign to follow.

Tariq held out his hand. A moment passed before Valdis shook it. Andris did the same, if only to prevent unnecessary trouble.

If they didn't know they were dealing with one of Europe's top gangsters, they fuckin' well did now.

chapter forty-two

Valdis stormed out and desperately flagged for a taxi.

'Who the fuck does he think he is? That was our wives. Our fucking wives!' he raged. 'This is not how things should be done. No respect. He has no fucking respect.'

A taxi approached and stopped a foot in front of them. It was dark, just above freezing and lashing it down. They got in and enjoyed the warmth the taxi had to offer.

'Where to, gents?'

'Tooley Street,' Andris replied.

Their hotel was a short walk from London Bridge station. He thought they'd frequent what Tooley Street had to offer by way of bars and restaurants before calling it a night. It had been a long day. They'd been to Nottingham and back, had meetings with two of the most feared criminals in Britain, and it wasn't yet seven o'clock.

'Look, we need to play this out. That was only a show of strength. We both spoke to our families earlier

– we know they're OK, and they obviously had no idea anyone was watching them.'

Valdis could not be placated. 'That is not the point. It's not how we do things. Why do the English always treat us like this? Why?'

'Maybe they treat everyone the same,' Andris replied.

'No, no, they don't. With us, they always think they can treat us like shit. Once this is over, we don't do any more business in this country. We do this job and that is it,' Valdis said, cutting his right hand through the air.

'Problems, gents?' the taxi driver asked. Even though his customers were speaking in a foreign language, he could sense their annoyance. 'Sounds like you're a little upset.'

'You should not be listening. Keep your fucking nose out,' Valdis said, in his best English.

'All right, all right, just making conversation.'

'Well don't.'

Andris lowered his voice. 'I agree that once this job is over we forget all about England. But we have to complete this. We can't risk failing.'

Valdis looked at his friend. 'We won't fail, but that piece of shit will get what's coming. He's not going to make idle threats involving my wife and get away with it. He doesn't know who he's dealing with. I'll show him we are not to be treated like that.'

Andris sat back, glanced at the taxi driver and prayed things would go to plan.

chapter forty-three

Archie was intrigued. Who were the two guys who had just been to see Tariq? He wanted to know. In fact, he wanted to know everything about Tariq's business dealings, his set-up and his routines. He made a call. There was one man outside of the family who he could trust with his life. One man who would never betray him.

'Bonnie, it's Archie. I need to talk.'

chapter forty-four

24th January 2020

'How the bloody hell did Frank ever go anywhere with you two? You're like two schoolkids. Honestly, I feel like we're off to the seaside. *Are we nearly there yet?*' Phoebe mimicked.

Pat and Brian laughed and winked at each other. Brian had managed to bag a place on the little trip over the border. Initially, Phoebe had suggested just she, Raquel and Pat go but seeing as she'd only managed to book a three-bedroomed cottage, with bunk beds in the third room, Brian had persuaded her he'd be fine on the top bunk. A two-night break had now become a three-night break, plus they also had to arrive on the 24th because Phoebe was only able to book Friday to Monday. They were staying in an old fisherman's cottage in Portknockie, one of the villages Valdis and Andris had mentioned right on the Moray coast, so Phoebe could really get a feel for the operation. She'd opted for a cottage so that she and her team could discuss things at length in private. Pat had driven as far as Carlisle, where they'd stopped to refuel and grab a bite to eat. They still had another five and a half hours to go.

'I remember those days. Great days they were,' Brian said, before taking another bite of his tuna sandwich. 'Kids in the back – no seatbelts either in those days – looking out of the window, playing 'I Spy' and 'Twenty Questions'. Mum would have the atlas on her knee and Dad would be praying the temperature gauge didn't go into the red before we got there. The radio would be crackling away, losing signal as you moved from one radio wave to the next. We'd be arguing over who had to sit in the middle and we'd always want to be the one who saw the sea first. Great days. Kids don't have all that to enjoy now. It'll never be the same.'

Phoebe, Pat and Raquel all listened intently while Brian reminisced. It was the first time any of them had seen this softer, thoughtful side behind his tough exterior.

'Sounds like a great childhood, Brian,' Phoebe said, with a warm smile.

'A simpler childhood. Not sure about the great.'

'No?'

Brian thought for a moment. Phoebe wondered what he was seeing in his head right now.

'Yeah, I suppose it was, ya know. I wouldn't swap mine for now, that's for sure.'

'What were your parents like?' Raquel asked.

Brian munched away, then said, 'Dad was a miner. All his family were. A hard man he was, but then I suppose he was fairly typical of his day. You know the type – worked all hours, weekends, loads of overtime. Us kids hardly saw him and when we did, he was knackered. Then he'd spend Friday and Saturday nights at the welfare drinking with the same men he'd worked with all week. We'd go on holiday, and it'd be like I've just said. Every year to Skeggy for pit fortnight it was, so the place was full of miners. The very same men he'd worked with all year and drunk with every weekend. Thinking back, it would've been cheaper to have all stayed at home and maybe we could've had a carpet on the stairs.'

'Your dad have a car then back then?' Pat asked.

'Yeah, very proud of that he was an' all. He was very independent, my dad. Never liked to be relying on others. That's why he always made sure we had a car, so he could go where he liked, when he liked. Most families went on the bus for the annual trip to Skeggy, but my dad always took the car. He always reckoned it was so if he fell out with anyone, we could all just bugger off back home early. Which we did once if I remember.'

'What about ya mam?'

'A diamond she was. And don't get me wrong, my dad was a good dad. He was just hard. Never cuddled us. That was always my mam's job. She kept house and the old fella brought the pennies in. My dad's only trouble was the drink. Liked it a bit too much, he did. He'd come home in a stupor most weekends and crash out in front of the fire. He'd get into scraps at the welfare after a gallon or two, but thing was, back then, they'd be drinking together straight after. The loser had to buy the round.'

'Was he ever handy at home with your mum?' Raquel asked.

'Never. Never laid a finger on her. He was a good fella, thinking back. You just don't realise it as a kid, do ya? He provided well enough but a gallon of beer always came before the stair carpet.'

No one thought to interrupt his trip down memory lane. All three of his criminal colleagues were enjoying this softer Brian.

'We were well loved, so yeah, I reckon my childhood was pretty good.'

'Not great?' Phoebe asked.

'Pretty good,' Brian said, nodding.

Pat got up and stretched his arms above his head. 'Well, enough of this reminiscing lark. We need to be heading up that long road north.'

Brian took over the driving and they headed up the M74, passing Glasgow an hour and a half later. As they saw the turn-off for Stirling, he and Pat couldn't help themselves shouting 'FREEDOM' in their very best Scottish accent. Phoebe and Raquel rolled their eyes at each other. They stopped at Perth for a quick coffee before heading up the A9 towards Inverness.

'Fuckin' hell, how long is this road?' Brian said, flinging his head back into his headrest. 'It goes on forever. It's still 55 miles to Inverness. How the fuck anyone ever comes up 'ere for a holiday is beyond me. By the time you get here, it's time to go home.'

'Imagine coming up here for pit fortnight,' Pat said.

'My dad's car would never have made it. We've still got about thirty miles till we turn off at Aviemore.'

'Can't you two just enjoy the scenery? It's absolutely breathtaking. Look.'

'Can't argue with that, Raquel. It's bloody marvellous. Best I've ever seen,' Pat said.

An hour and a half later they approached the turn-off to Portknockie. They all marvelled at the view out to sea as they turned off the main road.

'Looks a beautiful place. I love these crisp, cold days. A half hour later and we'd have missed that view,' Phoebe said. The daylight was subsiding fast.

'Good job you got us all up so early,' Brian remarked for the umpteenth time. He'd not been impressed with the 5:30 start. Phoebe ignored him.

'Here we are – nine and a half hours later,' he said. 'I'll never get through that door.'

The cottage was small and quaint.

'My head just about touches the ceiling,' Brian said, standing as tall as he could.

'Right, cup of tea first, I think. I wish Gloria was here. It would be all ready for us,' Raquel said, looking for the tea bags.

'What time is it we're meeting Valdis and Andris tomorrow?' Pat asked.

'Twelve. At a café in Cullen, for a bite to eat.'

'What about tonight?'

'What about it?'

'Well, we havin' a pint in the village?'

'You two can but I suspect me and Raquel will enjoy a bottle of something here. That log burner will be just the job, with a glass of wine in hand.'

Pat made up the fire while Phoebe and Raquel unpacked. He and Brian had more or less thrown their small cases onto their beds. After a nice cuppa and half a packet of biscuits each, they left to try and find a local beer. Phoebe and Raquel nipped to the local supermarket they'd passed on the main road, promising to have something ready to eat for 7:30.

'Bloody hell, it's cold mate, ain't it?'

'It fuckin' is, mate. I think that hotel and pub we saw are just up here.'

Fifty yards later, having turned a corner, they saw the Victoria Hotel and the Seafield Inn.

'Here we go Bri, just what the doctor ordered.'

Brian rubbed his hands together, in anticipation of both a good old pint and getting warm.

'Which one first?'

'Not bothered as long as they serve a decent pint.'

They walked into the Seafield Inn. There were a few men sat at the bar.

'Evening,' one of them said.

'Evening. Er, just after a couple o' pints, please,' Pat said.

'Any preference?' the barman asked.

'Not really, mate. Any suggestions?'

'Try this one. It's a local brew. You'll enjoy it, I'm sure.'

'Pour on then, pal. Sounds good.'

After downing that first pint, quickly followed by another, they said their goodbyes. They'd enjoyed an hour of great chat with a few locals and the guy behind the bar and by the time they left to sample the ales of the Victoria Hotel, they knew all about the Bow Fiddle Rock and the local area.

'Good craic in there, innit?' Brian said, as they took in the night air.

'Yeah, they had some good stories. Friendly bunch, they were,' Pat replied. 'Right, let's have a couple in the hotel before we go back to see what those two have cooked up for us.'

They walked through the front door and along a short corridor towards the bar at the end. They passed a guy coming the other way.

'Nice dog, mate,' Pat said, stopping to fuss the British bulldog plodding towards him.

'He'll stand that all night, mate. He loves a fuss.'

'I bet he gets loads in 'ere.'

'He does. And treats.'

They passed a door that said "Lounge bar", but it was clear the room to be in was the one at the end. They walked in and were again met with a warm welcome. They recognised one of the men from the Seafield Inn earlier.

'Thought I might see you two in here,' he said, laughing.

'Well, we couldn't exactly walk past, could we? Can I get you one?'

'No, it's OK, thank you. I'm off after this,' he said, pointing to the less than half a pint he had left to drink.

'What can I get you gentlemen?' the lady behind the bar asked.

'Er, two pints of that one, please,' Pat said.

'Cold tonight, eh?' she said.

'You can say that again.'

Pat looked to his right at two men sat at the bar, who he assumed were locals. 'Evening.'

'Evening,' they said in unison, as they nodded and lifted their pint glasses.

'You here visiting?' the barmaid asked.

'Er, yeah, just for the weekend.'

'You been up here before?'

'No, first time. Ah, cheers,' Pat said. He took a large swig, wiped the head from his mouth and replaced the glass.

'Nice drop again,' he said to Brian. 'I quite like Portknockie. Can't knock the beer.'

'We OK to have a game of pool?' Brian asked.

'Of course.'

'I'll play the winner,' a voice said from across the bar.

'You're on,' Pat replied with a nod.

Twenty minutes later than they'd promised, Brian and Pat strolled home.

'We'll try that chippie tomorrow night, eh?'

'Yeah, can do. Ages since I've had any chips. A chap in there said it's best to ring the order through, though. They come from all over apparently.'

After suffering the wrath of Phoebe and Raquel for being late, they tucked into a plate of spaghetti and meatballs. The next day, they were meeting the Latvians and things would get serious again. But for now, the four of them were enjoying a night off, chatting till late.

Brian's memories of his childhood had led to talk of those simpler times. The times ahead were going to be anything but.

chapter forty-five

Valdis and Andris were up early. They'd flown from Manchester to Inverness the previous day, hired a car from the airport and driven to a cottage in Buckie, about five miles from Portknockie. They wanted to be just far enough away from the Pearsons to avoid any uncomfortable scenarios, should things not go according to plan. For them, being able to come away and be in their own space was important. It meant they only had to play the game for so long.

Tariq had furnished them with some untraceable firearms, which he'd assured them would do the business. Andris, in particular, was nervous of having such merchandise in the hire car. Lester had met them on the A96 a few miles east of Inverness to hand over the hardware, which had angered Tariq, who'd expected them to meet in London and drive all the way up – some six hundred miles – with illegal guns in the boot. Valdis had stood his ground and made it clear that was not going to happen. After some threats and heated dialogue, Tariq had backed down. He needed them to play their part and was wise to the fact that without them, the whole thing was off.

The thing that unnerved Valdis and Andris was how Lester was "going to be hanging around up there" until both companies parted ways. Neither of them liked Lester. They both felt he'd sell them down the river without a moment's hesitation. Lester was one of those guys who hovered around the top man like a fly around shit, riding on the reputation of the man he served. He seldom spoke, always trying to give off a cool, threatening vibe. To those in the know, without Tariq he was a nobody. However, those same people also knew that while Lester had Tariq to ride with, he was a man they had to placate.

They drove along the coast road, through Portknockie to Cullen, keeping to the speed limit. With a boot full of firearms, they were keen to avoid unwanted attention.

'Two minutes and we'll be there. I know we'll be early but I could do with a walk,' Andris said.

'You're really nervous all of a sudden. Relax, we have it all under control. All we need to do is find out where they plan to take the goods once they've landed,' Valdis replied.

'I am nervous. Don't know why, but that Lester guy doesn't help matters. I hate all that moody shit. He needs a lesson in how to conduct himself. Anyone would think we were the enemy.'

Valdis shook his head as he passed the Portknockie shop. 'I wonder where in the village they're staying.'

'Some cottage, I don't know, but hey, I wonder who shagged who last night,' Andris said, his mood finally lightening.

'I'd do either of them. Phoebe's nice and classy, but I bet Raquel goes like fuck. She used to be a hooker back in the day apparently. I bet she'd still give you your money's worth.'

'Can't see either of us finding out, can you, especially after this is all over.'

After parking in the square in Cullen, they took a walk down towards the beach. Valdis stood on a patch of grass and looked out to sea, wondering what land lay ahead of them. Andris sat on a bench. It was quiet – just a few locals walking their dogs. People nodded and smiled as they walked past, a few offering a good morning.

'Makes you wonder what it must've been like for early man to venture out there into the sea. I mean, thinking the world was flat, wondering if he'd fall off the end. Brave thing to do when you think about it,' Valdis said.

'It's all about greed I reckon,' Andris replied, as he joined his friend.

'Greed?'

'Yeah, man is never satisfied with his lot. Always wanting more. Early man was no different. He must've sailed away with the aim to conquer whatever he discovered. History tells us that, doesn't it?'

'Yeah, probably. We're the same, I suppose. We're only here in Cullen today because we want more. Only difference is we know we won't fall off the end of the world.'

'Not if we find out the final destination. If we fail to do that, we might just get a gentle push over the edge – if you know what I mean.'

Valdis looked at his friend. Andris stared back. Neither spoke. Valdis turned to walk back up the hill towards the square. Andris stayed a moment to take in the view.

'Yeah, brave thing to do,' he whispered to himself, before turning to follow.

***

Pat pulled into the square and parked next to a tractor, which dwarfed the car he was driving. Tractors were not a regular sight in and around Nottingham and he could not help but marvel at the size of the tyres.

'Thinking of going into farming, are we?' Brian mocked.

'Bloody huge things, them tyres. They'd soon squash ya.'

The four of them took in the quaint village of Cullen. It was quiet, which, given the time of year, was not surprising. There was a car park both sides of the road, with a sprinkling of shops that all looked in keeping with the stone buildings they occupied. The Seafield Arms Hotel was to their left. No one knew where the café was.

'Excuse me,' Phoebe asked an elderly lady who'd come out of a shop on the corner of the car park. 'Do you know where the café is?'

'Which one, dear, there's more than one?'

'Ooh, er, no idea. I was just told the café in Cullen.'

'Well, there's one there, one over there and one round the corner up that way, away up the road. They've all got their signs ootside, so ya cannae miss 'em.'

'Thank you,' Phoebe replied. 'We'll have a walk,' she continued.

'You understood that then?' Brian asked.

'Just,' she said laughing. 'I'll ring Andris.'

She was just waiting for the call to connect when she heard a voice.

'Phoebe, over here. We're in here.'

Without saying a word, Phoebe led the way. By the time they'd reached the café door, Andris and Valdis had returned to their seats.

'Hello, can I help you?'

'Er, yes, we're meeting two friends here,' Phoebe replied, looking over the young lady's shoulder. She saw Andris and Valdis sat towards the back of the room. 'That's them there.'

'Then come on through,' the lady said, leading the way.

Valdis stood up to greet Phoebe, who shook his hand firmly.

'Hello. Good to see you again.'

'Likewise. Good trip?'

'Yes, pleasant enough. We flew. Arrived yesterday. You?'

'We drove. I was glad when we got here, let's just say that.'

Valdis smiled and sat back down. Andris shook Phoebe's hand, telling her how much they had been looking forward to this. Everyone else said hello to one another and shook hands.

'I'll give you a few minutes, and we'll be over to take your order.'

'Thank you,' Raquel said.

'So, how do you like Portknockie?' Andris asked.

'Spot on,' Pat replied. 'They serve a cracking pint.'

'Ah, excellent. We're staying in Buckie.'

'How far's that?'

'Five minutes, so not far.'

'Well, I'm famished, so let's have a look at this menu,' Brian said, before catching the eye of a young woman.

She walked over. 'Are you ready to order?'

'Ah, you're English. Where are you from?' Pat asked.

'Stoke. Well, Newcastle-under-Lyme actually, but I always say Stoke.'

'What brought you up here?'

'Love. Met a fella who worked on the rigs.'

'How long have you been up here?' Raquel asked.

'Three years. We live in Portsoy. That's about ten minutes, er, that way,' she said, as she spun round trying to figure out the right direction.

'You like it?'

'Love it. It's so peaceful up here.'

'Right, well, I'll have that Cullen skink thing,' Brian said, keen to move things on. His stomach was telling him it was lunchtime.

'Right, one Cullen skink.'

'Make that two,' Pat said.

'OK, two Cullen skinks. Any more?'

'Yes, I'll have the same, please,' added Valdis.

'I'll have the carrot and coriander soup, please,' Raquel said.

'Make that two, please,' Andris said almost immediately.

'And you?' the waitress asked, looking at Phoebe.

'I'll have the Cullen skink. We are in Cullen after all.'

Phoebe waited for the young waitress to disappear before saying, 'Well, we'll enjoy our lunch and then we can take a stroll and discuss matters. That sound good?'

Valdis and Andris nodded.

The waitress took their drinks orders and returned with them a few minutes later. They ate their lunch in between conversations about Scotland, Latvia and Mansfield, while enjoying the hospitality of the café.

Even the chef came out to ask if they'd liked their food. It turned out it was all homemade fayre, with Cullen skink being a firm favourite all year round.

They walked outside, taking in the cool, crisp air. Cullen, it transpired, had quite a few little independent shops, two of which they looked in. Once they reached the beach, which was very quiet – just one dog walker in the distance – the conversation turned to more serious matters.

'Right, gentlemen, I'm sure we can all agree that we have to be careful with what we discuss out here in the open, but are we good?' Phoebe asked, looking at Valdis.

Even though there was no one around, she lowered her voice so that it didn't carry.

'Yes, we are good. We have samples for you. We will show you later, yes?'

'Yes. That would be good, and you can also show us where you plan to land. I need to be comfortable with things on that score.'

'Of course. We understand. As soon as we have finished our stroll, we can go and I'll show you. It's a quiet spot. Good for what we need to do.'

'Right, we'll follow you then,' Phoebe said. 'Portknockie, yeah?'

***

Lester was sat in his car on the opposite side of the road. He'd watched them arrive and had stayed in his vehicle the whole time. He was under strict instruction to keep them in his sights. When Valdis had made it clear he was not prepared to drive up from London with a boot full of illegal firearms, Tariq had had the idea of sending Lester to meet them, with a view to keeping tabs on them the whole weekend.

Cullen was slightly busier now, with a few more bodies milling around, but from what Lester was used to back in London, it was dead. He was amazed how inconspicuous one could be in such a quiet little village. No one had noticed him. No one knew he was there. But then again, no one, including Lester, had noticed Archie parked a few cars behind. Phoebe and the rest had no idea they were being watched, and neither did Lester.

Archie rang Bonnie. 'Your guy was spot on, mate. They're all here – the two Latvians, my mum, Raquel, Pat and Brian.'

'He's the best there is.'

'Can't argue with that. The only surprise is that one of Tariq's blokes is here, too.'

'Which one?'

'Lester. Had a bit of bother with him at Jez's wake. Fuck knows what he's doin' here, but I'll find out. Anyway, I'll let you know what transpires. And thank your man for me. I owe him.'

chapter forty-six

They arrived in Portknockie and parked up by some tennis courts. They walked through the clifftop village, with its fishing harbour, pebbled bays and stone fishing cottages, some of which had a great view of the sea – the kind of village that changes little over time. Anyone they passed on their way to the harbour gave a cheery hello or good afternoon.

On seeing a washing line right on the cliff edge, Phoebe and Raquel looked at each other and smiled. They tried to work out whose washing it was, blowing frantically in the wind, but the line didn't appear to belong to any one house in particular. Raquel wondered if it was to use on a first come, first served basis. Phoebe marvelled at how quickly the washing would dry.

Andris pointed straight ahead and said, 'The harbour's just down here.'

They walked down a winding road that looked out to sea. Brian noted the "white horses" in the distance. They all became aware of the mesmerising power of the waves.

'Is that a swimming pool over there?' Raquel asked.

'No idea. Looks more like a paddling pool though. Be great that, in the summer. I bet the kids love it,' Brian replied.

'Be bloody cold now, though. I bet the local kids brave it. Hardy bunch up here, they'll be,' he continued.

They reached the harbour wall and walked straight to the other side, to what looked like a car park next to some grass. Andris led the way for a few metres.

'That's where we'll land,' he said, pointing to the waves lapping against the pebbles of the small bay.

They looked at the separate shoreline approached by a narrow stretch of water. It looked perfect.

'In what?' Brian asked.

'A boat. Don't worry, we have all of that in hand. The boat will stay out there and the guns will be brought to shore. Three or four trips. It'll be the middle of the night – no one'll see us. As we said, we have done some dummy runs.'

'Yeah, lovely here, innit, down by the harbour. Nice and remote. Great place for a picnic,' Pat said loudly.

Phoebe picked up on the change in conversation and smiled to the dog walker who'd appeared from round the other side of the rocks.

'Hiya.'

'All right, mate. Come here, you,' Pat said, bending down to stroke the very same bulldog he'd seen the previous night at the hotel.

'How old is he?'

'Six. Well, six and a half now.'

'He's a big lad.'

'Aye, he's a handful at times. Come on, lad, your mum'll have the kettle on.'

Pat nodded and the guy walked off.

'Good one, Pat ... anyway, as I said, we've done this before. No one'll know we're here. We'll bring the goods up from the shore, load it all into a van and drive off around that building there, which leads up a track into the village. The van will be gone, as will we, and the boat will be away. And the good people of this beautiful village will wake up the next day, not knowing a thing.'

Raquel could see Phoebe thinking hard. It all sounded too easy. Maybe it was, but she couldn't help feeling it was unprofessional and a bit off the cuff.

'What you thinking?' Raquel asked her.

'We need a dummy run ourselves. I need to see this play out in full.'

'That will take time, Mrs Pearson.'

'Well, you have tonight and tomorrow night, don't you? We go home Monday, so unless you can arrange a dummy run before then, I can't see us doing business.'

'That's impossible, Mrs Pearson.'

'Not my problem, Andris. Either make it happen or find someone else. You have my number, so I'll await your call.'

'What about the merchandise? Do you want to see it first?'

'I want to see the merchandise come in on the dummy run.'

'But we have it here with us, in the car. That was the arrangement.'

'You're not going to show us here, surely?' Phoebe asked, frowning in bewilderment.

'No, of course not. We'll have to take a trip in the cars. It's not far, on the road to Elgin. Before the big roundabout is a small car park leading into some forest or, how you say, er, woods.'

'OK, let's go now. But we go no further with this deal until I've seen exactly how you get the merchandise off the boat onto this little bay – and away.'

Andris spoke in Latvian to Valdis. Phoebe looked at her watch.

'It's cold, gentlemen ... can you do it or not?'

'Yes, maybe tomorrow night.'

'OK, well I'll hopefully hear from you soon to confirm, but for now let's take that trip and see the quality of the goods.'

Pat was looking at something.

'What's up, Pat?'

'That yellow barrier there. Says six foot along the top. We'll not get a van under it.'

Phoebe looked at Andris, then at Valdis. They tried to hide it, but when a face says "fuck", it's hard to disguise.

Andris spoke. 'It's OK. We'll just keep the van the other side of the barrier. We'll have to carry the goods a few extra metres, that's all. We have strong men. It's OK. It's under control.'

Phoebe stared at him, not masking her disappointment. She didn't like detail like this being missed. Her little voice spoke to her.

chapter forty-seven

Archie was at the railings overlooking the harbour, wrapped in a big, olive-green parka, his hat and scarf covering most of his face. He was confident no one would recognise him. He watched his mum and the others walk past the paddling pool, before Pat and Valdis nipped into the toilets. He walked back towards the village centre, stopping at the side of a house that gave him a good view of where he expected the group to appear. Three or four minutes later, he saw the top of their heads and followed them along Patrol Road, which ran along the clifftop. By the time he'd turned to where they'd walked up from, they'd disappeared.

He observed Valdis and Andris waving their ams around as though they were arguing. Lester wasn't there and Archie was aware he might be watching him. He'd seen his car enter the village, so he knew he was around here somewhere. On seeing the Latvians walk off, he scanned for any eyes looking his way. There was no sign of him. He fancied a walk. He'd seen a sign for Bow Fiddle Rock, which he'd been led to believe was a famous landmark in the area. The walk to it took him along a cliff edge, with a stunning view out to sea. He was thankful he'd wrapped up as the wind was strong. He reached the Bow Fiddle and took in the natural beauty of the place. He'd read how nature and the sea had sculptured it into what he saw before him. For a good five minutes he enjoyed the peace. Only the wind broke the stillness.

He carried on and saw a man sat on a bench. Although he could only see his shoulders and the back of his head, he knew it was Lester. Carefully, he made his way towards him, as quietly as he could. The noise of the wind helped mask his footsteps. Archie sat down.

'All right, Lester.'

Lester jumped up. 'What the fuck!'

'Surprised, eh? Amazing who you bump into round here. Gangster wannabes and even Latvians. Who'd've thought it, eh?'

'What the fuck you doin' here?'

'I could ask you the same question, you know – seeing as you're keeping tabs on my mum. Mind you, you'd struggle to keep tabs on her sat on this bench.'

'Tariq'll fuckin' kill you when he finds out you're here.'

Archie laughed. 'And here's me thinking he wanted to do that already. He'll be fuckin' chuffed with you when you tell him you've found me. He might even let you suck his dick. Now I'll ask you again. What are you doin' here?'

'Yeah, like I'm gonna tell you. You're outta your league, my son. You couldn't even hack things in that shit'ole of a place you come from, and that's a one-horse fuckin' town.'

Archie laughed for the second time, pleased Lester had taken a seat.

'Don't you just love the sea?'

'Not really,' Lester replied. 'Don't get much of it in The Smoke, if you get my drift.'

Archie looked around. There was no one else about. The houses that looked onto the sea were too far away to hear any shouts or screams.

'Nice beach over there, look. That's where you've just been, innit? Cullen?'

'You do know I'm gonna ring Tariq the minute we part ways, don't ya?'

Lester hadn't seen Archie unzip his coat. Archie pulled out a blade and sunk it into Lester's thigh. He then immediately put his hand over Lester's mouth, while he struggled.

'Calm down, for fuck's sake, it's only a flesh wound.'

Lester tried to bite his hand. Archie twisted the knife.

'Now now, we'll have none of that, thank you. Didn't your mum teach you it's not nice to bite? All you have to do is tell me what's going on with those two Latvians, my mum and that boss of yours. Tell me that and you'll live. If you don't, you'll die right where you're sitting.'

Lester's breathing was quick and heavy and his nostrils had widened, as he desperately tried to inhale.

'That's better. Now I'm gonna take my hand away – if you make any noise, I'll kill ya and I'll have to try and find out what's happening some other way. It's up to you. Understand?'

Lester made a valiant effort to tell Archie to fuck off.

'Do you understand?' Archie asked, a little louder than he'd have liked. He looked around. Still no one in sight. Lester nodded.

'So. What's the score?'

Lester had venom in his eyes, as wide as Archie had ever witnessed. He looked down at the knife in his thigh, then back at Archie, who raised his eyebrows as if to say 'I'll twist it if you don't start talking'.

'I'm a fuckin' dead man if I breathe a word of this.'

'You're a dead man if you don't. I won't tell Tariq if you don't.'

Lester continued to breathe heavily through his nostrils. 'Guns,' he said.

'What about guns?'

'It's why they're here – your mum and those two from Latvia.'

'And Tariq?'

Lester paused. Archie twisted the knife very slighty. Lester's nostrils flared.

'He's setting your mum up. The Latvians bring them in and sell them to your mum. Tariq then plans to take your mum and her lot out and take the guns for himself. It'll look like the Latvians have stitched them up, or whoever's supplying them. I don't know the details.'

Archie looked horrified. 'Why?'

'He hates you lot. Something to do with your grandad – something from way back.'

'OK, so why does he want the guns?'

'Wants to be the big man, the top gangster in the country. And he reckons having control of the firearms will do it. This way, it'll look like your mum was planning it all and he just slipped in to fill the gap. It's the only way he reckons London would allow it. Fuck knows what goes off in his head.'

'Thought he was your hero?'

'Yeah, well, when you have a father like mine, anyone can become a hero.'

'He ain't no father to you, Lester. What happened to yours?'

'He died five years ago. Drunk himself to death.'

Archie didn't want to hear this. He felt sorry for Lester, but he couldn't risk letting him go back to London. As much as Lester was talking from the heart, back in the bosom of his makeshift family it would be a different story.

'Are the Latvians in on it?'

'Don't think so. Couldn't swear to it, but I don't think they are. He chose them 'cos they've got beef with your lot from years back, too – with your grandad again. Though I heard your uncle stabbed one of 'em.

The one with the limp. Tariq said they'd jump at the chance to get one over on your family.'

'Sounds like they are aware then?'

'Nah, I'm sure they don't know he plans to take your mum and that out. I'm pretty sure they were just told to draw them in, do the deal, take a fuckload of money for their trouble and fuck off. They don't like him either, though.'

'No? Why?'

''Cos he's changed the goal posts as usual. Plus he got close to their wives, didn't he, to let them know how easy it was to get to their families if they didn't play ball. Used me to do it. They weren't happy, let's just say that. I'm sure they know Tariq has something planned, but from what I know, they're in the dark.'

Lester paused. Archie knew there was more.

'What?' he asked.

Lester took a moment before spilling the rest. 'They ain't part of the aftermath. Those two will be dealt with, too. That's just the way he works.'

'You're tellin' me a lot for someone who's supposed to be loyal,' Archie said.

'So would you if you had a knife in your thigh and were facing certain death.'

Archie pulled out the knife. 'Can you hobble?'

'You havin' a laugh? I've got a fuckin' hole in my thigh.'

'Get up for fuck's sake. I've had worse off our lass.'

Archie helped him up, taking as much of his weight as he could. He looked at the bench and saw blood on the wood, though surprisingly not much, considering it was now seeping from the wound.

'Where's ya phone?'

'In my coat pocket,' Lester said, nodding towards his left side.

'Stand there and look at me, with your back to the sea.'

Lester assumed he was about to take a photo and put all his weight on his good leg. Archie looked around for a third time. No one. He took a step forward, put his arm around Lester's shoulder and whispered in his ear, 'Make it up with your old fella when you see him.'

By the time he looked over the edge, Lester's body was on the rocks. The waves lapped over the top, more or less covering his entire body. He watched for a moment, wondering if the tide was coming in or going out. He didn't know, but realised that tide could very well help him out if luck was on his side. For the fourth time, he checked the coastline. For the second time, he wondered if anyone in Portknockie ever ventured out. For the first time in weeks, he wondered about making contact with his mum.

chapter forty-eight

The car park was secluded. It was cold and damp. They had to wait a few minutes for a car with a large Alsatian watching them to drive off. Raquel walked to the roadside and looked out for any cars indicating to pull in. She sat on the edge of a stump and wrapped her hands around herself. The road was quiet.

Pat and Brian looked over the merchandise. They had enough experience of guns between them to know if the quality was worth the risk. It was good. Everything seemed to be in working order.

'Once we've done the dummy run, we'll take these back with us,' Pat said.

'Not possible. I have to return them.'

'We can't really fire them here, can we, so let me make it clear – we are taking this lot with us when we go home. I need to hear these babies fire. Understood?'

Valdis was getting seriously fucked off with the changes to the arrangement and was struggling to retain his composure.

'That was not the fucking deal.'

His delivery made everyone take note. Frank always said that it's not what you say, but how you say it. Pat, having been in Frank's employ for many years, was well versed in that regard. He took half a step forward.

'Well, it fuckin' well is now.'

The air was tense while they waited for Valdis to respond.

'There must be no more changes to anything we agree. We will not be treated like this, Mr Steadman.'

'Agreed,' Phoebe said, keen to calm the atmosphere.

'CAR!' Raquel shouted.

The guns were quickly returned to the boot of the hire car. The door slammed shut, just as Raquel joined the group and a car pulled in.

'We will await your confirmation of the dummy run, gentlemen. Have a good evening.'

chapter forty-nine

Archie was in the little car park in the square in Cullen. He stared at the entrance to The Seafield Arms Hotel. He knew that if Pat and Brian were staying in Cullen, they'd call in somewhere for a pint soon enough. He knew his mum would have booked a cottage or a house for a trip like this – there was no way she would have stayed in a hotel. That would have been too public. Plus, she'd never have booked anything under her real name anyway, so even if she had booked a hotel, he wouldn't be able to ring up and ask if a Mrs Pearson was there. He wanted to speak to Pat and Brian first. He just felt more comfortable that way, with everything that had gone on.

Cullen was quiet. No sign of anyone. Archie was cold and hungry. He'd not booked anywhere himself yet, and the prospect of a night in his car didn't appeal. Given he'd murdered someone only a few hours earlier, he didn't want to be booking himself in anywhere. He got out of his car, wrapped his scarf around his neck, put on his woolly hat and walked over towards the hotel. He had to see if they were in there. He went in and followed the corridor round, into what looked like the main bar. There were two couples at the bar, a group of five chatting around a large table and two twenty-somethings just to his right browsing the drinks menu. They weren't there.

'Can I help you, sir?'

'It's OK. Just looking for someone, thank you.'

'If you fancy anything to eat, the restaurant's just through there.'

'OK, cheers.'

Archie walked out, slightly annoyed. He stood in the car park, pondering where to go. He saw a sign for the Grant Arms Hotel and went and checked in there, too. No sign of any of them.

'Fuck,' he said to himself, heading back to his car. He didn't want to ring anyone – he still felt let down – but contemplated having to. After checking in at the Royal Oak, and then the Cullen Bay Hotel on his way out of the village, he drove to Portknockie, hoping he'd have more luck there.

He tried the Seafield Inn first. No luck.

'If you're not in here, lads, I'll have to ring one of ya,' he muttered to himself, as he stepped into the Victoria Hotel. He walked into the lounge bar to see a couple enjoying a meal. He nodded to them, as they looked up, then heard a voice he recognised.

'Yeah, go on then, same again please, duck.'

Brian, you fucking beauty.

He was just about to walk into the bottom bar when he stopped. 'Fuck,' he said under his breath. If he walked in unannounced, Brian, or one of the others, would be bound to say his name in surprise.

He walked out the front door, took a right and reached the back door, where he could see Brian and Pat at the bar. Two others, who he assumed were locals, were to Pat's left.

He sent a text to Brian.

'I'm outside. Don't make a scene but we need to talk.'

Brian picked his phone up off the bar and immediately looked round through the window. He could see a silhouette but couldn't make anyone out. He knew it had to be Archie. Archie looked at his phone. *Two minutes.*

'Right, come on, let's go.'

'Eh? We've just ordered these pints,' Pat replied.

'I'm starving.'

'You what? You haven't long had fish and chips. I'm still stuffed.'

'Yeah, well, ale always makes me hungry. Come on, gerrit down ya.'

Pat sensed something was up. He downed his pint, finishing it a second or two after Brian.

'Right, see ya,' Pat said, getting to his feet.

'Will we see you again before you go?'

'Maybe. See what tomorrow brings, eh?'

He followed Brian outside, to find Archie a few feet away, next to the pharmacy.

'All right, lads.'

'Archie? What the fuck?'

'We need to talk.'

chapter fifty

'Pick up, ya piece of shit!' Tariq shouted, before slinging his phone across the room. 'I bet he's shaggin' some fuckin' whore up there. He should be answerin' his fuckin' phone!'

'Still no answer then?' Mo said.

'No. I'll try him again later.'

Tariq was not a happy man. Not only had Lester gone AWOL, but the Latvians were becoming a problem. They'd updated Tariq regarding the dummy run and how the Pearsons were insistent on taking the guns with them once the weekend was over.

'What we gonna do about the Latvians?' Mo asked.

'Fuck all until they've completed on the job.'

'What about the guns, though? We need to return them.'

'I know that. I ain't fuckin' stupid. Just leave that to me. I'll sort it this end. That won't be an issue.'

Mo could sense his boss was feeling the pressure. Trying to muster an angle that would not only take out one of the top criminal families in the country but open up a route to the UK gun market into the bargain was no easy operation. He was beginning to wonder whether Tariq had bitten off more than he could chew. He'd been with Tariq his entire criminal life and seen him rise through the ranks of the London scene to become one of the top players in the capital. That should be enough for anyone.

The London underworld was always a match strike away from blowing up, but in recent times the top three players had operated together successfully, because they'd stuck to their own areas – geographically and in business, too. With guns, they looked after their own affairs. It was a kind of unwritten rule, not just throughout London but the country as a whole, that the top table did their own thing. It meant no one tried to capture the market or gain a monopoly. Tariq was trying to push back, Mo knew that – and it concerned him. He knew the trigger for all this was Tariq's need to make himself feel better. Tariq had to prove to himself he could take out the Pearsons, the very family who had humiliated him so many years ago. He ignored the fact Frank was out of the picture. If he didn't, he'd struggle to accept he'd have never dared try anything like this while Frank was still able to draw breath. Mo knew it, too. Everyone did. And for those closest to Tariq Mali, it made them nervous.

'What's up, cat got ya tongue?'

Mo shook his head. 'Nah, just thinking where Lester could be. As you said, probably scored. You know what he's like. Jump anything in a skirt won't he?'

'Hmm. He never has his phone off, though. He's got one of those tracker apps on it, ain't he?'

'Yeah, he has. I forgot about that. I remember him showing it me. I've got the same one – never used it, though. But Lester told me if he ever lost his phone and the filth got their hands on it, they'd put him away forever.'

'See if you can track it.'

Mo logged into his app. 'Switched off. Last known location was Portknockie, though, so he must've been watching them. You don't think they sussed him, do ya?'

'Valdis and whatshisname – Andris or whatever he's called – would've said.'

'Maybe they don't know. What if the Pearsons sussed him themselves? They know what he looks like. He tried to frisk Alice at Carrington's wake, remember?'

'Nah, they wouldn't dare take out one o' mine. They know it'd start a fuckin' war. Nah, he's shaggin'. Gotta be.'

Tariq was unnerved. If Lester was dead and the Pearsons were behind it, he had a serious problem. That would send him a direct message that they didn't fear him – and being feared was all Tariq had ever courted.

chapter fifty-one

Pat shook Archie's hand firmly and pulled him close.

'I've missed ya, pal. But what the fuck are you doing here?'

Archie enjoyed the embrace for a moment before pulling free. He shook Brian's hand, brought him towards him and patted him on the shoulder blade.

'We need a serious chat, gents. Not here obviously, I'm fucking freezing, but we need to talk tonight. Anywhere in mind?'

'Not really. As you know, we're not from round these parts,' Pat said, smiling.

'OK, well let's go for a drive. My car's parked just in front of the hotel. We'll at least be warm.'

'So where you livin' now?' Pat asked.

'Castleton.'

'What, in Derbyshire?'

'No, I knew you'd think it was that one. Castleton in North Yorkshire. Not far from Whitby.'

'What took you there?'

'Long story.'

'Better be a long drive then 'cos we need to know it all, Archie. You ain't followed us up here for nowt, so this must be serious.'

'It is, but—'

'What's up?'

'I need some food. Just gonna pop into the chippie. You want some?'

'We had some earlier. Beautiful they were, and the fish were fantastic.'

Archie jogged over the road and into the Portknockie chip shop.

'Evening,' the lady behind the counter said.

'Hiya. Er, a portion of chips please, duck.'

'Large?'

'Yeah, go on, cheers.'

'Salt and vinegar?'

'Please.'

Archie handed over a note. 'Keep the change.'

'Thank you. Have a nice evening.'

'Yeah, you too, cheers.'

Archie put the chips on his knee, hoping they wouldn't burn through his jeans. He put on his sealtbelt and drove out of Portknockie, heading for the main road. It was now raining hard. He thought about how that would help wash away the blood on the bench. He'd been thinking about the tides and whether Lester's body would be taken by the currents. It could be found at any moment, certainly come daylight. He told himself what was done was done, but he had no one up there to call in any favours.

'Which way? Any idea?' Archie asked.

'I saw a sign for Aberdeen earlier. It's about fifty miles. Just head that way. It's bound to be a decent road. If we get there, we can just turn back.'

'How's my mum?'

'Fine. Misses you like crazy, though, and Sarah and Mary of course.'

'But she's doin' OK?'

'Yeah. So come on, no more small talk. What the fuck's happenin'?'

'Well, firstly, Tariq wants me dead.'

'Tariq? What, Mali?'

'Yeah, that Tariq.'

'What's that got to do with up here?'

'Try shutting up and I'll do my best to enlighten ya.'

'OK, sorry, you were saying...' Pat said, knowing he had to keep quiet.

'It's all to do with a job I did, or rather didn't do, in Spain. Anyway, you heard about Hugh I gather?'

'Yeah, your mum said. I'd heard of him, but never met him.'

'Well, he tells me before he shoots himself that this job was a set-up and Tariq was behind it all. He wants me dead for what went off at Jez's wake – you know, when I made a beeline for him.'

'Really? Mind you, you did threaten to kill him,' Pat said.

'Till I stopped ya!' Brian shouted from the back.

'So, I had to do one, didn't I? Had to think of Sarah and Mary. So we packed up and came back home. Well, to Castleton anyway. Lovely cottage, nice and quiet. Bonnie sorted it for me.'

'Bonnie? Fuckin' hell, he always pops up somewhere he does, bless him,' Pat said, shaking his head and smiling in admiration for the man who was a legend in their world.

'Anyway, I wanted to find out all I could about Tariq and his operations. Just to keep me one step ahead if you like,' Archie said, before laughing out loud.

'What's so funny?'

'Well, I saw, who it turns out, are those two Latvians coming out of Tariq's office. I didn't know them, but I was curious – knowledge is power and all that –and I realised I needed someone to gather the info on Tariq's business dealings, so I made a call.'

'To Bonnie?' Pat asked, knowing what the answer was going to be.

'Yeah, to Bonnie.'

'Finger in every pie, that fella, but he's no private detective.'

'No, but he knows the best around, and I wanted someone who we had no previous with. Put me in touch with a guy called Jake. Never got his surname, but anyway, he comes back to me, through Bonnie, and tells me about your little trip north with the two guys I'd seen coming out of Tariq's office. All Bonnie could tell me was that the two Latvians had had beef with Frank and my dad. Turns out Richie was involved, too. Stabbed one apparently.'

'Yeah, that's right.'

'So I decided to come up. I saw you all earlier but I was still in the dark about what this was all about. But then I came across Lester. You remember Lester from the wake?'

'Yeah, Tariq's man?'

'That's him. Well, he's no more, let's just say that.'

Pat flipped his head back into his headrest. Archie looked at Brian in the back, but it was too dark to make out any expression from him.

'Carry on,' Pat said, rubbing the top of his nose with the thumb and forefinger of his right hand.

'Well, before he fell off a cliff, I managed to persuade him to tell me the full SP.'

'And?'

'Tariq's behind all this. The guns, the Latvians, the whole thing. He's setting you all up and, well, the short version is, if you go ahead, he's gonna take you all out. He wants the guns for himself to take to market and plans to make it look like the Pearsons have been double-crossed by some foreign outfit, most likely from Latvia.'

The car fell silent. Pat pinched a couple of chips from Archie's lap. Brian leant over and did the same. 'Beautiful, these are. Piping hot an' all.'

'Fuckin' strange name for a town this – Keith. What sort of name's that?' Archie said out loud, as he drove past a sign.

'At least it's easy to pronounce. You want to try saying Finechty. Spelt Findochty, but for some reason beyond my comprehension, it's Finechty. Work that fucker out,' Brian piped up, still munching away.

'So the Latvians can't be trusted then. I fuckin' knew it. All that building bridges and the past is the past and all that bollocks. I'll fuckin' enjoy doing them two over!' Pat raged.

'I don't think they're in on it with Tariq, Pat. You know, part of the aftermath. I think they're just part of his overall plan. They'll likely get popped, too, once they've done their bit,' Archie replied.

'No, fuck that. They told us they were the brains behind this deal. Told us they got to know Janis and how it just happened to lead back to Pēteris and then, of course, to us. It was all a fuckin' set-up. They've played us like a right set o' cunts.'

'You've got to tell ya mum, Archie lad. You do know that?' Brian said.

'Yeah, I know. Blood's thicker than water and all that. I wanted to tell you guys first, though. Don't ask me to explain why 'cos I don't know, I just did.'

'Best turn round then. Here, there's a supermarket there. I need a piss. Pull in here and then we can head back.'

A weight had been lifted from his shoulders. He felt better, fitter and stronger than he had just thirty minutes before. It was nothing to do with the warmth of the car. It had everything to do with the fact he was back where he should be. Back with the family.

chapter fifty-two

Phoebe was on the phone to Valdis. The dummy run was on for tomorrow night. The boat would come in around 2:30 and anchor off shore. That would mean offloading some of the sample guns into a rowing boat and rowing in. Valdis and Andris would be parked down at the harbour near to the little car park. All under the light of the moon. This would demonstrate to her that the job was doable. The only difference on the real run was the quantity, and the fact it would be a van, rather than a car.

Valdis explained to Phoebe that they had other ways of getting to shore. One was near to another small village called Whitehills; the other at a place called Sandend. Both were just along the coastal road from Portknockie. There was no time to do others on this trip. It had to be Portknockie.

Phoebe needed to trust her two Latvian friends, but trust was something she struggled with, especially outside of the family. Her little voice was telling her to be wary. Her head was telling her that in their world there was always a risk and to put her big girl pants on and do the deal. Deals like this came with the territory. If she didn't, someone else would and the Pearsons would be left behind. She had given much thought to what Frank would have done in this situation and concluded he'd have done the deal. Frank would have known it was a way to progress and to improve the family's standing in the inner world of crime. The empire had grown significantly in recent years, especially since the turn of the century, and this was the kind of thing she'd signed up for in taking the top job. It didn't stop her being wary, though. She was about to wrap up the call with a recap of the timings when the front door of the cottage slammed shut.

About time, she thought, checking her watch. She stopped talking mid-sentence when she saw Archie walk in. Seeing she was on the phone, he immediately put his fingers to his lips.

Valdis had finished speaking. There was a pause.

'Mrs Pearson, are you still there?'

'Er, yes, sorry, my apologies, I thought someone was looking through the window. Right, that's all settled then. Pat and Brian will be at the harbour for 2:15 and will oversee everything. Enjoy the rest of your evening.'

Dropping her phone next to her on the couch, she jumped up and flung her arms around her son. He returned the gesture, squeezing her close. She didn't want to let go. They hugged for no more than twenty seconds but it felt much longer.

'What are you doing here?!' she asked, cupping his face in her hands. 'I've missed you so much.'

'I think we need a good cuppa, Mum. Where's Gloria when you need her?'

'Come on, come into the kitchen. Sorry it's so small, but you know what these old cottages are like. How is everyone? How are Sarah and Mary? Are they with you, are they up here with you?'

'No, Mum, listen – when you've brewed up we need to talk. You ain't gonna like what I have to tell you, but you need to hear it and you need to hear it tonight.'

The little voice was there, almost saying, *see, I told you, why were you not listening?*

'Is it about this trip up here?'

'Yeah. Where are the mugs?'

'There's three of us out here,' Pat said loudly as he walked back through to the lounge. Archie got the sarcasm, Phoebe didn't.

'In that cupboard behind your head. You go and sit down, luv, and I'll bring the drinks through. Go on, you look tired.'

Phoebe watched the kettle as it boiled. Her stomach was heaving. She had no idea what she was about to be told, just that it was not going to be good.

Archie hugged Raquel, before squeezing himself onto the settee next to Brian and Pat.

'Fuckin' hell, these sofas could do with being a bit bigger. Good job we all get on,' he joked.

'Wait till you get to bed!' Brian said, laughing out loud.

'Is there a spare bed then?'

'No, but me and Raquel will share. You can have mine,' Phoebe said, as she walked through. 'Right, there's no sugar in any of them, so you'll have to do your own. I'm no Gloria.' She sat down and straightened her skirt. 'Right, Son, over to you.'

Archie spent the next quarter of an hour telling his mum everything about Tariq, Hugh, Bonnie, the Latvians, and the reason he'd helped Lester on his way over the cliff. Phoebe listened intently. She didn't interrupt once while Archie held court. Raquel did but only to ask if there was any blood left on the bench.

'So, there you have it, Mum. Either we sort Tariq out or he sorts us out, but either way, there's gonna be more blood shed.'

Phoebe looked at Pat, Raquel and then Brian. She shook her head. 'Why am I not surprised? I just knew those two were not on a level. I should listen to my little voice more. Can we trust no one?' she said, throwing her arms in the air, before continuing. 'We only have one choice. We need to sort him out – Tariq, I mean – but how we do it without a war I do not know. Any ideas would be welcome.'

Raquel was the first to speak. 'I got the gist of your talk with Valdis earlier, so correct me if I'm wrong, but the dummy run is on for tomorrow night, early hours of Monday morning, right?'

'Yep, 2:30 the boat will arrive. I said you two would be there around 2:15 to see the operation complete,' Phoebe said, looking at Pat and Brian.

They both nodded.

'So we have to let that play out, don't we? We can't give anything away.'

'Most certainly, but what about the real run? By the sounds of it, Tariq plans to hijack the shipment at some point, and from what Archie says, he's looking to take us all out,' Phoebe replied.

'So we'll have to be ready for him. He won't know we know, so we have the element of surprise on our side. He'll be a sitting duck. We can just take him out before he knows what the fuck's hit him,' Pat said, ready and pumped.

The room went quiet. Pat knew that was because what he'd just suggested was either suicide or a vote winner. He was unsure which.

'That would be all-out war. It would bring too much heat down on everyone. The Old Bill would be all over both operations like a rash,' Archie replied.

'I agree,' Phoebe said, liking the fact Archie was arguing against meeting fire with fire. She had a suggestion. One that pinged inexperience, but would show maturity and leadership.

'What would Frank do?' she asked.

'He'd come out on top, I know that much,' Brian said.

'Exactly. He would. So how would he do it? What would his approach be?'

'He'd respond. He wouldn't react, but respond. He was always preaching that to me,' Archie replied.

Raquel smiled, looking at Phoebe as she did so. Phoebe was too engrossed in her own thoughts to notice, but as she often did, Raquel smiled inside at how much Frank had preached to everyone.

'Come on, Frank, we need ya help, mate,' Brian said, looking to the ceiling.

'I know another thing, too,' Pat said. 'Tariq wouldn't even be considering this if Frank was still alive.'

'Thanks for that, Pat,' Phoebe said. 'Nice to see my second has so much confidence in me.'

Pat regretted his point immediately and felt like a complete wanker.

'Phoebe, I didn't mean that. I know how it sounded, but it wasn't what I meant. I'm sorry and I take that back.'

'You're right though, Pat. He wouldn't have. He had plenty of time to do something like this. Apology accepted.'

Pat smiled. He felt a little better.

'What about Tweedledee and Tweedledum?' Raquel asked. Everyone knew who she was referring to.

'They'll be no problem. Tariq is an issue, a proper issue, but those two will be taken care of. They're of no concern,' Phoebe replied.

'So, Archie, what about you? What are you gonna do? Tariq wants you dead regardless of us lot,' Pat asked.

'I know. He's a twat, ain't he?' he said, laughing.

'We could pull out of the gun deal,' Raquel said.

Her four colleagues all looked at her in unison. She could see their cogs turning.

'Why?' Phoebe asked.

'Because that would be the last thing Tariq would be expecting, and that would be the sort of thing Frank would have done. He would be asking himself the question, what would Tariq least expect?'

Phoebe smiled. 'Hmm, I like that. I think you're right, Ms Bowrain, I think you might be right.'

The room fell silent for a third time.

'But, if we let the dummy run go ahead as planned and pull out in a day or two, just citing that it's not for us, we won't know what Tariq's planning next. At least if we proceed, we'll know what he's planning and be one step ahead,' Pat argued.

'So, for now, we do nothing. One thing I did learn from Frank was that if you don't know what to do, do nothing. The answer will come to one of us. It usually does,' Phoebe said in reply.

'We also have one other little problem,' Archie said.

Phoebe knew what he was referring to – Lester. A body in a small village like this would not go unnoticed. She wondered when was the last time Portknockie had a murder on its hands. She'd actually been about to raise the issue, but her son had beaten her to it. She wanted to help Archie, wanted to talk about it as *their* problem, thus making Archie part of the current predicament. It felt right, and a good time to test the lay of the land. It would allow her to see if Archie accepted the olive branch. However, more importantly, it would allow her to gauge the reaction of three of her most trusted.

'Lester?'

'Yeah, Lester. As I said, he went straight over the edge. Somewhere along the clifftop. I know the spot. It's right next to a bench.'

'There are a lot of benches along the top. Me and Raquel took a walk early this morning.'

'I know, I saw one or two myself, but trust me, I know the spot. I ain't likely to forget it, am I?'

'The rain will have diluted the blood, so that's one thing, but if a body's found on the rocks, fuck me will any outsiders be in the spotlight,' Brian said, stating the obvious.

Phoebe saw another chance to make the problem a collective one. 'What's done is done. Occupational hazard in our world, gents, as we know, but I would've preferred it not to have happened here. It's too dark now to do anything, but first light we find out if that body's still there. Hopefully the tide will have done our job for us, but either way we'll sort it together.' She paused before continuing. 'As we always do.'

To her genuine surprise but certain delight, Pat, Raquel and Brian all nodded, in both agreement and acknowledgement.

By 11:30, everyone except Phoebe had retired to bed. She needed to think. The problem with Tariq wasn't just unexpected, it was serious. Archie had elaborated as to why, but even taking all of that into account it still baffled her why it would still bother him after all this time. She knew, however, that Frank being out of the picture had made it all the more possible. As they'd agreed earlier, Tariq would have left well alone had Frank still been at the helm. That annoyed her. She knew how Tariq viewed women, knowing all too well where he thought her place was. In his mind, she should be at home, behind closed doors, looking after her man. She laughed at that. She'd not had "a man" for nearly eight years now. Not since her Daniel was murdered. She couldn't see herself with another man. Daniel was the only one for her. She'd loved him with every fibre of her being and she was still hurting. It would never leave her. Yes, time helped. The gap between her thoughts of him had grown longer as the years had rolled on. She still thought of him most days however. Recent events with Archie hadn't helped. A strained relationship with her only son had only increased her thoughts of the man she loved.

She smiled when she thought of Archie walking through the door. If only people knew how much she'd dreamt of that moment. She couldn't help but feel robbed, though. To have him return in such circumstances was not how she'd played it out in her head. It was as though he'd been forced to return, but for that, even in the predicament she found herself, she was thankful. Thankful to Tariq. Had it not been for him, Archie wouldn't be here.

She heard someone coming down the stairs. She hoped it was Archie. It was.

'I keep thinking I'm gonna bang my head on the ceiling. People must've been bloody small when these were built.'

He sat down on the chair opposite. Phoebe looked at him and smiled. Archie felt a little awkward but allowed her a moment. She patted the sofa. 'Come on, sit next to your mother.'

Archie smiled and sat down. Phoebe opened her arm and he snuggled in. She held him close. It reminded her of many years ago when he and Alice would be sat either side of her, cuddling in. She savoured the feeling, and enjoyed the warmth of his body and the smell of someone who had just had a shower ready for bed. That too took her back to when he was a boy. She closed her eyes, not wanting to think how long it would be before she was able to do this again.

'I love ya, Mum.'

'I love you, too, Son.'

'I'm sorry I've been a dick.'

'I'm sorry you have, too,' Phoebe replied. They both laughed.

'What we gonna do about Tariq?' he asked.

'No idea. I was hoping you might have one.'

'You disappointed in Valdis and Andris?'

'Not really. Only to be expected. I don't trust anyone outside of my inner circle. Why?' she asked.

'Something I forgot about. Something Lester said earlier about them two not liking Tariq. He's changed things apparently, changed the goal posts. And he got to their wives. That didn't go down well at all, as you can imagine. It was Tariq showing who was boss, you know, so they know how easy it is for him to get to their loved ones.'

'So what you thinking?'

'Well, I know they appear to have taken us for cunts, and they deserve what's coming to them, but in the meantime it may be worth trying to bring them on side. Yes, they have beef with us, but with respect, the three people involved back then are all, well, you know ... they've all passed away since.'

Phoebe glanced up, intrigued to hear what Archie had to say.

'I'm sure they'd much rather get one over on Tariq than us. He's threatened their family, remember. If we could play 'em, we'd have his ear.' Archie sat up as he spoke. 'Plus, it would put us one step ahead.' He watched his mum tap the arm of the sofa with her fingers.

Archie continued. 'We have a secret weapon, though.'

'What?'

'Pēteris.'

'I don't follow.'

'He's Latvian. He could be the one to approach them. Mutual trust maybe and all that. He could, with you and the others there, tell them we know, but that we also know about their beef with Tariq. If we get them on side, we could really be in the driving seat.'

'What, play our hand totally? Tell them "we know you've played us and were leading us to slaughter but hey, it's OK, we'll forget that, so now would you like to team up with us and pretend we're all friends?"? I can't see why we would do that, Son. We'd be wide open. They looked me in the eye and told me a load of rubbish. No way, absolutely no way.'

Archie was surprised his mum wasn't listening to reason. 'You seem certain of that,' he said, disappointed.

'I am, trust me.'

'It's your call, Mum, but let me just say this and I'll leave you to think about it. Grandad always used to say to me to keep friends close, but to keep enemies closer. Think about that. It may just be worth remembering. Anyway, I'm off upstairs. I've had a long day.'

He got up and kissed her on her forehead. 'Night, Mum.'

'Night, Son. Hey, tomorrow morning, early, you and Pat get up to that cliff edge. See what's happening up there. After breakfast we'll discuss Tariq and them two.'

'Will do, gaffer.'

They both smiled.

'Think about it, Mum.'

Phoebe looked at him. She loved him so much and was so pleased to have him here with her. It felt right. She felt complete. She felt it was where he should be.

Archie stopped in the doorway to the stairs.

'Blonde hair suits ya.'

'Thanks. Fancied a change. I always wanted to be blonde,' she replied with a smile. 'Hey, and before you go ... don't use the C word in my presence. I hate it.'

Archie nodded and mouthed 'sorry' before going up. He felt safe, warm and content. In the last few hours, his anger and despair had gone. His mum had included him, when she outlined the problems they had. He hoped she'd done it consciously. He was glad to be back. It appeared the others were glad to see him, too. He sent Sarah another text. *It's all fine. I think things are gonna be OK luv. Night xx*

Phoebe sank back into the sofa and looked to the ceiling. She thought about all sorts, but mostly she thought about what Archie had said.

chapter fifty-three

Tariq paced up and down his office, before looking out over the skyline. The sun was yet to rise above the horizon. He'd not been able to sleep and had arrived at work just after five. His breathing was heavy. He was mad. Either Lester was taking him for a mug or something had happened to him. He knew Lester wouldn't treat him with such disrespect, so the alternative was unnerving. There was still no answer from his phone. He'd left numerous messages. Nothing.

He'd sent three of his guys north in the early hours to bring back someone he wanted to talk to. He expected them back for seven thirty. It was now just gone six. He stood and stared at London. He just stood and stared.

chapter fifty-four

'It's fuckin' eerie along here at this time of day, pal,' Pat said hunched, trying to keep warm.

'Especially when there's a dead body around here somewhere, eh. It's just up here. Look, there's the bench.'

'Yeah, I see it. What you expectin'?'

'Fuck knows. He might be there, he might not. I've no idea, mate.'

'Well, come on, we'll soon find out.'

There were a few dog walkers out and about on the streets. Only one man, with a small terrier, had passed them along the clifftop. He'd said hello, but Pat and Archie had just replied with a nod, conscious their accent would be memorable. They were both well wrapped up, with their faces partially covered.

Archie stopped. 'This is it. This is where he fell.'

Pat indicated to the edge. Archie looked over. Lester wasn't there and there was no sign he ever had been.

'He ain't there, look.'

'You sure it was 'ere?'

'Deffo. He was sat right there.'

'No blood either. Looks like the rain and the tide were on our side.'

'You sure he was dead?' Pat asked.

'Fuckin' hell, Pat, have you seen the drop? And if he wasn't dead, where the fuck would he have gone? It's a long fuckin' swim,' Archie said, pointing north with his forehead.

'Must've been washed away then. Fingers crossed that's the last of him. You dodged a fuckin' bullet there, Archie lad.'

'Come on, let's get back before anyone spots us. Mum wants a meet, I think.'

'Yeah, she said.'

They'd walked about twenty yards when Pat said, 'What you gonna do while we're having our meeting?'

Archie stopped and looked at Pat. He could tell by his eyes he was smiling.

'Funny fucker.'

'It's good to have you back, mate,' Pat replied. He then stopped.

'Fuckin' hell, Pat, are we walking or what?'

'You are back, aren't ya?'

'Would it be a problem?'

Pat thought for a moment. 'It would've been, I'll be honest, but you comin' here and doin' what you did, I'm fine with it.'

'Doing what? Lester?'

'No, well, yeah that, but more comin' here and puttin' the family first. You could've stayed out the picture, and no one would've blamed you, I s'pose. Lines had been drawn and all that, but you did the right thing, Archie. If her in there says you're back, then that's OK with me. You're the real deal, mate. The life just came too early for ya. I'd have you on my team any day. In fact, I'd always wanna be on your team, too. I'd die for ya, you know that.'

Archie held out his hand. Pat shook it firmly.

'And me you, Pat.'

chapter fifty-five

Mo walked into Tariq's office, yawned and stretched out his arms. 'They're here, Boss. On their way up now.'

Tariq didn't reply.

'Boss, I said they're on their way up.'

'Yes, I heard.'

Tariq was still staring across the London skyline. The sunrise was beautiful. The landscape looked alive, as though London herself was yawning and stretching her arms for another busy day. He heard multiple footsteps.

'Sit him down,' he said, continuing to stare at the horizon. 'Janis, ain't it?' he asked.

'Er, yes, Mr Mali, but it's Janis, pronounced with a Y, rather than a J.'

'I couldn't care a fuck. You were the link to the Pearsons, weren't you?' Tariq said, still facing the window.

'Er, I think you may have me mixed up, Mr Mali.'

Tariq finally turned around. He walked over to where Janis sat. He looked at Si. Si took a step forward so he was now right behind Janis.

'Sorry, say that again, will you?' Tariq asked.

'I think you may have mistaken me for someone else.'

Tariq looked at Si again, who then put a plastic bag over Janis's face and pulled it tight. Janis struggled. Tariq showed no emotion as Janis's eyes widened. His arms flapped as he desperately tried to loosen Si's grip. Tariq nodded. Si let go. Janis ripped the bag off and threw it to the floor, then dropped to his knees and gasped for breath.

Tariq counted to ten. He nodded to Mikey, to Janis's right, who picked him up and put him back in his chair.

'Now then, would you like to say that again?'

'Honestly, I don't know anything about that. What link?'

Tariq held Janis's chin in his right hand. He then slapped him hard. 'The link between me, those two fellow countrymen of yours and that slag up north, Phoebe Pearson. You know the Pearsons. Whatshisfuckinname, Peter, or whatever he's fuckin' called – one of your lot. A mate of yours, ain't he? You were the way in, my boy.'

Tariq could see from Janis's expression he hadn't known about that. That pleased him. It meant Valdis and Andris had kept things from Janis. Maybe they could be trusted after all. Maybe he'd been wrong about them.

'You didn't know, did you?'

'I have no idea what you're talking about. All I know is that I first met Valdis in a club in Manchester. He was Latvian, and we got on. He introduced me to Andris and then a few weeks later they talked to me about bringing guns in.'

'They asked you about the Pearsons, though?'

Janis thought hard. How did Pēteris come into the conversation? He could only recall one of them asking him if he had any links with any criminal families, preferably a Latvian link. Of course, he'd thought of Pēteris straight away.

'Er, no, only if I had any links with a criminal family.'

'And that was Peter.'

'Pēteris. It's Pēteris and, yes, that was who I suggested.'

'Hmm. What do you do, Janis, to make your money?'

'Er, well, I supply a bit of foreign labour – you know, Eastern Europeans into the fields and the factories.'

'Human trafficking then?'

'Er...'

'Is it all above board, Janis? Do they have all the paperwork, or is it, under the radar, let's say? You know, not a lot of paperwork?'

'Well, yeah, I suppose.'

'So you're a people smuggler, a human trafficker. Let's not pretend here, my friend. If nothing else, own ya shit, especially in my company. There's no hiding places here, my son.'

Janis nodded. He didn't like to admit that's what he was – he preferred to call himself a "recruitment consultant". However, he knew that the people he helped bring in had no real choice in the matter. A mixture of people who were trafficked and people who had no option but to flee their homeland. Either way, there was very little consulting going on.

'How would you like to work for me?'

'Thank you, Mr Mali, but I much prefer to work on my own.'

'It wasn't really a question, my friend, but out of politeness and respect for a fellow criminal, a pretty poor one at that, but a criminal all the same, I thought I'd put it to you in a way that made you feel like you had a choice.' Tariq bent down, an inch from Janis's face. 'You don't, but I'll ask again.' He stood up and turned to face the window. ''Cos I'm like that, Janis. You'll love working for me. So, how would you like to work for me?'

Janis's heart sank. Whatever he did wouldn't end well. If he said no, he'd likely die right there. If he said yes, he'd regret it, probably sooner than he thought.

'That would be a privilege, Mr Mali.'

'Boss. Now that you're on the payroll, call me Boss, or Guvnor. But seeing as you're from up north, make it Boss. Guvnor's a London thing. It won't suit ya.'

Tariq was now sat behind a solid-oak desk. 'Now then, a few policies that I need to make you aware of. Look at this as your induction. You'll like that word, being in the recruitment game yourself. If I ask you to do something, you do it. If you don't, I'll have you killed. If you turn against me, I'll have you killed. If you breathe a word of my operations to anyone, I'll have you killed. Understand?'

Tariq was smiling like a Cheshire cat at the power he now had over Janis. One thing Tariq loved was to have enough control over people that they'd do anything to please him. He revelled in ridiculing. Janis was a tough cookie and well respected in his world. A hard man. Someone to have on your team. A man who would have your back. Someone who took shit off very few people. But, as Tariq knew well enough, in all walks of life, there are pecking orders. Big fish jump into another pond and often find that, in real terms, they're small fish. Janis had found himself in a very large pond indeed. He'd left the world of self-employment and was now very much an employed man.

'Do you understand?' Tariq said loudly, making Janis come back into the room.

'Yes, Boss.'

'Excellent. Now that your induction is over, you need to start work.'

Tariq put his feet on his desk, clasped his hands and put his fingertips to his mouth.

'I need you to find out what's happening with the Pearsons and your fellow compatriots. You need to get in touch with your mate Peter, or whatever you call him, and get him to find out. I need to know what the feeling is on their side. Do they suspect anything? Are they going along with it all? And, most importantly,' he said, rising from his chair, 'I need you to find out if any one of those bastards have killed my man Lester.'

'Who?'

'Lester. My man I sent up to Scotland. He's gone AWOL. No contact, and that ain't Lester. Find out what they've done to him. Report back to me.'

Tariq slowly walked over to him. 'And if you set eyes on the grandson, Archie, you are to kill him on sight. Do I make myself clear?'

'Boss.'

'Right. That's settled. But remember, Janis, I will have you killed if you so much as give me the slightest reason to distrust you.'

'Boss.'

chapter fifty-six

Archie and Pat walked into the cottage. Phoebe, Raquel and Brian were sat waiting for them. Before either of them had taken off their woolly hats, Phoebe asked, 'So, is the body there?'

Archie shook his head. Pat had decided to leave this to Archie. It was his shit.

'No sign of him.'

'Any sign anything happened?'

'Nothing. I couldn't see any blood. It's like it never happened.'

'Right. We assume the body's been washed out to sea. We never mention it. Tariq must know something's up. He'll be trying to get in touch with Lester – of that I have no doubt – so the fact he can't will mean he'll have his suspicions. Which brings me on to our Latvian friends.'

'They want taking out – and fuckin' pronto. We can't have them out there. We can't trust a fuckin' thing they say,' Pat said. 'Or do,' he added.

'I agree – we can't trust them. Not one inch.'

Phoebe looked around the room while she was speaking. Raquel was the first to acknowledge a *but* coming.

'So what we gonna do?' Raquel asked.

'Confide in them and try and bring them on side.'

Brian spat out his tea, spraying it all over Raquel.

'Fuckin' hell, Brian!'

'We're gonna do *what*?' Pat asked.

'Sorry, Raquel,' Brian said, as he wiped his mouth, then got up and fetched Raquel a cloth. 'I'll second that. We're gonna do what?' he continued.

Archie said nothing, content knowing his mum had listened to his suggestion.

'We're going to try and bring them on side. It's a risk, I know, especially given they've been happy to play us and lead us into war, but...' she said, with a dramatic pause, 'in our world, it's good sense to keep our enemies close. Frank always preached that and, may I add, was something he did on more than one occasion. If it works, we'll have people on the inside. If it doesn't, well, we'll have a fight on our hands. But I for one think it'll work.'

Silence.

After what seemed an age, Pat turned to Archie. 'What are your thoughts?'

'I actually think it's a genius idea.'

'Really?'

'Yeah. Look, think about it. They both have beef with Tariq. Real beef. I forgot to mention it last night, but he got to their wives. So they hate him nearly as much as we do. That's naughty. That's not what people like us do. We don't use wives and daughters to get at those we've got grief with. That's not the game. Frank would've died rather than do that. That will not sit well with either of 'em. They'll know there's not a lot they can do about it – Tariq's way above their pay grade – but if they had someone on side who could take him on, well, they just might cross over. It'll all depend on how we approach it.'

Archie could see their minds racing. 'Well, that's my take on it anyway. For what it's worth.'

Phoebe looked on in admiration at her son. Not only had he allowed her to plant this seed as her own, but he'd just, with that last line, made everyone aware he knew he was still an outsider. She wasn't the only one to notice.

'Well, I'll take my hat off to whoever can pull that one off, but I see what you're saying, Phoebe. I can't argue it makes sense,' Brian said.

'I think Pēteris is the man. He's their fellow countryman and speaks their language. So tonight we act as if nothing's happened. We do the dummy run as planned. If it all looks good and goes well, we invite them to Mansfield, for a "celebratory drink" or something, and we speak to them. With Pēteris, of course.'

'Right, well, what the fuck we gonna do today then?'

chapter fifty-seven

Monday 27th January 2020

Pat and Brian were waiting by the public toilets at the side of Portknockie harbour. It was 2:18. The night was still and the clear sky only helped to reduce the temperature to two degrees below freezing. Archie had been itching to join them, but so as not to give his presence away, he'd been told to stay put.

Andris and Valdis were at their side. The four of them had been together for eight minutes. Conversation had been limited. Valdis and Andris wanted this to go to plan. Brian and Pat wanted to shoot the fuckers. Pat was ready for anything that came. Brian, for the first time in his life, was feeling his age. He didn't want tonight to go tits up and for it to end up with him and Pat slugging it out. The row with Fletcher and his mob over in Manchester six months ago had shown him he was not as young as he used to be. He took a few shots that day. More than he normally would have. He was slowing up and he didn't like it one bit. His hands in his pockets, he looked up above.

'Look at that sky. How many stars are there? There must be millions and millions. How the fuck did we all get here, eh? Amazing when you think about it. I mean, we can't be the only poor sods in the universe, can we? There must be something out there.'

'You reckon?'

'Gotta be.'

Pat hopped up and down trying to keep warm. 'Well, if there is, I bet they're a damn sight warmer than me.'

'Is that a light? I reckon they're here.'

'Yeah, I think it is. Looks a fuckin' long way away.'

'It's OK, gentlemen. It's hard to tell in the dark, but it will be them,' Valdis said reassuringly.

Ten minutes later they could all just about make out the sound of something approaching. Other than a couple of green lights flashing around the harbour, which they assumed were to warn anyone off the harbour wall, the only light was from the moon.

'It's them. I can hear the oars,' Andris remarked softly.

Pat looked up at the houses that ran along the road at the side. There were no lights on in any of the windows. Portknockie appeared to be fast asleep. Brian made out the figure of a small boat and as it grew closer, he could see it was them.

Valdis spoke in Latvian. A voice spoke back. It annoyed Pat they couldn't understand what was being said.

'English, gents, please. I want to know what you're saying.'

'They don't speak English, Pat.'

'Well, translate then.'

Pat could see Valdis was struggling to stay calm, after being spoken to as if he was a piece of shit. Valdis, of course, didn't know the real reason why.

'He just said, everything has been like, how you say, a piece of cake.'

'Good, well, let's crack on 'cos it's fuckin' baltic out 'ere.'

Pat and Brian stood back while the two men in the boat unloaded two boxes. One of them tried his best to look threatening. Pat returned his hard stare. The other spoke in Latvian to Andris.

'He's just asked if we want them to do another trip to the main boat and back. They only brought two boxes to give them time to go back to the boat and get the other two. They're happy to do it, but as it's so cold they thought you might not want them to.'

Pat was desperate to say *no, it's fine* but he wanted to see them do it again to make sure they had all the guns and because on a real run it would involve more than one trip back and forth. 'Another trip,' he ordered. Andris, he assumed, told them in Latvian to do it again. After watching them disappear, he and Brian opened the boxes. The hardware was there. All four of them sat in their vehicles while they waited. Fifteen minutes later they saw the two men. Two more boxes were unloaded. Again, the hardware was good.

'So, satisfied?' Valdis asked.

'Yeah, I'd say so. Mrs Pearson will speak to you tomorrow,' Pat said, holding out his hand for Valdis and Andris to shake it.

Brian, who was loading the boxes into the boot, held up his hand in acknowledgement.

'We will need the merchandise back, you understand.'

'It's OK, Andris. We will hand it back, as agreed. Nothing to worry about on that score.'

Andris nodded and spoke to the two men in his native tongue.

Pat got in the car. 'Well, fair play. We have the goods and from what I can gather Portknockie slept all the way through it.'

Brian started the engine. 'Pity we might not be back. I like it here.'

chapter fifty-eight

While Pat and Brian had been freezing their nuts off at Portknockie harbour, Archie and Phoebe had had a good heart to heart. Archie told his mum how at such a young age he wasn't ready for the responsibility of running the family firm. Frank had fast-tracked him into the spotlight and the top job. He understood why, of course – Frank was big on family. Daniel was the natural heir, and when Richie turned out to be nothing but a vengeful narcissist, Frank put all of his focus onto Archie. It had to be him to take over at the top. No one else could do it. Not in Frank's eyes anyway. Archie said he'd always known he'd be running the show at some point, but he'd assumed he'd follow after his dad.

Phoebe listened to him talk about the immense level of expectation Frank and everyone had put on him. Like everyone else, she'd seen a strong figure coping with everything the job entailed. She was surprised when Archie said he'd known he wasn't ready. He let it all out about how he used to tell himself he wasn't the man everyone thought he was, about how he'd punish himself for not being good enough, when all the time it was just a case of not being ready.

He'd realised in the last week or two that he could have been as good as Frank, given more time. He cried as he said he wished his grandad had stayed on a few more years. He'd failed to recognise that Richie had killed Frank after passing Archie the mantle. Phoebe said nothing. She knew all Archie was saying was, that if things had been different, he wouldn't have run off like he did.

She cradled him in her arms, stroking his head. He snuggled into her for the second time in as many nights and apologised for the way he'd handled her excluding him from the family business. She let him talk. He needed to get it off his chest and she needed to hear it. She was pleased he recognised his reaction was because of his own stuff and nothing to do with her. Her decision that day was justified. To be able to look in the mirror and own his stuff was a huge breakthrough in their relationship moving forward. After speaking about going back to Spain before Christmas, he stopped. They both enjoyed the quietness of that moment together, but Phoebe knew it was her time to speak.

She kept stroking his head, while she told him she'd not realised his torment at being thrust into the limelight, about never seeing that side to the situation or, more importantly, never seeing it in him. He'd always appeared so strong – a leader ready to take on the world. She was disappointed in herself that, as a mother, she'd missed it. Maybe that was one of the consequences of her being more involved in the business. Had she remained nothing more than Daniel's widow, she might have seen his anguish. She apologised, but Archie told her she had no reason to.

He just wanted to hear that his mum understood, that she didn't blame him and, despite what happened, that he was good enough. He wanted her to tell him she was proud of him regardless and that whatever he did, none of it mattered. He needed her to tell him he would always be her son, she would always love him and she'd support him in everything he did.

Tears rolled uncontrollably down both cheeks, as she told him everything he wanted to hear. It was as if he'd given her a script he'd written himself. Phoebe's tears dropped off her chin into Archie's hair. She told him she'd always be proud of him and that she now understood why he did what he did. He felt content.

For the second time in the early hours of Monday 27th January 2020, they sat in silence, neither of them giving a thought as to what was happening down at the harbour. Archie enjoyed the warmth that only a mother's cuddle can bring and Phoebe, the strength only a cuddle from a son or daughter can offer. The one question neither of them had considered was, what happens now. Archie wanted to ask whether he could come back into the family business. Phoebe wanted to know if he hoped to come back into the fold.

'So, what I want to know, Son, is, are you happy in Castleton working as muscle for hire, or do you want to come back into the business?'

'Would you have me back?' Archie replied. He stared at the log burner, mesmerised, unaware that he was consciously taking everything in while watching the flames dance.

'That's not what I asked. What do you want?'

'Ideally?'

'Yeah, ideally. What do you want?'

'To be your number two.'

'There's no vacancy for a number two. I can't create a position that's not there.'

'I know. And I wouldn't want you to do that to Pat either.'

'So, in an unideal world?' Phoebe asked, keen to know what would come next.

Archie broke free and turned to face her. He wiped his eyes, laughing as he did so. 'Tariq would be laughing his head off if he could see us now. Two of the country's most feared gangsters crying like babies. What we like, Mum, eh!'

She held his gaze, enjoying the moment but wanting him to answer.

'In an unideal world, I'd just like to be back where I belong. I'd be happy to be back in the business working for you, Mum. I want to take over from you. I'll be ready when that time comes. I learnt so much from Grandad, but I'd learn just as much from you. Different things, but just as important.'

Phoebe smiled. 'Alice has no real position in the family. She's accepted as one of the top table because she's my daughter – and Frank's granddaughter, of course. She's there, in the background. Saying that, she's been far more in the foreground lately. Wait till I tell you about her latest escapade in Hull. You'll not believe what happened with that sister of yours. Anyway, I'll tell you all about that later, but my point is, because of her bloodline, she's accepted as a face in the business. She's respected as well as accepted, even though she has no real job and no responsibility.'

'Because of who she is,' Archie confirmed.

'Exactly. Because of who she is. And because she's a force to be reckoned with. You could be the same. I don't need to have a cabinet reshuffle, so to speak, to give you that place. You can have that because of who you are. No one would be moved aside, no one would have to make way – they would all just have to accept you there, at the top table, because you're a Pearson.'

'Would anyone have any issue?' Archie asked.

'Maybe, but it would probably be a quiet issue that they'd discuss between each other, but I have no doubt it would be short-lived. And if they don't like it, well, they can see me about it.'

Archie smiled. 'Or, as Grandad would say, "Go and start your own firm if you don't like it."'

'Exactly.'

'Thanks, Mum.'

'So, are you in?'

'I'm in.'

'One condition though.'

'What?'

'You move back in with me at Southwell. I can't have you up there in North Yorkshire.'

'I'll tell Sarah to pack.'

'I forgot about Sarah. How will she be?'

'She'll be fine. She was pleased I was out of it all, I'll be honest, but she knows I'm never gonna stack shelves for a living. I'm sure she'll be pleased to be back with the family. Well, I hope so anyway. Hey, I wonder how things are down at the harbour. You know I hadn't given it a thought. Those two could be shot dead, floating away to – where is it, Shetland, or wherever it is next up here.'

'Don't joke, Archie. Not about things like that.'

'They'll be fine, I'm sure.'

'You want a cuppa, Raquel?' Phoebe shouted.

Raquel had been in her room cat-napping to give Phoebe and Archie some time together, knowing they had things to say.

'Yeah, please. Can I come down now?'

'Yeah, sorry we've been so long.'

Archie looked out of the window. All he could see was the cottage opposite. He glanced at his watch. It was 2:42.

Brian and Pat soon returned. They told Phoebe and the others everything had gone well. Phoebe confirmed they would still invite Valdis and Andris over to Mansfield Tuesday night for a drink. She decided not to say anything about her and Archie's talk – she would do that in the car tomorrow. She tried hard to hide her excitement. She knew she was failing miserably when Brian asked her what she was looking so pleased about. Brian didn't usually notice anything.

'Nothing,' she said. 'Nothing.'

chapter fifty-nine

Tariq walked into one of his many brothels in West London. Whenever Tariq walked in, everyone was on edge. He treated his staff like shit and the girls who worked for him even worse. He was not a good man to work for. The fact he controlled the sex trade in Soho and beyond meant that anyone who was forced, or chose, to earn their money in London through having sex had no real choice but to work for him.

Today he was in an unpredictable mood. On the one hand he'd received some good news from Valdis and Andris – the dummy run had gone to plan and the Pearsons seemed to be fully on board. They'd told him they were going to stay in Manchester tonight, before making their way to Mansfield for a celebratory drink or two with Phoebe and her firm. That had pleased Tariq. It meant the Pearsons suspected nothing and his plan was coming together. On the other hand, the manager of one of his busier establishments was working her own clients under his roof. He was not going to tolerate that. Everyone knew the rules and tended to play by them. For those who chose to ignore them, retribution was swift and merciless. He'd normally send his enforcers, but this was a liberty he'd not had to deal with too many times and he wanted to dish it out himself.

'Where the fuck is she?!' he raged.

Bitsy was, shakily, smoking a joint. She knew she'd fucked up – and big time.

'What's up – that joint calm ya nerves, does it? Slag!' Tariq slapped her hard across the face, knocking her joint out of her hand.

'Fucking bitch!' he bellowed.

He picked up the joint and looked at Walt. 'Hold her face.'

Walt was 6ft 5in and had worked for Tariq for close to fifteen years. He was his man on the ground when it came to his gentleman clubs. Walt was the one who made daily visits and made sure no one was creaming off the top.

Tariq liked to think he catered for everyone. Some of his clubs were classy affairs; others not so much. At one like this, the front of house experience bore no resemblance to what happened behind the scenes. The plush rooms that looked out onto the street, where men in tailored suits sipped expensive drinks, were deceiving.

Walt placed his right hand under Bitsy's chin and pulled her hair with his left. Her tears smudged her eyeliner, making her look rougher than she was.

'No one pimps in here, Bitsy, you know that. How long?' he asked.

'It was just a one-off, Mr Mali. I felt sorry for her, so I gave her a couple of shifts. I know I should've said, but I just wanted to help her out.'

'Charity now, am I?'

Bitsy tried to wipe her nose but Tariq grabbed her hand. He positioned the end of her joint over her left eye. She closed both eyes tight shut. Tariq blew on the end and watched it burn, before shoving it onto her eyelid. Bitsy screamed, as it scorched her skin. He gave the joint to Si, who walked to the back entrance and threw it into the street.

Walt let go of her. She held her face in her hands and sobbed. She couldn't open her eye, the pain was so severe.

Tariq looked at Harvey, the head doorman, who gave a nod and stepped forward. Harvey picked Bitsy up by her hair and slapped her hard across the cheek, before letting her fall back into the wall. He pummelled her repeatedly, till she was an unconscious wreck on the floor.

Tariq looked at Walt. 'Bring her in.'

Walt brought through someone in her late teens. She had a fair complexion, with blonde wavy hair down to her shoulder blades. She looked different, in that she didn't have the look of the streets about her.

'Name?' Tariq asked.

'Shirley.'

'Nice name. Traditional, especially for such a young lady.'

'Where you from?'

'Cornwall.'

'Do you know my name?'

'Yes, it's Tariq Mali.'

'Mr Mali to you. Why you working here?'

'My mum passed away recently. We lived in a rented house. The landlord wanted me out, and I had nowhere to go. I only had my mum.'

'So you came to London to see the streets paved with gold, did ya?'

'No, I came to stay with my best friend from school. Turns out she was no friend. She nicked what money I had and her boyfriend kicked me out.'

'Shame, but life's tough like that. See Bitsy there?' Tariq said, pointing with his head.

Shirley turned, then immediately looked away in horror.

'That's what happens when you try and do me over. You won't see her after today.' He looked at Harvey. 'I don't want to see her again. Do what you need to.'

Shirley watched Harvey and another man pick Bitsy up and carry her through. Her face made Shirley's blood run cold.

'Still want to work here?'

'I have nowhere else to go – well, nowhere where I can earn what I think I can here.'

Tariq looked at Walt. 'Shout Christie through.'

Christie had been in the sex game for close to thirty-five years, since being pimped in her mid teens. She'd run one of Tariq's less profitable clubs for three years. This was her chance to run one of his busiest. She was trustworthy, had never married and would now joke she was as dry as the Sahara Desert.

'This is Christie. She now runs this place. Christie, this is Shirley, a new girl. Bitsy was pimping her, so make sure she knows the crack.'

Tariq turned on his heels, through the corridor and upstairs to his office. He knew within a couple of minutes a coffee would be brought up to him. Si and Mo followed.

'Still no information on Lester's phone?' he asked Mo.

'No, Boss. It can't've been switched on. I've tried everything.'

'Someone must've popped him, they must've done. And it's got to be the fuckin' Pearsons.'

'I can't see it. If they knew he was there, they'd be onto us. There's no way they'd be going through with the gun deal if they knew what you were up to. Any suspicions you were involved in this and there'd be hell,' Mo replied.

'So, what then? He's fucked off somewhere, has he? Lester was loyal. He wouldn't fuck off. Not from me.'

Si listened intently. He rubbed his chin, wondering what to do. He knew Tariq was unpredictable at the best of times.

Tariq caught his eye. 'Got something to say?'

'Er, well, I've been askin' around a bit and maybe Lester wasn't as loyal as you think...'

'Go on.'

'I've spoken to a few of our lads – you know, the ones who talk amongst themselves. You know how it is, it's the same in any organisation, people always talk about the boss—'

'For fuck's sake, spit it out, Si. What's up with ya!'

'Well, the word that's come back is that Lester was always callin' you. Sayin' you treat people like shit and never listened to him and, well, he was often sayin' how when he had a chance, he was fuckin' off abroad. He was done with all this and was looking for a way out. Maybe that trip north on his own gave him that chance.'

'Who's been sayin' this? Fuckin' bullshit, all of it. Who is it, Si? I'll fuckin' string 'em up.'

'Look, Boss, you don't need to know that. They told me in confidence. If you let everyone know I've told you, I'll never get to know anything again.'

'Did you know about this, Mo?' Tariq asked.

'Bits and pieces. As Si says, it's just what happens. I never take any notice.'

Tariq was seething. 'So, my two most trusted allow people to slag me off and do fuck all. Is that what you're telling me?'

Mo looked at Si as if to say *well done, twat.* He decided to take the bull by the horns.

'Look, Tariq, I've worked for you a long time. If I sorted out everyone who slagged you off, you'd have no one left working for you. That's the reality. It's just how it is. We can't change it. We never will. That's why we don't tell you. We tell 'em to shut the fuck up as they're normally just moaning about their wedge or the fact you don't acknowledge them, that's all. Same with Lester. He'd moan about you never listening to him, or that's how he felt anyway, but I'd just tell him to sort it with you if he had a problem. I never heard about him fuckin' off, though. Mind you, he wouldn't tell me that, would he, 'cos that would be something you'd need to know about.'

Tariq wasn't aware he was perceived like that. He thought everyone loved him. He'd always craved adulation and attention. Even as a young boy, he'd do anything to make people like him.

Mo continued. 'So, maybe he has fucked off. It'd make sense. More sense than Phoebe or any of her lot poppin' him. They wouldn't dare. It'd start a war.' Mo could see his boss processing it all.

'Yeah, well, if he has, fuck him. I want everyone to know that if they see him, they bring him to me. And if anyone hears of his whereabouts – even a rumour – I want to know. Is that clear?'

'Yes, Boss.'

'Where's my fuckin' coffee!' he shouted, just as Clara walked in, tray in hand with a pot of coffee and a plate of biscuits. She rushed over and placed it on Tariq's desk.

'I'm sorry, Mr Mali. The kettle broke. I had to run out and get another.'

'Forget it. It's too late, ya fuckin' whore!' he bellowed, smashing the silver tray out of her hands. Clara cowered and covered her face.

'Clean that up!'

She could feel his phlegm on the back of her hands. Thankfully, the backhander didn't come.

'Ya fuckin' slag!' he shouted, and stormed downstairs.

Mo followed, as did Si, but only after he'd picked up the tray and coffee pot.

Tariq walked through into the front of house. He greeted his regular clients, most of whom were in debt to him. Not in monetary terms, but because he hadn't divulged to all and sundry the dirt he had on them. They knew it and blew so much smoke up his arse, it was a wonder it never caught fire. He revelled in it. Tariq had people on the payroll whose job it was to find out such dirt, leaving him to ply his trade without interference from the authorities.

Everyone was happy. Everyone except Bitsy and Clara. Clara wasn't a whore – she only did admin work and made the odd cuppa. Bitsy – well, she would never see the light of day again.

chapter sixty

Phoebe and the others had set off just after ten o'clock. They were all pretty tired and no one had wanted to do the first drive, to Perth. After a bit of arguing, Raquel said she'd do it.

'Honestly, you two are like a couple of kids. Supposed to be tough men, you are. Stronger sex? I don't bloody think so.'

Pat and Brian looked at each other like scolded children. Archie laughed.

'Get in with me if you like,' he said.

Before either of them could answer, Phoebe said, 'Er, no, I need to talk with you three, so let's stay as we are. You follow us, Archie. There's a decent café at the second roundabout as you hit Perth, if I remember, so we'll stop there. If we lose you, just ring when you're a couple of miles away.'

'Will do. Keep 'em in line, Raquel, won't ya?' he replied, winking at her and laughing as he got into his car.

Phoebe knew that Brian would be asking what she wanted to talk about before they hit the main road. She wasn't wrong.

'So what's up? Must be serious.'

'Every time, Brian. Every time. I knew we wouldn't be out of Portknockie before you asked. It's about Archie. I need to talk to you all about Archie.'

She told them a diluted version of him pouring his heart out. Before she could get to why she was telling them, Raquel said, 'If this is leading up to you telling us Archie's returning to the fold, Phoebe, I for one will support it one hundred per cent. It took character and guts for him to return, given what's happened, and for me, his pedigree stands up.'

'Thank you, Raquel. He is returning. He's returning to the top table. As with Alice, not in any particular role, but as a family member, he will have his seat.'

Raquel waited for a response from the back, hopefully one that mirrored her own.

'Gents?' Phoebe asked.

'Fine with me, Phoebe. I told Archie as much when we went to look for Lester. My only beef would've been if he'd pushed me to one side.'

'That was never an option, Pat. Brian?'

Brian paused before answering. 'When you took the top job, Phoebe, you asked for me and Jez to continue as advisers. We're getting on, but you recognised we had a wealth of experience to offer. I'd like to think that means you'll listen to what I have to say.'

'I will.'

'Even though you made this decision without asking for my advice?'

'When I asked you to stay on as an adviser, Brian, that didn't mean I would seek that advice on every decision I have to make. I'll ask for it when I need it. I'm not asking for your advice on this one, I'm asking for your support. There is a difference.'

Brian looked out of the side window. He was unsure about all of this. Maybe he was more old school than the others. He was of an age and era where if you made your bed, you lay in it. He liked Archie, liked him a lot. Just as he would Phoebe and Alice, he'd lay his life on the line for him, but that didn't mean he agreed with Archie waltzing back in at the top table. However, he did recognise that blood is thicker than water. He tried to think what Frank would have done. Brian concluded Frank would have let his grandson back in and if he had, he wouldn't have questioned it. He'd have trusted Frank totally and supported him without hesitation. Phoebe deserved that same support.

'No issue, Phoebe. Apologies, I just had to process it. He's a good lad and someone I'd rather have with me than against me. We're a stronger force with him. You have my support.'

'Thank you.'

Everyone thought about what they'd just heard – Raquel, about the long-term future of the family looking good with Archie back; Pat, about how good it was to have his mate back and that his role as Phoebe's number two was secure; Phoebe, about how the rest of her top table would take it; and Brian, about why he had to think about it all before giving his support.

Archie was in the car behind, thinking about how it was all going in the car in front.

chapter sixty-one

Alice was in the Capo Lounge in Mansfield town centre with her friend Wendy. It was busy for a late Monday afternoon. They were sipping rosé on two very comfy chairs in the window, waiting for Wendy's boyfriend and his mate. Alice wasn't really that bothered, but since any physical signs of her clash with Billo had now healed, she felt comfortable having a drink and seeing what transpired. Wendy's boyfriend, Adam, was from just off Chesterfield Road. His mate Chris was from Sutton. All Wendy had said was that Chris worked in engineering for a company in Chesterfield, was twenty-five and had a fascination with classic cars.

The Capo Lounge was a very nice bar with a very nice clientele. Alice liked it. They did good food, had great staff and allowed dogs. Alice loved it when she was able to fuss a dog. She often wondered why so many pubs didn't allow them, especially when they were happy to have unruly children running around spoiling everyone's meals.

'Your mum back now then?' Wendy asked.

'Nah, doubt it. It's a ten-hour drive. I had a look on the map when they said they were going and it's about as far as you can go before you hit the North Pole.'

'Really? Wow. Yeah, seems a long way to go for a weekend. Who's she gone with again?'

'Just a couple of girlfriends. Mini break, she said.'

Alice had inadvertently told Wendy when they'd arranged to meet that her mum was in northern Scotland. She'd regretted it the second she'd blurted it out. She was confident she'd not made a big thing of it, though.

'You heard anything from Archie?'

'Nothing. I don't want to talk about it, to be honest. It just upsets me. I'll only have the face on all night if we talk about him.'

'OK.'

Wendy looked at her watch. 'Four o'clock, I said. It's ten past now. He's not normally late.'

'He's here, look,' Alice replied, pointing through the window with her glass.

Adam was tall and slender, with dark hair. He was a nice lad and treated Wendy well. He always seemed to be nervous around Alice and would watch how he behaved and what he said. Alice was used to it, but she just wanted him to be himself.

She looked at Chris and liked what she saw. He was fair-haired, stocky, around 5ft 10in, and had the most beautiful eyes. He was nothing like anyone she'd ever dated. She usually went for dark hair and guys who were a little taller. Chris was different. *Different is good* she thought.

'Keeping us waiting, are we?' Wendy teased, as Adam gave her a kiss.

'Hi Alice. You well?' he asked.

'Yeah, good, you?'

'Top o' the bill, thank you. Er, yeah, sorry, duck. Waiting for laddo here. He wasn't gonna come.'

'Hi, I'm Chris,' he said, holding out his hand to Alice.

'Alice,' she replied, taking his hand. He shook it firmly. Her grandad always said you could tell a lot about a man from his handshake. 'Didn't fancy coming then?' she asked.

Chris shook his head. 'Don't listen to him, he's telling porkies. I just had to nip and get some cash, that's all, but the first two machines we went to weren't working. Drink?'

'No, I'm good, thanks. I'll stick with this for now.'

'Wendy?' Chris asked.

'Same. I'm good, thanks.'

'Cheap round,' he mocked. 'Lager, mate?'

'Yeah, lovely.'

Wendy watched Alice check Chris out. She could tell she liked him. She knew how Alice had felt after Johnny disappeared without a trace. Wendy thought he'd have been in touch by now, but Alice had told her several times she didn't expect to hear from him. That had made Wendy quite sad. She'd liked Johnny and was surprised he'd just walked out of her life like that. What she didn't know, of course, was that Alice had shot him in the head. Johnny was never going to make a reappearance. But Wendy, being the romantic kind, had imagined him coming back into Alice's life, picking her up in his strong arms and making everything OK again. The fact he'd been fed to the pigs had never entered her sweet, innocent mind.

Like most people, Wendy was drawn to the mystery and intrigue of Alice's family. That they ran a criminal empire was known to just about everyone in Mansfield, but as you'd expect from the elite in that world, they were no bother to ordinary folk. Wendy secretly enjoyed the extra attention she'd receive if she was out in town. Even without Alice, if she was out with Adam or other friends, they never had to queue to get in a club or pub at the weekend. She never had to pay to get in and would get offered drinks by people she hardly knew – all because of her friendship with Alice. The friendship was real, though. They'd known each other since school, so no one could say she only hung around for the free drinks. Her colleagues at the council were forever asking about the family, which, to their regular frustration, always came to nothing. Wendy didn't know much really. Alice would never talk about what went on behind the scenes and to her credit, Wendy never asked. She always told herself it would spoil the fantasy and mystique that her ignorance allowed her.

She knew Chris would be a good fit for Alice. He was a young man very comfortable in his own skin. He had a good head on his shoulders and wasn't easily impressed. When he found out who Alice was, he wasn't fazed, nor was he overly excited. When they asked him if he'd like to sort of double date, he just replied, 'Yeah, OK.' When they told him it was Alice Pearson, he just replied, 'Yeah, OK.'

They finished their second round of drinks and headed to andwhynot, a classy bar and restaurant at the top end of town. They had a great selection of gins that Alice loved to sample and their Gin of the Week was usually one she'd never heard of.

While she was waiting for her mystery gin, she got a text from her mum:

Surprise for you when you get home xx

Ooh, can't wait. You home yet? Xx

Half an hour. What time you planning on getting back? xx

Won't be late. No later than ten. What's the surprise? Xx

Wait and see. Love you xx

Aw. Love you too Xx

'That was Mum. They'll be back in half an hour. I said I'd be back for ten,' Alice told Wendy.

'Where's she been?' Chris asked, as he sat down.

'Scotland. Girlie few days away.'

'Nice. Gin nice?'

'Hmm, lovely,' Alice replied, nearly choking, having spoken just as she was swallowing.

Chris gently patted her shoulder blades. 'You OK?'

'Thanks.'

Alice smiled at his eyes. He was a good-looking guy, but he had the kind of eyes it was difficult to see past. They were big and blue, and Alice just knew one day they'd get her into bed.

She never mentioned the surprise. She didn't know what it was and didn't want any questions about it next time she met up with them. Family business was just that – no one else's.

chapter sixty-two

Archie called Sarah and chatted to her on his way down through Scotland. She was torn. On the one hand, she was pleased and relieved the rift between his mum and him had been sorted out – she could tell how happy Archie was. But on the other, she knew it was back to the life. Back to wondering whether her husband would come home at night in one piece, or whether he would make it home at all. That life had taken its toll on her, but she was a gangster's moll and she knew that came at a price – the price being peace of mind. She had learnt to cope and play the supportive, dutiful wife and she would do that for Archie for as long as she had to. That was often the problem. She never knew how long that would be.

Archie arrived and quickly changed his clothes, which he left all over the bedroom floor, much to her annoyance. They had a quick cuppa and set on their way. They planned to return in a day or two for the rest of their stuff. Most of the furniture had come with the cottage, so one more trip would easily do it.

Archie pulled into his mum's driveway and parked up next to Raquel, who'd managed to get Pat and

Brian to share some of the burden, though they'd spent most of the journey snoring their heads off.

Gloria came running out, hardly able to contain herself. 'Ooh, my lovelies, come here! Oh, how I've missed you all!'

She was unsure who to hug first. Archie held out his arms. She instinctively navigated towards him. He hugged her close. He'd missed her, too. Even though she and Frank had never quite made it down the aisle, she was family.

'Missed you too, Gloria.'

'Ooh, Archie, luv, it's so good to have you back. I couldn't dare believe it when your mum rang me earlier to tell me to be here for when she got back. All she said was that she had a surprise for me. I just knew it would be you three. Come here, Sarah, ooh and Mary, let me give you a big kiss.'

Archie smiled and felt warm inside, seeing Sarah squeeze the life out of Gloria. He knew things were going to be OK. Phoebe was grinning from ear to ear. No matter what the future held with Tariq, it could never spoil this feeling she had seeing her family. She couldn't wait for Alice to get home later.

'Is that kettle on?' Pat said, keen to move things off the driveway and into the house. He was not one for long displays of affection.

'No, but it will be the second we get inside, luv.'

'Come on then, let's get in, we've had a very long day and I for one am shattered,' Phoebe replied.

'Where's Alice?' Archie asked.

'She's in town with Wendy. She'll be back around ten, though, she said. I told her there's a surprise waiting for her.'

'Whereabouts in town is she?'

'All I know is they were having a meal at Il Rosso, so...' Phoebe checked her watch. 'I imagine they'll be there around half eight.'

Archie looked at the clock on the wall. It was 7:23. 'I'll go and pick her up. She'll be gobsmacked when I walk in. I can't wait to see her. That all right, luv?' he asked Sarah.

'Course. I'll get Mary to bed and then me, your mum and Gloria can catch up.'

'Great. Right, where's this cuppa, Gloria? I can see I need to put some things back in place around 'ere.'

'Yes, sir, coming up.'

She laughed as she walked through into the kitchen. Even though she was in Phoebe's house, it was a given that Gloria made the tea. She always did and everyone hoped she always would.

chapter sixty-three

Janis was on the phone to Pēteris. He'd put off making contact because of who he was making the contact for, which he knew was silly because, Tariq or no Tariq, him making a call to Pēteris was perfectly normal.

'So you've got no idea how things went then?'

'No, but Phoebe has called a top table meeting for tomorrow lunchtime, so I'll get to know then. It must've gone well, though.'

'How do you mean?'

'Well, if it hadn't, I'd have been summoned on my own, or with you. It would've been just the two of us. A full meeting must mean it's gone well.'

'Yeah, probably. Let's hope so, eh. Will you let me know as soon as the meeting's over?'

'Course I will, my man, course I will.'

'Do you think Phoebe would let me attend the meeting – you know, 'cos I made the introduction?'

'No chance. You're not part of the firm, Janis. There's more chance of Frank coming back from the dead or Archie appearing out of nowhere and being there tomorrow than you, my friend.'

Janis knew that would be his response but he was under pressure to know what was happening inside the firm. His life could very well depend on it.

chapter sixty-four

Archie drove down Nottingham Road towards Mansfield. He passed High Oakham School before approaching the bend and seeing the sign for Il Rosso. He glanced at The Talbot, before indicating left into the car park. It was busy, but he managed to get one of only two parking spaces left. It was nine o'clock. He'd decided to head down early as he imagined Alice would be getting a taxi back and wanted to give her time to cancel it.

He walked in through the side entrance, unsurprised at how busy it was for a Monday night. He guessed Alice would be in the restaurant area and since he couldn't see her by the bar, he headed to the back of the pub. There she was, at a table of four, laughing. He enjoyed seeing her look so happy.

It then dawned on him his mum hadn't filled him in about her escapades in Hull. He'd meant to remind her but with everything that had happened earlier it'd slipped his mind. He made a mental note to talk to Alice about it on the way home. He walked to the restaurant area, where a member of staff came up to him.

'Hi, can I help you? Do you have a reservation?'

'I've just come to pick my sister up. She's there at the back. Can I go through?'

'Of course. If you need an extra chair, just give me a shout.'

'Thank you.'

Alice had her back to him, but Wendy clocked him. Her eyes widened and she put her right hand over her mouth. Alice and Chris turned round. Adam had his face in his risotto.

Alice squealed, as she jumped up and ran the few short steps to her big brother.

'What you doin' here?! Does Mum know?'

She practically rugby tackled him to the ground. He took a step back to steady himself.

'She does, yeah. How are you, little sis?'

'Ooh, Archie.'

A voice from behind him said, 'Would you like a chair, sir?'

'Yeah, please, I think I better had. Thank you.'

'So, come on, what you doin' here?'

'Firstly – Wendy, how are you?' he said, leaning over to give her a kiss. 'Adam – you all good, pal?'

'Hi Archie. Good to see you.'

They all heard the immediate nervousness in Adam's voice. Like a lot of people, he was mindful of watching his Ps & Qs in front of Archie Pearson.

'And this is?' Archie asked, holding out his right hand to Chris.

'This is Chris, Adam's friend.'

'Chris, I'm Archie. Like all big brothers, I look out for my little sis, so no offence, but if this is what it looks like, don't hurt her, will ya?'

Chris shook Archie's hand, aware he'd been given a gentle reminder of who he was having a meal with.

'No, of course not.'

'Oh, ignore him, Chris. It's me you need to worry about. Anyway, come on, tell me what you're doing here?' Alice asked for the third time.

'Well, to pick you up – when you're ready. I'll tell you the rest in the car. No rush, I don't want to spoil your evening. Just thought it would be good to give you a lift. Save you a taxi and all that.'

'Oh shit, a taxi. I haven't even booked one. Good job you're here, bruv.'

Twenty-five minutes later, Archie took a right out of Il Rosso car park, back up Nottingham Road. He told Alice a slightly edited version of his trip to Scotland, the reasons he'd fled Spain and what he'd learnt from Lester.

'That was him that tried it on with me at Jez's wake. Serves him right. I'm glad you done him, the perv, but bloody hell, that sounds like a right load of hassle for us with Tariq. How's Mum taken it all?'

'OK, I think. It's still early days with Mum. She's the only woman at the head of a family in what's really a man's world. She has a lot to deal with.'

He then told her about their mum's plans to get Valdis and Andris on side. Alice had difficulty processing it until Archie explained it all, as their mum had done in the early hours.

'Bloody hell, Archie, this could all end up really fucked up! It needs to be right. She's gonna need us, ain't she?'

'She is, sis, you're not wrong there.'

'So, are you back temporarily or is this more permanent?' she asked a little sharply. Archie knew if he said temporarily, it wouldn't go down well given what they were potentially facing.

'I ain't going anywhere. Me and Mum have sorted things. I'm not gonna steal her thunder – she'll announce it all tomorrow at the meeting.'

'What meeting?'

'Did no one ring you? Top table meeting tomorrow lunchtime.'

'This bloody phone,' she said, taking it out of her bag. 'It never rings. Look, three missed calls from Del and a voicemail. I'll let Mum know when we get back.'

She listened to her voicemail. It was Del informing her about the meeting. While she texted him to apologise, Archie asked her what happened in Hull.

'Mum not tell ya?'

'She was gonna, but with all that's gone off, she forgot. So, come on, who do I have to go and sort out?'

Alice laughed. 'No one. We are capable, you know. It's all sorted, but I'll tell you anyway. You might want to take the long way home, though.'

chapter sixty-five

Del and his brother, Michael, were the first to arrive. As usual, the meeting was in the boardroom at Frank's. Del stopped in his tracks when he saw Archie at the door.

'Well, fuck me.'

'All right, Del.'

'I am, son, I am. How the devil are you?'

'I'm OK, mate.' Archie opened his arms. Del walked in and patted his shoulder blades hard. Michael then did the same.

'You here alone or are Sarah and Mary with ya?' Del asked.

'They're in the kitchen. Kettle's on, as per.'

'Are you the reason for the meet then?'

'That and other things. There's a lot happening, mate, but that's my mum's bit.'

'Here, Ryan and Des will be here any sec ... speak of the devils!' Del said, as they pulled in, quickly followed by Trainer and Jase in Jase's car.

Archie greeted everyone and had a similar conversation with each of them. He was pleased they seemed genuinely happy to see him. He'd thought the new members of the top table – Gray, Jase and Knighty – might've been a bit frosty with him, but to their credit, they were glad he was there.

Phoebe, as she always did, took a moment, while everyone chatted over tea and biscuits, to survey her top team. It was strong. She had Pat as her number two and Brian, her trusted adviser. Her son and daughter were at her side. Raquel, Del and Michael, three stalwarts of the business, were there, as was Pēteris, a newer member of the top table. All as solid as a rock. Then there were Ryan and Des, two mirror images of their father; Trainer, who she knew would be at Archie's side in years to come; and the newest members, Gray, Knighty and Jase. Only three other people could make this team any stronger than it was, and that was Frank, Daniel, and Jez. Three people she'd do anything to have back. Phoebe knew she needed strength. Not just muscle power, but strength as a unit and strength of mind.

'Right, everyone, let's go through.'

Phoebe led her team in and they took their usual positions. Archie held back, waiting to see if there was a seat left for him. He was pleased to see there was.

'Take a pew, Archie,' his mum instructed. All of a sudden, he felt on show.

'We have a lot to discuss today, and I mean a lot, but I want to get Archie here out of the way first. Not literally, Son, of course ... but for those of you who don't yet know, Archie is back on the board. You'll understand why when we discuss the agenda, but for sake of clarity, he's back at the top table by his sister's side and mine. No specific role but, like Alice, he is here because he wants to be. And, most importantly, I want him to be. We've sorted things out and everything's fine. Everyone is to continue as usual, the only difference being Archie. He will advise and be there for each of you. That clear?'

'Good to have you back, Archie. We're stronger with you, pal,' Pat said, keen to start the accolades. He didn't want Phoebe to have to experience tumbleweed.

'Here here!' a few of them shouted, with others reiterating Pat's comments. Phoebe was pleased to see that any feelings towards him for disappearing were no longer apparent. She could sense they were genuinely happy about it.

She, Archie and Pat spent the next hour filling everyone in on recent events. They were astonished – angry – afraid. As you'd expect on hearing of a potential war with one of the UK's top crime outfits.

'So, gentlemen,' Phoebe said, smiling at Raquel and then Alice, 'there you have it. We need to sort Tariq Mali out. As Archie said, if we don't do it, he will.'

'Fuckin' hell, I didn't expect that. If we thought Fletcher was top league, Tariq is on another level,' Del remarked.

'So what's the plan, Phoebe? If he needs sortin', he needs fuckin' sortin',' Trainer said.

Phoebe smiled inwardly at Trainer. He was quite young as far as the underworld went, certainly for someone in his position, but he was as fearless as they come. She liked him. He had a good head on his shoulders for someone who would hit first and ask later.

'Well, first of all, we need to discuss Valdis and Andris. Some of you know them from previous, but most of you here today will only know them from our recent reintroduction.'

'They want a bullet by the sounds of it, too,' Trainer continued, looking at Jase and then Knighty. His colleagues both nodded. He then looked at Pēteris, who showed no emotion. Phoebe noted the exchange of looks. She knew Pēteris would be nervous. He didn't say anything.

'What are your thoughts, Pēteris?' she asked.

Pēteris had been sat there thinking how he might well cop some shit for this. He was the reason, or so he'd initially thought, they'd approached the Pearsons. He wondered how Janis would feel when he knew he'd been played all along. Janis had been quite in awe of his countrymen, singing their praises, and was evidently pleased he'd been the introducer.

'I'm shocked, pissed off and disappointed. And, of course, I'm sorry. I was the one who brought them to you.'

'No, you didn't, mate. You were just the pawn. You were used – that's what you were, used – so don't feel bad. You weren't to know,' Archie said, trying his best to reassure him. He liked Pēteris and knew how loyal he was. Frank had spoken highly of him and as far as Archie was concerned, he had nothing to beat himself up about.

'Too right you weren't to know,' Michael said, mirroring Archie's support.

Pēteris appreciated the comments, but looked at Phoebe for her reaction.

'That's correct, Pēteris. You've been played, both by those two and maybe by Janis, too.'

Pēteris had never contemplated Janis betraying him. He didn't believe it. Janis was solid.

'Not Janis. He wouldn't do that. I know him – he wouldn't do that to me.'

'Let's hope not, but until we know for sure, you keep him at arm's length. Tell him nothing. I'm sorry, Pēteris, but until we have evidence to the contrary we cannot trust him. Too much has happened and there's too much at stake.'

'Fair enough. I'm so pissed off, I can't begin to tell you all.'

'You'll learn, Pēteris, there are very few people who are on a level. It's a tough lesson, but something we've all experienced. People either wanna kill ya or they want what you've got. It's just how it is. Get used to it, pal,' Pat said, saying what others were thinking.

'I'm surprised you didn't just take him out, Archie. I can see you just marching in and putting a bullet in his head,' Trainer said, thinking that's what he'd have done if Tariq had put a price on *his* life.

'Now where's the fun in that, Trainer? We'll have much more fun with whatever the gaffer here comes up with.'

'Can we get back to the job in hand, please, gents?' Phoebe said. 'Now back to our Latvian friends...'

Archie raised his eyebrows at Trainer, as if to say *well, that told us.*

Phoebe continued. 'We plan to bring them into our confidence.' She paused.

'What?' Ryan said, speaking on behalf of those who hadn't already heard.

'As I said, we are going to try and bring them into our confidence.'

Ryan, Des and Jase all blew out their cheeks in bewilderment. Pēteris's jaw was on the desk.

'Just give me a minute, please, fellas.'

Phoebe, as she had the day before, in Scotland, explained the rationale behind her plan. As she progressed through her reasoning, the sense of it all dawned on her doubters.

'And you will be the man to help us sell all of this to them,' she said, looking directly at Pēteris. 'You are one of them, and by that I mean Latvian. They will feel more comfortable with you leading the way.'

'No problem, Phoebe. I will do all I can to get them on side, but it's a fucking risky situation. I can, though, see the, er, the...' Pēteris clicked his fingers, looking for inspiration.

'Benefits?' Raquel offered.

'Yes, that's it. I can see the benefits.'

'We deal with that every day, Pēteris. We live in a risky situation. We run the risk of lengthy jail terms and death every day, but we do it because that's the life we've chosen,' Brian said.

'Well said, mate. That's exactly what we do. We run those risks every day. This is no different. We plan, we plan and we plan. Then we execute. The main problem will be doing it under the radar. We can't risk taking out Tariq Mali in front of watching eyes. The rest of the underworld cannot know.'

'So why not just do what I suggested earlier? Just take him out. Bullet to the head. A hitman would do that. He ain't that hard to get close to,' Trainer said, annoyed he'd been reprimanded earlier for saying something that now seemed to make perfect sense.

Phoebe put down her pen and leant her elbows on the table, resting her chin on her clasped hands.

'Because I want HIM to know it was us. He doesn't get to plan to take us down, put a contract out on Archie – my son – and get away with a swift, painless bullet in the head. That's why. Understand?'

Everyone looked at Trainer.

'Perfectly. Makes perfect sense.'

'Good. Pat, Raquel, Del, Michael, Archie and I are meeting Valdis and Andris tonight at the main club.

We will all meet again here tomorrow morning at eleven. In the meantime, no one is to breathe a word about what's been discussed here today. Clear?'

Everyone nodded. They glanced across the table at one another, all aware of what they could be entering into. There was a mixture of excitement and trepidation.

Archie beckoned to Alice. 'You still going to Castleton with Sarah later?' he asked.

'Yeah, I'm picking her up straight from here, then we're going up. There's not much to get, is there?'

'No, not really. One thing I want you to make sure you do get, though, is Lester's phone. I left it zipped up in the inside pocket of my green parka. Bring the parka, but just make sure it's in there. I know it is, but just let me know once you get there, will ya?'

'Will do. Listen, I'm gonna get off. I think we'll stay over 'cos by the time we get there it'll be teatime.'

'Yeah, course. Is Sarah taking Mary?'

'Think so. She hasn't said she isn't, so I assume so.'

'Give her a kiss from me. And listen – be careful.'

Alice kissed Archie on the cheek. She was looking forward to catching up with Sarah. It had been ages and she was dying to know all about Spain.

chapter sixty-six

Pēteris was on his way back to the club at Mapperley. He had two missed calls from Janis. Knowing he couldn't ignore them any longer without raising suspicion, he rang him back.

'Janis – sorry, my friend, the meeting went on longer than expected.'

'So what's the score? What's happening? Is it still on?'

'Fucking hell, one question at a time.'

'Sorry, I just want to know.' He knew he had to rein his enthusiasm in a little.

'Look, mate, this is hard for me. I'm in a difficult situation, but I can't discuss what's been said. It's confidential. You understand, I'm sure.'

'Eh, come on, Pēteris, we're mates and remember – I brought them to you. In fact, I brought the whole operation to you. What you doing, fucking me off?'

'No, mate, course not, but you're not on the payroll, are you? Look, I'm sorry but I can't discuss anything.'

Janis was fuming. Scared, too. His stomach was doing somersaults.

'Well, thanks for fuck all. I never thought you, my mate, would do this to me. Remember what happened with Fletcher? Who was it that went and disarmed his CCTV, eh? I was there, remember, getting stuck in with you lot. Forgot that, has she, Mrs Pearson? Short fucking memory.'

Pēteris knew he was right. He was there for them with Fletcher. He stood his ground and showed his pedigree. He deserved better. Pēteris was sure he was on side.

'Look, all I can say is that, as far as I know, it's still on. Don't know where or when, but it's still on.'

He felt comfortable saying that. He'd not been told it was all off, so he wasn't lying. He suspected it might be, but as things were, he could say it was still on.

'So, all went well then? Valdis and Andris are happy, are they?'

'Yeah, as far as I know. I wasn't up there, remember, so I only know what I was told earlier, but yeah, all's good.'

'Great. Look, sorry about that just now, but I just want to make a good impression, that's all.'

'Forget it, I understand, but you need to know that I can't divulge much. It'd get me killed.'

'I know. So, er, nothing out of the ordinary happened up there then?'

Janis knew he had to try and find out about Lester but had no idea how to approach it. What was he supposed to say – "Oh, by the way, did Lester show up and has anyone bumped him off?"

'Like what?' Pēteris asked.

'I dunno, anything. You know what it's like in our world. Always something going off.'

'Is there? Never really thought about it,' Pēteris replied, stunned at the line of questioning.

'Ah OK, well, I'll wait to hear from you. Let me know when it's all on, mate.'

'Yeah, will do,' Pēteris replied.

He ended the call and drove along Mapperley Top. He slammed the brakes on just as he hit a red light at a pelican crossing. He held up his hand to a young mum with a pushchair. She put up her middle finger in reply and mouthed 'tosser' as she walked past his windscreen. He ignored her.

'What a strange thing to ask,' he said to himself, as he drove on. He glanced in his rear view mirror and saw the young mum light up a cigarette. He wondered what her day would be like. He also wondered about Janis.

chapter sixty-seven

'That's all he could tell me. I couldn't get anything else out of him.'

'Well, find out more. What am I fuckin' payin' you for! Find out about Lester,' Tariq raged.

'I'll try, but I can't make him tell me and if I push too hard, he'll get suspicious,' Janis replied carefully.

'If you don't push hard enough, you'll fuckin' wish you had, fella, so find the fuck out!'

Tariq ended the call. Janis felt like shit. He was out of his depth. On the one hand, he had to please Tariq or else his life was over. On the other, he was betraying his friend, which he didn't like one bit.

'Fuckin' useless he is. Fuckin' useless. He has one more chance. One more!' Tariq bellowed to no one in particular.

'Bring her in – let's see what she has,' he continued. 'Ooh, nice tits. Get them fuckers out and come and sit on my knee.'

chapter sixty-eight

Alice and Sarah were driving through the North Yorkshire moors. They'd stopped at Pickering for a coffee and to allow Sarah to feed Mary. The sat nav said they'd be at the cottage in ten minutes. Sarah had chatted to Alice all about their life in Spain, about Hugh and everything. Alice had listened through it all, hardly saying a word, and couldn't help think what a great adventure it had all been. She was glad they were back, though, especially Archie. She'd missed him.

'So, come on, tell me all about Hull. He sounded a right piece of shit.'

'Who, Barney or Billo?'

'Don't know. Which is which?'

'Well, they both were. I suspect Barney still is. A leopard never changes its spots, but Billo is no more. His sons were both tossers, too. The only half decent one out of the lot was Scratch.'

'Strange name,' Sarah commented.

'Yeah, but he was OK. In fact, Mum offered him a job but he stayed loyal to Barney. Don't know why, but then again loyalty goes a long way in our life. I liked him, though, there was just something about him.'

'Wasn't there a woman you made friends with?' Sarah asked.

'Yeah, Chloe. Nice, she is. In fact, I only messaged her yesterday to see how she's doing. I'll keep in touch with her. She was a classic example of someone who's in awe of us and what we do, and likes knowing us, but wants to keep far away from anything we do. She'll call for my help again some day.'

'And will you give it?'

'Course. I always help people I like. It's just the kinda girl I am,' Alice said, with a loud giggle.

Alice gave Sarah a brief rundown of the events in Hull before they reached the cottage. It was a traditional stone-built property, with original sash windows and a front door fit for a child that opened directly onto the street. Alice managed to park right outside. It was ten past six. The street was quiet, but well lit. Once Sarah had taken Mary in, she and Alice each took a large suitcase in with them. They'd only brought two, which would be enough for what they had to collect.

'Ooh, it's lovely. Very cute and snug. And I'm glad you left the heating on.'

'Wait till I get the log burner going – it'll be like a sauna in 'ere.'

'Fab, I'll just nip to the toilet. Where is it?'

'Upstairs, at the top, on your left.'

Sarah filled the kettle and Alice climbed the stairs. After using the bathroom, she had a snoop around. It had three bedrooms, though the third bedroom was downstairs, which Alice could not get her head round. She looked in what was Mary's room, before popping her head around the door of the main bedroom. As Archie had said, the clothes he'd worn up to Scotland were in a heap on the floor. His green parka was hanging by the hood over the opened door of the wardrobe. She patted the jacket down, took out the mobile and saw it was switched off. She smiled a devilish smile. She switched it on and watched it come to life, surprised it wasn't passcode protected.

'Tut tut,' she whispered to herself. 'Huge flaw that, Lester.'

There were fourteen missed calls from Tariq. She pressed the voicemail and listened. She laughed quietly, hearing Tariq ranting and threatening all sorts, stressed out of his head. She bit her lip, to stifle her laughter. She opened a new text and typed *Surprise*. She stalled for a moment, wondering whether to send it.

Oh fuck it she thought and tapped send.

She then quickly switched it off and put it back where she found it. She texted Archie from her own phone, saying *The phone's here safe and sound in your jacket. I'll bring it with me xx*

She walked downstairs just in time to hear the kettle switch off.

'Cuppa?' Sarah asked.

'Please, that'd be lovely. Nice bathroom.'

'Yeah, we liked it here. Mind you, we weren't here long. Biscuit?'

chapter sixty-nine

Tariq was in one of his clubs, holding court in between enjoying the lapdancers. His company consisted of Mo, Si, two wealthy businessmen from the city, and two aristocrats with large country estates, who all paid very handsomely to be honorary members of every single one of Tariq's clubs. The only thing that was still up for debate tonight was which of these four men would pay the most money to have all three of the ladies at the table at the same time.

Tariq was in conversation with one of the businessmen when, out of the corner of his eye, he saw his phone light up. He carried on listening as he picked it up. He waited until the guy had finished his sentence before he looked at his screen.

Surprise

On opening the message, he looked straight at Mo.

'With me – now.'

Mo got up as instructed. Si instinctively did the same. Tariq put his phone to his ear, which made Mo look at his own. He stopped. Si had to step to one side to avoid knocking into him.

'What's up?' he said, leaning into Mo's ear.

Mo showed him what was on his screen – an alert to say Lester's phone had been switched on. Mo walked quickly after Tariq and Si followed.

When they reached Tariq's office, Mo said, 'It's Lester, ain't it, my phone's just pinged.'

'Shut the door!' he shouted to Si. 'It most certainly is, my friend. Look at that.'

Mo looked at the text, then Si.

'So where does it say he is?' Tariq asked.

'Just a sec, let me open this up. Er, let's see. Well, according to this, it's somewhere called Castleton.'

'Where?'

'Castleton – er, just a minute – er, in North Yorkshire.'

'North Yorkshire? What the fuck's he doin' there?'

'No idea, Boss, but what can't speak can't lie. If he's still alive, he's in Yorkshire.'

'I've just tried his phone. No answer, straight to voicemail. He'll rue the fuckin' day he tried to take me for a cunt. I'll slit his fuckin' throat, then I'll set the fucker alight.'

He then looked at Mo.

'Get up there, Mo. I want you to go and bring that fucker back personally. Take Walt and Roach with ya and don't come back without him. How far is it to this place?

'Two hundred and fifty miles, I've just checked. Five and a half hours at least, by the time we get north of London.'

'How accurate is it, that thing on ya phone?'

'To within a few metres.'

'Right, leave now. Ring Walt and tell him to be ready with Roach. You'll be there for the early hours. You'll have to kip in the car. Keep tryin' his number, but whatever you do, do NOT leave a voice message.'

'Why?'

'Cos we don't know it's him. It probably is, but now I think about it, would he really send me that text? I'm not so sure.'

'Did you leave him a message just now?' Mo asked.

'No, but only 'cos I was in the middle of all that noise out there. I'm glad I didn't now.'

'Could be anyone – kids, anyone. They could've sent that message to all of his contacts,' Si said.

'Have you two had one?' Tariq asked.

They both checked. Neither of them had.

'So, as I said, could be him – and I hope to fuck it is – but if not, we need to know who has the phone.'

Tariq was thinking. 'When you get to within a few metres, just park up, wait, and see if he appears. If it's him, he'll be around somewhere. But what the fuck he's doin' up there, I have no idea.'

'Walt, it's me. Me, you and Roach are going on a little trip. Boss's orders. Get Roach with ya and I'll be out front in five,' Mo said.

chapter seventy

Archie smiled as he read Alice's text. He knew it would be there, but felt better knowing for sure. He replied *Thanks*. Within a few seconds his phone pinged again.

Can I have it? You know how mine's playing up xx

Can you hell. I want that in case anyone ever rings it

You'll need to switch it on for that dummy xx

Ha ha yes I know, I'll sort it when you get back. Just leave it in my coat

OK xx

Archie and the rest were waiting for Andris and Valdis to come through. Raquel was doing the honours.

'Ah, Mrs Pearson. How nice to see you again,' Valdis said, before kissing her hand, which now seemed customary every time they met. Andris did the same.

'Come in. Sit down, gentlemen. Drink?'

She saw how they both looked at Archie and then at each other.

'You're Archie, aren't you?'

'The very same gentleman.'

'So, er, are you back from, er, where was it?'

'No matter where. Yes, I'm back.'

Archie knew the reason for the interest. If they reported it back to Tariq, they just might be able to double their fee.

'That must be nice for you, Mrs Pearson,' Andris commented.

'It is, yes. Now, drink?'

'Yes, er, whatever you are having.'

'Tea all round then,' Phoebe said.

Raquel popped her head out of the door, shouting the order through to the bar area.

'We'll save the hard stuff for later. Hopefully we'll be toasting something,' she said while the others all shook hands. She noted how warmly they shook Pēteris's in particular.

'I think you know everyone here,' she said, looking at her team.

'Del, isn't it?' Andris said, shaking his hand again.

'Correct.'

'And you are?'

'Michael, Del's brother.'

'Ah, yes, very much alike. Nice to meet you, Michael.'

'Likewise,' he replied, shaking both their hands.

'So, are we all ready to set a date for the first shipment?' Andris asked.

Phoebe fixed her eyes on him. He looked around the room. Hard stares from all angles.

'Am I sensing a problem?'

'I'll cut to the chase, gents. We know you are working with Tariq.'

Andris sat back in his chair. He felt under pressure but couldn't let it show. He failed. He looked to Valdis, who said, 'And how do you know that, Mrs Pearson?'

Phoebe ignored the question. 'We know about your workings with Tariq, the deal you have with him, your input – and how he intends to do away with you both afterwards.'

She paused for effect.

'We also know how he changed the goal posts and that he got close to your wives. That must have been hard to take. You surely now see how he does business.'

Again, she paused.

'Go on,' Valdis said, amazingly calm given the conversation and the company he was in.

'We know he put you up to it all, and to be fair, I can understand you wanting to be part of it. You, in particular, Valdis must have painful memories of your last dealings with this family. But, as you said when we recently met, the past is the past.'

Phoebe leant forward as she continued. 'You need to decide tonight, gentlemen, which horse you're backing. But there's only going to be one winner.'

Andris looked at the faces staring back at him. 'And we have a choice?'

Phoebe gave Pēteris his cue.

'We want you to work with us. We cannot allow Tariq Mali to carry out his operation, you must know that. Mrs Pearson will take him down. If you work with us, you will be spared. If not, well, I think you know what the outcome will be.'

Pēteris delivered with authority. He held the room well. He had presence.

'Tariq will kill you both, be assured,' he continued. 'We know that from one of his own team. He will use you, then kill you. Your wives, too. Work with us and we can take him down together. It will look like a deal gone wrong. No one knows our involvement. Tariq has to keep it under wraps. We know that, too. Guns is the one area no one has total control over. If we work together, we can let him carry on and take him out when he least expects it, which we assume will be at our final destination. He'll think he's in control. It's your only chance of staying alive.'

Phoebe was impressed. Pēteris was doing well.

'Gents?' she asked.

They spoke in their native tongue, well aware only Pēteris could understand. He took note of everything they were saying.

After a brief exchange, Andris turned to Phoebe. 'Mrs Pearson, you are right. We did still hold a grudge against your family. Valdis here has walked with a limp ever since. It's a daily reminder and one we always said, given the chance, we would avenge. But you are also right that Mr Mali has behaved in a way we do not approve of. When we first met your father-in-law, God rest his soul, we were, shall we say, a little inexperienced in how to deal with you English. We were rather aggressive in how we spoke, but that is just the way we are. We learnt over time to be less so, and even though our relationship ended, we always knew that Frank would behave in an honourable way. He would never have threatened our wives. Neither would your late husband, God rest his soul. Richie, we are not so sure about.'

He paused to see how that went down. He was pleased to see Phoebe smile. 'But you understand what I am trying to say.'

Phoebe nodded.

Andris continued. 'Mr Mali on the other hand has proven to be very dishonourable. We have already vowed to never work in England again. With respect, we always seem to get, how you say, er, shafted. We always seem to get shafted.' He stopped for a moment. 'So, let me get this straight. Even though we were planning to help bring you down, are you now saying you can forget that and that we work together?'

'One thing my father-in-law always said was to keep your friends close but your enemies closer. He would also say that at times in life, certainly in the life we all operate in, you might have to work with the very people who are trying to kill you. It's the way it is. He would tell us all that if we were never prepared to work with those who would happily bring us down, we'd end up working with no one – we'd only work against each other. Every major criminal in the UK works with other firms at one time or another, often for a greater prize. I need to take Tariq Mali out, gentlemen. I will do it with or without you, but it would be a whole lot easier with you. So, yes, I am prepared to leave the past right here and look ahead to that greater prize. The question is, are you?'

'We are, Mrs Pearson. You have our word.' Andris held out his hand. Phoebe shook it. Valdis did the same.

Archie piped up. 'One other condition is you do not breathe a word to Tariq that I'm back. As far as he's concerned, I ain't around.'

'Put a hold on that tea, Raquel,' Phoebe said. 'I think we all need a stiff drink.'

chapter seventy-one

Mo, Walt and Roach had been driving for close to six hours. It was the early hours of the morning, the morning of 29th January 2020. They'd shared the journey, with Mo driving to Peterborough, Walt to Doncaster, and Roach the rest of the way. Roach was behind the wheel. His eyes were tired. He'd managed an hour or so in the back, but he was ready for his bed. If he was at the club, he'd be fine, but driving made him weary at the best of times. The cottage was just under an hour away. The moors were pitch black. He wondered how anyone could survive out here. He'd never been this far north before.

Roach was a city boy who never really saw the attraction of sheep in fields. As a youngster, his parents would take him on Sunday drives, but whenever he thought back to those times it just reminded him of being bored shitless. He left school and entered the world of criminality almost straight away. Initially, it was running drugs for the big players on the estate, but before too long he realised he wanted more. He was still only seventeen when he decided to go to London. His mum had cried buckets when he told her he was leaving. He was her blue-eyed boy and she idolised him. His father didn't even look up from the racing pages of the paper. Cigarette in mouth, he just said, 'Well, don't think you're ever coming back here. You walk out that door and I'll close it behind you for good.'

That was the last he ever saw of his father. He was killed one night walking home from the pub. No one knew why. Some said it was a debt that Roach owed. He knew it wasn't, but more importantly his mum did, too. He saw his mum once a month and always took her a wedge of rolled notes to make sure she had all she needed. He knew she hardly spent any of it, but he took it every month regardless. She would always tell him she was saving it for him for when she passed over. Leaving him something was important to her. Other than the money he gave her, she had nothing to leave. He loved his mum. Roach was a mummy's boy at heart.

Once in London he lived on the streets for a while. He then managed to live in a squat for a year. That was when he bagged a job in the cloakroom of one of Tariq's clubs. One night, a ruck broke out at the door just as Tariq was leaving. A bunch of out-of-towners, totally unaware of whose club they were in, who thought they were something special. Tariq was inches away from getting stabbed, when Roach, as young as he was, intervened and knocked the bloke out with one punch. While in the zone, he knocked seven bells out of two of the others, helping the doormen at the time. That was the start of him working for Tariq on a more personal level. He'd never looked back and was now regarded as one of his top team.

Roach didn't quite fit in, though. Most of Tariq's firm were psychopaths who thought nothing of inflicting unnecessary pain. They would happily slit the throat of their own families if it meant impressing the boss and adding to their credentials. The two men in the car with him were no different. Roach was wary of everyone. He wanted his own firm, but knew he'd have to leave London for that. Tariq would never allow it, so he was acutely aware that despite the money, the glamour and the reputation, he was trapped just like the vast majority of the rest of the country. Most were trapped because of living to their limit or beyond their means. People like Roach were trapped because of the life they led. He had more money than he could spend but he was no freer to do as he chose than the men he saw catching the Tube every weekday morning.

'Fuckin' hell, how much further, Roach? Can't you drive any faster?' Walt said, through his yawning.

'It's pitch black, dickhead, and what you in a rush for? We can't do anything till the morning anyhow.'

'Yeah, well, I've had enough. Where the fuck are we anyway?'

'No idea, North Yorkshire Moors, I think. Another forty minutes or so.'

'I don't know why he had to come here anyway, the fuckin' tosser. I've never liked Lester.'

'Fuck off, Walt – you like him. We all do. He's all right, is Lester.'

'Yeah well, he'll be a fuckin' corpse soon enough. I wouldn't like what's coming his way.'

'Go back to sleep, you're doing my nut in.'

Three quarters of an hour later they drove into Castleton. As nice as it looked, Roach still could not see the attraction.

'Where you reckon, Mo?' he asked.

'Just along this road. Park behind that Evoque.'

Roach pulled up. He looked behind him at Mo in the back. 'This it then?'

'According to this, Lester's phone is within twenty metres of where we are right now.'

'He must be in one of these three cottages then,' Walt said, looking out of his window.

Mo agreed. 'He must be. Look we can't do anything now. We can't see a thing and any noise will have the neighbours twitching their curtains. He ain't going anywhere, so let's wait till breakfast, knock on a few doors and see what comes. He must be in one of these here. If he moves, this will tell me, so let's get some sleep – I'm knackered.'

chapter seventy-two

It was 7:23 and Alice had showered and was wondering what to have for breakfast. Sarah was upstairs seeing to Mary. They'd bought a loaf and some eggs yesterday on the way up, but she fancied some porridge. Beside a real fire in a stone cottage, on a cold, crisp morning in the country, seemed just the place to enjoy a hot bowl. She put Archie's parka on. It was miles too big, but she was like toast wrapped up in it. She sipped her tea and looked at the phone wondering if Tariq had replied. She switched it on. There was a missed call but no voicemail. She smiled before placing the phone in the front pocket.

'Sarah, I'm just popping along to the shop to see if they have any porridge. Do you want anything?' she shouted from the bottom of the stairs.

'Er, no, we're good, thanks. Oh, mind you, can you see if they have any herbal tea. Any will do.'

'OK, not be long.'

Mo was staring at the three cottages, trying to work out which one it could be. It didn't really matter but it helped to relieve the boredom. Two of them had lights on, but he couldn't see anyone inside. The fact the windows were so small didn't help. Walt was also awake. Roach had nipped to the shop to get some kind of breakfast.

Mo saw one of the front doors open. A young woman walked out and looked both ways. He couldn't believe his eyes. The one and only Alice Pearson. When he slowly pressed his phone to ring Tariq, it was as if time had stood still. He watched Alice walk the same way Roach had a moment or two earlier.

'Boss, it's me.'

'What you got?'

'You will not believe who has just walked out of a cottage right by us.'

'Who?'

'Alice Pearson.'

Silence.

'Boss, you hear me?'

'THE Alice Pearson?'

'The very same.'

'Well, fuck me.'

'She's here, Boss. I'm watching her walk down the road right now. What do we do?'

'I'll ring you back.'

Tariq placed his phone on his kitchen worktop. He couldn't believe what he'd just heard. Alice Pearson *had* to have Lester's phone. 'This means they know,' he said to himself out loud very slowly. 'They fuckin' know,' he said louder. 'The bastards know!' he shouted.

He sat down on a kitchen stool and stared at the wall. *What did this mean? What the fuck are they planning?* This could be a game changer, but he needed to engineer things so that he was one step ahead. He rang Mo.

'Where is she now?'

'Er, she's walkin' along the street, to the shop I reckon.'

'Get Walt to knock on the door. They don't know him. I want to know who else is in there.'

'What – Lester?'

'Doubt it, but you never know. Either she's shacked up there with him, or they've done away with him, but they know, my friend, they fuckin' know. If Lester is in there, though, I want him. Ring me back.'

Tariq was buzzing with adrenaline. He could not believe fate had dealt him such a hand.

Walt knocked on the door. No answer. He knocked harder. He looked along the street and saw Roach walking back towards the car munching on a sandwich. He knocked again. This time he heard someone. The door opened. He was greeted by a young lady with a child in her arms.

'Er, is Robbie in? Sorry it's so early, and I don't know if I've got the right house, but I'm looking for my mate, Robbie.'

'No, sorry, there's no Robbie here. You must have the wrong house. There's just an old lady next door, and only me and my sister-in-law here. And this little one, of course. But a young man lives two doors along, so it might be him. I don't know his name, sorry.'

'Great, thanks. Sorry to have bothered you.'

Sarah smiled and closed the door. The fact she'd just told a total stranger she was one of only two women in the house didn't register. She'd always been the trusting type, forever seeing the good in people.

Walt rushed back to the car. Roach passed him a sandwich. Mo watched the app tell him the phone was switched on and, more importantly, moving.

'So?' Mo asked.

'Just another young lass with a young 'un. She actually told me it was just them two. Told me about an old biddy next door and some fella in that one there, but I'm sure Lester ain't in there with them two.'

Mo rang Tariq. 'He ain't there, Boss. Just young Alice and another lass.'

'Who's the other one?'

'Just a minute, there's more.'

'What?'

'Lester's phone's on the move. It was switched on a moment ago. Alice must have it on her. She has to.'

'Bitch. Fuckin' whore, I knew it. So who's the other one?'

'No idea. D'you know who the other one is, Walt?'

'No, no idea.'

'We don't know, Tariq.'

'OK, just come back now.'

'Eh?'

'I said leave. Now.'

Roach could hear his boss's orders, so started the engine.

'OK, but I need to ask, Boss, why?' Mo asked, confused as to why Tariq wanted them to leave.

"Cos they know. They have Lester's phone, so they know about me, they must do.'

'So shouldn't we do something? I dunno – nab her, or at least get Lester's phone?'

'No, absolutely not. Think about it. They must know I'm behind all this. If not, they'd have played their hand. They at least know Lester was tailing them. That alone speaks volumes. I bet those bastards from Latvia have grassed us up, or maybe Lester did, but either way, if they know, which I'm convinced they do, they don't know that we know they know.'

'You've lost me.'

'This puts us in the driving seat. This, my friend, is the best thing that could've happened. They think they can outsmart me. Ha, they're dealin' with the best, Mo. I'm the best there is and I'll kill the fuckin' lot of 'em. Hurry back.'

Mo managed to catch a glimpse of Alice outside the shop holding a box under her arm while attempting to get something out of her inside pocket. He watched the app confirm the phone was now moving in the opposite direction to before. She had the phone all right. He looked back but could only see the back of her.

Remembering she'd not switched it off, Alice took out Lester's phone from her jacket. She automatically checked for a text before switching it off and putting it back. She quickly walked back to the cottage. She was looking forward to her porridge.

chapter seventy-three

A week later – Thieves Wood, near Mansfield

Phoebe was walking through Thieves Wood, a couple of miles outside Mansfield. The clouds were thick and the air was damp. It was a cold February day. She and Pat had come to get some fresh air and to discuss the upcoming gun shipment. After their meeting with Valdis and Andris a week ago, it had been arranged that the drop would be made on Monday 17th February. If there was one thing Phoebe was keen to do, it was to get this over and done with. She had learnt that letting things drag on didn't suit her. She realised that she was someone who liked to grasp the nettle and squeeze it. If it stung, then so be it, but it wouldn't sting forever. She knew the next fortnight was going to be by far her biggest test, but she was confident that with Valdis and Andris on board she was a step ahead of her London rival. She knew she needed to be. How she wished Frank was there. She missed his rock-like stature more than ever, but she was prepared to take the fight to Tariq and deal with whatever came of it.

'You know, I was always unsure about those two, but to be fair to them, I'm convinced they're being straight with us,' Pat said.

'Me too. I mean, I was never as unsure as you, but yeah I think they are. It still makes me smile when I see them, though – Valdis with his limp and Andris with his glass eye. Honestly, they're like a double act.'

'Still remind you of Steven?'

'Nah, not any more. Initially, yeah, but no, I don't see him now, thank goodness.'

'You've done well, you know, Phoebe. I'm proud of ya.'

She smiled at Pat. He was one of the most sincere guys you could ever wish to meet. 'Thanks. I wish Frank was here, though.'

'Old Frank. I wonder what he would've done.'

They both privately pondered the question as they walked.

'Probably the same, you know. He'd have held back and weighed things up. You're in a position of strength, Phoebe. Tariq won't have a clue we know any of this.'

'Not even with Lester going missing?' Phoebe asked.

'I think with the timescale and us "going along" with his plan, he'll just think he's pissed off somewhere. Andris more or less confirmed that the other night on the phone, didn't he? He said that's what Tariq was thinking, so we're in pole position. Andris has confirmed to Tariq where the shipment's going to be offloaded this end, so we'll be waiting for him. He'll not know what's hit him.'

Phoebe smiled at him once more. He was now the rock she leant on.

'Plus, the van with the real stuff in will be miles away, so we're all sweet.'

'I'm still a little concerned about a fallout once it's known Tariq's been taken out,' she replied.

Pat could see she was concerned and it was his job to put those worries to bed. He had to be the voice of reason. It's what Jez always did for Frank.

'No one will know it's us. We've arranged for any bodies to be dumped outside London. The vans are untraceable and the fact Tariq is planning all of this without anyone other than Valdis and Andris knowing means no one'll look at us. We keep the guns for ourselves and forget the whole thing while crying crocodile tears at the funerals. Anyone in Tariq's firm who survives and knows the crack will never tell. It's foolproof. We know it is. We've gone over it so many times. It'll all be fine.'

'I know, I know, but it never hurts to go over it again.'

'I'm your sounding board, Phoebe. I'm always here to go over things. Anytime, you know that. Anyway, left or right here?'

'Er, right.'

'Any idea where it leads to?'

'No, but we're bound to hit a road sooner or later.'

Phoebe enjoyed the walk. They came across the A60 after an hour. The niggling feeling was still there.

chapter seventy-four

The early hours of Monday 17th February 2020 – Portknockie Harbour

Brian, Raquel, Knighty and Ryan were waiting for the boat to arrive. It was 1:24. Brian and Knighty were in a plain red van; Raquel and Ryan in Raquel's car. It was cold. Their engines were off to avoid unnecessary noise. Void of delay, the boat was due around 1:30. Andris and Valdis were in their own car. The two cars were parked in the little car park through the yellow barrier. The van was backed up as far as it could go before it would hit it.

Everyone was nervous. The plan was to load up and get straight off. No one wanted to hang around with a vanload of illegal firearms. On the journey back to Mansfield, Valdis and Andris would be in front; the van sandwiched in between them and Raquel behind.

Brian saw a light, just as he had a few weeks earlier. 'That'll be them,' he said to Knighty. 'Right on time.'

He got out and signalled to Valdis, who was in the driver's seat. He then did the same to Raquel. Brian knew it would be fifteen minutes before they hit shore, so got back in the van to keep warm. He'd been asked to come up again as the van he was in was going to a warehouse in South Normanton, a few miles outside

Mansfield. An empty, identical van would arrive at a warehouse on a remote, uninhabited farm a mile off the A614. That was where they expected Tariq to be. Access was via a dirt track, so it was easy to see who came and went. Phoebe's men, the best she had, would be waiting out of sight along the track. Whether Tariq turned up before the dummy van arrived or not was immaterial. They would be waiting for him.

No one knew about the tracker that had been put on the car Valdis was driving.

Twenty minutes later the first of the shipment was being loaded into the van. It took a further fifty minutes, after another trip to the main boat, to offload it all. By three o'clock that Monday morning Knighty was driving the van a few yards behind Valdis and his tracker up the road from the harbour. Ryan followed, driving Raquel and her car. The operation had been a success. A minute later, they were driving out of Portknockie.

Raquel rang Phoebe. 'It's all good, Phoebe. The van's loaded up, just in front of me. We're on our way back.'

'Drive safely. Is the van in the middle?'

'Yep, just as we planned. We'll all be sticking to the speed limit. Don't worry.'

'OK, good.'

'Phoebe?'

'Yeah.'

'Good luck later. I won't see you till it's over,' Raquel said with sincerity.

'I know. Just make sure you get in the van with Brian before you get onto the A614. I want Knighty and Ryan here if at all possible. The decoy van won't arrive until they're back at the farm. See you at mine tonight, as if nothing's happened.'

Raquel ended the call.

'You OK?' she asked Ryan.

'Yeah, all good, me.'

'Good. I'll have a snooze. Wake me up when we stop to swap drivers.'

The plan was to drive along the A95 though Aberlour towards Grantown-on-Spey and Aviemore before the long drive down the A9 to Perth. They would stop just before Aviemore and then again at Perth.

Valdis was humming away to the radio. Andris was asleep. They'd been driving for an hour. The roads were deserted. He'd only seen two cars in fifty minutes since coming off the A96. He approached a yellow road diversion sign, with the arrow pointing up a minor road to the left. He failed to recall it not being there when they drove up. He did what just about every other person would do and indicated left. Knighty did likewise, as did Ryan.

After three hundred yards, Valdis saw a dark-coloured van that appeared to have come off the road into a ditch and the figure of what looked like a lady flagging him down, so he slowed almost to a stop. As he did so, the person indicated for him to wind down his window. Without giving it another thought, he did just that.

Valdis still had his finger on the window button when the bullet went straight through his head. Andris was still asleep when a bullet from the same gun ripped into his temple.

Knighty tried to reverse. He'd only driven the van once and had forgotten where the gear was. He put it into first and stalled. Brian opened the glovebox to get his gun. He was dead before he managed to put his finger on the trigger. Knighty took off his seatbelt and rammed the driver's door into the man stood to his right, knocking him into the hedgeway. He managed to get out and was ready to fight, when a bullet hit him in the chest. He sank to his knees. He tried to get up, just as the second bullet hit him in the neck. Within twenty seconds of Valdis slowing down, all four were dead.

Ryan screeched the wheels of the Mercedes as he put it into reverse. Raquel was shouting at him to go. He had his left elbow over his headrest as he frantically sped backwards along the narrow road. Through the windscreen, Raquel saw three men in balaclavas. The fourth looked like a woman until she saw them rip off their wig and then realised it was a man. Ryan spun the car round on a track that led to a field where three cows were munching away. For a split second, everything appeared normal. He looked back along the road. They were a safe enough distance away.

'What do we do?' he asked.

'Drive, Ryan, just fuckin' drive!'

chapter seventy-five

Phoebe had thought about going to bed, but she knew she'd never sleep while they were en route. She was on the sofa, drifting in and out of consciousness, when her phone rang. It was Raquel.

'Hi, everything OK?'

'We've been ambushed. The guns are gone, Knighty's dead. I think Brian is, too. Me and Ryan are somewhere, but fuck knows where.'

'Woah, slow down, say that again.'

'We've been ambushed. We'd been driving for like an hour when, out of nowhere, three or four men in balaclavas started shooting. We slowed right down, no idea why, as we were at the back. I couldn't see properly in the dark, but I heard two or three shots, then another three or four. I saw Knighty fall. He's dead. Didn't see Brian but he was in the van with Knighty.'

Phoebe struggled to take it all in.

'Phoebe, are you there? Did you hear that?'

'What about Valdis and Andris?' she replied.

'No idea. I assume they took bullets, too. They were in the car in front.'

'When was this?'

'Literally just now. We reversed and managed to get away. We drove for like thirty seconds before I rang you.'

'Is anyone chasing you?'

Raquel looked behind her. There were no headlights.

'Don't think so.'

'Fuck, fuck.'

'We can't go back, Phoebe, we have to keep driving.'

'But we can't leave Brian and Knighty's bodies there – how the hell would we explain that?'

'Shit. Right.'

'You'll have to go back. We can't leave the bodies there, Raquel. You'll have to drive the van back, too. We've got to clean this up. We cannot leave any mess.'

'Gotcha. Shit, OK, leave it with us.'

'Raquel.'

'Yeah?'

'Don't get yourself killed, but we need to clear up any mess. Understand?'

'I do.'

Phoebe's mind was racing.

Archie came in. He'd been lying on his bed upstairs still dressed. He couldn't sleep either. He could see the expression of horror on his mum's face. 'What's up?' he asked.

'Raquel, ring me back,' she said.

'OK, will do – as soon as I have something to tell you.'

Phoebe looked at Archie. 'They were ambushed. A few minutes ago. Knighty's dead. Brian too, probably. Gunshots.'

Archie ran his hand through his hair. 'Fuckin' hell! I'll kill him, Mum, I'll fuckin' kill him. Today. He won't see another sunrise that bastard.'

'Who?'

'Tariq, of course, who the fuck else?'

'Know it was him, do you?'

'Well who else would it be?'

'The Latvians? We don't know if they've been taken out, too, yet. They were in the front car. They could've set us all up just as easily as Tariq.'

Archie sat down. His mum was right. They knew nothing for sure.

'Fuckin' Brian. Why did it have to be him? Been in the game forever and he gets taken out like this. We should've all been there. They were sitting ducks.'

'Hey, we all agreed who would go. There's no point saying that now, it won't change anything.'

'I know, I know. Poor old Knighty. In his prime, he was. He'd've gone far, that one. Ryan and Raquel got away then?'

'Yes.'

Archie ran his fingers through his hair again. 'We didn't see this comin', did we? Fuckin' hell.'

Phoebe rang Brian. She knew he wouldn't answer, but until she knew for sure there was always hope. No answer. She rang Valdis. No answer from him either.

'Knighty definitely dead?' Archie asked.

'Raquel saw it with her own eyes. Brian was in the front seat of the van. She was behind, in her car, so she couldn't say for sure about Brian.'

Her phone pinged. A text. It was Brian. Phoebe stared at a photo of him with a bullet in his right temple. Fighting back tears, she passed it to Archie. Underneath, it read *See you in hell.*

'We have to take him out, Mum. Today. Let me do it.'

Phoebe sniffled, wiped her nose and then said, 'Archie, we can't do that. We cannot, for no reason or without justification, take out one of the top crime bosses. It'd cause all-out war.'

'No reason? Unjustified? Look at that – is that reason enough?'

'Think, Son, think. What did your grandad teach you? Have you forgotten what he always said?'

'He said all sorts of things, Mum, so you'll have to enlighten me,' he replied, fraught with frustration.

Before Phoebe could answer, a voice from the other side of the room said, 'He always said, if you ever take on one of the others, make sure you have a fuckin' good reason and can explain why. That way it would be accepted. Otherwise, the whole country will be gunning for you.'

They both looked up to see Alice in the doorway.

'That's exactly what he would say. Word for word in fact. Alice, sit down, luv, I have something to tell you.'

'I heard most of it. They've been ambushed and Brian and Knighty are dead.'

'Come here,' Phoebe said, with her arms outstretched.

The three of them hugged one another, feeling the warmth and comfort it gave.

'So what we gonna do?' Alice asked.

'Think. That's what we need to do – think,' Phoebe replied. 'Thing is, we have nothing. This was all done under the radar, remember? No one, other than the select few involved, knew anything about it. Tariq would just deny it. We don't know who these men are, who sent them or anything. Yes, we can put two and two together but we need to make sure they add up to four, and at the minute we can't. If we take Tariq out, we'd have to answer for it. We can't go in all guns blazing on a suspicion, on word of mouth or anything else. If I'm wrong, tell me, but from where I'm standing we have nothing at all to tie Tariq to any of this. All we have is the word of Lester, who's dead, and the word of two Latvians, who may be dead but if they're not, might have orchestrated everything. Plus whatever Hugh told you in Spain.'

'And he's dead too, ain't he?' Alice said.

'Yeah, surprise surprise, he's dead as well. And that's it. We have nothing else. Or am I missing something?'

Neither Archie nor Alice could offer anything.

'So I'm right. We have nothing. Nothing to justify taking out Tariq Mali. Nothing at all. Yet we have two of ours dead and a shipment of guns on the loose.'

The reality of how they'd been played hit Phoebe like a tonne weight.

If only Alice had not switched on that phone.

chapter seventy-six

Tariq lifted his glass. He rarely drank, but this was a celebratory moment. He'd just had word from his men in Scotland that they'd pulled it off. The guns were now in one of his own vans on its way back to London; the bodies were in a separate van on its way to Mansfield; the van that Knighty was driving had been burnt out; and Valdis's car was being driven back to London, too. The Scottish police would assume the van had been dumped and set on fire after some sort of joyride or robbery, but as far as the rest went, no one would have a fucking clue. Just as he'd planned.

It was a good day's work and the sun had yet to rise. He'd achieved a lot in one fell swoop. Managing to get rid of Valdis and Andris, knock off two of Phoebe's most trusted and acquire a shipment full of illegal firearms he didn't have to pay for was a master stroke. He was disappointed there hadn't been more of Phoebe's men to take out but, as he said out loud before sipping his whisky, 'You can only shoot the fuckers in front of ya.' The only thing he'd not managed to achieve was taking out the entire Pearson outfit. That annoyed him, but he had to settle for them knowing he knew about their involvement. That day would come, though. He would bide his time. He'd quite enjoyed thinking this all up and was sure he could do it all again someday. His only slight issue was how he was going to explain the shipment of guns he now had in his possession. When the time came to introduce them to the market, he'd have to have a story. Guns were a hot topic amongst his fellow elite, so he needed to think this one through. He made a call. 'All's good. Take him out.'

Ten minutes later, at a house in Manchester, Janis was woken by a loud banging at his front door. He yawned as he shouted, 'Hold on, for fuck's sake!' He opened the door and tried to focus on the person in front of him. He was dead before he hit the ground.

chapter seventy-seven

At eleven o'clock that same morning, everyone was at Gloria's – everyone except the four who'd been up to Scotland. Phoebe's top table now knew about Brian and Knighty's fate. The atmosphere, on losing two of the team's strongest, was one of anger and despair. Pēteris, in particular, had taken it hard. He took responsibility not only for bringing this down on the firm but for the loss of two of his dearest friends.

Phoebe knew she needed to lead from the front. She'd already spoken to Pēteris separately and assured him he had nothing to worry about. She trusted him and had no doubt he was not involved. This morning's meeting would, she thought, be a difficult one to chair. People would be wanting revenge and might not be too fussy about when and how to deliver it.

She was expecting Raquel and Ryan around midday. They'd informed her the van had been set alight and Valdis's car was missing. Raquel was sure there were no bodies in the van. Whoever had done this was a professional outfit, who'd cleaned up properly. Other than a burnt-out van, there was nothing to say what had happened.

Phoebe opened the meeting. 'Gentlemen, and Alice, last night we lost two of our best. Brian, bless him, went out the way he always wanted to, in a blaze of glory. Knighty, a father of three, was taken far too early. I know you will want revenge, as do I, but – and I need to make this very clear, folks – BUT we have nothing to go on.' She paused, looking everyone in the eye. No one showed any emotion. 'So, until we know for sure who did this, we have to bide our time. But rest assured, we will have revenge and when we do, I will make sure every single one of you sat here today is there to witness it. This will not go unpunished. Someone will talk, they always do, but until that time we have to accept what's happened and plough all of our energy into finding out who's behind it.'

'It has to be Tariq, Phoebe. It can't be anyone else.'

'I have two theories. One is, of course, Tariq. We have strong evidence to suspect he's behind all of this, but – and again, I emphasise the but – we have nothing to prove it, so we have no justification to take him out. The other theory is Valdis and Andris. Raquel suspects they were also gunned down, but until we know their fate, they're suspects.'

'Who's your money on, though?' Michael asked.

'Tariq.'

'So that's where we focus our attention?' Pat asked.

'Yes, BUT – I won't do it a third time – we need to tread carefully. I will go and see him personally. I want him to know we fully suspect it's him and if we get any proof, we will take him down.'

'Won't he see that as a threat, especially from you?'

'A woman?'

'Yeah, you know what he's like.'

'Maybe, and he'd be right. He can take it as he likes, but he will be under no illusion.'

'And if that leads to war?' Trainer asked.

'Then we go to war. We cannot take a war to him, gents. The other top tables wouldn't tolerate it without reason. But we can defend if he brings it on top with us. That I have no issue with.'

'Who's going with you?'

'No one, just me.'

'A bit risky that, innit?' Del said.

'Quite the opposite, Del. Me on my own will show strength on my part. He needs to know I am not to be intimidated.'

'When you goin'?'

'Tomorrow morning. Catching the train from Newark.'

'How do you know he'll be around?

'I don't, but I'll find him. Once he knows I'm looking for him, he'll come to me. I know he will.'

'I don't like you goin' on your own,' Pat said.

'I know, Pat, but I'm going. I'm a big girl, so don't worry.'

'What do you want the rest of us to do?' Del asked.

'To be honest, Del, there's not a lot for you to do. Tell your teams what's happened but leave out the gun operation bit. That's to be kept under wraps. All you need to divulge is that Brian and Knighty were on a job for me and, well, it didn't go to plan. That's it. Nothing else. Once word gets out, we'll have the Old Bill on the phone, so I'll leave that with you, Pat.'

Pat nodded.

'In fact, I think we should inform those on the payroll. They'll hear soon enough, so make sure they keep the others away. We don't need any heat from them at this stage.'

He gave another nod.

Phoebe continued. 'The other problem is, we have no idea where the bodies are, or where they've been dumped, if anywhere. That could be a problem. It'll take a hefty wedge to keep that quiet, so make that known, Pat – that if any bodies are found anywhere on our manor, it's not to cause us a problem. Pay whatever it takes.'

'Will do. I know those to call, don't worry.'

'We will avenge their deaths, gentlemen, I promise, but it may take time. Keep your wits about you and look out for anything suspicious. Whoever is behind this may strike again. We don't know, so be on your guard.'

She looked at Alice. 'Tell Gloria she can bring the tea through.'

'Last of the old guard he was, Brian. You know, in just over six months we've lost Frank, Jez and now Brian,' Archie said.

'At least you're back, Archie, so we'll be OK,' Trainer said, trying to lift the moment.

Archie smiled at the intent. 'No one could replace those three, pal.'

'I know, I was just—'

'We know, we know.'

'What about Knighty's missus?' Jase asked.

'She's in bits. Angry, as you can imagine. I've only spoken to her, but she blames us, as you'd expect. I just let her talk. She'd calmed down by the end of the conversation, but I said I'd go and see her later. Pat's coming with me,' Phoebe replied.

'We'll take care of her, though, yeah?'

'Of course, Jase – we always do.'

Gloria came through. She was not her usual jolly self. Even after Jez passed away, she'd managed to remain upbeat but this, so soon after, had rocked her. She was pouring the teas, when they heard footsteps. Pat and Del rose immediately and headed towards the door. In walked Raquel and Ryan. Pat flung his arms around Raquel. She squeezed him tight, unable to hold back the tears any longer. Del pulled Ryan close to him and threw his arms around his son. The memory of losing Paul was all too much and he too broke down. Ryan managed to hold back his emotions while he hugged his father.

Once they'd all shaken hands and had their cuddles, Raquel told them of the night's events. She looked as though she'd not slept for a week. For the first time, her face showed her age. Ryan then took over.

'A professional job then?' Gray asked.

'Yeah, most certainly. It was over in seconds. They knew what they were doing.'

An hour later, everyone was gone – Raquel and Ryan to get some sleep, Pat to make some phone calls before joining Phoebe in Derby to see Knighty's family, Phoebe to have a good old cry before Pat joined her, and everyone else to start the task of trying to find out anything they could.

chapter seventy-eight

Alice and Archie were on their way back to Southwell. The talk was all of Tariq. Archie wondered how he could've known. It was the one thing he could not get his head round. Alice was unable to offer anything to help him piece any of it together. His phone rang.

'Sarah, luv, calm down, I can't make out what you're saying. Just take a breath. Now tell me again.'

'They've just dumped them, Archie, right here.'

'Who has? Dumped what?'

'Two bodies on the drive. I daren't go out.'

'Sarah, stay in the house – lock all the doors and sit tight. Do not go out, do you hear me? We won't be long.'

'Hurry, please hurry.'

'Five minutes, luv, five minutes.'

'Brian and Knighty, innit?' Alice said.

'Must be. I fuckin' knew it, you know. I knew they'd be dumped there. I wish I'd said something now. I shouldn't've left Sarah alone when I had that feeling.'

He suddenly swerved to the left. 'Fuckin' hell! Woah! Watch where you're going, ya fuckin' tosser!'

he shouted at a van careering round the bend. He looked in his rear view mirror. *Black van* he thought. *I'll remember that next time. Wanker.*

He rang Sarah back. 'Hi luv. How did they get through the gate?'

'They must have followed me in when I came back from the Co-op. They must have. I took Mary in and was just going out for the bags when there they were, dropping them out of the back door of their van. I'm just glad they were able to get out back through the gates, or else I dread to think what would've happened, Archie.'

'What colour was the van?'

'Black.'

Archie screeched to a stop. Alice looked at him in horror. He spun the car around and drove towards the roundabout at Rainworth where the A617 meets the A614. Three exits to choose from. He could see part way along towards Arnold, and part way towards Ollerton, but not towards Mansfield. There was no sign of the van. He opted for Mansfield. He drove into Rainworth and along to the junction at The Widecombe Fair. Nothing. He thumped the steering wheel.

'Fuck. It was them, Alice.'

'I know, but we need to get back. Sarah's on her own.' She stared at him.

'Archie, the lights have changed.'

He turned round in a car showroom car park, before heading back to Southwell.

chapter seventy-nine

Tariq was contemplating his victory. He tapped his phone on his desk as he looked out over the London sky. He was expecting contact. How or when he could not decide, but he knew they'd be in touch. He'd play it down, of course – they had nothing to tie him to any of it, especially the deaths. He'd purposely changed his mind and disposed of Valdis's and Andris's bodies elsewhere, knowing that without their bodies Phoebe would suspect them. That would play right into his hands when she came knocking.

He brought up that last text from Lester and smirked at who was now getting the "surprise". And then it dawned on him who'd sent it. The person who sent the message had to be the person who had the phone, and the person who had the phone was Alice Pearson.

He smiled as he said out loud, 'I'll show *you* fucking "Surprise".'

chapter eighty

Phoebe was on her way home with Pat. They'd had to put off seeing Knighty's wife until later that day. If she was honest, she could do without it but she knew she'd never forgive herself if she didn't go and see her. Tomorrow she was off to London, so today it had to be.

She'd bought an open return since she didn't know how long it would take to see Tariq. Knowing Tariq like she did, though, he was likely to be out of the capital. One thing she was sure of was that he'd be back to see her without delay. Probably to gloat, and probably to deny everything, but he would not be able to resist having his fifteen minutes.

She pulled into the driveway to find Archie wet through from the rain and standing over the two lifeless souls. She and Pat rushed over.

'Come on, pal, I'll give you a hand to move them. Let's get them into the garage out of the way.'

'Been waiting for you, Pat. I couldn't drag 'em. Just didn't seem right. They deserve better.'

Phoebe couldn't help but look at their faces. Despite the circumstances of their deaths, they looked peaceful. It made her wonder whether everyone achieved peace in death. She hoped so.

'Archie?'

'Yeah?'

'You made any calls?'

'Alice has.'

'To Ted?'

'Who else? He's the only one we'd call.'

They carried Brian in out of the rain.

'Anyone else?' she asked.

'Yeah, I rang Sheryl after I checked the CCTV. Got a number off the van but it's false. She's just confirmed. Quick as a flash she was, as usual. She'll go far that one, I tell ya.'

Phoebe agreed. 'You say the same, Pat, don't you?'

'Deffo. She'll be running the force one day.'

'So all we know is that it was a black van,' Archie said, shaking his head.

'I can't believe you nearly had 'em, pal,' Pat said, patting his back.

'Minutes away I was, Pat. Fuckin' minutes, that's all.'

'I won't be long,' Phoebe said, and walked quickly towards the house. Once inside, she rushed straight upstairs.

'Mum, that you?' Alice shouted.

'I need a moment. Let me be.'

Phoebe ran into her bedroom, lay on her bed and sobbed. She needed to. Grief had to play out – she knew that. After a bloody good cry, she'd be fine. She couldn't let her team see, though. She had to be strong. She *was* a woman in a man's world, and it was time to stand front and centre and show she could mix it with them all. In full view of everyone, she would take on all comers.

Phoebe cried for twenty minutes solid. She would shed no more tears after.

chapter eighty-one

Phoebe arrived in London King's Cross just after 11:30. She'd slept most of the way and had had to be woken up on approach. She grabbed a coffee on the go, before heading to flag down a taxi. Her first port of call was Tariq's main club. She'd never been in it before but knew where it was, in the heart of Soho. It was allegedly the biggest and best club in the West End – if sex was your thing.

The driver made no attempt to engage in conversation, which suited her. She was playing out scenarios of her meeting Tariq. Would he be engaging, would he give anything away or would he be his usual obnoxious self? She guessed the latter.

As the taxi weaved through the traffic, she observed the people. London was busier than she could ever remember it. She peered at the landmarks as she passed them by and noted the number of homeless people and ethnicities. London was so different to her world. She loved Mansfield, the people and the area. But she recognised that in certain places and communities, being different simply meant you either supported the striking miners or you didn't. People were very much the same.

'Here we are,' the driver said, clicking the meter to stop the fare going up by the second, as it had done throughout the ride.

'Thank you. Keep the change.'

'Lovely. You workin' here, are ya?'

Phoebe laughed, secretly flattered he thought she still could.

'No, not here.'

'You have a nice day now.'

She watched the taxi drive off and wondered how many people the driver would come into contact with today. She thought about the virus that had been on the news, now causing deaths, and hoped he'd be OK. She was pleased she'd not taken the Tube.

She stood back and took in the outside of the club. It looked OK, but nothing special. As she walked in, a man in his forties came up to her.

'You OK there, sweetheart?'

Phoebe could see he worked there, but wasn't impressed by his customer engagement. 'I'm here to see Tariq Mali.'

'I bet you are, luv. A lot of women like you would like to meet Mr Mali.'

'Women like me?'

'Yeah, you know.'

'No, I don't. Now kindly inform Mr Mali that Phoebe Pearson is here to see him.'

'Well, he ain't 'ere, so you're outta luck.'

'I think if you were to kindly get in touch with him, he'd be here soon enough.'

The guy looked her up and down. 'I doubt it. They all like to think that, but wait 'ere.'

Phoebe took a seat on one of the leather sofas that adorned the reception area. The interior was far nicer than the exterior. In fact, she was impressed by the quality of the place. No expense had been spared. She could sense the woman behind the counter, dusting everything in sight, was curious as to who she was. She was wearing the customary tabard and had more wrinkles than Phoebe had ever seen. That aside, she didn't look too bad.

The woman somehow managed to dust her way over. 'Be careful, my love, he's a bad 'un. If he asks you to perform anything sexual, make sure you give a good account of yourself or else you'll never work in this town.'

'Thanks. I'll make a note of that. Is he here most days?'

'No idea. I just clean here and the one round the corner – which is a dive compared to this. Half the price, though, so some prefer it. You know, same thing for less dough. Means they can come back again, see. You're too classy for that place, though. He'll have you working here, lady like you. Cut above, you are.'

'You haven't seen any guns, have you, in the last day or two?'

'Only me fella's biceps. He's sixty-two, he is, and has guns on him like a thirty year old. I love 'em, I do. He still does it for me, bless him.'

'Mavis, fuck off out of it. Go and clean somewhere else.'

'Sorry, Mr Davis, I was just chatting.'

'Go on, fuck off.'

The man who Phoebe now knew was Mr Davis smiled at her. 'Mr Mali is otherwise engaged at one of his other venues, but he asked me to take you through and to ensure you're given whatever you need. He said he will be no more than half an hour. Are you happy to wait, Mrs Pearson?'

'Yes, I'll wait. Thank you.'

'Right, this way then please. And please forgive my manners just now. I didn't realise who you were.'

Phoebe looked at him in disgust. 'That should not matter,' she said curtly.

Mr Davis said nothing as he took her through, but then stuck his fingers up at her behind her back.

The décor behind the door was even more impressive. The place was dripping with money. It reminded Phoebe how much more money could be made in the capital. For all her wealth – and she was a very wealthy lady – she felt in awe of the sheer decadence of this club.

'If you would like to take a seat at the bar, Mrs Pearson. Anything you like is on the house. Juan here will look after you.'

'Thank you.'

She enjoyed two glasses of mineral water while waiting close to forty minutes before Tariq made his entrance. As expected, he was loud. And he wanted everyone to hear his phone call.

'I don't care who you come across, just get her and bring her to me! That lady needs a lesson in how to behave. Ring me when you have her.'

He finished his conversation just as he reached the bar.

'Phoebe, what a surprise. I like surprises.'

'Do you? That's nice.'

'Yeah, love 'em. Especially when you get a message out of the blue saying *surprise*. Always does it for me, that. Especially when you can return the favour – that's the best bit. What a world we live in, eh? Now then, to what do I owe the pleasure?'

Phoebe stared at him, momentarily speechless. She knew he could be strange and off the wall but she wasn't here to talk about surprises.

'Trouble?' Phoebe asked, diverting her eyes to his phone. The call had evidently been for her ears.

'Oh, nothing I can't handle. Just a young upstart that needs teaching a lesson. You know how it is. Now what can I do for you? Have you been looked after while you've been waiting?'

'Yes, thank you. But not here. We need to talk privately.'

'OK, whatever you say. How's that son of yours? Well, is he?'

Phoebe was just about to say he was fine, when she remembered Tariq had put a price on his head. Plus, as far as she knew, he didn't know he was back.

'I couldn't tell you, I haven't seen him. We no longer speak.'

'Hmm, shame that. Give him my regards if you do. In fact, tell him to give me a call. I hear he's an enforcer these days. I may have a job for him from time to time.'

Phoebe didn't reply.

'Well, follow me,' Tariq said, before walking off in front.

Phoebe followed, flanked by Mo and Roach. Mo she knew. Roach she didn't. Mo totally blanked her. Roach smiled and said hello.

chapter eighty-two

Joseph, Ed and Isaac were three of Tariq's enforcers, who'd all worked for him for more than ten years. They all liked inflicting pain and operated wherever he needed them.

Isaac put his phone back in his pocket. 'He says he don't care a fuck who we encounter, we're to bring her to him. No excuses.'

'Where the fuck is Mansfield anyway?' Ed asked.

'It ain't Mansfield – it's a place called Southwell.'

'Where's that?'

'Fuck knows. Somewhere near Mansfield, I guess.'

chapter eighty-three

'I would take you into my own office, Phoebe, but I only use that for important meetings and my most important guests. For everyone else, I use this one,' Tariq said, as he opened the door.

Phoebe ignored his poor attempt at humour. She'd expected nothing less from him. She stepped into a very plush office with an oak table and high-backed chairs with red cushions. *It was good enough* she thought to herself. She took a seat, noting Mo and the other guy, whose name she didn't yet know, each standing either side of the door.

'You don't need them in here, Tariq. There's only me.'

'Where I go, they go. Mo follows me everywhere. Roach, well, today's his turn.'

Roach she thought. *Strange name.*

'I'd prefer it to be just me and you.'

'And I'd prefer it not to be,' he said, smiling a sarcastic smile.

Phoebe had played out this moment so many times over the last twenty-four hours and wondered how best to tackle it. Tariq had got to her. She now thought, *oh fuck it, just put your cards on the table, girl.*

'As you wish. I'll come straight to the point.'

'Good, 'cos I'm a busy man.'

'Two of my men – two of my most trusted men – were gunned down two days ago. Ambushed. Were you responsible?'

Tariq played his poker face. That alone told Phoebe he'd been prepared for that question and had rehearsed his response.

'Phoebe, you're new to this, I understand that, but you need to understand something very important if you're going to survive in this world.'

He expected a reply, but Phoebe said nothing.

'And that is, that if you come to me or any other of your opposite numbers and make wild and serious accusations such as that, you will find yourself fighting battles you will not win.'

'I made no accusation. I simply asked you a question. Were you responsible?'

'Phoebe, I'm a serious businessman, who has control of the sex trade here in the capital. I do not need to bother myself with petty squabbles you get yourself tied up in. I have no idea what you're talking about. I'm sorry to hear of your two men – I'm sure they will be a loss to you – but it has absolutely nothing to do with me. Now I would leave if I were you, before I do something I may regret.'

For the first time since taking over the reins, Phoebe felt vulnerable. She'd been prepared for his denial, but was now unsure what to say. She wished she'd brought Pat with her. Lesson learnt, she told herself. It was futile to try and labour her point further, not being in a position, here on her own, to threaten him. He needed to know, however, that when she found out who was responsible, they'd have a war on their hands. Just before she opened her mouth, she changed tack.

'Do you know two gentlemen called Valdis and Andris?'

'Never heard of 'em. Now are we done?'

'It would appear we are. Someone has taken out two of my men. Someone is trying to play me. The world should know I do not play games. I'm not one for making war, I think we all know that, but if it's a war it has to be, then so be it. I'll find out who it is. Someone will talk or something will come to light. As you will know too well, it generally does. But thank you for your time and hospitality, Tariq. It's been, how shall I say, enlightening.'

The fact he'd denied even knowing Valdis and Andris told her enough. Archie saw them coming out of his club and they'd admitted their involvement with him. Whether he was behind everything remained to be seen, but he was lying. And people only lied when they had something to hide. She was convinced it was him, but she needed something concrete.

'Show Mrs Pearson out please, Roach.'

Phoebe knew it was time to leave.

'You,' he said sharply, 'will always be in the shadow of men. This is a man's world, not a place for the likes of you. You'll do well to remember that.'

'Really? Interesting viewpoint, Tariq, but one I've heard before. Just make sure you're out of the way if I ever come out of that shadow, won't you?'

Roach escorted Phoebe down the stairs and out through the main entrance. He said nothing, but she sensed he was not in the mould of Tariq. His presence reminded her of Archie – a presence that said he was not to be messed with but was honourable. Not many people in her world had that, but Roach she concluded did.

'Thank you, Roach,' she said, adjusting her eyes to the daylight. It was surprisingly dark in the club.

'A pleasure, Mrs Pearson. Take care and have a good day.'

'You too.'

***

She walked through the streets of Soho, along the main drag and down the alleyways and back streets. It was a world away from her empire back in Nottinghamshire and Yorkshire. Her streets weren't littered with activity like these were. There weren't sex shops and live shows on every street corner.

She needed to walk and think. It was strange how the noise seemed to be in the background – like the radio being on when you're sat deep in thought in the kitchen. It was there like company but it didn't impact on the job in hand. Soho, she decided, was like her radio. It was there, but it didn't heed her thinking.

Tariq was going to be a difficult one. The fact he was one of London's elite made it all the harder. Sorting Barney and Billo out wasn't the same. This was London. It was different. Tariq was guilty and he knew she'd come. She wondered if she'd played right into his hands going to see him so early. Frank, she confessed, would probably have waited. That would have made Tariq nervous. Frank would've responded; she'd reacted. Now she was on the back foot. She'd been to see him but had achieved nothing. Other than maybe convincing herself of his guilt. A harsh lesson, but a valuable one all the same.

Her phone rang. It was Greg West, one of the other two London main players.

'Greg?'

'Phoebe. I hear you're in London.'

'Yes, I am. Who told you?'

'No matter. Where are you?'

'Soho.'

'Be on Dover Street, just off Piccadilly, in twenty minutes. I'll pick you up.'

'I'm intrigued,' she replied.

'So am I.'

chapter eighty-four

Two black cars drove up Dover Street towards her. It had been eighteen minutes since the phone call. She knew it would be Greg, but for a moment she wondered if it wasn't. Then a rear door opened. She peered in. Sat in the back was Greg West. She got in.

'How's Tariq?' he asked.

'His usual obnoxious self.'

'Figures.'

'So what's this all about? How do you know I've been to see Tariq?'

Greg looked out of his side window and began. 'There's something you need to know, Phoebe. I run London. Tariq and Paul, as you know, have their manors – and to the outside world, we run it between us. But what you need to know is that I run this city. People like your father-in-law knew it, the Burbanks brothers know it, Rory up in the West Midlands knows it. The people who need to know, know. They don't need to be told. Frank never needed me to tell him. He was wise enough to recognise the way things are. You know of the top table, don't you? I know it was a term

Frank used – maybe you do, too. Every table needs a head. The head of the table, the one who everyone else knows, is the top man.' He turned to Phoebe. 'No offence intended. Just a turn of phrase.'

She smiled in acknowledgement.

'I'm the head of the top table. When I go, someone will need to assume my role. It's a bit like natural selection. One of you assumes the position and, God willing, the rest accepts it. If not, you have carnage. The world we operate in cannot live with carnage. There needs to be order, and I'm the one who keeps it.'

Greg paused to allow Phoebe to take in what he was telling her.

'Nothing happens without me knowing about it. I know Tariq has beef with you – he's not one to let things go – and I know you now have beef with him. I won't allow him to control the gun market, as I wouldn't you, had the outcome been different. Why he thought he could do what he did without me getting wind of it is, well, disrespectful.'

'So you know what he's done?'

'Only just, which has fuckin' annoyed me. Sometimes it takes a while for word to filter through. You must understand it's not Tariq who feeds me the information.'

'Of course. But you know about my two men Brian and Knighty?'

'I do, which puts a different perspective on things, but you need to understand two things, Phoebe.'

'Go on.'

'If you take him on, you have to have proof. I cannot allow you to take out one of the top players without justification. It will upset the order of things.'

'And number two?'

'Make sure you win.'

'Do I not have justification given he's murdered two of my top table – my friends?'

'Justification, yes. Proof, no. It's how we do things, Phoebe. It's how Frank did things. He knew with Fletcher, for instance, it'd be accepted. He had no choice. Fletcher's drugs were all over his streets. It's the way it is.'

'Are you aware he's put a price on Archie's head?'

'Tariq?'

'Yes. Wants him dead.'

'Have you proof?'

'Well, no. Just the word of a dead man.'

Greg was still looking out of his window.

'You'd have supported Frank making a move with what I have,' Phoebe continued.

'But you're not Frank, Phoebe. It's an insult to his memory to think you are. You will be one day, but not yet. I'm doing this out of respect for Frank. He was one of the best. He understood the bigger picture. If you'd have gone in all guns blazin', it wouldn't have been a quiet word in your ear we'd be having. Understand?'

She nodded.

'Tariq Mali has been somewhat of an irritation for a while now, Phoebe. I would not be sorry to see him go. But Frank left Manchester to George and Ivan after he took out Fletcher. You need to do the same. Walk away and leave London to me to sort out. Someone will take his place. I need to ensure it's a round peg.'

'So when you say Frank and the Burbankses didn't need to be told, what do you mean?'

'I naturally assumed the position and they, by virtue of their silence and lack of protest, accepted it. There's always got to be a captain of a ship, Phoebe. Even the ship that sails the underworld of this great country of ours. Remember that.'

The door opened. She hadn't realised the car had stopped. She was back on Dover Street. She laughed as she realised.

'We're back. It's like that chat never happened.'

She closed the door and straightened her skirt.

The window wound down. Greg popped his head out. 'It didn't,' he said.

chapter eighty-five

Phoebe decided to stay over in the capital. She quite liked the idea of some alone time and booked into a boutique hotel in Mayfair. She was enjoying a hot soak when her phone rang. It was Pat.

'Pēteris has just rung me. Valdis and Andris are missing. He's made some enquiries in Latvia and they were expected home yesterday. No one can get hold of them. Their wives are convinced they're dead.'

'That puts that little theory to bed then. They must've been straight with us.'

'Looks like it. But that's not all.'

'What?'

'Janis is dead, too. Shot through the head, point blank range. Definitely a hit by the sounds of it.'

'We were maybe right about him then. How's Pēteris?' Phoebe asked.

'Mad as hell. Feels used and abused by Janis. He was a good mate of his.'

'We all liked him. I'm never totally surprised, though. OK, well look, I'm having a soak, so I'll speak later.'

Phoebe submerged herself for a few seconds before resurfacing and wiping the water from her face. She relaxed into the headrest and thought about the order of things and what Greg had told her. It made sense. Greg was right. Without order, even in their world, there'd be carnage. Frank had never told her, or Archie as far as she was aware, about the way the order of things was controlled. But contemplating it all, she realised she'd never questioned it. The lack of mayhem and disorder within the top level of organised crime was, when she thought about it, quite remarkable. It worked. It worked because there was order.

chapter eighty-six

Sarah was trying to keep Mary amused. She'd hardly slept since the two bodies were dumped. She was finding motherhood quite a challenge today.

'Alice, can you do me a favour and watch her while I go for a nap? I can't keep my eyes open.'

'Yeah, course, go on. Me and Mary will be fine. Won't we?' Alice said, taking both of Mary's cheeks in her thumb and forefingers. 'We'll have a great time. Come on, let's go and watch your favourite cartoon and let Mummy get some sleep. You wear her out, you do. You little rascal, you.'

Sarah climbed the stairs, grateful. No sooner had her head touched the pillow than she fell into a deep sleep.

Alice had Mary on her knee, pointing and giggling at the TV. The intercom buzzed, indicating someone was at the gate. Alice put Mary down and walked into the hallway.

'Hello?'

'Delivery for Mrs Pearson.'

'Eh, what is it?'

'No idea. Just a parcel.'

'OK, just leave it at the gate.'

'It needs a signature.'

'Is it heavy?'

'No, not really.'

'OK, I'll come up. Wait there.'

Alice walked up the driveway. By the time she'd reached the top, she wished she'd asked them to drive down. She pressed the button for the gate to open. As soon as she saw the black van, she knew, but was too late to react. Isaac and Ed bundled her into the back and before she knew what was happening, the van was screeching away. She kept calm and stared at the two men looking at her, determined to show no fear. It was like Hull all over again. Despite her perilous situation, she laughed inside at how her life had changed. This was the second time she'd found herself in such a predicament since no longer making the tea, though she feared this would be far worse than Hull. She knew who they were. Only Tariq would do such a dishonourable thing to the daughter of the head of the Pearson family.

'You do know my family will hunt you down, don't you? Whatever you do to me will be nothing compared to what they'll do to you.'

'Hey, little lady, you have no idea what's in store for you, so I'd keep those opinions to yourself for now.'

'Whatever – but don't say I didn't warn you.'

Ed was impressed. The youngster had class. He liked her. *This is going to be interesting* he thought.

chapter eighty-seven

Sarah stirred. She opened her eyes and stretched her arms out as wide as she could. She looked at the clock. It was 6:15. She'd been asleep for just under an hour. Not long, but she felt so much better. She walked out onto the landing to hear Mary crying. *What are you doing with her?* she thought, as she quickly went downstairs.

'Bloody hell, the front door's wide open!' she said loudly, hoping Alice would hear her and get the message.

She closed the door and went into the lounge. Mary was on her own, on the floor crying. The TV was still playing. Alice was nowhere to be seen.

'Come here, sweetheart,' she said lovingly, as she scooped her up. 'What's Auntie Alice done with you, eh? Where is she?'

Mary snuggled into her mum. She immediately stopped crying and sunk her face into Sarah's chest.

'Alice! Alice! Did you not hear Mary crying? Where are you?' she shouted, as she walked through into the kitchen.

She'd fully expected Alice to be in there making a cuppa or something. Sarah slowly turned round on the spot. This was strange. She peered through the door of the downstairs bathroom. Nothing. A feeling of dread came over her. *The door,* she remembered. Sarah ran through into the living room and looked out into the front garden. She looked to the side and as far up the driveway as she could. Alice's car was still there. *Had she gone to meet someone at the gate?*

Sarah was scared. This didn't feel right. For no reason, she looked around the room. She saw Alice's phone on the table next to the large sofa. *She can't be far,* she told herself. She put Mary down, and got her shoes from the downstairs cupboard. She picked Mary back up and walked to the gate. Maybe Alice was speaking to someone there. *Yes, that'll be it* she thought. *That's where she'll be.*

'Come on, Mary, let's go and find Auntie Alice. She'll be getting a piece of Mummy's mind, won't she, eh?'

Tentatively, Sarah headed up the driveway. Her heart was pounding. She kept telling herself that Alice would be chatting away without a care in the world. *Oh, sorry! I didn't think* she'd say. She walked round the bend and stopped. The gate was open. Desperate to find Alice, she picked up the pace. But when she was only a few yards away, she concluded she wasn't there. She bit her lip. She went out onto the road and looked both ways. Nothing and no one. She was alone. She stepped back inside the gate and pressed the button to close it. Having to close it manually told her that Alice had walked up to it. The sensor would have picked up a vehicle and opened automatically – and closed behind it. She jogged back to the house, Mary in her arms.

She rang Archie.

'Hi luv, I'm just on my way home. Been chattin' with Del and Michael. I won't be long.'

'Archie, Alice has gone.'

'What – gone where?'

'I don't know, but she's gone. I was having a nap, she was looking after Mary, but when I woke up she was gone and Mary was on her own in the living room, crying. The gate was open at the end of the drive.'

'Have you tried her phone?'

'It's still here, on the table in the living room. Her car's here, too.'

'Where are you now?'

'In the house.'

For the second time in as many days, he told her to stay put, make sure all the doors were locked and wait. He'd be home as soon as he could.

chapter eighty-eight

Alice had purposely said nothing on the way down. Ed, in particular, had tried to engage in conversation, but she'd blanked him, not wanting to give him anything. That had annoyed him. He'd threatened to hurt her but she'd remained resolute. She was unaware of her final destination but guessed it would be London. Her mum was in the capital and even though she didn't know where, that gave her comfort.

Three and a half hours after being snatched, she was taken out of the back of the van straight through the rear entrance door of a run-down building. She was pushed and shoved along a dark corridor, up a flight of stairs and into a room, where the door closed behind her. Then locked.

Curled up in a ball on a bed was a young girl of about eighteen.

'Where am I?' Alice asked.

The girl was sucking her thumb and gave no response. Alice looked around the room. It had one more single bed, a poorly put together chest of drawers with a lamp placed on top. There was another door that led through to a toilet. She tried the main light switch. Nothing.

'It don't work,' the young girl said.

'Just the lamp then?' Alice asked.

'Yep.'

'What's your name? I'm Alice.'

The girl looked at Alice out of the corner of her eye. She could see she was weighing up whether she should tell her.

'Toni.'

'Nice to meet you, Toni.'

'Is it?'

'I hope so. So where am I?'

'London.'

'Thought as much. Where exactly?'

Toni sucked her thumb again. She looked so childlike. Alice sat next to her.

'I don't suppose you have a phone on you, do you?'

Toni smiled.

'What's so funny?' Alice asked, fully aware why.

Toni sat up. She was wearing a thin black top that was at least two sizes too big for her, black leggings and pink socks.

'I don't know where we are,' she said.

'That's a Brummie accent, isn't it?'

Toni nodded. 'Black Country actually.'

'Where's that?'

'Well, it is Brummie, I suppose, but I'm from Dudley, in the Black Country.'

'Right. So you don't know where we are?'

Toni shook her head. 'Only that it's London.'

'So how do you know that?'

'I came here a year ago. Me mum left us, and me dad just beat us. Me and my sister, I mean.'

'So you came to London?'

'Yeah. She's in the next room.'

'Your sister?'

'Donna.'

'So what do you and Donna do here?'

'Sleep with men.'

'What?'

'That's what we do. Every day we sleep with men.'

'In here?'

'No, twice a day we get taken to what we call The Den. Me, Donna and about ten to fifteen other girls. We basically stand around and get picked out. Whoever picks us out takes us into a room and, well, I'm sure you can guess the rest.'

'And you want to do this?'

'Yeah, right. Course we don't, but we have no choice. Neither will you. We'll be getting picked up soon.'

The horror of what was likely to happen to her hit Alice smack in the face. Her mouth became dry. She licked her lips. Her heart raced.

'What do you mean we'll be picked up soon?'

'Just that. We've done the afternoon one, but not the evening one. You'll get used to it. It takes a while but you just become numb to it.'

'Why don't you run?'

Toni laughed. 'You'll see why soon enough.'

Alice realised that no matter where in London her mum was, it was a million miles from her.

chapter eighty-nine

Archie was on the sofa stroking Sarah's head. They'd said nothing for at least twenty minutes. Archie was thinking about Alice, his mum and how they were going to get to Tariq Mali. Sarah was thinking about Spain. He rang his mum as soon as he realised Alice was missing. Her being in London made matters worse. They needed to be together. They were stronger together. Archie felt useless sat on the sofa. He should be doing something. But what could he do? He thought about why Alice would be targeted. Had they targeted her? He'd said to his mum they'd known she'd be in. Why would they risk it, knowing he was back there? Phoebe had reminded him Tariq – if it was him behind it – didn't know he was back. As far as Tariq knew, only she and Alice lived there. She was in London, so any female in the house was likely to be Alice.

Archie was so pent up he couldn't speak. He was glad Sarah was happy to just lie with him. All he could think about was his sister. Where was she and who was she with? He'd always protected her and so he now felt as though he'd let her down. Revenge was at the forefront of his mind. He had to get revenge. He had to get to Tariq Mali.

chapter ninety

Phoebe checked out of her hotel. She couldn't stay in London after what she'd been told. Her baby, her youngest, was missing. All Archie could obtain from the camera on the gate was the rear of a black van with a false registration plate. The men in question had been wise to the camera. The one who'd told Alice he had a parcel had kept his head to the ground. All you could make out was his dark hair. Other than that there was nothing. Phoebe was annoyed. She'd been meaning to upgrade the camera on the gate and install CCTV to give her a better view of who came and went. How she wished she had now.

Things had changed. If Tariq had Alice, Phoebe was not going to wait for any green light from Greg West. She wouldn't wait for anything from anybody. She couldn't believe Tariq would do this. She'd been in London after all, in his company. On the taxi ride to the station, she thought about where Alice could be. She had an awful feeling about this. She recalled Tariq's entrance into the club and the way he was talking on the phone. *Was that Alice he was talking about?* She put her hand to her mouth. *Could he be so callous and have that much front to do that? Would he say that, knowing the mother of the woman he was talking about was sat only feet from him? Was he that brash?* She replayed the conversation and remembered his eyes. *Of course he was* she told herself. *Of course he fucking was.*

This was personal. This was unforgivable. This was war. A war she could not lose.

chapter ninety-one

Alice was on her bed. It was now approaching ten o'clock. Her mind was racing and she didn't like her thoughts. The door unlocked. Two men walked in. One grabbed Toni by the upper arm and dragged her outside. The other got Alice by the hair and dragged her off the bed towards the door. She lashed out and caught his chin with her forearm. He flung her against the landing wall and slapped her hard with the back of his hand as she tried to steady herself.

'Bitch! Fuckin' bitch!' he shouted.

Grabbing her by the hair once more, he marched her down the stairs. She struggled, but it only made it hurt all the more. They reached the bottom, where she noticed the other girls in a room on the right. She was taken left through a separate door, along a corridor, up a different flight of stairs and into a dark seating area. She was pushed to the floor and the door was locked behind her.

She gently put her hands through her hair to see if any came out. Only a few fine hairs did. She was in a box of some sort, like at a sporting venue. In it were two rows of five seats. She looked through the glass. All she could make out was a kind of dimly lit room. She wiped her mouth to check for blood but there wasn't any. She sat down on the front row.

The door unlocked and in walked Tariq, with two men either side of him. Alice got to her feet, conscious she was more vulnerable sat down.

'Evening, Alice, how are you? Room OK for you?'

'Piss off, Tariq.'

'Ooh, feisty! They'll like that. You'll be a good earner for me, Alice.'

'I don't know what you think is gonna happen here, Tariq, but let me tell you, I won't earn you a fuckin' penny.'

'Well, let's see, eh.'

He walked over to her and put his face right into hers. 'Don't put any money on it, will ya, ya fuckin' whore.'

Alice took a step back. 'You need to brush your teeth.'

Tariq slapped her hard with the back of his hand, then yanked her back by her hair. He then licked her cheek very slowly. 'You, young lady, need a lesson in manners.'

He pulled tighter. She wanted to scream, but resisted.

'Sit there!' he barked, as he pushed her down into one of the front row seats. He sat himself to her right. The two men, Mo and Si, sat behind them.

'Now I just want to give you a little insight into what your life is goin' to be like from now on. You've met, er, who was it?' he asked, turning his head.

'Toni,' Si confirmed.

'Ah yes, Toni, one of our two girls from the Black Country. She'll be on in a second. Toni, her sister...' Tariq paused.

'Donna,' Si again confirmed.

'Yes. Toni, her sister Donna and the rest will be parading around any second now. Ah, in fact, here they come. They're for my, let's say, less fussy guests, who pick the one they like and take them through into our specially designed rooms for a good old-fashioned fuck.'

He turned to Alice. 'Or whatever else takes their fancy. It's a no holds barred outfit here. Anything goes, Alice.'

Alice looked straight ahead. Toni seemed to be enjoying the attention, but Alice guessed it was more a case of her doing what was expected of her.

'But *you*, my good little earner, *you* will not be doing this, here in this room. Oh no, I have bigger plans for you. *You*,' he said, squeezing her chin and pulling her face to his, '*you* are going to Amsterdam.' He smiled a wide smile. 'What do you think of that, eh? Amsterdam! Yes, you will be one of the window girls, day after day, seven days a week, getting fucked out of your tiny mind.' He squeezed her lips hard. 'And your fuck face of a family will not have a fuckin' clue where you are. Oh yes, they'll come down 'ere shoutin' the odds, tryin' to find you, but you won't be 'ere. Brilliant, innit?'

He kept her face on his. 'Now then, what was it you said in your text?' He tilted his head towards the ceiling. 'Oh yes, that was it – "surprise".' He turned back to face her. 'Is this surprise enough for ya?' He then burst out laughing and let go of her cheeks.

Alice stared at the girls being chosen. Some had already gone, including Toni. There were five left. A woman came out from behind the darkness and took another one through some curtains.

Alice felt the fight slowly drain from her body. She recalled pausing before sending that text. She knew sending it would lead to something – never for one second thinking it would be her going to Amsterdam. Here in London, she had a chance of being rescued. A very good chance. The thought of her mum, Archie and the others bursting through the door at any moment had never left her mind. But Amsterdam? That was a different scenario altogether.

'Cat got ya tongue?' Tariq laughed. 'What's up – finally dawned on ya, has it? Tell you what. I'll give you a way out. A chance to put Amsterdam right out of your pretty little head.'

She turned to him.

'Tell me where that brother of yours is and once I've put a bullet in his head, I'll set you free.' He leant in towards her. 'But you mustn't tell Mummy about any of this. Deal?'

Alice was a Pearson. How dare he talk about her brother like that. She spat at him and roared, 'Fuck you, Tariq Mali!'

Tariq wiped the phlegm from his face. 'You'll regret that.'

He turned to Si. 'Bring her!' he barked.

Tariq jumped up and walked swiftly out of the door. Si picked Alice up by her upper arm, then tugged her head back by her hair. He marched her a few paces behind Tariq, along a corridor and up a flight of stairs that took them to the second floor. They stopped halfway along a landing and entered a room of seven or eight men. Alice quickly realised these were the men choosing the women below.

'Who wants this one? No charge – it's her first time. Who wants her?'

Every hand went up. They all wanted her.

'Roger, she's yours,' Tariq said with a smile.

A man in his fifties stood up, grinning like a Cheshire cat.

'Si, take her with Roger. Stand outside the door until he's finished, then take her back to her room and lock the fuckin' door. I'll be in my office.'

Tariq marched off, followed by Mo. Alice looked at Roger. He stopped in front of her and stroked her hair.

'Nice, very nice.'

Alice kicked him hard between his legs.

'Fuckin' hell!' Roger shouted, bending over holding his groin. 'For fuck's sake!'

Si was unsure what to do. He'd not expected Alice to do anything. He pulled her outside and looked down the landing. Tariq was marching back.

'What the fuck's she done?' he bellowed.

'Kneed Roger in the bollocks.'

Tariq looked in. Roger was taking deep breaths, still leant with one hand on the wall. Some of the men were sniggering. One or two were looking on in horror.

'Gentlemen, it would appear we have a feisty one here. Please accept my apologies, Roger.' He looked at Mo. 'Bring Roger to my office once he's got his breath back.'

Mo nodded.

'Si, with me.'

Alice was hauled into an office that bore no resemblance to the rest of the building. *This was Tariq's office.* Expensively kitted out.

Tariq was looking out of the window into the night sky. Alice said nothing as she tried to work out whether he was playing her about Amsterdam or if his threat was real.

The door opened. She expected Mo and Roger, but it was a man she'd not yet seen.

'Boss, er, sorry, you busy?'

'You could say that, Roach. What's up?'

'Just Christie wanted to know if you needed any more girls up here tonight?'

'No, we've enough.'

'OK, I'll tell her.'

Roach was just about to leave when Mo and Roger came through.

'Roach, stay here a bit, I might need you,' Tariq ordered.

Roach didn't question it and took a few steps further inside the office.

Tariq walked over to Alice. 'You need to realise your place, young lady. Women your age should be looking after their husbands. Those who aren't are nothin' more than whores, just like the women we have here. There's no in between. Seein' as you're not married, you must be a whore. So you'll be treated like one.'

He looked at Roach and then Si. 'Hold her down, gentlemen. Roger here needs to get what was promised him.'

He then looked at Roger. 'All yours, sir.'

Si seized Alice by both arms and pressed her down to the floor. She tried to fight him off, but Si was far too strong.

'Giz a fuckin' hand then,' he said, looking at Roach, as he tried to flatten her arms.

Roach looked at Tariq.

'Hold her fuckin' down!' Tariq ordered.

Roach looked at Roger, who was undoing his flies. He punched him so hard on the jaw, they heard it break. Roger fell to the floor, out cold before his head bounced off the thick carpet. Roach then punched Mo, who was transfixed on Roger. Mo fell back into the door, but got to his feet. Si let go of Alice and threw his arms around Roach. Mo hit Roach hard in the face, then the body, before hard on the jaw again. The second punch to his face knocked the back of Roach's head into Si, which allowed him to shake him off.

'Fuckin' stop her!' Tariq shouted, as Alice bolted for the door.

Mo lunged for Alice. Si hit Roach in the kidneys. Tariq was now in on the action. Roach battled hard but was overpowered. They threw him to the floor and booted him again and again. Out of breath, they eventually stopped. Roach lay curled up in a ball.

Si stood over him while Tariq, gasping for breath, made a call downstairs. 'Get up here, all three of you. I've got a piece of shit for you to dispose of.'

***

Tariq told Mo to take Alice back to her room. Roach had saved her from being raped and the three men who'd kidnapped her had taken him away. She had no idea what happened to Roger. Toni was yet to appear.

chapter ninety-two

Roach was in an alleyway half a mile from the club. He knew he'd be killed and his body dumped or buried. The only thing he could do was throw himself out of the back of the van he'd been bundled into. As soon as he realised only Isaac was in the back with him, he knew he had a chance. It took all his strength, but Isaac wasn't the biggest of blokes, and a headbutt had given him that small window of opportunity.

Slumped against a cold stone wall, out of a job and aching all over, he told himself he was lucky he was still alive. The one thing he did have was his principles. Roach was a lot of things. He'd done his fair share of illegal activity and he'd been involved in the sex trade for a good few years. He was mainly muscle and protection for Tariq, but by association he was part of Tariq's business dealings. Despite battling with it, to his eternal shame, he'd pretended it was all OK, these women having no choice in what they were subjected to. One thing he would not do, however, was stand by and watch a woman be raped. If he'd allowed that to happen to Alice, he'd never have been able to forgive himself. He got up, wincing, and walked slowly out onto the street. He had something to do. He needed to make a few calls.

chapter ninety-three

Phoebe was on her way home, weary and seriously angry. The train journey back to Newark had allowed her time to think. She thought of the fracas at Jez's wake, which involved Tariq, and Archie fleeing to Spain, which was also down to Tariq. The opportunity to import illegal firearms, which turned out to be a plot to take her and the family down, was all because of Tariq. Brian and Knighty being gunned down was Tariq's doing, and Alice being bundled into the back of a van was, she had no doubt, down to him. This one man was causing all the grief in her life. She had to sort him. How she was going to do it was the biggest question of all.

Tariq was well protected and would be hard to get hold of. She didn't really want to go in mob-handed and take him out in full view of onlookers. That would only serve to bring unimaginable pressure and hassle for her and the whole Pearson empire. She wouldn't be able to talk her way or indeed pay her way out of that one. But, she conspired, it might be the only way. She knew nothing of Tariq's general movements, his weaknesses, or ways of tempting him in. For what seemed like the millionth time recently, she wondered what Frank would do. Would he go in gung ho and shoot his way out of the problem? She doubted that very much. Would he wait and bide his time? Not with his granddaughter missing and at Tariq's mercy he wouldn't. *So, what would you do, Frank? What would you do?*

She looked out at the night sky. It was cloudy, but she could see the moon shining brightly. She realised that no matter how big her problems were, the moon would still shine and the sun would still rise in the morning. The world would keep spinning and life would go on. Archie had told her something similar that Hugh had said to him when they were looking at the sea. It struck a chord with her. She now realised what Hugh was talking about. Despite the weight on her shoulders, she was really quite insignificant in the grand scheme of things.

She was looking for inspiration, but it appeared Frank was not listening. She concluded she'd just have to do this on her own. Whatever the outcome, she needed to find her baby. She rested her head on the window, hoping and praying Alice was OK. She needed something, anything, to give her an edge.

The train approached Newark station. Phoebe had opted for Raquel to pick her up, knowing that if she asked any of the others the journey back to Southwell would be filled with ideas of *let's just fuckin' do 'im, fuck the consequences.* Phoebe didn't need that. Raquel would be more measured. It rankled Pat, but as she'd tried to explain to him, sometimes she just needed a girlie chat – even if that girlie chat was about taking on Tariq Mali.

Raquel was waiting on the platform. She put her arms around Phoebe and told her things would be OK.

'Don't suppose there's any news then?' she asked.

Raquel shook her head. Once in the car, she said the one thing Phoebe needed to hear: 'Everyone's chomping at the bit, everyone wants to help – and I mean everyone.'

'Who knows?'

'Just the people you'd expect. We haven't broadcasted it. By everyone, I mean Gloria.'

'Gloria?'

'Yep. In fact, her exact words were "I don't care who he thinks he is, if there's anything you want me to do, just say the word".'

Phoebe smiled. 'Frank would bloody love it if Gloria was the one to bring him down. He'd be made up.'

'Don't dismiss it, you know. They don't know her in Tariq's circles. All I'm saying is keep your options open.'

'He'll know her from Jez's wake and from Frank's funeral. Daniel's, too. He'll know her, he's not daft.'

'Fair point, but she's in the background is Gloria. Done up in some sort of disguise, well, you just never know. Anyway, we won't need her to do anything, I'm sure.'

Phoebe just could not see Gloria being of any use. 'It's nice she wants to help, but I won't put her in any danger. She's not like us, Raquel.'

'So what's the plan?'

'Oh, fuck knows. I just keep coming back to thinking we have no option but to go in all guns blazing, but then I think go in where? We don't even know where Alice is. Tariq would rather die than tell us, and as much as I want to kill him – and I will, mark my words – my main focus is to find out where Alice is. She must be scared out of her wits.'

'Thing is, Tariq and maybe Mo are the only ones we know who could tell us. I know he has two or three other guys around him, but I don't really know them.'

'Nor do any of us. If this has taught me one thing, it's to know your enemies and their entire set-up. It's no good us just knowing about Tariq and his sidekick, Mo. We should know his whole operation. Knowledge is king, don't they say?'

'Yeah, that was one thing Frank was not overly good at – sharing information like this. I know he and his opposites shared stuff like that, but he never did with us. He took that information with him unfortunately.'

'We've got to find her, we just have to. I dread to think what might happen to her.'

'How was your meeting with Tariq anyway?' Raquel asked.

'Well, put it this way – if I thought he was a prick before, he more than confirmed it. He's so far up himself. He came waltzing across the floor on his phone, shouting so everyone could hear that "she needed a lesson" and to bring her to him.'

'All for your ears then.'

'Yeah, I'd say so. Thing is, the timing all ties in with Alice. I'm wondering if he was talking about her 'cos he was striding towards me, looking me straight in the eye, when he said it.'

'Unfortunately, I can see him doing that. Well, look, everyone's coming round at ten in the morning, as you requested. Let's hope someone has something.'

'Anything.'

'I thought you might go straight back to see him – you know, while you were down there.'

'It did cross my mind, but to be honest, that's what he wants me to do. I just could not give him the satisfaction, and he'd only deny it. Frank taught us to keep the likes of him guessing, so pardon the pun, but I guess that's what I'm doing.'

It was quarter past one in the morning when Phoebe arrived home. She had a cup of tea with Archie and Sarah, and had a similar conversation with them to her one with Raquel. Archie struggled to keep his anger in check. Phoebe wondered if it was because he felt he had something to prove. Was this his opportunity to show the world he was back and the past few months had been nothing more than a blip? She decided not to tell him her concerns, but was determined to rein him in. A man like Archie feeling he has something to prove can be dangerous – a loose cannon. A loose cannon can get people hurt, especially those closest to them. Phoebe was not about to let Archie's ego put Alice in any more danger.

chapter ninety-four

Alice had hardly slept a wink all night. Toni reappeared just before twelve. Alice couldn't help ask about her previous couple of hours. It had been a fairly normal client she said. Someone who wanted a blow job and a jump. This one, though, had also wanted to lie and cuddle her for an hour afterwards. She told Alice how that sometimes happens, usually when they don't get that affection from their dreary home lives. Alice was surprised. She'd assumed the clients would all be wealthy. Toni confirmed some were, but others were fairly normal blokes who had boring jobs and boring home lives. They didn't get their needs met at home, so came to The Den. Toni concluded the reason they came here, in particular, was because it gave them a sense of power having women parade in front of them. It added to the kinkiness, too. Most got off on seeing their prey paraded before them. That's why most came within a few humps, they were already that excited.

Alice asked her about Amsterdam, saying she'd overheard a conversation about a girl being sent there. Toni said it did happen, mainly when the girls were no longer being picked regularly. They called it being sent to the knacker's yard – if you're no good for the bottom rung of the Soho ladder, then life in Amsterdam had to be pretty grim. This did nothing to allay Alice's fears or to assure her Tariq had just been playing her.

She stared at the ceiling, wondering what plan her mum and Archie had. Little did she know they didn't yet have one.

chapter ninety-five

'It's the only option we have. We've discussed it for how long now, an hour and a half, and the only option we have is to take the bull by the horns and torture it out of him. Or we go and talk to him. But, as we've said a number of times this morning, that'll be a waste of our energy,' Phoebe said, confirming everyone's thoughts.

'When and where is the only question,' said Del.

'That's two questions,' Ryan quipped.

'Twat,' Del mouthed to him.

'Ideally, we need to nab him on the street and take him somewhere secluded.'

'So we need to watch every one of his clubs, see when he's in which one and pounce when we get the opportunity.'

'Take a lot of manpower that, Phoebe. And time. Time Alice may not have,' Trainer pointed out.

'Fair point.'

Archie's phone pinged. It was a notification that someone was at the gates in Southwell. He'd only installed the function yesterday. The guy who set it up for him couldn't believe he didn't already have it. He said the system they had was ancient. It brought home to the family that they'd taken security very lightly over the years, with not feeling at threat in their own community. Recent events, however, had highlighted danger could come from anywhere.

Archie shot up. 'Someone's at the house. Who the fuck's that?' he said, showing it to Trainer, who was sat next to him.

'No idea, mate, but he's been in the fuckin' wars whoever he is. Ask him. You can talk through the intercom there on your phone, remember. Giz it 'ere.'

Trainer held the phone to his mouth. 'Hello?'

'Er, hello, I'm looking for Phoebe Pearson. Is she in?'

Archie grabbed the phone and looked at his mum.

'Who wants her?'

'She'll know me as Roach.'

'Who?'

'Roach. Tell her it's Roach.'

'Never heard of you, mate. She ain't in.'

Phoebe got up and walked the couple of paces to stand behind Archie. She took the phone from his hand and looked at the face of the man who was asking for her.

'Roach, this is Phoebe. What can I do for you?'

'It's more of what I can do for you, Mrs Pearson. Well, more for you and Alice. Can I come in?'

chapter ninety-six

Archie, Trainer and Jase arrived at Phoebe's house in Southwell. As they pulled up outside the gates, they saw who they assumed was Roach inside a dark-blue Range Rover. They all got out, as did Roach.

'I'm on my own, gents – you have my word.'

'I'm sure you are, but you won't mind a quick pat down, will ya?' Archie said.

Roach opened his arms.

'How did you find us?'

'Once you get round 'ere, it ain't gonna be hard to find out where Phoebe Pearson lives, is it? Not exactly the bright lights of London.'

'He's clean,' Trainer said.

'What do you know about Alice?' Archie asked.

'Look fellas, I'm freezing my nuts off here. There's no hidden agenda. I ain't come all this way for nothin'. I want to talk to Mrs Pearson, or else I'll get myself off back south.'

Archie studied him while Jase checked the car. He'd certainly been in a fight of sorts.

'All good,' Jase shouted.

'So, can we go?' Roach asked.

'OK, I'll come with you,' Archie said, throwing his car keys to Jase.

'No problem.'

'I'm Archie by the way.'

Roach laughed a little.

'What's funny?'

'Tariq'd pay good money to be here with you. He hates your fuckin' guts. Wants you dead, don't he?'

'Apparently. You're not plannin' on collectin', are ya?' Archie said sarcastically.

'Nah. Outnumbered anyway, ain't I?'

'What happened to ya face?' Archie asked.

'A result of saving Alice.'

'Is she OK? Where is she?'

Roach looked over at Archie before concentrating back on the road. 'Look, she's in serious danger. I ain't gonna sugarcoat it, but the reason I got this,' he said, pointing to his face, 'and the rest you can't see, is 'cos I saved her from being raped.'

He paused, aware that last sentence would be difficult to hear.

'Raped?'

'He's a nasty fucker, Archie. He needs stoppin'.'

'So what can you offer us and why you here?'

'I can tell you where she is, for now.'

'What d'you mean "for now"?'

'I heard he has plans to send her to Amsterdam.'

'Amsterdam? When?'

'That's the thing, I've no idea. It could be a bluff. He's threatened girls with it before, but 'cos it's your sister, my guess is she'll be on her way soon.'

'Fuckin' hell. Can we get to her today?'

'Depends on how quickly he moves her. If he does, given I'm not flavour of the month, it'll be hard to track her.'

Archie stared out of his window. He couldn't remember the last time he felt so angry.

'So why you here? You never answered.'

'Cos it ain't right. I'm no saint – fuck me, I've worked for Tariq for long enough – but that ain't right. Asking me to....'

'Go on – don't hold back.'

'Asking me to hold her down while some dirty fucker rapes her is not my style.'

'I don't know you, Roach, but if what you're sayin' is right, we owe you.'

They exchanged looks.

'And you did save her, yeah?'

'She didn't get raped last night. I broke the dirty fucker's jaw and then had a row with two of Tariq's men, Mo and Si. Even Tariq landed a few blows, and he normally just sits and watches. I was supposed to be popped but I managed to get out. Had a chat with the tarmac in the process, though.'

'Does he know you're still alive?'

'No idea. Depends what the lads said when they got back. If they blag it, they'll regret it, cos I ain't one for sittin' in the wings. He'll get to know I'm still breathin' soon enough and then they'll pay for it.'

It took twenty-five minutes to get to Frank's house, in Papplewick. They drove through Oxton and Roach commented on how nice it was.

'So this is where the legend lived then, eh?' Roach said, as they drove up the drive.

'Yep. A true legend. They don't make 'em like him any more,' Archie said. Roach could sense the love and pride he had for his grandad. 'I hear he was one of a dying breed. I'd've loved to have met him.'

Roach admired the house. It was grand but it had a real warm, family feel. He'd never been in a house like this before. Tariq's was big and luxurious, but compared to this, his had no soul. If the house was a measure of Frank, he could see why people said what they did about him.

'This is my mum,' Archie said, as Phoebe came out to greet them.

'Mrs Pearson,' he said, holding out his hand. 'Nice to meet you again.'

'Come in. Tariq do that to you?' she asked, looking at his face.

'Him and two others.'

'This is Gloria, Frank's better half.'

'Hello, luv, would you like a cuppa?'

'Tea, two sugars please. Thank you.'

'Coming right up.'

Gloria was desperate to ask about Alice, but knew to leave it to Phoebe and the others.

Roach walked into the boardroom behind Phoebe. He saw a sea of faces that all looked like they wanted to kill him.

'Roach, this is my top team. I won't do names because you'll only forget, but let's get straight to it. You said you could help us and Alice?'

'Yes. I know where she is.'

'Go on.'

Roach was impressed by Phoebe's presence. As hard as these men in the room were, she most certainly held authority. He waited for Archie, Trainer and Jase to take their seats before continuing.

'You know the club where we met the other day?'

'Yes.'

'Well, she's in another one a few streets away. A smaller club, down one of the back streets.'

'We need to get to her quickly, Mum. He reckons they might take her to Amsterdam.'

'Amsterdam?'

'I believe so, yes.'

'When?'

'I don't know, Mrs Pearson. I said to Archie it could be a bluff, but given who she is, I reckon she'll be on her way soon enough. But if she ain't, she's still in serious danger.'

'Go on.'

'Well, the club she's in may be small but it hides a murky secret. It's where Tariq houses some of his girls. They're never allowed out.'

'What do you mean?'

'They're basically imprisoned. They sleep there, eat there, and work there. Twice a day they get paraded to men who pay for the privilege of choosing one of them for however long they've paid to have 'em. The girls never see the light of day, which is why most of them end up in Amsterdam – it don't take long for looks and smooth complexion to start disappearing.'

'And that's where he has her?'

'It is.'

'How do we know we can trust you?'

'You don't, you only have my word – but my word's good.'

'Who gave you your beatin'?' Pat asked.

'I got it after savin' Alice from being raped.'

Phoebe looked horrified.

'So let's just say I ain't welcome back.'

Phoebe straightened her skirt. Roach knew it was her way of composing herself.

'So how do we get to her?'

'Well, I can take you to the club, but you must appreciate she might not be there. The sooner we get there, the better.'

'Is there no way you can call someone to see if she's there?' Michael asked.

'No chance. I was supposed to be killed. If I make a call, he'll get to know about it and she'll be in more danger.'

'How many men does Tariq have at that club?' Phoebe asked.

'Oh, thank you,' Roach said, taking his tea from Gloria.

'Some biscuits there for you, luv, if you want them.'

Roach smiled. 'Thanks.' He looked at Phoebe. 'Two or three. He gets no grief there, you see. The women are all ex-druggies or found themselves with nowhere to go. He likes to think he rescues them. Once they get past their best, he ships them to Amsterdam.'

'So muscle is light?' Pēteris asked.

Roach looked around the table. 'You shouldn't have any problem. Time's crucial, though. He could have an army there pretty quick if he gets wind of anythin'.'

'So why the conscience all of a sudden?' Pat asked.

Roach sensed his tone. 'I'm a lot of things, pal, but I ain't gonna stand by and watch a young lady get raped. He asked me to hold her down.' He was starting to get annoyed. 'Imagine that. I don't know about you but that ain't my bag.'

'But seeing women abused daily is?'

Roach looked at Phoebe. 'I'll get myself off, Mrs Pearson. Things are gettin' uneasy and, well, I'm at a slight disadvantage, if you get my drift.' He got to his feet.

Phoebe had allowed Roach his moment and understood his annoyance. She looked at Pat, who held Roach's stare. He held out his hand. Roach shook it.

'Fair enough. Just had to ask.'

Phoebe needed to intervene.

'Well, from me, Roach, thank you. And I'm sure I speak on behalf of everyone here when I say that if we get Alice back, we'll owe you.'

'I had my line, Mrs Pearson, and it's just been crossed, that's all I'm sayin'.'

She smiled before addressing her team. 'Right, folks, we know what we need to do, but once we have Alice, I want Tariq. How do we get to him?' Phoebe asked.

'If I was you, Mrs Pearson—'

'Phoebe, please call me Phoebe.'

'If I was you, Phoebe, I'd do it at the same time. If you manage to get Alice, he'll know about it before she's in whatever vehicle you put her in. He'll up his security and, well, it'll be full-blown war.'

'Where will he be, though?'

Roach took a deep breath. He'd thought about what he was about to say long and hard, but it was the right thing to do.

'If I make my presence known before you spring Alice, he'll be distracted with me. Wherever I turn up, Tariq will be there very quickly. He either thinks I'm dead or wants to finish the job off. That'll give you a chance to get your daughter. Remember, it won't take much muscle to get her out. Once she's with you, the rest of your guys can go for Tariq.'

'You'd put yourself up as bait?'

'More of a distraction I'd say but, well, maybe bait too, yeah. Why – you got a better idea?'

'Why would you do that?'

'He wanted me to hold your daughter down and watch her being fucked against her will. That's unforgivable.'

No words were needed. The looks said it all.

'Pat – you, Michael and Del get Alice. I'll be with you. I want to be there. Archie – you and everyone else will be with Roach, waiting to get Tariq at his main club. Once we have Alice, I'll ring you,' Phoebe said. 'I want Mo, too. Anyone else, Roach?'

'I ain't gonna go to his main club.'

'Why not?'

'Too many eyes. It'll be busy, it always is.'

Phoebe frowned. 'Why would you not want to be around many people? Surely that would make you safer? He's less likely to put a bullet in your head.'

Roach could feel the stares. He'd already sensed Pat distrusted him. 'It ain't about me, is it? It's about you gettin' your daughter and then takin' out Tariq.'

'What – are you suggesting you turn up where Alice is?'

'No, definitely not. What I'm sayin' is that once you have Alice, you won't be able to just walk in his main gaff and take him out. Well, you could, but can you seriously see that playin' out? You've been in that club. How d'you think you'd get to him? There are access codes on all doors from the main floor, with doormen on them, too, remember.'

Roach then did a quick count-up. 'There's twelve of you 'ere. It'd be too visible, even if four of you were busy gettin' Alice. Eight men like you lot waltzin' in and tryin' to get to him without attracting attention – impossible. You'd have to shoot your way to him.'

Phoebe could see his point. She'd been so wrapped up in getting Alice, and so consumed with taking out Tariq, she'd forgotten Frank's golden rule: *respond*. Phoebe was *reacting*. She needed a response.

'Good job you're here, Roach. I see what you're saying. Everyone agree with that?'

Most of them nodded. A few said 'yeah'.

'So which club?' Archie asked.

'Three streets away from where Alice is, is a members-only club. It's small and kept for, let's say, the more elite members of society.'

'The posh knobs then.'

'Yeah, you could say that. It's down one of the quieter streets, away from the crowds. That's why the clientele like it. I'll go there. It'll be easier for you to get in, far easier. There'll be two doormen – there always are – a fella on reception, and maybe two bar staff. The waitresses won't be on till later tonight.'

Phoebe studied Roach carefully. His face told her to trust him. Her heart told her to trust him. But her head had a niggling doubt.

'That could make you a sitting duck,' she said.

'I know. Life can be shit like that, can't it?'

She held his stare.

'All I have is my word, but my word's good. Sometimes you just know it's the right thing to do. You need your daughter back and I need my life back.'

That niggling doubt went.

'So, as I said a moment ago, who else should we target?' Phoebe asked.

'A guy called Si, so-called 'cos he's a psycho. He was holding Alice down, waiting for me to join him. Get him, too.' Roach took in the room. 'You've got a large top team, Phoebe. You may be surprised to hear Tariq only has four top men around him. Get them and the rest will fall. For all his power, I can now see he's actually quite vulnerable.'

'Who are the four?' Archie asked.

'Mo, me, Si and Lester.'

Archie had his moment. 'So what about Lester?'

Roach smiled. 'I thought you guys might tell me.'

chapter ninety-seven

Alice was woken by two men barging into the room. With nothing to do other than worry about her predicament, she'd succumbed to the tiredness. She was grabbed by one of the men, while Toni more or less stood to attention when they walked in. Toni walked in obeyance along the landing. Alice was dragged. She assumed they were being taken to The Den for the first session of the day, so was surprised to be herded into a shower block. There were four shower cubicles and four toilets. Alice counted fourteen women of varying ages.

'What's happening?' she asked Toni.

'We get showered once a day, every day. We can clean our teeth, too.'

'Are these all the girls you were with last night?'

'Yeah. There should be fourteen of us if everyone is here. Fifteen with you.'

Alice stared in bewilderment while the first four women showered.

'I'd start getting undressed if I were you. We don't get long. The shower gel and shampoo are in that tall cupboard there. There's razors, too, as most of us like to be clean shaven. It helps with hygiene.'

Alice opened the cupboard door to find rows of shower gel and shampoo, razors, which she was pleased to see were individually packaged, and tampons. *What else could a girl need* she thought. Though she was not going to let anyone touch her, she was not about to let the opportunity of a shower pass her by.

'Any toothbrushes?'

'In that small cupboard there. Toothpaste, too.'

Alice followed Toni's lead. She introduced her to her sister, Donna, who looked older, but not by much. Noting the women were now sharing the showers, she sneaked in with Toni.

'At least they're hot.'

'Not always.'

They quickly dried themselves before taking turns to brush their teeth.

'No chance of a hair dryer, is there?' Alice asked.

'We've been promised one ever since I came here. Just towel dry it and do your best.'

Ten minutes later, they were being led back along the landing to their rooms. Alice felt much better, amazed at how invigorating a hot shower could be in even the grimiest of places.

'We'll be collected soon,' Toni said.

Alice said nothing, praying that her mum and Archie were doing something. The thought of being paraded in front of leering men did nothing for her mood. The thought of having to fight them off did even less. And the thought of Amsterdam scared her shitless. Her family had no real ties there, save a few contacts, so tracking her down would be hard – that's if they knew she was there of course. Tariq would never divulge that, so they'd be left thinking she'd basically disappeared off the face of the earth. *Amsterdam can't happen* she told herself.

To avoid thinking all sorts of horrible things, she chatted to Toni. She found out she'd wanted to be an actress. Her plan was to come to London and walk the boards of the West End. Donna was a singer, and she too had dreams of singing to nightly audiences. The worst thing they could have done was walk into one of Tariq's clubs and get talking to one of the doormen. Like others before them, they got swept away by his promises of introductions to contacts within the industry. Their biggest regret was agreeing to meet him the next day. That was the last time they tasted freedom. It was a sad tale of dreams and ambition, but a tale, according to Toni, that was all too common.

'Rose-tinted glasses affect your vision,' Toni said. And her glasses were removed the minute she walked into that room.

'You sound as though you've given up the fight?' Alice said, saddened by what she'd heard.

Toni laughed. 'I gave that up within a few days of being here.'

'Has no one ever escaped?'

'Not since I've been here. I mean, how could you? Why, do you think you can? Something special, are ya?' She sounded resentful.

'No, there's nothing special about me,' Alice replied, not wanting to give any false hope.

She did have hope – hope that included her mum and her brother – but it didn't feel too strong. The longer the clock ticked, the more likely Amsterdam was becoming. She couldn't quite believe that she was hoping she'd be paraded along with the rest of them today. Anything but Amsterdam.

chapter ninety-eight

'Come on, Mum, we need to go!' Archie shouted from the doorway.

The cars were ready. Each one untraceable. It had taken less than an hour to get the vehicles required. When the Pearsons needed a favour, there was no shortage of people willing to assist. Association with the Pearson family was enough to get them the street cred they craved. For the Pearsons, it was another reminder of their power.

Phoebe came through. She was on her phone.

'I won't forget this. I owe you.' She listened for a moment before finishing. 'Well, that's very good of you, but as I say, I won't forget it.'

'Who was that?'

'No one. Just something I needed sorting.'

chapter ninety-nine

Tariq was in the office of his most exclusive club. He was in a jovial mood. He'd heard nothing from Phoebe, which unnerved him slightly, but his inner circle weren't going to know that.

His phone rang. It was his main contact in Amsterdam.

'Albert, I hope this ain't bad news,' he joked.

'I'm afraid it is, my English friend.'

Tariq took his feet off his desk and sat up.

'What d'ya mean?'

'We will have to wait. Now is not possible. It's not good time.'

'Like fuck we will. What d'you mean it's not a good time? Says who?' Tariq shouted.

'Tariq, we know each other long time. We do good business. Do not spoil the relationship. Now is not good. She cannot come. We have to wait.'

'Look, Albert, I have no idea what the fuck is goin' on with you, but we're all set. She's comin' later today – we agreed, so do not fuck me about.'

'I not argue with you, but my men will not be there to meet. She not come. It is final. If you bring her, we do no more business, ever.'

There was a pause. 'And Tariq, do not fuck me about either. You show me disrespect again and I cut off your balls.'

The line went dead. Tariq threw his phone against the wall. 'That fuckin' bastard is trying to dictate to me! Who the fuck is he?!'

He looked at Mo. 'Who the fuck is he, eh?' he shouted again.

'What you gonna do?' Mo asked, having got the gist of the call.

'Sort that fucker out next time I see him, that's what.'

'I mean with Alice.'

'I know what you fuckin' mean.'

Mo knew now was a good time to remain tight-lipped. He picked up Tariq's phone. It worked, but looked like it had been stamped on.

Tariq made a call.

'Put her in the fuckin' mix with the rest for now.'

Mo could almost see the anger rising through his body.

'Just fuckin' do it,' Tariq reiterated. He looked at his phone. 'Get me a new one,' he ordered.

Tariq stared at the wall, his hands on his hips. He needed to think. This was a setback all right, one he'd not planned for. He'd never been told it was not a good time. He'd never had to postpone trafficking his women over the Channel either. And Tariq Mali had never been told he'd have his balls chopped off. He was in uncharted territory and he didn't like it one bit.

chapter one hundred

Roach was in the lead car with Phoebe, Pat, Archie and Raquel. Phoebe wanted him to be with her, to find out his story and as much as she could about Tariq. She knew Tariq's history to a degree – that he'd started off providing women on some sort of rental scheme back in the day to the likes of Barraq and Akrad from Leicester, two men who had felt the wrath of Frank. Other than that, she was largely unaware of how he'd risen to become king of the sex trade in the capital. On speaking with Roach, it turned out he knew as much as she did about Tariq's past.

'I've only known what he's like since I first started working for him in that club cloakroom. If I'd not intervened that night when he was about to be sliced, I don't know where I'd be now.'

'You'd be doing something similar. It draws us in, does this life. I mean, look at me. I was just one of the women, married to Daniel. I never imagined I'd be heading the family business – never in my wildest dreams – but once you get that buzz, it never leaves you.'

'Like chasing the dragon, I s'pose.'

'Probably. Always chasing that feeling.'

'When did you first get it?' Roach asked.

Phoebe was instantly transported back to the nineties, when she plunged a knife into the back of the guy who'd tried to rape her. He was one of the men Barraq and Akrad had sent up to the house she had with Daniel. Richie had saved her, but had taken a beating. At first she was terrified she'd spend the rest of her life in prison, but on discovering she wasn't going to have to answer for it, she realised she'd enjoyed the adrenaline rush. She had crossed the line.

It took her a few years to process it and accept who she was but after Daniel was murdered, she found herself wanting to be involved in the family business. Chasing the dragon, as Roach put it.

'A long time ago, let's just say that,' she told him.

Roach nodded. She wasn't going to spill the beans on her past to him.

'So Tariq's route to the top remains a mystery then, eh?' Archie said.

'He did it out of sheer brutality,' Raquel piped up. Raquel had been a whore close to thirty years ago, prior to meeting Daniel one night off the train at Nottingham.

'You know then?' Roach asked.

'I know enough. I was part of that life back then. Not one of Tariq's women, but I had a pimp, so I knew the players in the game.'

'Tariq was one, was he?'

'He was small fry back then. The Tariq of the day was a totally different guy. Tariq filled the void after he retired, but he filled it with torture, bloodshed and death. The Soho sex trade was never the same again.'

'Well, he ain't mellowed with age, let me tell you,' Roach said. 'He's as ruthless as ever with the women.'

The car went quiet. Roach eventually realised that was not what they wanted to hear. He wanted to explain what he meant, but thought it best not to. He didn't want to dig himself a hole.

He'd left his car in Papplewick, to not risk it being spotted. He was nervous about what would unfold when he met Tariq. He could well be shot on sight. Tariq was likely to do that. He couldn't quite believe what had happened in the past twenty-four hours, but for the first time since entering the gangster world, he felt he was doing the right thing. He'd only ever experienced Tariq's world. It was all he'd ever had to go on.

Being in the company of Phoebe and her team, he was now seeing a different side to the people who controlled organised crime. It was a side he liked. It was who he wanted to be. As he looked at the roadside whizzing past, he prayed he'd be around to be that man.

chapter one hundred and one

The door flew open. Alice was manhandled out of the room. Toni followed. While Alice was marched along the landing, women came out of their rooms waiting for instruction, as if they were in the armed forces.

On passing the separate door she'd been taken through the previous night, Alice realised she was going with all the others. She put her brakes on. A man with a ridiculously long beard yanked her hair and dragged her along. Finally, she was shoved into a chair. Within the space of a minute, every single seat was taken.

No one spoke. Everyone looked haunted. Some looked like they were craving their drug of choice. Others looked like they'd been in the sex trade for years. She looked at Toni, then at her sister. They were as gaunt and drawn as everyone else. Alice wondered why anyone, given the choice they had around the streets of Soho, would pay to sleep with any of the girls here. It really was a pitiful sight.

In the room with them were two men. The one with the beard, plus one other, who Alice had clocked the previous night. She couldn't understand why the women hadn't grouped together and fought back. Fifteen against two were very good odds. But none of them could weigh more than nine stone. They weren't just physically weak, they were mentally weak, too. Not one of them looked like they had any fight in them. The two men in the room, on the other hand, were tall, solid, tough-looking.

A woman came in through a door in what was a false wall. Behind it were velvet curtains. She opened them to reveal what Alice recognised to be The Den – the arena where they would be paraded. She felt fear she'd not felt for a long time. Alice made a decision. There was no way anyone was parading her. If she was going in there, she was going in fighting. And she banked on no one wanting the girl making a scene. What she wasn't yet aware of was what a fucking scene it was going to be.

chapter one hundred and two

Phoebe was parked up a few yards from where they expected Alice to be. She rang Archie to ensure all was going to plan. He'd swapped cars at London Gateway Services. Roach had done the same. In the lead car, driven by Raquel, were Phoebe, Pat, Del and Michael. Raquel was to stay in the vehicle. Pat, Del and Michael would rescue Alice once Roach had sent the text. If Roach's information on the muscle was correct, they should have no worries. The rest of them were parked in two cars fifty yards from the club Roach was to walk into.

Roach was right – the street was quiet. It was only metres from the hustle and bustle of Soho, yet it seemed miles away. Roach would enter on his own and give the green light to Phoebe. She felt as though everything had been rushed – it had, but time was against them. She needed luck to be on her side.

'You guys all set?' she asked.

'All good, Mum. You?'

'Same. Stay safe, Son.'

'And you.'

Archie turned to Roach. 'You're on, pal.'

'Good luck, gents,' he said, as he opened the door. He checked his phone as he walked towards the club entrance. His text to Phoebe was ready: *Good to go.* All he had to do was press send.

Trainer was in the front next to Archie. 'You trust him?'

'He was the edge we were looking for,' Archie replied.

'Not what I asked. Do you trust him?'

Archie looked over. 'Yeah.'

Roach walked through the main door. He'd expected Russell, the head doorman, to be on duty – and he was.

'Russ,' Roach said confidently.

Russell, evidently surprised to see him, blocked his way.

'Kieran not on today with ya? Thought you two were joined at the hip.'

'You've got some front, ain't ya?'

'He in?' Roach asked.

'Nah, but he will be any minute. You do know I have to contact him.'

'Course. I'll wait in the bar. Nice and visible, if you know what I mean.'

Roach stepped aside to walk through the next set of doors. Russell grabbed his arm.

'He'll kill ya, Roach – you do know that.'

'We'll see. You never know, I might catch him on a good day.'

He then looked down at Russell's hand, as if to say *do you mind?*

Russell loosened his grip.

Roach walked in. Russell made a call. Kieran was still shagging one of the cleaners.

Archie had eyes on Roach all the way to the entrance to the club. All twenty-seven seconds. In these situations, people hardly spoke. Even though they were all seasoned criminals, everyone preferred to sit with their own thoughts – trying to work out how things would go, trying to second-guess the reactions of those they'd face, trying to see themselves coming out on top. Negative thoughts would creep in, but they were quickly pushed to one side.

Roach ordered a drink. He could see the nervousness on the barman's face. Russell's reaction told him Tariq knew he was still alive and that Isaac and the others hadn't tried to cover their tracks. He looked around the club. There were five punters in. He placed his phone on the bar next to his glass.

Roach had been in the club for seven minutes when Archie saw two cars pull up outside. He leant towards his windscreen to see Tariq walk in, with who he thought was Mo. One other guy followed a step behind. The cars stayed where they were.

'He's just walked in,' Archie said.

'Clocked him,' Ryan confirmed from the back.

'Those motors ain't movin', so we can expect a bit of muscle to be sat in 'em.'

'Do we sort them before we go in?' Trainer asked.

'No. When we get the nod, we just walk in as if we're punters. Give nothing away.'

'That'll mean the weapons'll have to stay in the cars,' Trainer pointed out.

Archie hesitated. 'It does, but fuck it, we'll be OK.'

No one had really noticed that Archie was the one making the decisions. He'd assumed the role of the one in charge, with everyone following his lead. It was as though he'd never been away.

Archie rang Pēteris, who was in the car behind. 'Get ready, gents. Game on soon. But see those cars?'

'Yeah.'

'Well, they mean you leave the weapons in the boot. We walk in as though we're paying customers. If they get wind, well, we'll just have to deal with 'em.'

Tariq stopped on clocking Roach sat at the bar. Roach kept his eyes on him and placed his hand on his phone. He glanced at the screen. The text was there. As discreetly as he could, keeping one eye on Tariq, he tapped send. The room was dimly lit. Tariq didn't notice.

A few streets away, Phoebe's phone pinged.

Good to go

chapter one hundred and three

'Gents, you know what to do. If Roach is right, we shouldn't encounter any grief, but take no prisoners. I want Alice out quickly and safely.'

'If she's in there, Phoebe, we'll get her, make no mistake,' Del said.

'I know. Right, let's go.'

Phoebe led the way through the main doors of what looked to be a very dingy club. The entire entrance area was painted black and there was a black curtain. It was a depressing place for anyone to frequent.

A man of an unfortunate disposition was on some sort of reception. He immediately rose from his chair. Phoebe did a double take, momentarily startled at how ugly he was. She'd seen some sights in her time, but this fella was something else – tall, gangly, with the most severe acne she'd ever seen. His teeth, what was left of them, looked as though they'd never seen a toothbrush and his hair, being so wiry, could well be used to scrub the inside of an oven. With a pointy nose and similar chin, she couldn't help but think that if he was an animal, he'd be a rodent crossed with a stork.

'Can I help you?' the man asked.

Michael whacked him hard in the face. The guy was out cold, but Michael slammed his face into the counter anyway.

Phoebe led them along a dark corridor, where they eventually came to some stairs. On reaching the top, she heard voices. She held out her hand for them to be quiet. She listened. Del pointed up a second set of stairs.

'Up there,' he whispered.

Phoebe walked quickly to the top, where the voices got louder. Whoever they were were jeering.

'Go and see,' she said to Michael. 'If it's the punters, try and get in. Say that's what you're here for. We need to know where the girls are – I think the events are under way.'

Michael nodded. He passed three doors before opening the fourth. Inside were twenty-odd blokes cheering over a balcony.

'You all right, mate? Get held up, did ya?' said a man dressed in black trousers, a black bomber jacket and black boots. Michael sussed he was in charge of this little room.

'Sorry, mate – traffic,' he replied in his best Cockney accent.

'Yeah, well, you best get a look quick. Viewing time's almost over.'

'Cheers.'

Michael made his way to the front and assessed the floor below. He now knew what the jeering was about. Two men had Alice by her wrists and ankles. She was making it as difficult as she could for them.

He walked back towards the door. 'She's a handful,' he said.

'Special case, that one. Think she's something special.'

'Toilets anywhere?'

'Yeah, back out the door, second on your right.'

'Cheers, back in a sec.'

Michael rushed back to the others. 'Yeah, that's the punters. I saw Alice – she's on the floor below.' He didn't feel the need to furnish Phoebe with the finer details.

'Is she OK?'

'We need to go,' he said.

Pat and Del were already halfway down the stairs. They ran along the corridor below, listening out for noise but all they could hear were the faint shouts from upstairs. Pat tried a door. Locked. Del tried the next. Expecting it to be locked, he ended up bursting through and almost falling over. In the room were lots of chairs. He glanced up and saw moving bodies through an opening in the wall. He waited. Pat joined him and Phoebe and Michael soon rushed in.

Del pointed through into the room on the other side. Phoebe tentatively poked her head through.

She frantically scoured the room, then spotted Alice. It took all her strength to go against her motherly instinct and rush in and grab her daughter.

'How many other than punters upstairs, Michael?'

'One.'

'You take him?'

Michael looked at her, slightly disappointed she'd had to ask. She nodded in recognition. He ran out and back upstairs. Phoebe waited for the commotion to ensue. Within ten seconds, it was evident Michael was in the room above.

'Go get her!' she ordered.

Pat and Del ran through and Phoebe texted Archie: *Go get the bastard.*

On seeing two men running towards them, the two guys dropped Alice. Pat rugby tackled one into the wall, winding him, and pounded his head. Del had already whacked his man twice and knocked him to the ground. As big as they were, the element of surprise had given Phoebe's men the advantage. They were taking no prisoners, as Phoebe instructed. Both Pat and Del beat their targets into submission.

Alice hugged her mum. Phoebe held her tight, not wanting to let go.

It was pandemonium. Women were running everywhere – towards the exit, upstairs to the safety of their rooms. Michael threw the man from upstairs over the balcony and he broke his neck. Upstairs, punters were running along corridors and up and down landings in a panic, worried their dirty little secrets would be out in the open.

'We need to get these girls out, Mum.'

'Are you OK? Has anyone touched you? I'm sorry we were so long,' Phoebe said, raising her voice above the chaos.

'I am now,' Alice said. 'I fuckin' am now.'

Both she and Phoebe laughed. It was all they could do.

'Where's Archie? And the others?' Alice asked.

'Hopefully having similar success three streets away.'

'Tariq?'

Phoebe nodded.

Alice looked for Toni. 'Mum, wait here. I'll be two minutes.'

'You're going nowhere, girl.'

Alice was already on her way. She ran back towards her room. It was empty. She checked the room next door. Donna was gone, too, but the girl she shared with was rocking back and forth with her knees under her chin, crying.

'Come on, let's go.' Alice held out her hand.

'Where? I have nowhere to go,' she sobbed.

Alice wanted to take her with her, but knew she couldn't. She could hear at least three or four other women's voices. Women who either had nowhere to go or were too scared to try. She couldn't save everyone, and for the first time since she'd arrived, she thought maybe some didn't want to be saved.

'Take care,' she said. 'And good luck.'

The girl carried on rocking.

Alice turned to run back to her mum. Phoebe was right there. She'd followed her, not wanting her out of her sight.

She hugged her tight once more. 'I love you, Mum.'

chapter one hundred and four

Archie approached the entrance to Tariq's club. He was glad to be back. This was what he lived for. He'd enjoyed his time in Spain – he'd needed to go and rediscover himself. He was comfortable with who he was and, more importantly, who he wasn't. He wasn't Frank Pearson. He wasn't Daniel Pearson. He was Archie – Archie Pearson. And that wasn't Archie, head of the family. Not Archie the heir apparent. Just Archie Pearson, one of the top table members of the Pearson crime family. Son of the leading lady. The man who would probably one day take over the reins. Probably was the key word in all of this. Not expected to be, not the one who was always going to be, but the one who may, if it was right for him, take over at the top. Only when the time was right. Not now, but maybe sometime. That was who he was. The *maybe sometime* man. Right now, however, he was the bloke who was walking into a club of the very man who'd ordered a hit on his life.

He and the others headed towards the door, chatting as though they were on a lads' jolly. To anyone not in the know, they looked like a bunch of blokes looking for a good time. Their attire, somewhat out of place for the type of establishment they were walking into, didn't catch the attention of the men in Tariq's cars. In fact, they hardly noticed them.

On barging in, Archie cracked Russell straight on the jaw before he'd had time to register who he was. One thing Archie was good at was connecting sweetly with people's chins. Kieran, who had by now returned to take his place on the door, swung for Archie and caught his temple. It stunned him, but Ryan and Des grabbed Kieran and threw him up against the wall. Des headbutted him. Ryan punched him twice in the head. He swung back and got Ryan on the jaw. Des whacked him to the side of the head. He rocked, but stayed on his feet. Pēteris caught him with a righthander that sent him flying back into the wall. He slid down and slumped. He was out.

Archie walked into the reception, where he met a lady in her early fifties with dark-brown hair down to her waist, dressed in a fawn jumper with a very expensive brooch on her left breast. She'd have looked less out of place in an antique shop. Archie slowed his pace.

'Hiya. Er, first time here. Do we just go through?'

'No, most certainly not. This is a members-only club.'

'It's OK, we know Tariq. Long-standing friend. I believe he's in. We'll find him, don't worry.'

'I'm sorry, but no membership means no entry.'

Archie walked in, followed by Trainer and the others. Cecelia got up, unsure what to do. She knew Tariq was there – he'd just strutted in. She sat back down and tapped the desk with her fingers. She put her hand to her mouth. This could be trouble. She rang Walt.

The club was well appointed, with seductive lighting and Chesterfield-style sofas and chairs. Five wealthy-looking men were sat having a drink. Roach was nowhere to be seen.

'Yes, gentlemen?' one of the barmen asked.

Archie saw a door marked *Private*. 'It's OK, we know where we're going.'

He marched through the door, followed by the rest, pleased to see there were no access codes.

The barman looked at his colleague, who was cleaning some gin glasses. They both shrugged their shoulders. Neither of them wanted to get in the way of any bother. They didn't get paid enough for that.

Two of the men supped up and walked out. Getting caught up in anything unsavoury would not assist their climb up whatever ladder they were ascending.

Archie turned left and walked along a corridor. He listened for any voices. Nothing.

'Try this way,' Jase said, pointing in the opposite direction.

Archie again took the lead. Knowing Tariq wanted him dead made him want to walk in first. They passed the entrance back into the bar, and walked on towards two doors, which they found to be both locked. Archie was beginning to think they'd disappeared out of some back door, when he heard voices. At the end of the corridor was a left turn. The closer they got, the louder the voices became. Archie tried to control his breathing, which he could hear and feel getting heavy. His nerves had kicked in. He looked back over his shoulder to the men he had with him and indicated to Trainer to wait.

Archie walked into a very large room that was evidently an office to find Tariq. Roach was on the floor, having taken another beating. Two men were stood over him – Mo, who'd taken a few hits, and the other one, who Archie didn't know.

'Well, well, well, if it isn't the man himself. I've been lookin' all over for you. Do come in.'

'Why, thank you, Tariq, that's most kind. You won't mind if my mates come in, too, will ya?'

Archie took a few steps further into the office, then Trainer and the rest filed in.

He cracked Mo hard, sending him into Tariq's desk. Tariq rushed over to a cabinet and brought out a long knife. He swung it towards Archie, shouting, 'I'll fuckin' kill ya!'

Archie managed to move just enough that it only slashed him on his upper arm, where he went to protect his head. Trainer was now fighting with Si. Gray jumped through a gap and onto Tariq's desk. Tariq caught him with his knife and sliced him along the stomach. Gray saw the blood and dropped to his knees. Pēteris grabbed Tariq around the neck from behind. Ryan helped Des tackle Mo. Trainer was still slugging it out with Si.

Jase shouted, 'There's more!'

Walt, Harvey and the men from the cars were now in the corridor. Jase stood in their way and traded blows with Walt. The corridor was so tight there was no room to fight.

Pēteris managed to stop Tariq waving the knife around. Archie then punched him hard in the head and the body.

Si tried to get to his boss but Trainer fought hard to stop him. Mo was on the floor, having been beaten to a pulp by Ryan and Des, who were now in the corridor with Jase. Gray's wound was not as bad as he'd thought. He was cut, but not deep.

The fighting had now moved into the main bar. Walt and Harvey had retreated with the others to allow them space. All the drinkers had left and the two barman were cowering in the corner while chairs, tables and glasses smashed around them. Jase, Ryan and Des were outnumbered, even without Russell and Kieran, who were yet to reappear. They were starting to lose the fight and were using furniture and glassware for help, when the door flew open and Russell, holding his head, walked in. Des clocked him. They were now three against six – the odds were not good. Just then, through the door came Del, Pat and Michael, launching themselves at Tariq's men. The numbers were now even.

Raquel, in the midst of the mayhem in the next room, was seeing to Cecelia, who was sobbing into her chest, telling her she only came as a temp three months ago to get her son through university. Raquel missed Kieran, who had by now recovered, slip past. Cecelia, with her head in Raquel's bosom, was in no position to spot him either. Luckily for Raquel, the noise from the main room drew his attention far more than a woman being comforted.

Kieran ran in, still a little unsteady, but ready for more of the same. He saw Harvey on the floor, alongside two of the others. Walt, Russell and the sixth guy were backing off under the pressure. The odds were stacked against him, so he sat down to rest his head.

Phoebe made her way to the rear office, where she found Tariq being restrained by Pēteris. Trainer looked like he'd taken a pounding, but Si had come off worse. Mo was slumped in the corner. Roach was next to Archie, who had blood seeping from his upper arm. Gray was in Tariq's seat, smiling, pleased he'd not been stabbed to death.

The noise had quietened down in the main bar. The fight appeared to be over. Phoebe opened her bag and took out three firearms. She gave one to Trainer, before walking through and passing one to Pat. The other she kept herself. The bar was a war zone.

She looked at Alice, who had stayed close to the door. 'Come with me, sweetheart.'

She took Alice through to see Tariq. They both faced the man who'd dared take them on. The man who'd told Phoebe she'd always be living in the shadow of the stronger sex. The man who'd tried to take both of her children from her, and take her and the entire family business down. The man who had totally underestimated her position, power and strength in the criminal arena in which they operated – a place that had changed, and a world that had no place for Tariq Mali.

Alice glared at the man who'd told her she'd be taken to Amsterdam to be abused daily. The man who was prepared to watch her be raped and who'd told her not being married meant you were a whore. A man who despised women, thought they were inferior, and didn't want one at the top of the table. He'd put a price on Archie's head – their son and brother – and was responsible for killing their dear friends Brian and Knighty.

The two women Tariq Mali had tried to destroy were now standing over him, in pity. Phoebe could see he was in denial. He was doing everything he could to appear unfazed.

'I told you not to be around when I stepped out of the shadow, Tariq, didn't I?' Phoebe said, knowing that would hit a nerve.

'Fuck you, fuck both of you!'

Phoebe smiled at him and turned to Roach. 'Thank you, Roach.'

He looked as though he'd been through a meat slicer. It hurt to smile, but he wanted Tariq to see it.

'Ah, I get it … you fuckin' slag, Roach!' Tariq shouted.

'You should've put better men on me. Those three were no match for a man of my pedigree.'

Alice took a step forward and looked him up and down. She wanted to scream and shout – tell him what she thought of him. Instead, shaking her head, she said, 'And *you* were no match for us, Tariq.'

Tariq had nothing to say.

The power of reducing a "powerful" man to silence was inspiring.

Tariq spat at her thigh. She looked down, then back at him. A moment passed before she turned on her heels.

'Bring them through,' Phoebe ordered.

While Tariq and his men were assembled in the main room, Phoebe walked through to see Raquel. Cecelia was now telling her about her daughter, who worked for a big financial outfit at Canary Wharf.

'Phoebe, this is Cecelia.'

'Cecelia, what's your daughter's name? I know people who work there. I may know her.'

'Michaela, Michaela Ward.'

'Sorry, I don't know her. I just need to ask you one more question. Now that I know your daughter's name and where she works, did you see anything here today?'

'What – you mean what's happened in there?'

'Yes.'

It took a second or two for the penny to drop. 'No, I didn't see anything. I was in the loo the whole time. Weak bladder since the hysterectomy.'

'Good. And you saw no one, I presume?'

'No one.'

'So we understand each other?'

'Yes.' She held Phoebe's hand. 'You won't harm my daughter, will you?'

'Who? I don't know your daughter.'

Cecelia smiled. 'Thank you.'

'Now then, we need to clean up here, so I need to know where the keys are. That door needs to be locked. We don't want any more customers coming in, do we?'

'We've knocked two back already,' Raquel confirmed.

'The keys are in a drawer under the till. Here's the key to the drawer.'

'Thank you. Now it's time for you to get yourself off, Cecelia. Early finish. And remember – if anyone ever asks, you saw nothing.'

Cecelia got her coat and kissed Raquel goodbye. Phoebe went to get the keys.

'Will anyone come knocking?'

'I doubt it,' Raquel said. 'Now look after yourself.'

They followed Cecelia out and watched her turn right when she hit the main street.

'I can't believe that's just happened.'

'What – that in there or Cecelia telling you her life story?'

'Cecelia. It was, well, surreal.'

They each took a petrol can from the boot and Phoebe a pack of tie wraps. On locking the door to the club behind them, they placed the cans on the floor before walking back into the main bar. Pat and Trainer had their guns pointed at Tariq and his men. Archie and Alice bound them to their chairs with the tie wraps. Only Tariq and Si made a noise.

'Roach,' Phoebe said, 'you told me to also make sure I had someone called Si. Is he here?'

'Yep. That's Si there.'

She walked over to him. 'You were going to hold my daughter down while someone raped her, I hear.'

'So?'

'So I just wanted to know who you were, that's all. Didn't want you to miss out on all the fun.'

Phoebe nodded to Raquel to get the petrol cans. She gave one to Alice, who unscrewed the top before walking over to Tariq. His eyes were wide. His breathing erratic. She liked that.

'What's up, Tariq? Scared, are we? I'm only a girl.'

No reply.

Alice poured petrol over his head before doing the same to Si, who pleaded with her to stop.

She shook her head. 'I don't think you'd have told Roger to stop, would you? No matter how much I pleaded.'

She stepped back, placed the cans on the floor and noticed two of the men she didn't know had wet themselves. She took the gun from Trainer and, without saying a word, shot Kieran, Russell and the three men from the cars in the head.

'I think you deserve a bit of petrol, Mo. You'd've watched, wouldn't you?'

'Look, I ain't the gaffer. I just do as I'm told.'

'You should've taken a leaf out of Roach's book and grown a pair.'

She then poured petrol over Mo, who begged her to stop.

'OK, time to go, folks,' Phoebe ordered.

'Shouldn't we show Tariq what's in store for him first, Mum? Be a shame not to – you know, seeing as he's such a main player. He deserves that at least.'

Phoebe took a moment. She could see the fear in Tariq's eyes. 'What a good idea.'

Alice took one of the cans and, calmly, without averting her gaze, trailed its contents from Mo to Si. She then lit a match and threw it on Mo. He screeched as he ignited. Within seconds Si was alight, too. The noise they made was piercing.

Alice had stepped back to watch at her mum's side. She then turned her attention to Tariq, who was sat, head bowed, a shadow of his former self. Before the screams became intolerable, Alice walked over to him. Holding a match in one hand and the box in her other, she waited for him to look at her. 'Surprise,' she said, as she struck the match and threw it in his lap. Together with her mum, she watched Tariq wail in agony.

'Time to go,' Phoebe ordered for the second time.

By the time she'd closed the passenger door, the screams of all three had subsided.

The three cars drove through London, attracting no attention whatsoever. The tinted rear windows hid the fact most of the people inside looked like they'd been in a war. Within ten minutes of setting off, Phoebe made a call.

'Greg, it's me. It's done.'

'On fire?'

'Oh yeah – burning well.'

'And Alice?'

'She's fine.'

'You?'

'Yeah, I'm fine, too, but Greg...?'

'Yeah.'

'Thanks.'

The line went silent for a moment before going dead. Greg West wasn't one for sentiment. He'd heard her – and appreciated it. The pause told her so.

chapter one hundred and five

Two days later

Phoebe was waiting for her top team. Today was a time to reflect and consolidate, and to remember two men who had given their lives for the family. She was determined to give Brian and Knighty a send-off. It had to be low key, however, away from prying eyes. It reminded her so much of what Frank did for Paul and John. It was the least she could do. It was what she wanted to do.

She'd hardly had time to process the last week. It had been a lesson in how life at the top could be. Forty-eight hours after her daughter had set fire to Tariq, here she was having to cremate two men she loved dearly. Brian had been part of her life ever since she'd first come into the family. But he'd gone the way he'd always imagined going. He'd often say that he'd die on the job. Something Trainer said he'd like to do, too. Different job of course.

She arrived at the crematorium with Archie, Alice, Sarah and Gloria. Ted had arranged things with the staff to allow them some time after the official cremations for the day had been completed. They had fifteen minutes to say their goodbyes. The only other people coming were Knighty's wife and children. Phoebe hoped things would go smoothly.

She looked at her family. Firstly, Alice, who she worried was in denial. The experience of the past few days would leave a scar. Having the mental strength to cope with it was to be admired, but she needed to process it. Phoebe was concerned she was blocking it out and doing what her grandad would have told her to do. *Give yaself a shake, gal,* he would have said. *It's just part of the deal.* Alice seemed to have done just that. She'd picked herself up and dusted herself down. Maybe she was made of sterner stuff. Maybe she had more of Frank in her than Phoebe realised. Or, Phoebe feared, maybe the fallout would show itself further down the line. For now, though, Alice was her usual bubbly self, showing no sign of trauma from meeting Tariq Mali. Her little princess had grown into a fearsome young lady. She'd been subject to not one, but two, traumatic experiences and if you took her at face value, she'd come out unscathed. Phoebe prayed that would be the case.

Then she turned to Archie, the prodigal son. He was the Archie of old. A young man who, for the first time since Frank's death, was showing a glimpse of who he would turn out to be. Interestingly, she'd recognised that her top team, who'd been pleased he'd been ousted from the family meetings, were happy he was back. They'd not said as much but they'd make their feelings known if needed. Only Pat and Raquel, when they were in Portknockie, had said they were pleased to see him back, but that's because they were there when he arrived.

In the last few days, she'd found herself watching him, admiring his presence. The best thing about Archie was that he seemed happy. He'd dealt with his demons, processed his feelings, and by his own admission had found comfort in who he was. He was happy to be in a position within the family that had no defined role. He was content to be at his mum's side by virtue of who he was. He was comfortable being himself.

Sarah, too, appeared happier. She'd been through the mill of late – seeing two bodies dumped on the drive. Phoebe was worried about what that would do to her and that Archie might think it was too much and be persuaded to return to sunnier climes. Thankfully, that was not the case. Sarah was a Pearson wife and accepted Archie's return.

She found it inspiring that people still naturally looked to him for leadership, and just as pleasing that he would take on that role. She had no worries about Archie. The business was in good hands. If Alice could grow into a more measured criminal, she was sure the bloodline would stay intact.

She finally looked at Gloria, the mother hen who never asked any questions – Frank's rock, who the rest of the family would continue to lean on. Gloria was the kind of woman families were built on. One half of the rock on which they all stood.

Taking out Tariq, rescuing her daughter and removing the hit on her son's head in the process had been a monumental test for Phoebe. She'd been told repeatedly she was a woman in a man's world, living in the shadow of men and that, to quote Barney, the running of a criminal empire "was no place for tits and make-up".

She observed how her top team behaved with composure and dignity. They'd all put their lives on the line for her and her kin. Her team was solid. Full of men who would die for her. She was no match for any of them, but she was in charge of arguably the best firm in the country. She'd never been in anyone's shadow. She didn't operate in a man's world. She operated in a tough world and one where sex only mattered in the bedroom, or wherever else it happened to take place.

While she was welcoming her team, she saw Knighty's family arrive. This, she was not looking forward to. She walked over to greet them.

'Hi, how are you?' she asked.

'Bearing up. It's so hard, though, Phoebe.'

'I know, believe me, I know,' Phoebe replied.

'How long's it been now?'

'Coming up to eight years.'

'Does it get any easier?'

'Yeah. It never goes, but, yes, it gets easier.'

Knighty's wife smiled. Her resentment and anger towards Phoebe had gone. They held hands as they made their way, along with Knighty's children, to the chapel door.

Pat, Archie, Phoebe and Gloria were the bearers for Brian's coffin. Trainer, Raquel, Alice and Jase carried Knighty's. The service was short, given the time restraints, but both Phoebe and Raquel were able to say a few words. Knighty's wife gave Phoebe a hug outside. A warm, meaningful hug that told Phoebe she didn't blame her. A hug Phoebe would remember for a long time.

They had a few drinks at Gloria's, in Papplewick, where they mainly talked about London and how both Brian and Knighty would have loved it.

Life was returning to normal very quickly for the firm. The only difference was that Roach was on the payroll. Phoebe had earmarked him for replacing Knighty in Derby. He was a solid player, who commanded respect, and she wanted to repay him for saving Alice. She'd liked him from their first encounter, but the fact he didn't expect any favours in return had only endeared him to her further.

Alice, in particular, was in awe of him. When she found out what he'd done, she shed a tear – the only tear in the whole process. The two of them were in the kitchen talking.

'D'you think you'll miss London then?' she asked.

'Probably, but I can always visit. It's a different life up here. Hard to put into words, but London is a place of its own.'

'I like it, but only for a few days. I like the buzz of the place, but I'm always keen to get back,' Alice said.

Roach stared at her for a moment. She could tell he had something to say.

'What?' she asked.

Roach came out of his trance. 'Oh nothing, it's nothing.'

'No, come on, tell me. What were you gonna say?'

Roach lowered his voice. 'I assume you deleted the text?'

She looked at him quizzingly. 'What text?'

'Surprise,' he said. 'That text.'

Alice's face changed. 'I don't know what you mean.'

'Really?'

'OK, what about it?' she asked.

'I'd just make sure you delete it from the phone. I assume no one here knows about it?'

'Not as far as I know.'

'Our little secret then.'

Alice didn't like secrets. She didn't like the fact Roach knew about it either. As far as she was concerned, it was still in Archie's parka pocket.

'Back in a mo,' she said, giving Roach her drink to hold.

Roach smiled as she scurried off.

chapter one hundred and six

Two weeks later – Monday 9th March 2020

Since Tariq's exclusive little club had gone up in flames, Phoebe had spoken to Greg West four times, in addition to the call she'd made immediately after.

The first time was him confirming there would be very little investigation into the fire and the deaths. It would be reported as an accident, with the main focus being on how lucky it was that there were no customers in at the time.

The second was for him to explain to her, as a top table member, that the rest of the UK's elite were comfortable with the situation and had agreed she had no choice given Alice was in danger.

The third was to explain who was going to take over Tariq's operations. It was to be one of his own top table. She had assumed Greg would take control, but he said it would upset the balance of things. She was learning quickly that power needed to be shared to keep order. As Greg had told her, it was all about the balance of power.

The fourth call he made, which was only yesterday, was to ask her if she was interested in a shipment of guns that had been uncovered in a warehouse owned by Tariq. At first, she thought he was asking her if she wanted to buy them, but it soon became apparent he was letting her know where they were. They were her guns after all. Trainer, Michael and Roach had gone to acquire them. She liked Greg. She liked the way he did things. She saw Frank in him, which did everything to cement their relationship.

Today, she was meeting a friend. It was a kind of date. After all that had gone off, she and Alice had had a couple of nights away in the North Yorkshire moors the previous weekend. Archie had arranged for them to stay in the cottage in Castleton that he and Sarah had lived in. It was when they were walking the route from Commondale to Castleton that they bumped into a familiar face.

Today was the first date. They were meeting at The Brown Cow in Mansfield before having a meal in town. Alice had wanted to double date with her new fella, Chris, but Phoebe had insisted, for now, she wanted a little privacy. She walked in, took the left door into the snug and immediately saw Scratch sat in the corner supping his pint. Since the events in Hull, he'd lost a stone and a half and had been visiting the gym four times a week. He looked trim and fit, and his new, streamline figure added to his appeal. Phoebe had liked him in Hull, but she liked him a lot more now that he'd lost the excess timber.

Things with Barney hadn't worked out. He was still struggling to recover from the effects of dealing with

Phoebe and her firm. Scratch was more or less at a loose end. If things went well, she was planning on asking him if he'd like to reconsider her offer of a job.

Scratch got up. She could tell he was nervous. He scratched his head.

'Drink?'

'Gin, please.'

'Righto. Er, I would've got you one, but you know, I wasn't sure what you'd have.'

She smiled. 'It's fine.'

'Any gin in particular?'

'You choose. I'll sit down. Slimline tonic too, please, but on the side.'

'Gotcha.'

They chatted effortlessly for over an hour before strolling the short distance into town. Phoebe linked arms with him. After their meal, they had the slightly awkward moment of whether to kiss. Scratch was out of his comfort zone. He'd never been a ladies' man. Phoebe took the lead and kissed him gently. He was even unsure whether to put his arms around her. Eventually, he did.

'Right, well, er, I better get off,' he said.

'Where to?'

'Hull.'

'Southwell's closer.'

'Is it? Where's that then?' he asked, knowing exactly what she meant.

'You make me laugh, Scratch! How can one so innocent be mixed up in our world, eh?'

He followed her lead back towards The Brown Cow. They talked some more, never once touching on the subject of Southwell again. Scratch just assumed that's where he was going to spend the night. And he was right.

chapter one hundred and seven

Two days later

It was approaching ten o'clock in the morning and Archie was making a cup of tea. He'd slept in after a heavy night with Ryan and Des and his head was still rather fuzzy, though not enough to keep him from doing anything. He buttered his toast, poured his milk in his tea and sat at the kitchen table. He flicked on the TV, taking no note of what was on. He only really wanted the background noise.

He'd just finished his first slice when his ears pricked up.

A body has been washed up on a beach on the Moray coast in Northern Scotland. Dog walkers reported the body on Cullen beach just after seven o'clock this morning.

'Oh fuck,' he muttered, choking on his toast.

The End

Acknowledgements

As always, there are people behind the scenes, in the background, helping and assisting me as I write my books.

I'd like to thank the following people for their help and support, without which, producing what you read, would be so much more difficult:

My wife, *Debbie*, forever my rock, who sits and listens to me read chapters to her for hours. Someone who critiques my work along the way, never holding back with her views. I love you *Debbie*, more than ever.

Heather Brown – a very good friend who has read every one of my books as it's being written. Thank you, *Heather*, for your support and feedback.

Bob Hart – a stalwart of valuable feedback, who provides honest and frank opinion from the start.

Andy Brown – again, *Andy*, your support is always appreciated. Thank you for your input.

Nick and Mandy – our old next-door neighbours. By that, I don't mean they're old, just that they used to be our neighbours ... lol. Two people we enjoyed many drinks with and who are always there to read my books and give positive support.

Tracey Carver – a lifelong friend, who, along with her husband, *Dave*, is always there when we need her. Thank you for reading this, *Tracey*, and for your support. Appreciated as always.

Paul Gibbons – *Paul* has offered inspirational feedback on all my books, and taught me many moons ago the art of chairing a sales meeting! Thank you for the many conversations we had while you read *Killing Shadows* and, of course, for the many ideas you allowed me to bounce off you while I tried to come up with the title.

And finally to *Yasmin Yarwood at Meticulous Proofreading* and *Alexa Whitten at The Book Refinery* for their help in making this a novel I am immensely proud of. Without your help, it really would not have happened.

About the Author

Where do I start?

Probably best to start at the beginning, but to make sure this section is nowhere near as long as this book, I'll keep it rather brief.

I was born in Newcastle upon Tyne in 1970, but spent my childhood in Mansfield, Newbury and Carlisle. I had a fantastic time as a child – great parents, who always made sure my sister, brother and I were well looked after and, most importantly, well loved.

I was a confident young fella, always front and centre, with bags of energy, and as a young man, I always had my glass half full. I spent most of my working life in sales, using that confidence and chat to make quite a successful career for myself.

One event that changed my life forever was when I first set eyes on my wife, Debbie. People sometimes say 'I just knew she was the one for me' or 'It was love at first sight'. Well, I can honestly say I knew as soon as I saw her that I'd marry her. And we did – in

1994. We have two wonderful daughters, Heather and Georgina, and three grandchildren, with one more on the way.

In June 2022, Debbie and I made the move 471 miles north from Mansfield to Northern Scotland, to live in a lovely clifftop fishing village along the Moray coast.

So, what about my novels, you may ask? My writing came about after saying for many years that I'd like to write a book. As with a lot of writers, it just never materialised. After deciding to leave full-time work and take life a bit slower, Debbie persuaded me to put pen to paper and write my first novel – the first in this trilogy – *The Wrong Man*.

I'm also a funeral celebrant. This is something I do on a part-time basis and which allows me to help many wonderful people at such a difficult time in their lives.

So, that's me in a very small nutshell. The life of M J Elliott on one page.

I hope you enjoy *Killing Shadows*, but whatever you do, please ensure you read *The Wrong Man* and *New Blood* first!

Take care and look after yourselves.

Contact Michael

Email: michael@mjelliottauthor.co.uk
Facebook: mjelliottauthor
Instagram: @mjelliottauthor

Other titles by M J Elliott

The Wrong Man

Frank is at the top of his game. He has grown through the ranks of the criminal underworld and is now at the top table. Born into violence, for Frank's twins, Daniel and Richie, there are certain expectations. Yet, there can only be one heir to the kingdom.

Frank doesn't see any of it coming. He has to face his demons and look at himself for once. Just maybe, Frank is the one who is ultimately responsible – responsible for it being the wrong man.

New Blood – The Wrong Man part 2

Frank has ruled the criminal underworld of the East Midlands and parts of Yorkshire for over thirty years, but he needs a successor. He sees Archie, his grandson, as the only man who can fill those shoes.

Fletcher O'Brien rules half of Manchester. He sees Frank and Archie as vulnerable and wants to take them out. Can Frank and Archie take him on? Can they hold onto the family empire?

As they battle with Fletcher, neither of them sees the threat from within, a problem far bigger than anything they've had to deal with before.

A Bitter Pill

Anna Fox has been in an abusive marriage for far too long. Desperate to find a way out, a chance to change her life presents itself in the most unexpected way. Is Anna willing to do anything to escape? She must dig deep if she is going to succeed, but she soon realises that her husband has other ideas.

Anna used to be a bubbly person. Then she met Jonathan. She wants to be that person again. She wants to be free. She sees a chance, and takes it. She's scared, but excited. Jonathan is smart, cute and plays the long game. Can Anna outwit him and play the long game too? Can she finally get her freedom and meet her Simon? It will take courage and it will take help. Has Anna got enough of both?

Available on Amazon.co.uk as a paperback and Kindle edition and, of course, on his author website, www.mjelliottauthor.co.uk